DEAD GIRLS NEVER TALK

SJ SYLVIS

WELCOME TO

WHERE

DEAD GIRLS NEVER TALK

S.J. SYLVIS

PROLOGUE

JOURNEY

My skin was still warm from the sun blanketing me earlier in the day, only for the warmth to escape to a balmy night that smelled of wildflowers, pine, and bad decisions. The note crinkled in my hand as I stood underneath the glittering stars, waiting for him. I glanced back down at the messy scribbles again, rereading it for the fifteenth time in the last hour.

Meet me in the courtyard after curfew. 9pm. I want to talk in private before summer break.

There was always the option to stay at St. Mary's Boarding School during breaks, even one as long as summer. A lot of the students here didn't have much of anything, but there were some that had grand homes all over the country. Why they would stay here was beyond me. If I had somewhere to call home other than a poorly lit fortress and a crappy orphanage with what seemed to have a revolving door of adoptions for everyone *but* me, I would go. But I didn't have anything to my name. Nothing but the uniforms the headmaster had graciously handed over and the blanket that Sister Mary knitted for me when I was too young to remember such a gesture.

Despite all of that, I was still leaving for a couple of weeks. The orphanage was never supposed to be a permanent home for someone like me, which was why I was sent to St. Mary's in the first place. Sister Mary was the only family I had, and now that I was older, I knew she needed extra help to run the orphanage smoothly. The relief in her tone the first time I called her from Headmaster Ellison's office to tell her I would like to come visit and help her during the summer was groundbreaking.

Except, this year was a little different. I wasn't looking forward to going back to my old, creaky bed with chipping paint falling to the wooden floor every time I shifted in my sleep. I wasn't looking forward to seeing Sister Mary's rosy, chubby cheeks curve at the sight of me. I wasn't even looking forward to her scowling when I pretended to pray at the dinner table each night, knowing that I didn't believe in such blasphemy. If there was a God, and he called me up to heaven after my unavoidable death, the first thing I'd ask is *why*. And he'd know exactly what I was talking about.

A light gust of wind wafted around me as I stood alone in the courtyard, open for anyone to see. Most of the students were already gone, as the school year had ended, but Cade always stayed. He and the Rebels never strayed too far. They liked order, and those boys had secrets that went as deep as the core of the earth. I was certain there was a reason they stayed behind, although I hadn't asked Cade.

We were very much a *beat-around-the-bush* couple, hidden behind stone walls covered in dust and cobwebs, with lingering touches and scorching kisses. The note crinkled in my hand again as I grew anxious. I didn't usually feed into the feeling of hope or excitement because when you've been hurt and disappointed enough times, you began to grow a thick skin with the realization that there wasn't much point, but with Cade, things were different.

Maybe that was why I allowed him to keep me a secret.

I kept him a secret too, too afraid that the first whisper about what was happening between us would break everything we'd created.

So, what does he want to talk about?

Was he ready to stop hiding me? Was I ready for that? Was I ready to let myself feel something so big I couldn't even fathom how it would break me if I was forced to let it go?

I shifted on the sandals that Sloane had lent me, glanced up to the high tower of St. Mary's Boarding School, and felt a shift in the air when the clock showed it was past the time Cade was supposed to meet me. Nibbling on my lip, I looked over to my left and then to my right. Did he get caught by the duty teacher? We weren't allowed out of our rooms after seven, but the Rebels never followed the rules.

Just as anxiety began to settle in my belly, I heard the breaking of a twig. Hope soared in my heart, and I didn't have the strength to shut it down—just like it had always been with Cade. One tiny grin from him in my direction turned my world upside down, and that was the most terrifying thing I'd ever felt.

"You're late," I said, still keeping my back to him. A smile slid onto my cheeks as I flipped my long hair over my shoulder.

I stood there with my heart in my throat, waiting for his large hands to grip my waist. He'd spin me around and press his lips to mine, silencing every thought in my head, and I'd relish in the feeling he'd give me, because no one else had ever given me such a thing in my life. *Ever.* It was hard to ignore the feeling of being wanted when you had waited years for someone to want you.

Another twig snapped, and then another, and with each sound hitting my ears, my smile grew bigger and bigger. I was seconds from turning around because I couldn't wait a single beat longer to see the slight glimmer of need in his warm eyes. But just as I tipped my head over my shoulder, a crack of shocking pain blinded me, and I fell to the cobblestone, still warm from the afternoon sun.

Slight glimpses of twinkling stars met me when my eyes began to flutter again. My head rolled to the side, my hair half covering my face. Stomach acid bubbled deep in my belly as I tried to figure out what had happened. The shuffling of foot-steps snagged my ears, and I shut my eyes because the sky was spinning too fast.

Something heavy landed on me, but everything was blurry. There was a figure above me, but my vision strained too much to focus on anything except the glint of something shiny, and then my eyes were shutting again. When my head rolled to the side as I grasped for consciousness, I saw a set of black, shiny shoes. I was confused because I felt fear, and I wasn't usually afraid. I was quiet and submissive to most, but I was tough on the inside. I had lost the ability to be afraid at the ripe age of eight, when Sister Mary told me that I likely wouldn't be getting adopted because of my age. No one wanted an older child who often had screaming fits.

I had stopped allowing myself to be hopeful, and I'd

stopped allowing fear to take me under. It always sent a shiver down my spine when adoptive parents would look at me out of the corner of their eye as Sister Mary told them about my history—which was nearly nonexistent. I was a ghost to most.

But I was afraid right now, and I had no idea why.

Why does that hurt?

My eyelashes fluttered again, and I cried out, pulling my arms back.

"Ow," I said, but my voice was weaker than usual. I sounded like a mouse, barely making a noise. Slowly, I began to sit up, but my stomach rolled like I was tumbling down the green hills behind the orphanage again. I was dizzy, and there was a stinging pain. My fingers dug into the cobblestone courtyard, and they were wet. When I glanced down, righting my vision, I went to scream at the blood, but nothing came out. I laid my head back down, rolled over to my side, and tried to get up, but my arms were Jell-O. Wet streaks of blood trailed down to my hands, covering my fingers in a sticky mess of red. Tears fell and mixed with my cut flesh, and I knew right then...I'd been lying to myself from the very beginning.

I had hope.

I had hoped that, one day, I would be loved, and *wanted,* and have the life that I had always dreamed about on those cold nights at the orphanage where I thought I'd been fooling everyone with my ability to act bored and uninterested. I knew that, because fear like no other slammed into me the second I fell back down to the cobblestone, washing away every single ounce of hope I had.

I was going to die.

And I didn't want to.

CHAPTER ONE

CADE

BEING selfless was embedded into my DNA the second I was thrust into the Walker family, butt-ass naked, screaming for my mother's tit. Although, could you truly consider yourself a selfless being when you only thought of one person above all else? Being selfless was to think of how your actions could affect others, to put their feelings before yours, but the only person I had ever thought about was Tommy-motherfucking-Walker. *My father*.

He beat my mom in front of me, and I allowed him to do so.

It wasn't because I agreed with it. No. In fact, it felt like a waging war of fire was occurring inside my body, burning me alive with each thudding punch to her skin. But now that I was legally an adult and had been through more shit than I ever cared to discuss with a therapist, I knew that I had been brainwashed from the second I could say the word *gun*. I was born into a scheming, illegal, gun-running business, and unfortunately, it had always been the plan for me. Isaiah and

Brantley, too, but now things had changed. Alliances had shifted, trust had been broken, and more targets were inflicted on the three of us due to sending our fathers to prison for the very business we were set to inherit.

Tommy Walker, my own flesh and blood, the man who I had been devoted to, was locked behind bars, and there were a lot of angry people, but especially him. My father, along with Carlisle and Frank, were likely planning our deaths at this very moment.

Think of the business, son. Don't fuck this up for me. Be a man. Watch as I cut this man's throat out, because you'll be doing the same one day. You are loyal to one, and that is the brotherhood.

Looking back, I should have listened to him a little more intently. I regretted the second I became devoted to another. And again, not because he deserved my devotion or loyalty, or because I agreed with the business I was forced into, but because the second I let my guard fall—and trust me when I say it fucking fell—that was when shit became real. Selfishness typically led to regret, and regret was what I'd been feeling since Journey left.

The cool winter wind pelted through my crisp, white dress shirt as I stood in the exact spot I was standing in when I realized I'd fucked up. The cobblestone was slick with ice, and the tattered, faded, maroon flag atop the skyscraper boarding school I called home blew as angrily as my heart was beating. The car door slammed, and the thundering muscle climbed up to my throat. I knew why I was angry to see her again. It wasn't because I wasn't thankful she was here, because even though I knew she'd never be mine again, I was glad that she was back. I was angry because I'd spent every waking second of the last eight months trying to rid her from my brain, and now she was here, and there was no way I was going to be able to scrub the memory of us when she was no longer just a ghost striding down the halls of St. Mary's, holding my entire being in her small hands.

Chills scraped over my arms and chest, and it had nothing to do with the wintry breeze. Her pretty, wavy hair flew over her shoulder, and it pissed me off that she didn't have a coat on. Her jeans were looser than normal, no longer hugging her edible curves like before. I knew, without even looking, that the light in her smoky eyes was dull. They were empty just a few weeks ago when I saw her standing in the foyer of St. Mary's with a war brewing around us. Time was subjective, and some would say that eight months wasn't much time at all, but to me, it was a lifetime. An entire eternity had passed since the last time I'd felt her lips on mine. She was different. And I was, too. There was so much to say, but nothing would ever leave our mouths.

My hands dove into the pockets of my pants as she moved up the front steps of the school, not even looking back at the town car that had dropped her off. She'd been staying at the orphanage since escaping from the psych hospital, and I knew that because I had left St. Mary's and checked on her each and every night, not caring if Tate—the headmaster who despised me and the rest of the Rebels when we called him by his first name—tried to stop me, which was exactly why he didn't. I could see her pretty face from the glow of the candle inside the far-right window of the tall, brick building that was close to ruins. I felt her hopelessness and despair from across the street, and it made me sick.

I liked to pretend that I was numb on the inside—a walking fucking Frankenstein, if I might—but it was all a ploy.

I had feelings for one person, and now she was back, and I wasn't sure how I was going to unbury myself from all that had happened. Because the truth was, I still didn't know what had happened other than the fact that, for the first time in my entire life, I was selfish, and it had hurt us both in the end.

So, if there was one thing that I could take away from my fucked-up father, it was that he was right: being selfless was better than being selfish, because when you thought of only yourself, people got hurt.

And she got hurt. *Literally*.

My hand came up, and I swiped at my bottom lip as I watched her stand in front of the school as if she were preparing for a battle. I could almost taste her sweet lips on mine, even from the far distance that separated us. Everything tightened when her head snapped over and her gray eyes landed on me. I swore I could feel her tender hands squeeze my soul. I stayed still, watching her as she watched me. The wind blew her hair all around her, like she was an enemy, unmoving as she towered over her opponent. I took a step forward, as if she were a siren calling me from afar, as soft snow began to fall from the sky, but the second I moved, she was like a fearful rabbit, running away at the first sound of distress.

She disappeared into the two heavy doors of St. Mary's, and I dropped my arm down to my side, preparing myself for death.

Because that was what Journey was going to be for me.

A slow, dreadful calling to my death.

CHAPTER TWO

JOURNEY

HOME.

The smell of the glossy wax on the black-and-white-checkered floor brought me back to the one place I had considered home above all else. The scent of the dining hall that lingered to the front doors, past the headmaster's office, filled my senses, and my stomach growled from hardly eating over the last few weeks. Wasn't it funny how a smell could take you back to a memory, as if you traveled back in time to relive it? The scent and warmth of this old, dusty building propelled me to last May, when I felt untouchable and hopeful for the first time in my entire life. But now, *home* felt more like a burden. There were secrets here and memories that tarnished the good. St. Mary's didn't feel like home to me any longer.

I glanced over my shoulder as the wooden doors slammed behind me, shutting out the rest of the world—shutting out *him*. I knew Cade was looking at me. I could feel him from a mile away. I had always been able to feel him. I saw him when he came to the orphanage, too, and I almost opened the window to tell him to leave, but I didn't.

Fear began to creep up my chest, replacing the cold I felt in my bones from winter with a burning heat of anger and confusion, which were the two most dominant things I'd been feeling since I was closed in a padded room at The Psychiatric Covenant Hospital. It was a hospital that allowed demented people to be in charge of patients who had no business being evaluated for a psych test. That place was so corrupt, and in exchange, it corrupted me, too.

"Journey?" I swallowed the memories and allowed them to scatter like the melted snow droplets from my boots over the floor. "Is that you?"

Headmaster Ellison rushed out the door and breathed out a sigh of relief when he saw it was me. He ran a hand through his unkempt hair. "Oh, good. I'm getting an alarm for that door as soon as the SMC approves it."

The SMC—St. Mary's Committee—held the power of this school in their hands. Every decision was run through them, and I briefly wondered what they thought of allowing me to come back here after finding me with my wrists slit in the courtyard last May. Surely everyone at this school was apprehensive with me walking the halls again, since they all thought I'd tried to kill myself instead of being viciously attacked like I'd said.

The headmaster turned around and waved me into his office, and I followed after him reluctantly, my wet boots squeaking over the floor. As soon as he sat down at his desk, I stood against the back wall and crossed my arms over my chest. "Gonna give the code for the new alarm to the Rebels? You know how they like to sneak out occasionally."

Headmaster Ellison's brows crowded as he eyed me cautiously. I knew what he was thinking. *What happened to you?* I was being snarky and completely unlike myself. Even admitting that I knew the Rebels—Cade, Isaiah, Brantley, and Shiner—and their rule-breaking tendencies was out of the norm for me. But Headmaster Ellison and I both knew that things had changed between us. Although, standing here looking at him as he rested his elbows on his cluttered desk, I knew that just because he and I were aware of the psych hospital and its underground *"business"* that landed many people in jail, not much had changed from the previous school year when it came to him. He was still as overworked as before, likely too deep into everything else in his life to really care much about the Rebels and what they did in their spare time—unless, of course, it had to do with a student being kidnapped and taken to the same place I had been kept for the last eight months.

"Let's talk, Journey."

I blinked, unmoving against the wall. "About what?"

Headmaster Ellison removed his elbows from his desk and clasped his hands together, eyeing me with something that made me feel extremely uncomfortable. I swallowed a gulp and pushed back on the girl that I was before everything had happened. "You. I want to talk about you."

I shrugged. "There isn't much to talk about." *That's a complete and utter lie.* Headmaster Ellison had already made up his mind about me from the second he saw my wrists cut—just like everyone else at this school.

His eyebrow raised. "Journey–"

A knock on the door sounded, and our conversation was cut short. Headmaster Ellison straightened in his seat and smoothed out his wrinkled tie. "Come in."

The door slowly swung open, and a head popped in. "Is this a good time? I gathered all my things."

I know that voice.

Gemma Richardson—or should I say, Ellison—walked into the headmaster's office, and I immediately scanned her from head to toe. Gemma and I had an unspoken bond that she probably wasn't even aware of, but I was. When two people shared the same kind of trauma, it automatically linked you, regardless of if you acted upon it. It felt like I knew her, and I'd never even spoken to her. Maybe it was the fact that I was so close to her twin brother, Tobias, who I hadn't seen in several weeks, but there was something about Gemma that I felt connected to. And with the way she was staring at me, like she could read everything going on inside my head, I think she felt it, too.

Gemma eventually cleared her throat, and we broke our eye contact. I still stayed leaning against the far wall, right beside an overly full bookshelf, if there was even such a thing. Gemma was wearing dark jeans and had on a black hoodie that made her green eyes even more vibrant than I remembered from that stark-white room I found her in several weeks ago.

"Oh, great." Headmaster Ellison stood up and rounded the desk, showcasing his gentle smile that I'd seen a time or two in the past. "Do you want the key to your new room?"

I glanced at their exchange. "New room?"

Gemma peered over her shoulder, encasing the same exact smile that her father shared. "Yes, I'm moving down the hall so you can have your old room back."

My heart thumped hard as blood rushed to my fingertips. "No!" I shot away from the wall and felt my legs wobble.

The headmaster and Gemma shared a questionable look as a set of keys lingered in between them. They jingled as the headmaster's fingers tightened. "No?"

Gemma turned all the way around, giving me her full attention. "We thought you may be more comfortable in your old room with Sloane. Is that not the case?"

I felt the blooming of anxiety but tried to keep my face as even as possible. I was proud of the way my words flowed with ease out my mouth. "I would like to have my own room, if that is possible." I shifted my gaze to the headmaster, and I knew he was trying to figure me out, just like those doctors—who I was certain had cheated on their MCATs—did at the psychiatric hospital. *Were they even real doctors?* They couldn't have been.

"Are you sure?" Gemma asked quietly. There was a sweetness surrounding her, and it was really no surprise that Isaiah had fallen for her. She was pretty and had a softness to her. She was completely opposite of her brother, Tobias—at least the version I knew of him.

"I'm sure," I answered.

"Can I ask why?" The headmaster raised his chin, waiting for my answer. I didn't blame him for being so curious. Last we saw each other, I'd had blood all over me and was in and out of consciousness. For all I knew, he was placing me with Sloane because he thought I was going to fall into old habits. After all, everyone at St. Mary's assumed I had tried to kill myself. What else should he have thought? I didn't blame him or anyone else for their assumptions. I knew he came from a place of concern.

Gemma cleared her throat and gave the headmaster—*her father*—a look. Her eyes widened slightly, and her small jaw tightened. I almost laughed at how hard the headmaster was trying to figure out what she was trying to tell him.

He wanted to know why I wanted to room alone, but I wouldn't tell him.

I wouldn't tell him that I didn't trust a single person at this school, not even my old roommate, because the last time I was here, someone had tried to kill me, and I had no idea who it was.

xxx

. . .

"SORRY ABOUT THAT," Gemma said, glancing over at me as we walked down the quiet hall. "He is so oblivious sometimes."

I huffed out a polite laugh, even though nothing was funny. "It's okay. I wouldn't have told him even if he didn't drop the question."

Gemma rolled her lips together as she clutched her box of things in her hands. She seemed to be deep in thought as we rounded the steps to the girls' and boys' halls. Everything was exactly the same in this school, and I'd be lying if I said I didn't miss it, even if I didn't feel as safe. *What's the fun in feeling safe anyway?* Made life more exciting when you were constantly on edge. I'd been on edge since the second I left St. Mary's, and that feeling wasn't going anywhere.

I ran my fingers along the wooden handrail, feeling the intricate details engraved in the dark oak as Gemma and I climbed side by side. A heavy silence was surrounding us, and with each step that took me closer to the hallways full of students tucked away in their rooms, the pit in my stomach grew wider and wider. My eyes flicked to the boys' hall, knowing that Cade was in one of those rooms. Or maybe he was still out in the courtyard, standing in the same spot that I was brutally assaulted in and left for dead.

Fear slithered up my spine and wrapped itself around my neck, making me itch. It was scary not knowing what had happened. It was unsettling when your thoughts were disoriented and your mind came up with scenarios that may or may not have been true. Every time I fell asleep in that locked room at the psych hospital, being fed drugs that I didn't need for a suicide attempt that didn't actually happen, it was as if my brain would construct a story in my slumber that was the worst of anything I could have thought consciously.

Cade. He was the only one who knew I was out there that night, and that was a mountain I couldn't quite climb over. In fact, it felt like I was on the very tip of the mountain, dangling over the edge, with him holding me back with his pinky finger. My curiosity begged for me to look back and ask him if it was him, if he had something to do with my attempted death, but something stopped me from doing so. Something that resembled fear. I was fearful that he *did* have something to do with it.

I cleared my throat and straightened my chin as Gemma and I began our walk over the soft, red carpet. The hallway grew darker the farther we went, and there was a looming shadow hanging over my head. Being back at St. Mary's, after the entire school knew something about me that was so far from the truth, felt like being trapped in that dull room at the Covenant Psych Hospital all over again.

A chill ransacked my body with the thought, so I quickly put an end to the silence. "So, is Tobias here yet?" We came to a stop at Gemma's door. She placed her box of things on the ground and continued walking farther down the hall—I assumed toward my new room, considering she had the keys.

She sighed. "Not yet. He's at Tat—I mean, the headmaster's house, down the road. He should be starting soon."

I nodded quietly, wishing that I had at least one person in this school that I trusted. Tobias, Gemma's twin brother who everyone thought was dead, had actually been stowed away at the same place I was, and he was honestly the only thing that kept me from losing myself to misery the last several months. I had done okay by myself. I learned who to trust and how to get my way—survival of the fittest at its finest—but when I came in contact with the broken boy in the basement of the psych ward who was abandoned and tortured for reasons unworthy, things changed. Tobias was the longest *'patient'* that the Covens had housed. The Covens was the disguised program veiled by the Covenant Psych Ward. It was the lowest level of the psych hospital that housed criminals and turned them into real-life monsters and the leaders desperately tried to turn Tobias into their ultimate black-market killer. He was being molded to do the dirty work of bad men, like his and Gemma's uncle, but we made it out of that fucked-up place alone, trusting no one but each other.

"I should say thank you," Gemma whispered, glancing at me briefly as the sconces on the walls flickered with our slow stride.

"Thank you?" I asked, my heartbeat growing increasingly fast. It made me anxious to talk to anyone about the last few months and what Tobias and I had done to get out of that place. Sister Mary tried getting me to open up, concerned with my well-being after learning that I didn't get placed with a foster family like she was told, but I couldn't. I couldn't talk about it because I was half-ashamed but also half-proud. And feeling proud of the things I did probably wasn't normal.

"Yes, thank you. Thank you for helping Tobias get out of that place."

"We helped each other," I answered quickly, tucking my hair behind my ear. I caught her soft smile just outside my new door, and although my fingers were shaking with the thought of everything that had happened and everything to come, I still grasped onto her gaze and allowed myself to bring up the one thing that tied us together. "About what you saw…"

Gemma's eyes dropped momentarily. "You mean when you came into where I was kept at the Covens?"

I nodded. "Yes."

Gemma huffed out a laugh, and her lip curved. "Journey, you don't have to explain yourself to me. I know a fighter when I see one. You do what you have to do to survive."

Gemma held the keys out between us, and I took them

tentatively. The second she let go, I clenched my fingers together, the keys digging into my palm to erase the things I'd done and touched at that corrupt place. "It's like looking in a mirror, yeah?"

I could see the white of her teeth as she smiled wider. "It's something only you and I will ever understand, Journey."

Silence passed between us, and she slowly began walking backward. "If you need someone, you know where I am. Okay? Sloane, too."

I nodded and turned around, heart beating wildly inside my chest. A slippery breath left my mouth as I canceled out the past and entered my room, making sure to check the lock twice before sitting on my bed, feeling just as trapped as before.

CHAPTER THREE

CADE

Dust flew from the inside of my book when I slammed it shut with one less-than-steady palm. My chest was tight with the questions buried deep below, and the second Journey was tucked away inside her room, I stepped out of the small cavity at the end of the hall that was blanketed in moonlight and whispered my best friend's girl's name. "Gemma."

A half-silent shrill left her as she spun around. "Cade! What are you doing?"

I snickered as I passed by Journey's room, forcing myself not to bang on her door. *She is so close, yet so fucking far away.*

I shoved the bent and worn paperback in my back pocket, not really in the mood to share my newfound hobby that I'd hidden away from prying eyes, and began walking in stride with Gemma. It was after curfew, but that didn't really seem to enter either of our minds—and I knew she was headed in the same direction I was. Gemma was basically my third roommate as of late, and most of the time, I had to go stay in Brantley's room because Isaiah and Gemma didn't hold an ounce of respect of not fucking with someone else in the room.

I take that back. Gemma tried to be respectful. Isaiah did not.

And he didn't take no for an answer in most aspects of his life. I could only assume it was hard for Gemma to deny him. Head Rebel and once the heir of the biggest gun-running business on the West Coast, he didn't like to be told no. Although, Gemma was the only one that got away with it.

I stared down the long, dire-looking girls' hallway, knowing I'd spent way too much time here in the last few months, trying to rid *someone else* from my mind. My question came out fast, like I was racing for an answer I wasn't sure I wanted. "What was Journey just referring to?" Gemma didn't talk much about being at the Covens, and I didn't blame her. When the Rebels and I entered those doors just over a month ago, it wasn't my first time in there. I knew what that place was: *hell*.

Gemma stopped dead in her tracks and angled her dainty little chin up to me. "It shouldn't surprise me that you were spying."

"Then, why do you look so surprised?" I countered, peering down at her.

Gemma rolled her eyes but couldn't hide the little grin on her mouth. "You Rebels are so invasive."

"Only with those that we love."

"I thought that word didn't exist for the rest of you."

I rubbed my jaw together, feeling the muscles in my temples hinge back and forth. "It didn't exist for Isaiah a few months ago, and now look at him."

Gemma stopped walking and turned to face me just a couple feet from the break in the hall. The light from the staircase that separated the boys' and girls' dorms shined on her face, and the pity lingered. Gemma was the only person at this school, other than the Rebels, that knew me well enough to know that I was completely fucked in the head over Journey. Her memory haunted me when she was gone, and now that she was back, I was pretty certain the Grim Reaper was the one haunting me now. Death from one glimpse of her gray eyes was what awaited me in the morning when she walked into the dining hall for breakfast—I just *knew* it.

"It's not my place to tell you, Cade. If Journey wants to discuss what happened at the Covens, then she will."

My heart thumped one hard, thundering beat. "She wasn't at the Covens. She was on the top floor, remember?" *Please tell me you haven't been fucking lying to me.* It wouldn't shock me in the slightest if Isaiah had withheld some of the truth from me regarding Journey. He knew I was a smidge unstable when it came to her, but it still bothered me, nonetheless. He didn't like to be kept in the dark, and neither did I. Although, there was a burning truth in the back of my head that singed me from the inside out, knowing I wasn't exactly brimming with honesty.

"Answer me," I said in a low voice as I thought about Journey in that place. The Covenant Psychiatric Hospital was an actual psychiatric hospital on the outside. There *were* people there that needed psychological help for numerous reasons, Journey being sent there for a suicide attempt, which was hard to even fathom. But the bottom floor housed criminals that were viciously turned into black-market killers, amongst other things. As far as I knew, Journey wasn't a part of that, but looking down at Gemma and the nervousness she was eliciting, I was starting to get antsy.

"Gemma," I warned. "She was on the top floor, right?" My throat began to squeeze, like a rope being tied around my neck. The knot dug deeper and deeper, cutting off my air supply every second that Gemma stayed silent.

She shrugged as my ears began to ring. "I don't really know, Cade. Yes, I think she was truly just a patient on the top floor." She glanced away, but I continued to stare down at the curve of her left cheek. "But she knew my brother, and he wasn't on the top floor—*ever*." Gemma's eyes flicked to mine, and anger coursed just at the mention of her brother.

I had no right to be jealous of him and his friendship with Journey, but *fuck,* I was jealous. Foaming-at-the-mouth jealous. I wanted to rip him to pieces, which was completely and utterly fucked up, because from what I had learned from Isaiah, Journey and Tobias had escaped that place *together*. He helped her, and for that, I was thankful.

My skin was hot to the touch, and my ears burned with an impatience that was close to panic. "What was she talking about, Gemma? What did you see while at the Covens that had to do with her?"

"Cade." Gemma rolled her lips together, fear and remorse drowning her green eyes. "Don't make me betray the trust of a girl who has no one on her side."

I was quick to step forward. "I'm on her side."

Her shoulders dropped. "I'm not sure she wants you on her side." She nibbled on her lip. "I'm not sure she wants anyone on her side."

Gemma and I stood in the hallway together, staring in silence. A wave of something crashed over me, and I clenched my jaw tight. No one had been able to understand why I'd been torn to pieces since that night. No one but Journey knew that I was supposed to meet her on that warm night and that I had stood her up. Not a single soul in this school understood the dark, raging guilt and confusion I'd been stewing in for the last eight months because Journey ended up severely hurt, and I wasn't sure exactly what had happened, but regardless, I knew it was my fault.

"Hey." Gemma's soft hand landed on my arm, and I flinched out of my thoughts. "Just give her some time, okay?"

"Babe?" Gemma kept her hand resting on my arm, and neither of us moved. Isaiah rounded the corner and stopped in his tracks. "There you are. You know I don't like you wandering the halls alone."

"Relax. Bain hasn't even glanced in my direction since being back, and plus, I'm with Cade."

Isaiah stepped forward, placing his hands in his pockets. His eyebrow flicked. "Yes, I see that. Brings me back to that time you were panicking in the forest after running for your life, and Cade had to bring you back down to the present."

I chuckled as Gemma's hand fell. Her tiny fists clenched, and she placed them on her hips, turning fully toward her boyfriend. I stood back with a half-grin on my face, momentarily letting the black pit in my stomach shrink.

"I wonder what would have happened if you didn't show up that night to take over?"

I watched as Isaiah's eyes darkened, and I sighed. "Will you two fucking stop it? Do not bring me into this. I have never wanted to fuck Gemma."

"Chill." Isaiah laughed, pulling Gemma into his chest in a single whoosh. "We're just messing with you."

"Sounds more like foreplay if you ask me."

Isaiah shrugged. "Maybe it is."

"Isaiah!" Gemma tried to act stern, but there was a ghost of a smile on her face.

I huffed. "I'll give you twenty minutes, and then you two better be done fucking."

"Done." Isaiah winked at Gemma, and she slapped his chest.

"Isaiah, I swear! Cade, come back to your room. We can all just hang out."

I crossed my arms, looking from my best friend to his girl-friend. "Isaiah's face is telling me differently."

"Yeah, Isaiah's face *is* telling him differently."

Gemma turned around in his arms and peered up to look at him. "Cade needs us right now. Let's be good friends."

Isaiah leaned down, his mess of hair hanging over his fore-head as he kissed the tip of Gemma's nose. "Okay, baby."

"*Jesus,*" I muttered. Neither Gemma nor Isaiah spared me a single glance as I leaned back onto the far wall. "I have something to do. I'll be back to the room in an hour. *Go*...you fucking love birds."

Gemma glanced behind her shoulder as Isaiah kept his hands along her hips, not bothering to look at me as he asked, "What are you up to?"

"Nothing."

"Cade. Give her time. Trust me."

I shook my head at Gemma. "I'm not going to Journey's room."

Isaiah barked out a laugh. "Fucking someone else won't help you forget about her. Especially now that she's back. And you couldn't last an hour fucking someone if you tried."

No fucking shit, Isaiah. I wouldn't even be able to get it up for someone now that she was back and looking just as down-right edible as ever.

I sensed the confusion and leeriness from Gemma even as I turned my gaze away and stared at the wall across from me, ignoring Isaiah's dig at my stamina. It was a nice wall. It would be a shame if I rammed my fist through it to feel *something* other than what I'd been feeling for the last several months.

As soon as Gemma and Isaiah turned around and sneakily walked back to the boys' hall, I turned my attention down the long hall and stared so hard at Journey's door I was half-surprised it didn't burst into flames. The door wasn't visible in the dark corridor except for every other beat as the candle-light seemed to flicker in a direct line of the dark wood.

Pushing off the wall with a loud huff, blood rushed to my fingertips as I stalked over to the linen closet that housed much more than extra bedding and towels. Just as my hand hit the cool knob, I heard the sound of a door opening. The iron-clad chains bounced off one another just as quickly as my heart thudded to the floor. I craned my neck and saw her small frame standing in the doorway of her new room.

Too many things hit me, and it was like being doused in gasoline. *Fuck.* I turned, knowing damn well I needed to go read my daily reminder that was tucked underneath the towel-lined shelf in that supply closet instead of walking toward her, but as soon as I squared my shoulders and caught a glimpse, she froze. Even from far away, I felt something shift in the air, and the next thing I knew, she was gone, and her door was slammed shut.

I swallowed the lump in my throat, fingers digging into the doorknob, and I rushed into the linen closet to get out of the suffocatingly empty hallway. I craned my neck back and breathed a heavy breath, blowing out the air inside my lungs to fill the tiny area. *This is exactly what you need.* I nodded, leveling my head, and walked two feet over to the left and bent down and shifted so I could push my fingers underneath the shelf. The tattered edges of the papers snagged with my rough skin, and I pulled the torn pieces toward me and sat back on my ass, resting my head along the soft towels. I pulled my cell phone out of my pocket, and the flashlight illuminated the words that I needed to read over and over again so it forced me to stay away, even if I wanted nothing more than to pull Journey into my chest and allow us to bleed together. Because that was what it felt like when I thought of her. Like I was bleeding and the wound just wouldn't fucking stop.

I scanned each piece of paper, one by one, folding them in half and putting them into my trusty little pile of secrets, until I got to the last one, knowing it was from the day that I last saw her.

HER DEATH WILL BE *on your hands*.

AND IT NEARLY WAS.

CHAPTER FOUR

JOURNEY

I THOUGHT I was through with this part. I thought that the first time I stepped foot in St. Mary's Boarding School my freshman year, it would be the last time I would ever have to face the uncertainties of being *that* girl, but here I was, once again, standing in the middle of the dining hall with a mask full of feigned confidence. Their eyes were following me, every single one of them. Voices were being shushed; whispers were being shared. The faculty was looking at me funny, too. My bare knees wobbled as I took a step forward, bypassing old groups of friends to get to the breakfast line. I grabbed a tray quickly, keeping my chin level as the blood drained from my face. Random food items were placed on my tray, and I was too blinded by my ability to stay focused on not running out of here to deny any of it. When I slowly turned around and realized that I had to find somewhere to sit, my stomach twisted.

The only good part about my day so far was the fact that

the Rebels weren't in the dining hall yet. But everyone else was, and I didn't trust a single one of them.

"Journ!" Sloane waved at me from across the dining hall. She was sitting at our—*my*—old table, and my eyes dropped to the open seat in between her and Mercedes. I recognized every face that stared back at me. It was like there was a giant spotlight above my head, and everyone was waiting for me to make a move with their breath trapped behind their lips. I knew time wasn't on my side. I shifted my gaze to the large, curved, dining-hall doors, expecting to see Cade walk through them any second now with a punch straight to my chest.

When I stared back at Sloane, my legs grew even more unsteady. I bit the inside of my cheek to keep the frustrating amount of emotion on lockdown that was clogging my senses at seeing my old roommate again.

Sloane was such a good friend to me, and it didn't feel fair to cut her out now that I was back, but I peered down at my covered arms, knowing there were long, pink scars running up and down each one, so instead of stepping toward her, I turned around.

I don't trust you anymore, and I'm sorry.

My chin raised again, and my shoulders straightened. My plaid skirt, that felt all too familiar to me, swayed as I made my way to the far-left table that housed not a single person. St. Mary's was usually a cluster of students sitting at each long, dining-hall table, the longest and middle table for the Rebels and most of the lacrosse team, along with some girls. Of course, Gemma was sitting there, and that was for obvious reasons.

I grew cold as I placed my tray down on the polished top. My fingers shook with nerves as I reached for my spoon, as if I were actually going to be able to eat, and that was when I felt a presence behind me. Sloane's perfume grew stronger the longer she stood there, and my mouth dried out with each passing second.

"Journey?"

I tipped my head back, just slightly, and caught her shiny dark hair resting over her shoulders. Her tone was soft and hesitant, as if she were approaching a timid hare, and I couldn't blame her for that.

"Hi, Sloane," I said as she sat down beside me. She straddled the long bench, facing me head on, but I kept my gaze locked onto my spoon.

"Are you okay?" she asked, leaning in so her voice was more of a whisper than anything.

Am I okay? No, not really.

"Yes, I'm okay. How are you?"

She laughed, and that was when I turned my gaze over to her. The hazel color of her eyes was muddied with something I couldn't pinpoint, and there was a crack right down the center of me that hurt. I was glued to my seat, completely unmoving.

The laugh disappeared from her lips quickly. "I know what you're doing." Her head shook, her glossy strands swaying softly back and forth. "It's not going to work."

"What are you talking about?" I asked, feeling the nerves duplicate in my stomach.

"You're protecting yourself."

I stayed silent because she was right, and it was no surprise that she could see right through me. She always was observant when she needed to be. When her hand landed on mine, I fought the urge to jerk away and allowed the fleeting thought of hugging my old best friend to vanish right from my head. "You don't have to protect yourself from me. I would never judge you, Journ."

The nerves in my stomach turned to hardened stone, weighing me down with each breath I held. I wanted to turn toward her and blurt out the truth right there in the dining hall, but after a few more seconds, Sloane stood up and shot me a soft smile. "I won't give up on you even if you are pushing everyone away. I'm here for you."

Tears stung the backs of my eyes as she slowly walked away, leaving me at my empty table with nothing but too many feelings surrounding me. If there was anyone left at this school to trust, it would be Sloane, but she was right, I *was* protecting myself. The only problem was that I wasn't sure who I was supposed to be protecting myself from.

My hands were still shaking as I reached for my spoon again. My back was to everyone, just the way I wanted it, and I was so far away from the dining-hall doors I was surprised I heard them open. *Round two, here we go.* Even if I hadn't heard the faint creak of the door, I would have known that *he* had walked in. A wave of awareness went through the dining hall like a tsunami. I felt his stare before I turned my head. He always could find me in a crowded room. My long, wavy hair brushed against the wooden table with the tip of my chin, and when we locked eyes, it was an arrow to my heart. I sucked in a breath even though all the air in my lungs had whooshed out.

Last night, I saw him from a distance. A lingering, dark shadow impeding the hallway like a vivid nightmare, probably sneaking into the room of some girl that would drop to her knees within seconds of him stepping foot inside, because he was a *Rebel*. When I saw him on the street at the orphanage, it was always a fleeting glance so he wouldn't see me staring back at him. I wanted to pretend so badly that I didn't notice him, or that his presence didn't affect me, but it did in the worst way. I felt pain when I saw him. Tangible, ground-shattering pain. His honey eyes were what kept me from closing mine at the psychiatric hospital, but the comfort that I felt with Cade from before was no longer as I stood in a place that I once called home, not sure if it would ever feel that way again.

The whispers in the dining hall grew more frequent as Cade remained unmoving just barely inside the archway. I could almost read the things being hushed on the tips of my classmates' tongues.

Cade and I were *never* exclusive, and I was too afraid to ask for more. It wasn't like I wanted the attention of being mixed up with someone like him—a ruler of the halls, a bad boy by default, a sinner amongst a school with many rules. Some knew that Cade and I had *something* going on, but it was never of confident certainty.

Now, though, I thought they may have guessed because he and I were at an impasse, and the longer we kept ahold of each other, the more my heart raced like a bull toward a red flag. His sandy hair was messier than ever, a little longer on top and cut short on the sides. His jaw was angled in stern determination, and the arches of his cheeks were slightly flushed. My stomach tightened at the sight because I'd seen his cheeks flushed on more than one occasion. Only now, they weren't because of me. *Is he with someone? Is that why he was late?* I swallowed the frustration at the one thought that came through, knowing it was the last thing I should have been thinking about, especially given the fact that I wasn't sure if he had something to do with the fact that I had almost died. Cade's chin raised, and it looked even sharper. His eyes bounced back and forth between mine for a split second, pinning me right there as I leaned over the desolate dining-hall table, until he shifted his gaze down to my arms that were covered by my maroon uniform.

Disgust was the first thing that came to mind, but what I saw when he looked back up at me was a visceral guilt, which sent me into complete fight-or-flight mode. Fear shocked me to stand up straight, and my arms crossed as my fingers dug into the soft fabric of my uniform.

Was it a mistake to come back here? It was surely better than the alternative, but at least at the psych hospital, I knew who the foes were.

My nervous gaze moved from Cade, and it traveled around the dining hall as heat rained down over my head, seeing just about every single person staring at me. All except one. *Bain.* I hadn't forgotten about him, not even for a single second. Bain was a mystery to me, but then again, everyone was a mystery to me now. He was cryptic, always watching me from afar but never getting too close. All I knew was that Bain and the Rebels didn't get along and that he had an interest in me, but never one that he had acted on. Cade despised Bain, but looking back, I wondered if maybe Cade was just afraid I'd slip through his fingers and Bain would be the one to catch me.

Nevertheless, it didn't look as if Bain had an interest in me now. He was the only one in this room that wasn't looking at me or Cade. He and I were like a car crash—no one could turn away, even though they knew they were invading. Bain's short, cropped head of hair was tipped down as he stared at his phone with a furrowed brow. His jaw was as tight as a bolt, but he didn't even spare me a glance. A part of me wanted to go sit with him because everywhere else I looked, I felt *seen*. And I knew my peers could likely smell my fear from a mile away even if I did have a straight spine and an impassive look on my face. I used to wear my emotions on my sleeve, but now, I knew when to hide them.

Instead of giving Cade or anyone else any more to feed off of, I turned my attention from Bain, pulled out the long bench at the empty table that I now considered mine, and sat down. I pulled my tray of food that I knew I wouldn't eat closer to me, and slowly, chatter began to fill the large room again, and my heart slowed from a marathon-like pace to a light jog.

Fear and anxiousness slowly left the base of my throat as I flung my hair over my shoulder, and the second I felt myself relax, I peeked to my left to make sure Cade had moved from the doors to his seat beside Isaiah, but when I snagged his attention again, the nervousness was right back to where it was before.

Why hasn't he moved? He was just staring at me, unmoving, like a blood-thirsty wolf ready to strike.

I turned away, and not even two seconds later, I jumped when I heard the creak of the door again. The slam of it echoed throughout the entire dining hall. A fork fell and clamored to the ground, and when I realized it had fallen from my shaking hand, I cursed under my breath and bent down to snag it, only to see it had already been picked up. My head tilted, and I was met with two warm green eyes that held entirely too much knowledge of me in their depths.

"Headmaster Ellison," I breathed out. "I didn't see you there."

Headmaster Ellison had always been on my side. He'd always been on every student's side, and when I saw him again, just a few weeks ago, covered in filth from running away from the psych hospital with Tobias, I couldn't deny the comfort that filled me. But that may only have been because I had been starved of parental figures my entire life. I take daddy issues to an entirely new level.

No one I knew had ever been able to truly relate to me because I'd *never* had parents. I'd never known unconditional love, and even though the other girls at the orphanage didn't have parents either, they always got adopted, and I was always left behind. To love and to lose was a burden, but to never have loved or been loved at all was even worse.

"Yes, well, there was quite the elephant in the room a few

moments ago. I won't hold it against you." Headmaster Ellison winked, and I felt the tiniest smile drawing itself on my face. "I just came by to give you this." He held out a piece of paper in between us, and I took it slowly, glancing at the contents. "Your new schedule. I know you've missed a few lessons this year, but your teachers are willing to give you extra credit or even tutoring if you need help catching up."

I shook my head. "That probably won't be necessary." I peeked up at him, trailing past his striped tie. "There was a library at the hospital. I spent most of my time there." *When I wasn't doped up on medication that I didn't need or sneaking through the halls to find a way out.*

Headmaster Ellison stiffened at the word hospital, and I quickly snatched the paper and laid it beside my tray. "Did you make su—"

"Yes," the headmaster interrupted me, and I was thankful he didn't make me say it aloud again. It was already hard enough asking him face to face to take me out of Cade's classes, if I were placed in any to begin with. The soft glint in his eyes that morning we'd discussed coming back to St. Mary's softened even further as he studied me in my vulnerable state. "If you need anything else, Journey, please do not hesitate to come to my office. At any time of the day." He lowered closer to me, placing a gentle hand on my shoulder in what I felt to be a fatherly gesture. "You are safe here, and I promise you that I will not let anyone take you away again, as long as you can promise me that you'll be open with me, yes?"

I knew why he was being so secretive with our conversation. The entire situation was so taboo and fragile, and it was likely something the headmaster never wanted to repeat in his life—ever. Neither did I.

The bell rang above our heads, and the headmaster quickly took his hand off my shoulder. He gave me a tight smile. "Have a great day, Journey. Don't forget, you do have friends here, okay?"

He turned around without giving me a chance to respond, and my eyes went directly to Sloane. She was in between Mercedes and Gemma, smiling at something one of them had said. I shifted my hesitant gaze over one more spot and held back a smile when I saw Isaiah's hand creeping underneath Gemma's short, plaid skirt, and I had to fight a laugh when I watched the headmaster hastily make a curve to the left to smack Isaiah on the back of the head.

Isaiah's voice carried all the way over to me. "What the fuck, Tate."

The headmaster's face was stern, but he stood in such a lax manner. "Hands to yourself, Isaiah, and quit calling me by my first name."

Jutting laughter fell upon Brantley and Shiner, two of the four Rebels. I didn't miss the fact that Cade was nowhere to be seen.

Relief filled me, but the disappointment buried deep beneath layers and layers of protection was like a slap to my face.

CHAPTER FIVE

JOURNEY

My eyes looked grayer today than they had yesterday. They looked more alive than I'd seen in the last few months, but I could also see the loneliness lingering inside them, too. The whites clashed with the red-rimmed almond shape, and although I did throw a little bit of mascara on this morning, I knew my eyes were bloodshot because of lack of sleep and from the day's events.

It was exhausting keeping everybody at arm's length. It was even more exhausting cutting people out that were confused by your behavior or misjudged your behavior for something that it wasn't. I remembered learning in the psych hospital that most mentally ill patients were some of the loneliest beings, unable to connect with others because they had such a heavy burden to carry.

That wasn't the case with me, but I knew that was what people thought.

My classes were full of nagging stares. My peers' curious thoughts hit me from every other angle. Mary's Murmurs, St.

Mary's secretive gossip blog that was somehow *still* a hot commodity at this school, had me featured right in the first paragraph. I couldn't even hold back the eye roll when Callie snuck her phone out from her blazer pocket and passed it around her little group of friends, all of whom discussed *me* in ghostly whispers.

The hallways were even worse than the actual classes. My stomach climbed to my throat as everyone gawked, and I rushed to every class quickly, in hopes of avoiding the Rebels, which only ended in me appearing like a fearful mouse, running for my life at the first glance from the boys who alluded authority with one curve of their rebellious smiles. They were hard not to notice. *Cade* was hard not to notice. He always had been, but now it was even worse.

Blowing out a deep breath from my pale, puffed-up cheeks, I tucked my wavy, sandy hair behind my ears, showing off my fake-diamond-studded ears, a gift from Sister Mary on my sixteenth birthday. My head dropped as I gathered my books off the ledge of the sink, ready to be one of the only students here that would rather hole up in their room instead of hanging with their friends or watching the lacrosse practice that was probably minutes from starting.

That was what I used to do. Sloane and I, and sometimes Mercedes, would drop our books off, grab a snack from the dining hall, and then sit out on the bleachers and watch the boys travel up and down the field in their hot dynamism, grasping onto their large crosses, laughing and being as carefree as I wished I could currently be.

My eyes would automatically find Cade. His tall, lean body frame, tight shoulders, and rigid muscles along his forearms would dance with a fluidity that only a strong athlete could have. His cheeky grin would meet me from across the field, and my cheeks would burn with giddy happiness.

"Who wants you gone, Journey?" I whispered, staring at

myself no matter how uncomfortable it made me feel. I hardly recognized the girl staring back at me. I was equal parts confident and uncertain. I was whole but also scarred—both metaphorically and literally.

I sighed once again as I turned and headed for the bathroom door, hoping that the hall had cleared out all the way so I could make it up to my room alone without a single stare pelting me in the side of the head. I was exhausted from pretending they didn't bother me. I wasn't sure I had the energy to fake anything else today.

The door slammed behind me, and although the hall was empty and echoed nothing but my thoughts, my heart began to thud quickly against my ribs. *Thump, thump, thump.* My teeth gritted as I relaxed my shoulders and evened my breathing, climbing the steps to the dorms one by one. Relief hit me when I reached the top, but I couldn't help the way my eyes traveled down the boys' hall. Cade was likely at lacrosse practice, so I knew he wasn't tucked away in his room, unknowingly squeezing my heart with his bare hands, but the memories of us meeting in this exact spot after classes to disappear for a short burst of time hurt all the same.

The feelings were still there. The ones that burned as bright as the stars and were as sharp as a hunter's knife. A flick of his eyebrow and the curve of his lips were a delicious cut to my skin, and his kisses were the balm that soothed them. Cade and I were a discreet type of chaos that only he and I were the center of. But our secrets had turned to hardened calluses all over my body, and the betrayal that he may or may not have been a part of grew tougher and tougher every second I was back here.

My eyes grew watery as I traveled down the girls' hall, only a few clips of chattering here and there from some of the cracked dorm doors. I kept my posture relaxed and only paused for a moment outside of my old room, wondering if

Sloane understood why I'd been distant and unforthcoming. There was a big part of me that wanted to reach out to her, to have some type of comfort, but the secrets remained, and I was more careful than before. Relief came next as I got closer to my *new* room. My eyes dried instantly as I pushed the ugly feeling of hurt away, but as soon as my hand hit the door-knob, the blood from my face drained.

"Journey."

A thick bundle of butterflies swarmed up my throat, suffocating me at the sound of my name coming from his hushed, abrasive voice. It rubbed me completely raw from the inside out.

Fear was present, but so was burning confidence. I spun around slowly, my knees brushing against one another as the plaid fabric of my skirt fluttered over my skin. Cade took a step forward, and my heart hiccupped, sending a flash of pain to my chest. His messy blond hair had a small wave in the front as it fell over his forehead, and his strong hands were shoved deep inside his pockets in the most relaxed manner that I'd ever seen.

He wasn't at all as affected as I was, and that was both alarming and disappointing.

"You're not going to talk to me?" he asked, taking another long, sinuous step toward me. My back hit my door in a single breath, and my books were pushed up against my chest like a shield of safety. I didn't miss the way Cade shifted his atten-tion to them, then back to me, and the way his head tilted just slightly in confusion.

Say something, Journey. I thought back to the girl I had turned into, if even momentarily, at the psych hospital and began lifting my chin, pushing back on the fear, but nothing came from my mouth. I'd thought over what I'd say to him, given the chance, every single lonely night that I was trapped inside a room that was sterile and homely, but now that he was standing in front of me, I couldn't hide away from the painful assumption that I was too afraid to know the truth.

"Nothing?" Cade whispered, mouth parting with ragged breaths as he erased the space between us. "And you keep running from me. You won't even look at me."

My eyes dropped even farther, and I stared at the St. Mary's crest covering the top left part of his maroon uniform blazer. My heart thumped faster, and when I let out a shaky breath and allowed his scent to crowd me like I was locked in a room with nothing but *Cade* on the inside, I shut my eyes.

There was a sound of shuffling first, and then his hand landed on my chin, and my eyes flashed back open at the speed of light, burning with something on the inside. *No.* I heard nothing but the vicious sound of blood rushing to parts that I wanted to shut off, giving life to things that I thought were dead. My chest climbed so quickly and swiftly that it brushed over parts of him, and his hand on my chin tightened. His eyes bounced back and forth between mine, the warm, golden flakes glowing with more intensity than I'd ever seen.

"Why, Journey?"

That single word carried such a punch that I nearly gasped. *Why? Why what?* There were far too many answers that could have climbed out of my mouth, and not to mention, I could have asked him the same. *Why didn't you show up that night? Why was Isaiah the one to find me with my wrists cut? Why did you keep me a secret for so long? Why did you keep coming to the orphanage after learning that I was back? Why didn't you try to find me after I'd left?* The answer to the last one cut me up inside because, for all I knew, he could have been the one who wanted me gone.

I felt the wobble of my lip before Cade noticed. His eyes widened momentarily before I slashed back at my vulnerability. "I could ask you the same, Cade."

His brow furrowed beneath the single lock of hair, his grip on my chin tightening enough to notice the bite to my skin. Fear was present, but all of a sudden, I was fed by this interaction like a starving animal. I wanted to scream at him. I wanted to bang my fists against his hard chest and ask him if he had something to do with it. *Did he want me dead?*

"Let go of her, Cade." Both Cade and I turned our attention down the hall, and I gulped up the comfort I felt at the sight of my old best friend walking down the long hallway like she was ready to strike out at the first appearance of a fight.

Cade let out a feral growl, and I felt it go straight in between my thighs. My cheeks flushed, and I hoped that, with the lingering darkness of this gothic school, he didn't notice that I was still twisted up over him. I didn't want to be. I didn't want to *want* anyone—especially not someone that held more secrets than a Pandora's box that went as deep as the ocean. My entire life was based on secrets. I didn't need any more.

"Or what, Sloane?" Cade took a step back, but I still could feel his anger as if it were my own. His arms crossed over his chest, and his jaw locked. "In case you haven't noticed, Journey is back. You can stop hating me now."

Sloane stopped right beside me and angled her slender body toward him with her arms crossed over her chest, too. "Yeah, no thanks to you. I have no doubt in my mind that you had something to do with what happened."

With what happened. Sloane was referring to my *suicide attempt.* My heart screamed inside my chest with the realization that everyone at this school thought I had tried to end my own life and that I had done it because of Cade. *Does he think that? Does he think I tried to kill myself because he stood me up?*

My brows furrowed as I moved my gaze from Sloane's little

sparring match to Cade's *very* alive stare. His entire body was facing me, as if Sloane wasn't three feet away from him, spewing insults. "Trust me," he whispered, placing his hands back in his pockets and slowly walking backward. I ignored the jab of pain I felt with his departure. It was like my entire soul had sung for him, and now it was screaming because he was leaving. The gap was forming again, and I needed to leave it open. Just before he got too far away, he finished his thought. "I know it's all my fault, Sloane. You should fucking know that by now."

Then, he spun on his heel and left me pushed up against my door with my heart in my stomach. Sloane stood beside me, as if she was my bodyguard, with her small hands bundled by her sides, until Cade was long gone, likely headed to his lacrosse practice that I knew he was now late for. Watching him walk away made me realize how much I missed him. How much I missed the way he made me smile and feel things other than the feeling of being jilted. I'd been abandoned when I was an infant, and it was a suffering that I had been surrounded in like a needle poking my skin every time I let myself feel.

"Are you okay?"

A shaky breath floated out of my mouth, and I nodded curtly. "Yeah, I'm fine."

Silence was shared by both of us. A jutting, painful, awkward silence that I hated. My eyes dropped to the red floor, and when I slowly peeked back up, I saw Sloane in a different light than before. Vulnerability looked good on a tough girl like her. A girl who wasn't intimidated by much— not even the Rebels.

"It's not you, Sloane," I admitted, thinking about our earlier conversation. It was something that I'd been thinking about since this morning at breakfast. I nibbled on my lip just like she was. "It's me."

Sloane dropped her gaze and nodded. "I'm so sorry, Journey."

"What? You're sorry? For what?"

My shields were still up, but they were shaking, like they were seconds from tumbling down.

"I should have been there for you."

I reached forward unknowingly and grabbed onto Sloane's warm hand. *This feels right.* "You were." I squeezed once and let go quickly.

Sloane peeked up and shrugged. "Maybe. But not everything is what it seems on the outside, Journey."

I huffed out a laugh, and Sloane's lips twitched. "You have no idea how true that is." I sighed, looking back down the hall again at Cade's no-longer-there shadow. "Trust me."

"I do trust you," she started, bringing my attention back to her. "But do you trust me?"

Do I?

"Hey, Sloane! Are you ready?"

Sloane and I turned at the voice of Gemma leaving their room. She was standing in the threshold of their door, wearing two black stripes on her cheeks like a football player ready to take the field. Her warm, chestnut hair spilled out from beneath her black beanie with a fuzzy ball on top, and she was wearing a large jacket over a St. Mary's t-shirt with Isaiah's number in the center. How did I know it was Isaiah's? *He is number one, always.* One of the first things I remember him saying when I met him.

"Yeah, I'm coming!" Sloane said, zipping up her jacket. She turned to me, and I saw the question before she said it. "Do you want to come to the game with us? We were gonna stop and get some hot chocolate from the dining hall before braving the snow to watch the guys." *There's a game today?*

I shifted uncomfortably at the hope in her eyes, knowing that Sloane was nearly begging me to go without actually doing so. "Still have the lunch ladies wrapped around your pretty little finger, huh?"

The white of Sloane's teeth gleamed in the thick darkness of the hall. "Of course. You know I'm Betty's favorite."

"Come with us, Journey," Gemma said, walking closer. "We can be stared at together. It'll be fun!"

I nibbled on my lip again, feeling the familiar feeling of friendship bloom inside my dismantled chest. "I know why people are staring at me, but why are people staring at you?"

Sloane busted out a laugh. "Because someone let it slip that the headmaster is Gemma's father, so now the entire school thinks that Gemma and Isaiah are incestuous."

"What?" I said, mouth dropping.

Gemma rolled her eyes, pulling a pair of mittens out of her coat pocket. "Mmhm. Everyone knew that the head-master was Isaiah's uncle—"

"But they're not blood related, right?" I knew that from when Tobias and I popped in unexpectedly a few weeks ago.

Gemma nodded, looking up from pulling her mittens on. "Yes, so take comfort in knowing you are no longer in the spotlight. Just me and my incestuous relationship."

A laugh flew from my mouth without being quick enough to hold it back. Gemma and Sloane shared a look, and it reminded me of better times. Happier times. Before I was leery of everyone and their true intentions.

Gemma's lips curved as she stared at me, probably knowing that I was teetering with the idea of falling into old friendships even if my guard was still up. "Now go get some-thing warm to wear and come hang out."

Sloane nudged me with her shoulder, softly coaxing me into hanging out. "You know Betty misses you. And I do, too."

I bit my tongue. There were unwanted feelings swarming me from every direction, and my heart beat harder when I thought about sitting up in the high bleachers on the lacrosse field with the sun setting behind my back, watching the one boy who made my world spin down below.

Only this time, he wouldn't be sending a hot grin in my direction followed by a wink that set my core on fire with anticipation. No, instead of that, this time I would be sitting in between two girls who didn't know a single ounce of the truth, while looking over my shoulder at wandering eyes that could have been the catapult to getting me taken from St. Mary's all those months ago.

No matter how comfortable I seemed being back at St. Mary's, I would never be able to relax until I found out the truth.

CHAPTER SIX

CADE

THERE WAS a calmness to the snow that I relished. The stark whiteness, the bone-cold lingering touch of the air that cooled your heated skin, the pliable feeling of it as you stood over it. Even in the middle of a lacrosse game, with the havoc of two teams fighting for victory and the mayhem of the student section that sat high up on the snowy hill, it was still calming to feel the cold flurries falling on top of you. Except, I wasn't calm. My heart was thumping violently, and my head was spinning like a car sliding too fast on black ice. Blood rushed to my flesh, and even if I lay down on this snowy field, it wouldn't cool me down in the slightest.

Journey was back, and I was in complete disarray.

She said one single sentence to me, and that was all it took for me to need a tourniquet to stop the bleeding. Her skin was soft against my hand, and it took every ounce of self-restraint not to push her farther into the door and swallow her words. The beating muscle that I tried to ignore, nestled deep inside my chest, flipped with the parting of her lips, and her warm gasp hit me like a sucker punch to the jaw. She felt so delicate in my grasp, but she felt heavy, too. There was a fleeting glimpse of fear buried deep in her gray eyes, and it sucked every bit of worry that I could produce from me and made an atomic bomb from it.

Why is she afraid of me?

Where was the girl who chased after the bright, fiery glow of disobedience with me? Where was the girl who drank off of my rebellion to feed her own? Where was the girl that gave every inch of herself to me?

But had she?

There were questions unanswered and assumptions that had been made. Trust had been broken, and a wedge of hushed secrets formed between us, thus leading to this moment right here, with her avoiding my gaze as I stared up at her from the middle of my lacrosse game.

"What the hell are you doing, Cade?"

I ignored Coach's gruff voice and kept my eyes on the top bleacher. His voice had pissed me off from the very beginning because it reminded me of my father, and any reminder of him was one too many. A small, scarce feeling of happiness filled me over the fact that Journey was back in her rightful spot on those bleachers with her friends. Sloane sat on one side of her, Mercedes on the other, and then Gemma to the left. If there were other groups of girls around, I hadn't noticed. Journey stole my attention. My gaze always seemed to find her, and I'd watch with pure, rapt attention, focusing on the smallest of mannerisms. Like the way her now-hollow cheeks and tiny nose were dipped in pink from the bite of winter air. Even when Journey was gone, I still followed the ghost of her, seeing a whiz of long, sandy-colored hair behind every lurking corner of St. Mary's, or hearing her voice late at night as I stood in the middle of the courtyard, wondering what had happened to cause her to leave.

A whistle blew, and my eyes flared when Journey's attention came directly to me. The whirl of the ball flew over my head as I gripped my crosse with my numb fingers.

"Cade, snap the fuck out of it."

There were cheers erupting. Everyone around Journey jumped up and clapped, all gleaming down at the field. Journey didn't stand, nor did she clap. Instead, she stared directly at me, and I stared directly at her. *What's got you so scared, Journ?*

Her head turned at the same time Brantley's wild eyes popped up in front of my face. "Cade, Coach is about to snap you in half. You just stood here for the last twenty seconds of the game like a fucking pussy-whipped bitch."

I grumbled, feeling a growl tear out of my chest at the fact that Journey looked away. "I'd like to see him try."

Brantley sighed agitatedly, annoyed down to his core. "Goddamn, here we go again. Two Rebels down, two to go." He threw his hands up in the air and stalked off the field, ripping off his gloves with frustration.

The next time I looked up at the bleachers, the girls were gone, and the disappointment was heavy. I dropped my head, evening my breath so I didn't punch Coach in the face, which would take a great deal of control—something I'd been mastering since Journey left. Because let's be honest, I'd like to punch just about every person I came into contact with.

I hastily turned around, the light dusting of snow that surrounded me disappearing with my heavy steps. My crosse was glued to my hand as a way to bring me back to reality, and instead of feeding Coach's ego and allowing him to yell at me for not playing the last twenty seconds of the game, I swiftly walked right past him, keeping my eyes on St. Mary's so I could dive into the shower to wash away the buildup of regret.

Isaiah caught up within seconds. I felt his eager questions before he even stepped in stride with me.

Isaiah had technically been set to be my boss before everything had gone down with Gemma just a month ago. Together, the Rebels and I sent our fathers to prison, but there were lingering whispers of threats from people in the business, and Isaiah was still brimming with authority. Who could blame him? We were all raised to be replicas of our fathers, and that shit went down to the fucking bone.

"Have you talked to her?"

I kept my gaze level, heading for the school so I could stand under a hot stream of water that would do nothing but burn my flesh even more. "Hardly," I grunted out, holding my crosse even tighter in my grasp. I could see Isaiah's head drop slightly out of the corner of my eye, and when we made it to the locker room with our teammates close behind, he quickly turned around and eyed me sternly.

"So, what are you going to do about it? Are you here to take your girl back? Or not?"

I scoffed. "It doesn't seem like she wants me to take her back." Spinning around, I put my back to him and calmed my erratic breathing. My eyes closed, but instead of calming down, all I could see was her in my head with bloody wrists and a faraway expression on her face.

I spun around quickly, throwing my crosse across the locker room with pent-up anger that was ready to be unleashed. "I need to just leave her be."

Isaiah shrugged nonchalantly, placing his crosse on the bench before sitting down. "Then, leave her be." He scanned my face closely, watching me like he was looking for a gateway to something deeper.

"You're not going to ask why?" I asked, treading with suspicion.

"I know why."

Our conversations were always short and to the point, but it felt like he was beating around the bush. "What is this? Are you trying to act like Ms. Glenburg? Trying to analyze me as if you are some psychologist?"

He smirked, and I rolled my eyes.

"If only you hadn't seduced our only school counselor months ago, then maybe someone with an actual psychology background could analyze me and my feelings."

Isaiah smirked. "As if you'd let someone get close enough to you to analyze your feelings."

He was right, but I went back to our earlier conversation and said, "You don't know why," before ripping my jersey off along with the long-sleeve shirt underneath it.

Isaiah threw his head back as he rested on the bench, stretching his long legs out in front of him. "I do know why. You're trying to protect her, just like I was trying to protect Gemma. Staying away isn't always the best form of protection, though. And it's up to her. Not you. Tell her the truth about you, and our past, the threats that are lurking like moles out there in the fucking dirt of this corrupted earth, and see if she wants you."

I turned around slowly, putting my back to him as I walked over to the showers. "You don't even know the truth, Isaiah."

The sound of his long strides came next. "What do you mean I don't know the truth?" I didn't have to look back at him to know he was expelling anger from every pore. That was just Isaiah, and to be honest, I was the same. "Cade, is there something I need to know? That you haven't already told us? Did someone contact you? Your father?"

I turned around, now fully naked. "My father is in prison. So is yours."

Isaiah threw his head back in mock laughter, stripping down to take the shower beside me. "We both know that just because those fucks are in prison, it doesn't mean a single thing. What about your mom? Has she reached out?"

I almost laughed at the thought. Although my mother was totally coherent, unlike Isaiah's, who had suffered brain damage from being a casualty in his father's sick games, my mother left me high and dry. She wasn't sticking around to deal with the laced threats of retribution of my father's future behind bars, and she didn't bother asking me to come with her. *Must have slipped her mind.*

The water fell like pelting rain droplets of fire along my skin, and I bristled under the scorching burn. It was surely better than feeling the icy sting of Journey's and my earlier run-in, along with the fact that my entire family was nothing more than a speck of dirt on the bottom of my shoe.

"Burying shit never works, Cade. What's going on?"

The pressure wasn't leaving my chest, and the thought of tonight's claiming party—which usually gave me a minor escape—was doing nothing but making me antsy. *Will she go?*

"Cade."

I shut my eyes under the stream, allowing the water to drown me for a moment. When I opened my eyes back up at the sound of the locker room door opening and the chattering of my teammates, I gave Isaiah a quick look, and he met my gaze instantly.

"You afraid it'll happen again?"

"Am I afraid what'll happen again?"

Flashes of that night were coming back, and it made my skin itch under the heat. She was lifeless, and the regret and guilt were so heavy that night I could hardly stand after the paramedics took her.

I shut my eyes again, trying to shove away the visual of her and the way my heart screamed in agony, but the more I stood under the hot water, the heavier the memory grew.

• • •

THE NOTE CRUMPLED *in my hand for the fifteenth time, and the pen was smeared from the constant crushing and smoothing. My back rested along the hard wall of the hallway, hidden away from everyone that would become suspicious about what I was doing out of bed after curfew. Not that I didn't leave my room after curfew often—we all did—but I was sitting here like a recluse, holding a crumpled piece of paper in my hand, feeling as if I were the one torn instead of it.*

I knew that Journey was where I told her to go, and I had no way to tell her that I wasn't coming, which would ruin everything anyway. She didn't have a phone, and with the threat laying in my shaky fingers, I didn't even want to risk going out there. Someone wanted me to leave Journey alone, and I had no fucking idea who it was, which drove me mad. I'd eyed everyone with total distrust, even my friends, which was complete and utter bullshit. I needed to tell them what was going on, but I'd found myself in a position that went against everything I'd promised.

I wasn't supposed to get attached to someone. The Rebels and I didn't have plans of settling down with anyone, especially not at this godforsaken boarding school full of misfits and girls who were daring enough to break the rules. It was supposed to be a one-and-done type of thing, but...Journey. She was different. The slight curve of her lips sent me into overdrive. The blush on her cheeks did nothing but push me to make her blush deeper. The sweet sound of her laughter as I flirted with her in secret was like a rehabilitation to what I was raised to become. She and I were a ticking time bomb. I had known it from the beginning.

My stomach tightened even though I knew I was doing the right thing. Pushing her away was necessary. It hurt me to do so, which was scary because I didn't often feel pain. For someone that had been punished for feeling much of anything his entire life, pain was always brief. But tonight, it was staying, and it was potent. I had to force myself to swallow the guilt of hurting her, because this was going to fucking hurt.

I glanced down at the note again, knowing I had a dozen more stored away in the linen closet. For a while there, I was just waiting like a wolf, prowling the forest for its prey. I figured whoever was fucking with me would slip up eventually. I'd been raised for this: to find a threat before it was even created and destroy it immediately with my own bare hands. But no one had slipped up, which made me wonder if my father had somehow gotten wind that I had something that I cared about. I wouldn't put it past him to take her away from me just like he took everything else.

My head flung back onto the hard wall behind me, sending a jolt of pain through my skull. My fingers clenched tightly, and a sweat broke out along my temples. The longer I sat here, knowing that Journey was out in the courtyard with a heart full of hope and eyes burning with excitement of spending her night underneath me, the more I wound up. I was strung as tight as the metaphorical noose around my neck to the point that I stood up and was seconds from pounding on her and Sloane's door. Sloane could go out there and get her. Sloane wasn't stupid. She knew something was going on with Journey and me. Half the school likely did. My friends did, too; they just thought it was the typical fuck-and-done deal. But it wasn't. It wasn't at all. I wanted to keep her forever.

I turned on my heel, shoving the torn paper in my back pocket, but I paused at the sound of sirens. My brow crowded, and I rushed over to the window of the small nook I was hidden away in and peered outside. Who needs an ambulance? My heart was twisting as it fiercely beat against my ribcage, and the second I landed on a limp body in my best friend's arms, it died all together.

"No," I muttered, turning and rushing down the girls' hall. My feet skidded against the carpet, and I skipped steps with suffocating panic filling my lungs. I couldn't breathe, and my vision was growing blurry with stress. What the fuck happened? My plans were going up in flames at my back, and I suddenly didn't know right from wrong or what direction I was supposed to be heading in.

The warm night hit my heated face as I rushed past the headmaster's open office door and out to the front of St. Mary's. Not a single *stone step hit my feet as I leaped over them all to land on the hard ground, and the second Isaiah rounded the side of St. Mary's, holding the only thing that had ever made me feel something in his arms, I had to physically force myself to stand.*

The ambulance was flying up the winding road, rushing past the iron gates of our stowed-away, castle-like school, but the only thing I could hear was the echoing words of the note stored in my back pocket and the rushing of my blood to every inch of my body like a dam being broken in half.

"Journey," my voice cracked as I stared at her lifeless body. Isaiah was speaking to me, yelling something, but I couldn't move. Journey's head was flung backward, and her pretty, long locks of hair had flakes of dirt in them, as if she was thrown on the ground in the courtyard as she waited for me. Her flawless, kissed-by-the-sun skin was no longer a golden tan but pale with streaks of blood covering both arms and her shirt.

I tried to rush over to Isaiah as time passed too quickly but too slowly all together. The headmaster's hands wrapped around my torso, stopping me, as I clawed to get closer. "Wh—what, what happened?"

The sound of my yell broke the silence around me, and suddenly, I was met with Isaiah talking with the paramedics as he handed off something that belonged to me, with Headmaster Ellison telling me to look away.

"Why is she bloody?" I asked, still struggling to get out of the headmaster's grasp.

Isaiah rushed over, but I stared past his shoulder at the paramedics jumping into the back of the ambulance and watched in defeat as it flew down the winding drive to leave St. Mary's all together.

"Cade." Isaiah's hands were around my face the second the headmaster let go of me. I tumbled forward and gripped onto Isaiah's shirt that was covered in blood. Vomit burned the back of my throat as he looked me dead in the eye and said, "I found her with her wrists slit." He looked away briefly toward the courtyard. "It looked—"

The headmaster interrupted my best friend, and I had no energy to throttle him for what he'd said. "It looked like she tried to commit suicide, Cade. Now, both of you get inside. We need to talk."

THE SHOWER BEING TURNED off brought me back as I blinked through the water droplets clinging to my eyelashes. A surge of intense emotion clung to my bones as I revisited the one night in my memories that I pushed away until I couldn't any longer. Isaiah flung a towel at me as I stepped out of the water, and he finished our conversation.

"You know exactly what I'm talking about. I can see it in your eyes. We still don't know what really happened that night. Maybe you should find out. *From her.*"

I gripped the white cotton towel roughly and wanted to throat punch Isaiah for bringing up that night, even if I was already thinking about it. It was like a black cloud always hanging over my head, and the mere sound of her name on anyone else's lips made me recoil on the inside because every time I heard it, I was brought back to the last time I saw her. *Bloody.*

Anger filled me as I rushed to get dressed. I didn't make eye contact with a single person, not even Shiner or Brantley as they joked and tried to pump me up for the claiming party where everyone assumed I'd pull my normal shit and fuck a willing girl in one of the dirty, hidden rooms. We had more freedom lately. It was the first claiming party that Isaiah, Brantley, Shiner, and I didn't have to watch Bain—our former rival's son who we were all sent here to *watch*. Bain was no longer a threat that quite literally fucked with our futures. Brantley and Shiner were ready to let loose, and I would have been, too, if *she* wasn't here.

Instead of losing myself in someone for the mere twenty minutes of solace, I was going to be consumed with Journey —even if she didn't show up. Because I knew if she didn't show, I'd be in that hallway, waiting for a mere glimpse of her to pop out of her room like the previous night.

Shiner's hand slapped on my shoulder, and every muscle in my body tensed. Something clicked into place, and if it weren't for the tiring game I'd just participated in and the practice of self-control over the last several months, I would have broken his arm in half.

Goddamn, I'm on edge.

"You ready for tonight? Or are you going to stand back against the wall like a fucking freshman at his first party all because Journey is back?"

I bared my teeth, and Shiner's wry smile stroked my anger and poked at my temper. "Oh, we still can't say her name? Sorry. Party starts in an hour. There's a flask tucked behind the portrait of my ol' pal Abe Lincoln in the east hall. Have at it. You need a fucking drink."

I shook Shiner's hand off my shoulder, knowing very well he was right.

———

DAMP, mildew-infested dirt mixed with spicy cologne and fruity perfume filled my lungs. I nearly gagged on the scent. The taste of tequila was persistent on my tongue, and I instantly regretted tipping the flask back before prowling down the veiled hallway that led to the private claiming party, because the taste pushed me right into purgatory.

The last time I had tequila was on the roof of St. Mary's with the one girl that I was looking for at the moment. I wasn't sure if she was coming tonight, but I had a hunch because Isaiah kept his eyes on me every time the door to the party opened. The way these parties worked, since they were after curfew, was that everyone had an allotted time to travel the halls to miss the duty teacher. It wasn't hard to eclipse the authority in this school. Most of them didn't want any distur-bances, so they didn't really *look*.

"They'll be here soon," Isaiah said as he walked past me, heading for the table of open shots. The lights were flickering back and forth like a rave, and everyone was high on rebellion and drunk on bad decisions. The guys were scoping out the girls, deciding who was making eyes at them and speaking silently of their plans for the rest of the night. I'd been there, done it. Multiple times. I wasn't in the mood for any of it tonight.

The burn of jealousy surged through me like a hot, metal rod pinning me to the wall. I scanned every guy in the dark room that I knew would make a bad decision and try to pull something with Journey.

I settled on Bain's group of friends.

He was nowhere to be found.

I knew a rat when I saw one, and although Bain had been quiet for likely the first time in his entire life, and he had helped get Gemma back from the Covens, I didn't trust him enough to even blink when he was in front of me.

"Where's Bain?" I asked as Isaiah came and stood beside me. Brantley and Shiner were on the floor, slinging shots like this was their first go-around. To be honest, it sort of was, because we weren't working for our fathers tonight. There was no true need to find Bain or to follow his moves like before. Except, I would anyway.

"He was here somewhere." Isaiah scanned the crowd along with me. The thudding of my heart matched the upbeat song climbing from the speakers.

"I still don't trust him," I grumbled in a low voice, clenching my jaw.

Isaiah's eyebrows crowded as he searched further. "For good reason. He helped us, but that doesn't mean I trust him either. I don't want him around Gemma. Ever. And he fucking knows it."

I didn't have to say it for him to know that I didn't want Bain around Journey either. The way he used to gaze at her made me recoil with something much stronger than jealousy. He always had his eye on her, and no matter the threats either of us sent his way, he didn't budge.

Some could say I was paranoid due to my upbringing, but I didn't believe in coincidences. Too many fucked-up things had been stemmed from *coincidences*. Nothing was ever coincidental.

"I don't see him." My irritation kicked up a notch the longer the girls weren't here and the longer Bain was missing. Old habits never died. *Where the fuck is he?*

"Me neither," Isaiah said, a roughness to his voice as he shouted over the music. I knew he was ready to travel back through the underground hall that we used to get down to the lower level of St. Mary's, but a second later, he breathed out a hefty sigh. "It doesn't matter. The girls are here."

I was doomed from the very second I caught her standing inside the doorway of the party with her little group of friends.

My stomach fell to the cold, damp ground, and my eyes flared with angry heat. I had no right, but I was pretty certain Journey had just declared war with me. I was already on my way to her, ready to shove her back through the bleak, empty hall all the way up to her fucking room to change her outfit.

Absolutely not.

"You have no right, Cade." Isaiah was in front of me before I could even take a step. "Are you leaving her be? If so, turn the fuck around. She can wear what she wants."

"Says the guy who broke down fucking doors when he was supposed to be leaving a certain *good girl* alone."

Isaiah's jaw ticked. "If you want her, then go fucking get her. But an hour ago, you said you didn't."

I seethed under my breath. "Oh, I fucking want her, Isaiah. I just can't have her."

Isaiah's hands never left my chest, and I was sure he could feel the angry beat of rage thumping on the inside. "You're not telling me something. I can see right through you. This goes further than the shit with our fathers."

I grunted. "The shit with our fathers isn't as clean cut as you're making it out to be."

He shook his head as the song changed in the background. People were likely gawking, and I hoped every guy in this room could feel the uptick in my blood pressure and *knew* not to fuck with her. "There's something else going on. Keeping secrets won't get you anywhere. Especially not with her. You should know this by now."

"Keeping secrets is how I was taught to survive." I shoved Isaiah's hands off my chest, stalked over to the far back wall, and leaned my back against it, keeping my eyes on a set of toned legs that sent a wicked dose of desire into my bloodstream.

CHAPTER SEVEN

JOURNEY

GIVE them something to stare at. There was a piece of motherly advice that I would hold onto for dear life. And I meant motherly advice as in *Cosmo* magazine, because I didn't have a mother, but I'd like to think she was confident and fiery and gave me up for a reason and not for her own selfish desires. Maybe it was the dreamer in me that chose to cling onto something as optimistic as conjuring up some far-fetched fantasy of a mother that I never knew, or maybe it was a way to protect myself from the feeling of rejection, like my existence was unpalatable to those who created me.

Regardless, I was giving the entire student body of St. Mary's Boarding School something to stare at tonight. This claiming party was officially *claimed* by the version of Journey that none of these people knew, except maybe Gemma. She saw me in that place. That corrupt, sterile hospital that was quite literally what nightmares were made of. But other than her, my peers wouldn't look at me like the girl who tried to kill herself. At least, that was the plan.

I knew I'd made the right choice as I pulled down the articles of clothing from Sloane's closet while getting ready for the party. It'd been so long since I'd snuck out of my room and actually sought out *fun* instead of survival. Each time I snuck out of my room at the psych hospital, it was for a reason that far outweighed drinking mindlessly in a damp basement full of teenagers partying and kissing like there was no tomorrow. Although, tonight I wouldn't just be turning heads and causing whispers. The second the lights went out, I was going to travel on an entirely different adventure—one that didn't include Gemma, Mercedes, or Sloane.

"Good choice on the outfit," I heard a sultry voice pop up behind me and the girls when the door to the party shut behind us. I didn't look back because the tone of voice didn't really match the compliment. Gemma's hair tickled my arm as she peered backward, seeing who had spoken, but before she could say anything, the voice started up again. "It'll take away everyone's first impression of you—for a moment, at least."

I side-eyed Gemma as she fully spun around, and I was half-thankful for the distraction. I knew I would gain attention tonight, like I'd been gaining since the night they found me bleeding, and I knew I wouldn't enjoy it. I would just rather people saw me as confident instead of clinging onto some false idea of me. "And what impression is that, Aubrey?"

Aubrey. I knew the name. She was one of Callie's friends. I'd never had an issue with girls before, and considering I was the oldest at the orphanage, no one dared to get bratty with me. The little ones looked up to me like a big sister, and they were the closest thing I had to a family—until they were adopted. But Aubrey's tone hinted at an insult.

Her light scoff hit the back of my neck, ruffling my hair. "It's just that everyone sees Journey and thinks *emo*. We wouldn't be surprised if she wore thick eyeliner and black polish on her nails." Her laugh irked me, so I quickly spun around, making sure to keep my eyes away from the crowd in front of me. Aubrey was pretty, but forgettable. She didn't stand out, but I kind of envied that at the moment. I'd never liked much attention, which probably stemmed from years and years of gaining attention from potential adoptive parents only for them to reject me in the end. If no one noticed you, then you could protect yourself from the hurt of being the only outcast.

I shrugged, looking Aubrey in the face as she watched with humor. I pulled my freshly polished, black nails up and gazed down at them. "Looks like I'm already halfway there."

Gemma, Mercedes, and Sloane stayed quiet as everyone watched our little spar, along with most of Aubrey's friends—Callie being one of them. They had never been anything but nice to me before, but apparently, something other than just me had changed over the last eight months, and I had a hunch I knew what it had to deal with. It made my stomach sour at the thought.

Aubrey rolled her eyes at my choice of shiny black nail polish and scanned my outfit again. I did the same, stopping at the tiny peek of skin against my flat belly that stood out beneath the tight black crop top, and then traveled down to the mini-skirt that was a little loose along my hips. I wonder what she'd say if I took off the black leather jacket and showed off my scars.

Sloane stepped forward as we all scanned my choice of clothing again. Part of me wanted to take the heel of my boot and slam it on Aubrey's toe for becoming one of those girls who tore down others to make themselves feel better, but that'd make me just as bad as her, so I stayed silent.

"I know what this is about." Sloane's smile slithered across her face as she crossed her arms over her own tight tank.

Aubrey's blue eyes flickered with annoyance as she turned to Sloane, waiting for her to finish.

"You're jealous."

Aubrey nearly squealed. "Jealous?" She looked over at me again. "Of her?"

Sloane tried to suppress a laugh. "Now that Journey is back, you know your late-night visits with Cade are no more. You're mad that she took your fuck buddy."

I stepped forward, the toe of my boot hitting the front of Aubrey's stripper heels. I plundered the jealousy right from her full chest and gripped it in my tight fingers as I reverted to the girl who thought she meant more to Cade Walker than she probably ever did. "You can continue your late-night visits with Cade. I'm not here to steal him back from you."

The blush on her already pink cheeks ripened. "I wasn't aware that you had him to begin with, *freak*."

I laughed at her attempt to wound me and did nothing but speak the truth back. "I didn't, and neither will you."

Turning around and leaving Aubrey's next insult to linger at my back, I grabbed onto Sloane's hand, and together, along with Gemma and Mercedes, we walked farther into the party. As soon as we were out of earshot from the other girls, Mercedes breathed out a sigh of relief. "I've never seen Aubrey act like that," she huffed, looking back once with a dirty look on her face. "It's not like she hasn't had sex with other guys. I know she's slept with Shiner."

Sloane snatched a couple of drinks off the nearby table, and I made sure to keep my eyes down because I knew, without a doubt, that there were a set of eyes on me that were just begging me to look.

"Keeping tabs on Shiner, are ya?" Sloane grinned, and Mercedes bristled at the assumption.

"What? No. It's not that hard to know who he sleeps with. He fucks everyone."

"Apparently, so does Cade." I ached from just saying his name aloud. My heart screamed with rushed beats, and I hated myself for feeling the jealousy. *He was mine—'was' being the operative word here.*

"Hey, baby." Isaiah sauntered up seconds after my lapse in rationality and kissed Gemma right on the lips. My brows shot up in surprise as he wrapped his hands around her waist and plunged his tongue down her throat. A growl of pleasure left him, and it must have been normal for them to show so much PDA, because no one seem fazed by the scent of sex in the air. *Okay, then.* Tobias was going to lose his mind when he saw his sister getting tongue-fucked. His love for his sister went deep. It had kept him alive in the shithole we both called home once upon a time.

I leaned into Sloane's ear with my eyes set on the prize, pushing away the untrusting thoughts when it came to anyone but myself. *You can trust her.* "I'm going to disappear when the claiming starts. Don't worry about me, though. Okay?"

Her eyes widened slightly, and I wasn't sure if she was surprised I was confiding in her after being so standoffish, or if she was just worried. "Where are you going?"

I may have let my guard down *some* when it came to Sloane, but not that much. "I just need to be alone. But I'm fine."

Sloane came and stood in front of me, placing her hands on my shoulders. She bounced her gaze back and forth between mine, and I saw the conflict there, and the only thing it did was push me to trust even more. "Sloane, remember what I said earlier? That not everything is what it seems?"

She nodded, her black shiny hair catching the blue strobe light from above.

I leaned in again, whispering in her ear. "I'm not suicidal." Her gasp was subtle, but it was there. "And I never was."

Pulling back out of her space, I felt her hands tighten on my shoulders. Her thick, black eyelashes fluttered in confusion. Before she could say anything, I turned my head to the left and caught him immediately. I knew where he was the second I stepped foot in here, which was why I had avoided that side of the room. We were two unmoving beings stuck in a pandemonium of sorts. Loud music, gyrating bodies dancing, shots being spilled on the dirty floor, hushed conversations happening. And there we were, staring at one another, locked and loaded like a pistol being held to both of our heads.

His warm eyes were as dark as the night, and sharp, jutting shadows covered his features, showing off his angled jaw and full lips. He wore a white t-shirt and dark jeans, and the second I let my gaze travel his body and found his eyes again, it felt like his hand was around my throat, suffocating me. He glared at me, jaw ticking like a clock that was timing us, and my breath hitched when he scanned me just as I had him. I nearly jumped when his gaze snapped to mine again, the warmth I always found myself latching onto turning into icy disappointment. His lip snarled, and something burned on the inside. One shake of his head, and just like that, I found myself becoming angry. Almost as angry as I had been that first month in the psych hospital when I blamed him for what had happened to me.

I would have never been in that courtyard alone if it weren't for him.

My lips twisted upward as I kept ahold of his stare, pushing away the sliver of fear and reserved caution I held with almost everyone now, and shook my head right back at him. He had no authority over me, especially not now.

The longer Cade and I stared at one another, the more my

body tensed. We were halted, both of us too stubborn and full of quiet confessions, and maybe even a little hate, to look away from one another. Maybe it was my choice of outfit or the constant whispers and gossip that had been happening since I came back, but the skittish, fearful Journey was no longer in sight tonight. I suddenly wanted to bang my fists on Cade's chest and take out every bit of resentment I had on him. If I didn't have undisclosed plans for tonight, I may have found some guy to lose myself in *just* to dig the knife a little deeper into both of our chests.

I silently growled like the muzzle was finally off, and when angry lines formed on Cade's face, along with an overpowering stench of dominance following his every step, I steadied myself for the impact. We were seconds from exploding, and things were going to be said that I hadn't braced myself for, no matter the confidence and anger that I was exuding at the moment.

The scratching of the speaker sounded overhead, and the music cut off. Cade stopped mid-step with his hot gaze full of too many things I couldn't decipher set on me.

A voice reverberated through the room. "Remember the rules, St. Mary's. And watch out for the Rebels. We're on the prowl tonight." There was a pause, and I swallowed the words that were reserved for Cade.

Isaiah shouted from behind me. "Except for me. I'm only here for one girl."

Some of our classmates laughed, but Shiner, who was the one speaking through the mic, ignored Isaiah's comment.

"Turn the lights off. *It's claiming time*."

MY FOOT SPLASHED in the same puddle I'd slipped in when going through the thin door to the underground hallway. The faint glow of the candles along the wall warmed me as I shut out the claiming party and *other things*. I took off my boots, gripping them by the laces, and continued on my path to the headmaster's office.

My toes were chilled against the tiled floor, but I knew it was crucial to be as quiet as possible when out of bed after curfew. Not so much at St. Mary's, but at the Covenant Psych Hospital, being found out of your room when you weren't supposed to be ended badly. *Always*. So, take it as you will, but I did learn some valuable skills at that psychotic place.

Rounding the hall, I listened past the beating of my heart as I grew closer to Headmaster Ellison's office door. I glanced at the two tall oak doors that led out to the cold, wintry air and realized just how easy it would be to slip out of them and just leave.

But where would I go?

It was a special kind of torture not having a family or a place to call home. It was precisely why I was breaking into the headmaster's office to uncover the secrets of my life. I was doubtful there would be anything useful in my school file, but I had to try. When I'd first asked Sister Mary about my past before I ended up at the orphanage, she said there wasn't much to tell. I was young and naive, and I believed everything that everyone told me. It took me years to fully grasp the concept that people lied, and things weren't always what they seemed.

If you wanted to find out the truth about things, you had to sort through the secrets and lies on your own, and I was certain my life had a load of them that I wasn't even aware of. And just maybe it had something to do with what had happened eight months prior.

Tucking my softly waved hair—thanks to Mercedes— behind my shoulder, I placed my ear up to the door of Head- master Ellison's office. My heart feasted on fear, but there was a hint of delicious rebellion that followed softly behind each beat. When I felt confident that Headmaster Ellison wasn't inside and likely back at his new home down the winding road from this school, playing the role of *father,* I took the hairpin out of my jacket pocket and began working the door like Tobias had taught me to do.

Three misses, but the fourth one would do. I stood up straight, feeling proud of my achievement for a brief second, before turning the handle and quickly darting inside to shut the door behind me. A sigh of relief filled the expansive yet cluttered office. It smelled of burnt wood, the husky, leftover smoke causing me to cough. My boots were placed beside the door, and I walked over the soft carpet and flipped on the lamp on top of his desk. Papers were flung all over it, covering every inch of dark wood. Another small smile found itself on my lips as I laughed at how unorganized Headmaster Ellison always seemed to be. He was in over his head 99% of the time, and it was probably even worse now that he had the newfound responsibility of being a father.

But what would I know about being a father? Or daughter? *Nothing.* I knew nothing, and Headmaster Ellison seemed like a decent guy from what I could tell. He had a special kind of charisma to his persona, and if you paired that with his warm expression and caring nature, he was about as fatherly as you could get.

My quiet footsteps traveled around the headmaster's desk as a thrill raced up my spine. I'd missed sneaking around. A sort of calmness found itself nestled inside as the solace of this messy office surrounded me while looking for anything related to me or my past.

I wasn't naive enough to think there was anything useful in here. It wasn't as if there would be a giant red arrow pointing to some boogie monster in my past that led me in the direction of whoever tried to kill me, but I had to start somewhere, and this was a good beginning. I sure as hell wasn't going to ask Cade if he was the one to do it, or if he knew what had happened to me that night. *No way.* Not yet. I wasn't sure my heart could take either answer.

After shuffling through the papers scattered on the desk, peeking at Tobias' school schedule that, thankfully, was very similar to mine, I tried to pry open the two drawers near the bottom ledge, but they were locked. My hairpin kept getting caught, and a fine line of sweat began to trail over my hairline, so I moved past those and tiptoed over to the bookshelves that surrounded the fireplace. I coughed again, covering my mouth from the lingering smell of burnt wood. There were lines and lines of books that went all the way to the ceiling, and I was suddenly very jealous that the headmaster got to spend his days here instead of the glamorous halls of St. Mary's where gossip was the pulse that allowed this school to live.

Rushing over to the chair that I sat in just a day ago, I pulled its heavy mass over to the bookshelf and climbed on top, trailing a single finger over each spine of the archaic books that gave me comfort in the simplest of ways. I'd always found myself reading as a young child and even now as I entered adulthood. Books were an escape—a way to live a different life at a different time. And when your days were filled with unwanted visits from future adoptive parents who didn't want you, they came in handy when you had to reconstruct that feeling of disappointment into something else.

My eyes shut as I breathed past the smoky scent of the fire and inhaled the dust of history and a thousand lives. The thought already occurred to me that I may sneak a book or two from the shelf—maybe one that I didn't think the headmaster would miss—and spend my evenings reading instead of snooping through the school for any indication that there was someone here that wanted me dead. Just as I opened my eyes, staring at the files that were on the very top shelf, I froze. My hand stilled against the spine of Jane Austen's *Emma*, and fear rushed down my spine like dominos falling to their ending.

"I see your love for books hasn't died." His voice stacked those dominos right up, and they pounded me in the back until they thudded straight into my chest. My eyes were locked on the tattered book in front of me, one leg up on the shelf as my other stayed on the arm of the chair, stretching as far as it could without causing me to buckle. The door shut quietly behind him, and I swore the headmaster's office kicked up another degree. "What are you doing here, Journey? You know there is a library full of books, just like the one you're stealing...free for you to read."

Annoyance blinded my shock of him following me, which irked me to oblivion. I should have known that he'd somehow find me. He had the skills of a true predator.

"Ah," he said, voice much closer. I didn't dare peer over my shoulder to meet his gaze. It wasn't that I was too stubborn. It was because I was afraid for many, *many* reasons. "Jane Austen? There's an entire section of Jane Austen novels in the library...*remember?*"

Fire erupted inside my core, and memories flooded me so quickly that my foot slipped. A gasp rushed out of my mouth, and when a large, warm hand landed on my bare thigh, every amount of oxygen rushed out of the room through any crevice it could find. His fingers dug into my flesh, biting the skin so roughly that my nerve endings fried, leaving a trail of heat all the way up to the spot between my legs.

"Breathe," Cade commanded. The whisper left his mouth and landed on my bare flesh. His fingers stayed glued to my skin as mine dug into the shelf in front of me. My nails scratched along the wood as I let my eyes fall, landing on his steely expression. His pupils were dilated, and I couldn't see the golden flakes I was used to.

"You do remember, right?" he asked as his fingers undug themselves from my skin. Chills rained down over my smooth legs as he pushed my leg back up to its rightful spot on the shelf edge. The goosebumps were replaced with heat as he slowly brought his hand down past the curve of my knee, all the way to my ankle, before dropping it all together.

His chest was rising, but mine was unmoving. My lungs burned to breathe, but I kept them closed off until he took a step away, and that was when I finally turned and let out a held breath.

Cade sounded nothing like the boy I was used to as he swiftly turned around and leaned his back against the same shelf I was half-climbing. "Is this how it's gonna go, Journ?" His words were laced with something gravelly—like hate. I'd heard this voice before, and it wasn't one he *ever* used with me. "You're gonna run away when I try to talk to you, pretend like you don't see me staring at you?"

I said nothing. Instead, I continued on with my search of scanning the tiny letters that were printed on the ends of the files up on the top shelf. *Cade Walker does not exist, and your heart does not beat for a boy who potentially set you up for death.* I glanced down fleetingly with my last thought, catching him peering up at me with the muscles against his temples rocking back and forth.

I flinched internally when his eyes narrowed. "Nice outfit."

"Do you have a problem with it?" I bit back, likely shocking him. *My heart hurts, and I don't like it.*

He scoffed as I leveled my chin and found the letter S, making my way down to the last name *Smith.* Despite there being over two million people in the world with the last name *Smith*—which was given to me by Sister Mary—there was only one file with that printed on it. My fingers gripped the manilla folder with a tight grasp, and I jumped down from the shelf, landing with a soft thud right in front of Cade.

We were on level ground now, our chests almost touching, and that was when he scanned me from head to toe again, making my heart beat a little faster than before. *I miss him.* It was the one emotion I couldn't seem to turn off when it mattered the most. I also liked his eyes on me, and that may have meant I had a death wish.

Cade ignored my question as he flung himself from the bookshelf in my direction. Panic fled me from behind, and I quickly turned around, taking his spot with my back pressed to the books. They weren't so comforting now. In fact, I wished one of those books would open up and swallow me whole at this very moment.

"Why do you keep running from me, Journey?" His tone had subdued a little, like he was curious rather than angry, which only caused jitters to enter my belly. He was suddenly hiding his emotions, and I'd learned the hard way that it was better to know what someone was feeling rather than not. "Are you angry with me? Or are you afraid of me?"

He could see right through me. Cade knew me, and even though I'd been gone for most of the school year and some things had changed, my heart was still the same.

"I'm not afraid of you." *Am I?* Standing here, looking at him, I knew the answer to that question. I should have been afraid because the truth of that night was buried deep underneath a layer of snow and dirt out in the courtyard. But I was feeling something other than fear, and the only way I knew how to crumble it before it grew into an avalanche was to get angry.

Cade's head tilted, and my soul begged to see those dimples on his cheeks that were like a glimpse of sunshine. "You're not?" His eyebrow lifted as a slight grin laced with deception curved onto his cheek, like he was ready to prove me wrong.

"I think it's the opposite, Cade," I whispered in a low voice, chest rapidly gaining traction.

"You think I'm afraid of you?" he asked, fully skeptical. He took a step forward, and I gritted my teeth as I dropped the file to the ground, allowing its contents to float over the soft carpet.

My voice was shaky, and it proved right there that I *was* afraid. Just a little. But not for the reason I should have been. My fingers trembled as I pulled one sleeve down over my hand and pushed it over my bare shoulder. I had to admit, my outfit *was* skimpy, and it was even worse with the leather jacket falling to the floor. My confidence wavered as cool air hit the thick, red lines running vertically along my forearms, realizing this was different than before. At the psych hospital, I didn't care who saw them. No one cared about scars at that place, on the outside or inside. But here? Standing in front of Cade with his stern expression glued to my face instead of my arms bubbled with goosebumps? I wasn't feeling so sure of myself.

I dug the heels of my feet into the carpet below me, pushing myself further into the bookshelf, and met his gaze for what it was. "I don't think you're afraid of me," I whispered. "I think you're afraid of these." I dropped my head, staring at my arms with too many emotions, none of which were shame, like most people would assume. When I peeked back up at Cade, with my heart thudding in my chest like a drum, his jaw was tight, and his face was growing red with rage. "You're afraid of them, right? You won't even look at them."

He made no move to glance down. Instead, he snapped back a response. "Is that why you won't even look at me?

Because you're afraid of me? It's safe to assume that's the reason if you can assume just the same about me."

Annoyed that I wasn't winning this...*argument*, I raised my hands and pushed them against his hard chest like I wanted to do earlier at the claiming. Resentment and anger outweighed my suspicions, and my insides rioted. "I'm not afraid of you!" I gritted, shoving hard.

Cade didn't move.

He didn't even flinch with surprise.

Instead, his hand wrapped itself around my slim neck, and he suddenly crowded my space, taking all the air with him. A gasp got stuck in my throat as he quickly moved me to the side to avoid a falling book from the top shelf, only to put me back in my rightful spot with his knee tucked in between my bare legs.

My hand gripped his wrist tightly, so tight my nails dug into his skin, but he didn't wince. His hand around my neck wasn't so hard that I couldn't breathe, but hard enough to gain my full attention. My throat bobbed against his palm, and angry breaths left me as I stared into his darkened eyes. "Why are you afraid of me, Journey?" His warm, slightly intoxicated breath hit my face, and I inhaled like I was starving for him. The slight movement of his finger rubbing against the side of my neck that he'd marked once before caused a familiar feeling to nestle itself into my core. "Why is your pulse racing? Is it fear? Or something else?"

Both. And I was certain that meant I was completely insane.

"I thought you may be angry with me." Cade looked away, his hand still curved against my neck. I knew he was strong enough to strangle me if he wanted, but I also knew he wouldn't, which probably should have told me right there that, deep down, I wasn't as afraid of him as I originally thought. "I even thought you might slap me for standing you up that night."

I swallowed against his palm, and I knew he could feel my pulse racing even faster the more he talked about that night. I jumped in his grip when he whipped his attention back to me quickly.

"But I never, *ever* fucking thought you'd do *this*..." A small whimper left me when Cade's other hand slapped my arm up above my head, causing another book to fall beside us. His long finger sent sparks to the raised scar as he trailed the length up and down again. "To yourself."

Anger and desire swarmed me, and I curved my chest and pushed it against his, causing his already dark eyes to darken further. He was hard against my front, and there was a wicked part buried inside of me that wanted to move against him, like no time had passed at all. Only, time had passed, and I wasn't the same girl he was used to, and I wasn't quite sure I knew him like I thought.

A strained, sarcastic laugh left my dry mouth as panicked nerves fought against the excited butterflies. "That's hilarious."

His hand tightened again like he had tied a rope around my delicate skin and pulled on the end. Dust flew from the bookshelf as I pulled back, and it landed on us like little specks of embers from the fire we were creating. "Hilarious? You think it's fucking funny what you did to me?"

My jaw unhinged, and I pushed against him again, bucking with anger. "What *I* did to *you?*"

I dropped my eyes to his lips that pulled back into a snarl, like he was just as angry as I was, and it confused me. I bounced my attention down to his rapidly rising chest, feeling his heartbeat through the thin, white shirt. "You really don't know, do you?"

"Don't know what?" he gritted.

He doesn't know.

"I thought you knew me better than that, Cade." I swallowed, sliding my arm down and out from his grasp. Both of my small hands wrapped around his thick wrist as he continued rubbing over the pulse point on my neck. "You truly think I'd tried to kill myself because you stood me up?"

His hand left my neck as he pulled back quickly like I'd branded him. His strong browline hooded his eyes even further, hiding every emotion on his face. "And here I thought you were the only person who truly knew me. I thought you knew me down to my very core." My eyes prickled from behind as I swiftly bent down and grabbed the scattered papers from the file along with my leather jacket. Wavy tendrils flew into my face as I stood up and rushed over to the office door. "You didn't know me at all, Cade Walker."

The straightening of my spine was the only thing I allowed Cade to see as I turned my back to him to shove my leather jacket on. My shoes were like boulders in my shaking hands, and the file with messy papers shoved inside crinkled between my fingers. A cool rush of air entered the suffocating office as I opened the door, but before I could breathe it in, a loud slap against wood hit the side of my ear, shutting out the hall, and I was suddenly flipped around.

His hands were around my face, and my heart clawed as it climbed to my throat. It was a race to see who could make their move first, and I let him win as his lips crashed to mine in the most intimidating, intimate way possible. *Mine.* That was all I heard when his tongue dove in, lapping up my mouth like he had been dying without my taste. The prickles were back behind my eyes as something deeply intimate filled me up to the brink of death. It was a silent type of death—the kind you couldn't escape from but didn't want to. His hand wove into my hair as he continued to kiss me and suck me, making me lose all train of thought as desire and warmth swarmed me. I was so close to kissing him back just as fever-ishly, allowing the flame to quicken from his mouth against mine, but he pulled on the long strands of my hair, and we broke apart.

Through rushed breaths and a flushed face, he bit out his next question. "I do know you. Now, tell me why you've been afraid since coming back?"

Emotions clogged my senses, and my voice was strained. "You don't get to do that." I glanced away, stomping on the hurt and disappointment from constantly being let down. I was disappointed in myself as I let myself enjoy his kiss a little too much. "You can't just demand answers from me. You don't deserve to know, and unless you care to explain your reasoning for standing me up that night, you never deserved me to begin with."

Silence was shared, and it was so loud I wanted to cover my ears. My lips were swollen, and my soul felt branded, and suddenly, *I felt seen.* Cade's fingers untwined themselves from my hair, and he took a step back. I couldn't look at him. I didn't want to, so instead, I bent down and grabbed my shoes that had fallen, turned around, and stalked out of the office.

His hoarse voice hit the back of my head as I began trav-eling back down the hall. "I sure as fuck don't deserve you, Journey. But I want you."

And what Cade wants, Cade usually gets.

CHAPTER EIGHT

MY TEMPLES THROBBED as I rested my head against the head-master's office door. My entire body was vibrating with the thudding of blood to every open vein, and the shallow breaths told me just how much I wanted Journey, despite the look of pure betrayal that dominated the slate color of her eyes. My lips tingled, and my tongue was tinged with the sweet taste of her mouth, and I was completely out of sorts because Journey gave me nothing but another riddle to decipher, just like those fucking threats that were burning a hole in the floor of that linen closet.

You truly think I tried to kill myself because you stood me up? Her sharp-as-the-winter-wind laugh full of sarcasm echoed around the office, slapping me with confusion and concern. What did that mean? My heart pumped out doses of unsettling misfires, and the wheels were turning viciously. I quickly stood up and began pacing back and forth from Tate's desk to the door that I'd just had Journey backed up against with my tongue halfway down her throat. When I reached his desk again, I violently pounded my fist on top of it. Papers flung through the air and landed all over the soft carpet, which had me craning my neck to the bookshelf.

I stomped over to a paper that was resting underneath a fallen book, grabbing it along with something that read *Smith*. My eyes scanned the contents quickly, realizing it was something that had fallen out of the folder that Journey had dropped when I bombarded her. *What was I thinking? Putting my hand around her neck like that?* The feel of her pulse against my fingers drove blood straight to my dick. I wanted to feast on her body more than ever before because I knew it would be different this time around. You appreciated something a little more when you lost it. I'd lost Journey, and although she was back at St. Mary's, she was no longer mine.

She was different. The gray in her eyes hardened to stone as she tried to act intimidated, as if she were in charge of our conversation. Even through her lie of saying she wasn't afraid of me, she still wasn't the one on top. I could see right through her. The pale skin on her cheeks tinted with red as she pushed up against my front, feeling how hard I was for her, and I hoped like hell she knew that I didn't give a fuck about the scars along her arms. I gave a fuck about her, and her alone.

Why did she lie?

She *was* afraid. Maybe not of me, but she was afraid of something, and a familiar feeling of protection flooded me like a tidal wave. I hadn't felt protective over much since she left. In fact, I hadn't felt much of anything since that night— not as deeply as I felt when she was near, at least. It was like Journey, herself, was my beating heart that kept me alive.

Leaving the office even messier than before, I headed straight for the girls' hall while reading Journey's lost paper. It seemed to be a summary of her life in what I was pretty sure was Headmaster Ellison's handwriting:

. . .

JOURNEY SMITH - ASSUMED BIRTHDATE: 10/18/2004

Arrived at Clemency Orphanage as a newborn on October 18, 2004 (given birthdate) bundled in a pink blanket with a note that read: In danger - keep safe and do not trust anyone. *She has been at the orphanage since birth. Sister Mary did not allow anyone to adopt Journey due to the note, fearful that she was sending Journey with someone who shouldn't have been trusted. Journey had issues as a young child with anger and feeling abandoned but slowly stopped discussing such issues as she grew older. She is very loving and smart. Sister Mary has asked me to educate her and to keep her safe until she graduates. At that time, Sister Mary said she would tell Journey of the note/threat. Sister Mary said there was never another note to be found regarding Journey, and all traces stopped at the original note tucked into her baby blanket.*

MY STOMACH KNOTTED as I peered down the girls' hallway, wondering how I'd even gotten there from the headmaster's office. If the duty teacher was out and about tonight, I wouldn't have known, because I was solely focused on what I'd just read.

What the fuck?

My eyes flicked to the linen closet that veiled the other threats that Sister Mary had seemed to be waiting for, except they came to me instead. Something sticky, like impending doom, had sludged up my veins and had me in a chokehold as I stood in complete and utter confusion. *Did someone hurt her?* I replayed the anger-laden conversation that I'd just had moments ago with a girl who smothered herself in every nook and cranny inside my brain, always showing up in between the empty spaces of dark and light. I began prowling toward her door as my heartbeat slowed, but it was hard, rocking against my ribcage, gearing me up for round two, until I heard a shuffling of feet and saw the flickering of a flashlight.

Fucking shit.

Part of me wanted to stand and wait to come face to face with the duty teacher, prepared to get detention, but the other part of me felt the need to be alone to gather my thoughts, so I slipped inside the very linen closet that held my secrets and rushed out leveled breaths until my pulse calmed.

The shine of the flashlight basked the floor of the darkened closet as it swayed by, and soon, the footsteps disappeared down the hall. I placed my shoulder against the door and tilted my head, my messy hair falling over my forehead. The longer I stood in silence, the more the threats laying just a few feet away underneath the shelf taunted me. Each one raced around my head, along with the new information I'd just stumbled upon, causing me to think very carefully about my next move.

My body was pushing me to go to her room, to slip inside and demand she explain her cryptic message followed by her condescending laughter, as if I was the malleable one in the situation. Did she think I was going to take her little warning and become pliable underneath her biting words?

If she thought I'd back off from her, she didn't know me at all.

A quiet huff left my tight chest at the thought. Journey was likely just as confused about me as I was her. I *did* leave her out there that night. The moon was our witness.

It didn't matter if I had good intentions backing my decision to cut her off or if they were justified at the end of the day. It didn't matter if I was trying to be chivalrous and put her safety first. She ended up hurt, and it was my fault.

Only now, I wasn't sure *how* she had gotten hurt, and she

wasn't really in the mood to tell me, and all that did was make me want to try harder. The perseverance ran deep.

Walking over to the pieces of paper that I would continue to keep under lock and key, I shoved the missing information from her file underneath my trusty keeper of a shelf and went back to the linen closet door, knowing I would retire to my room for the rest of the night and toss and turn in my bed until morning when I could see her again.

I'd keep my distance, but that didn't mean this was over.

This was far from over, and deep down, she knew it.

My hand stilled on the doorknob as I cracked the door, hearing something in what should have been the still hallway. There was a rush of air that swept inside the stuffy crook full of blankets and sheets that caused prickles to hit my neck.

"What are you doing out of your room?" The voice of Mr. Cunningham filtered through the tiny opening of the door, and my brows crowded. *Did Journey not go back to her room?* I almost stepped out into the hall to save her, although I had a feeling she didn't *want* to be saved, but when a different voice hit my ears, I stilled.

"Needed to clear my head."

Motherfucker. The skepticism smacked right into me as I wondered what Bain was doing in the girls' hallway when the majority of them were at the claiming. He had always snuck away—that was, if he hadn't found a girl to feast on—to do his father's bidding. And although the Rebels and I were technically out of the gun-running business due to turning our backs on our fathers and betraying them, Bain was not. His father now reigned over the western part of the United States and had taken past clients of Isaiah's father and scooped them up under his wing, meaning Bain was still sneaking away occasionally and running guns.

My pulse began thudding against my neck as I rubbed the back of it tightly, trying to uncoil the tightened muscles that were bundled there. I couldn't see much through the sliver in the door, but I could hear their conversation clearly.

"In the girls' hall?" Mr. Cunningham asked suspiciously.

It was a true shame that it was Mr. Cunningham on duty tonight. Usually, if it were a female teacher, they were easier to sway. One quick grin and a well-thought-out excuse that was born before even being caught, and you were off the hook. It sounded sexist, but it was what it was.

It wouldn't be that easy with Mr. Cunningham. Not that Mr. Cunningham was intimidating in any way whatsoever. I mean, the man wore wrinkled khaki pants to class nearly every day, and I was certain his arms were made of pudding instead of hardened muscle, but he wasn't stupid by any means. He was a man, after all, so he suspected that Bain was sneaking into a girls' room to screw around, and if it were any other male student, his suspicions would have been correct.

Except, this was Bain we were talking about, and he was a part of a life that Mr. Cunningham only read about inside the pages of those fictional books he stored away in his desk at the start of each class.

"Oh? Is this the girls' hall? I had no idea. I apologize, Mr. Cunningham. I'll head back to my rightful hall." Bain's voice was deceiving at best. Confusion hinted at the edges of his words, and if I liked him, I would have laughed. But I didn't. So, it wasn't funny.

"You'll do right to do that, Bain. You'll do right to spend detention in my classroom for the rest of the week, too."

A haughty laugh left Bain, and their voices grew closer.

"You boys think I'm stupid."

"Not necessarily stupid, just a little dull-witted."

My eyes leveled with their darkened silhouettes, and they narrowed further as Bain stopped right outside the opening of the linen closet door. Mr. Cunningham stopped, too, his hands on his thick waist.

"Excuse me?"

Bain shook his head, his shadow moving slowly behind him. "It's just that it takes you a little while to catch on, and sometimes, time isn't on your side. You assume things that aren't true, and when you realize your error, it'll be too late."

The whites of Bain's eyes clashed with mine, and I suddenly felt as if I were in the middle of a war, grenades firing off in the distance, a sword being thrusted in my hand. *What the fuck are you playing at?*

Mr. Cunningham turned, and I stared at the side of his long, crooked nose instead of Bain's beady white eyes full of deception and fallacious, misguided truths. "I have no idea what you're talking about, but add on another week of detention for calling me dull-witted."

He walked away agitated, and Bain tipped his chin at me, showing off the thickness of his jaw before placing his hands in his pockets and following after him. Unease began to settle, and the anger that had been quiet since shutting out my father came back roaring like a fucking lion in the wild. Bain had been a distant thought in the last month, and it was welcomed, but now, things were shifting again.

I whipped the door open with a clenched jaw, and an agitated feeling of discomfort hit me as I looked down the hall to where they disappeared and then down to Journey's door in the distance.

Was he here for her?

My lungs screamed, and my feet carried me farther and farther away from my daily reminders that warned me to stay away from Journey. The pressuring decision of right versus wrong was at my back, and her door was at my front. I could hear her inside her room, rummaging around with the papers she had stolen from the headmaster's office. My head rested along the door, and my hands planted themselves firmly against the solid wood that separated us, along with too many other things, and I breathed out a full breath. Seconds later, I backed myself up against the tiny crook that I'd found myself in the previous night when I listened to her and Gemma's conversation and pulled out my worn paperback from my back pocket and slumped down with my legs in front of me.

Except, I couldn't read a single word on the pages.

Instead, all that echoed in my head were Bain's words and Journey's attempt to wound me, which wasn't an attempt after all.

CHAPTER NINE

JOURNEY

THE PANCAKES TASTED nothing like they should have. With each syrupy bite, I had to force them into my mouth and down my throat. The layer of lip gloss over my lips didn't help either.

I could taste one thing and one thing only: Cade.

He kissed me. His lips had been on mine, and it was the only thing I could think of for the rest of the weekend. His hand around my neck and how a burning chill bellowed in my core, making itself known in between my legs, replayed when I shut my eyes that night and continued to do so the next day when I sat in the lounge area with Sloane and Mercedes.

Cade was in there, too, staring at me from across the room with his hand rubbing mindlessly over his chin as he likely thought about the previous night.

Things were so different between us now, and it was hard to know the rules to our little game. A part of my ruined heart hated him and blamed him for the scars along my arms. But the other part, the part still intact, wanted to reach for him in the worst way. My fingers had nearly trembled when he walked into the dining hall this morning, his eyes set directly on me at my little table in the corner, away from everyone. I shifted my gaze to Sloane, and she gave me a soft smile. She wanted me to sit at their table today, and when I declined, she said she was going to sit with me instead, but I refused, telling her I needed to review some notes for English. I knew she didn't believe me, but Sloane knew when to give space.

I saw everything through a cracked lens now, second-guessing everyone in the room, focusing on the way someone would stare at me for a little too long and how their eyes would linger on my covered arms. *Were you the one who put them there?* Skepticism was born from broken trust, and my trust at this school was shattered like the window that Tobias and I broke out of that chilly evening not so long ago.

I shoved my food away and rubbed at my lips that were somehow still tingling from just the mere thought of Cade and me in the headmaster's office—which ended up being a total blow; there wasn't anything useful in my file. My grade cards and special notes from teachers. That was all, and it frustrated me.

My back was to Cade, as I continued being the school hermit, when I heard the door open and close with a loud thud.

Did Cade leave?

Without being able to stop myself, I flung my eyes over to Aubrey, seeing if she was following after the person who left. She was too busy shoving a breakfast burrito in her mouth to notice me, and whoever had left the dining hall didn't seem to gain her attention, so I knew it wasn't Cade.

The jealousy was there, burning brighter and brighter at the thought of his mouth on someone else while I was away. My throat closed at the visuals my overactive imagination was painting, and I wondered if he had said the same things to her that he used to say to me. The fork in my hand clattered down to the wooden table, and I clenched my eyes, wishing away the thought of being jealous of a boy who stood me up, which then landed me in a literal psych hospital.

There were more important things to focus on, like who wanted me gone from St. Mary's. Or who brutally attacked me and left me for dead. But *Cade*. The teenage girl that I still was at my core lived and breathed and rolled around in resentment like a pig in mud at the irrational thought of Cade never caring about me at all.

I refused to believe it on the inside.

He and I were *too* real. What we had was vehemently intimate.

Tobias' words floated around and brought me back to reality. *"Maybe it was only real to you, Journey. To people like us, love is easily manipulated and can often be one-sided. When you're desperate for something, you likely believe it at the very first glimpse."*

His words hurt at the time, but he did a good job at snapping me out of heartbreak when I needed it the most.

I wish he was here. He'd wrap his forever blood-stained hands around my face and bring me back down to the *real* and shove away the *what-ifs* and the past. Tobias was skilled at turning off emotions. In fact, I think I'd only ever seen him elicit emotion once or twice, and it was in this very school that I saw the slip in his mask.

After leveling my breathing and remembering the wise words from the only person who I knew had scars that went much deeper than mine, I opened my eyes back up and stared down at my half-eaten breakfast. I placed my hands on my plaid skirt and gripped the fabric to keep me present, but that was when I realized the entire dining room was near silent.

I could hear myself breathe and the heavy beating of my

heart in my ears. *What's going on?* There was a screeching of a bench nearby, and when I finally peeked through the wavy strands of my hair, I found Cade staring directly at me.

I *would* find him in a sea of students all dressed in the same damn color. My stomach bottomed out as if I had been flung from a cliff, so I pulled my attention away, hiding my half-snarl to disguise my present hurt. I followed a blur of maroon as it rushed through the dining hall toward the door.

A gasp left me, and my head whipped up, causing my hair to whiz away from my face. *Tobias.* Gemma's arms wrapped around her brother's middle, and tears pricked the backs of my eyes like a million little needles trying to show the entire school that I wasn't as strong as I was pretending to be. Not that it mattered. They already had formed opinions of me before I came back hiding my emotions like a chameleon.

Tobias looked the same. Still expressionless, even with his long-lost sister's arms wrapped around his slender middle. His shoulders were as muscular and broad as they were at the Covens in that underground bunker-like room that I found myself in way too many times when I couldn't sleep through the nightmares. His one solace in that place was the constant building of muscle as he'd do hundreds of push-ups while I lay on his bed, willing my eyes to stay open so I didn't have to deal with the past as it came for me in my sleep. The little scar was still there on his eyebrow, and his jaw was as tight as a rubber band as he stood right inside the dining hall, wearing the same uniform as the rest of the guys, looking more of a brute-like soldier than anything else. Tobias was what bad boys were made of. If we were here under different circumstances, I bet he'd fall right in line with the Rebels in a heartbeat.

I could already hear the slow murmurs of St. Mary's as they took in our new student. I was pretty sure there was a collective shift of girls as they crossed their legs and parted their lips at their shiny, new toy.

I had news for them, though. Tobias was off limits. Not because *I* wanted him—we were never anything more than two broken teens trying to save our lives and each other at the same time—but because Tobias' heart was just a single organ keeping him alive. Nothing more than that.

Before I knew what I was doing, I pushed myself out from underneath my lonely breakfast table and locked right onto Tobias. Gemma was still hugging him around the middle, and he didn't quite reciprocate the motion, but as soon as we caught onto each other, he let out a breath and gave me a subtle nod.

We're okay.

The closer I got to Tobias, the more my body grew warm. I knew everyone was shifting their attention from Gemma and her twin brother to me as I walked on quiet feet over to them. Gemma must have sensed that Tobias was relaxing a little, because she pulled back briefly, dropping her arms.

"I told you she was fine," she whispered as I grew closer. Gemma peeked over her shoulder at me and shot me the warmest, softest smile I'd ever seen, and it sent something gooey into my heart. *I like her.*

"I like to see things for myself," Tobias said with no intention of lowering his rough voice. Gemma half-rolled her eyes and stepped away.

I shrugged, crossing my arms as if there was a chill in the air, and there was...coming directly from the table to my right. "She's right. I'm fine."

Tobias' icy eyes narrowed slightly, the small scar over his eyebrow dropping down like a shadow covering his emotions. "I know you better than you think." His glower immediately sliced over to the table that held the one person he had a grudge with in this room, and his body heat hit me like stepping too close to a fire.

"I can take care of myself. You know this." I lowered my voice so no one would hear me, because, trust me, *everyone* was waiting with bated breath and ears on full alert to hear our conversation. Almost no one knew the full story of Tobias and me and how we'd managed to escape a psych hospital, but we were surely gaining attention. It had already been on Mary's Murmurs that Gemma Richardson was related to the headmaster and that she had a secret twin brother who'd soon be attending our school. The rest was speculation, and this little show would soon gain traction.

Tobias half-shrugged as he continued to glare over my head at what I could only assume to be Cade. Gemma was still standing there, nibbling on her lip. "Doesn't mean you should." There was a little growl that paired with the teetering of his temples before he moved his attention back to me. "Can you get the hug over with? I want every girl in this fucking school to think I'm taken so they don't try to spread their legs for me."

A soft laugh left me as I took another step closer. Gemma's head came in between us as she angled away from the rest of the dining hall. "That won't stop them, trust me."

He grunted. "Great, a pack of fucking savages."

Gemma and I both laughed under our breath as the three of us corralled together. Although Gemma wasn't at the Covenant Psych Hospital as long as Tobias and I, we were all connected in a way, sharing something no one else ever would.

Placing my head against Tobias' hard chest, hearing his eerily calm heartbeat against my ears, I wrapped my arms around his middle and felt the way his spine went rigid like the unbending walls of this school.

"You're going to have to hug me back if you want people

to think you're off limits, Tobias. Or at the very least, stop standing there like a cactus. I feel like you're going to sprout a spike and make me bleed."

There was a rumble in his chest that vibrated my ear as Gemma smashed her lips beside us. His strong arms wrapped around me, and it was the first time he'd ever hugged me. It may have been the first time he'd hugged anyone since being thrown into the Covens. "As much as I hate such a pointless gesture, the face your little boyfriend is making nearly makes it worth it."

My cheeks flamed, and I was thankful the bell overhead rang out. It seemed to snap everyone out of their stupor, and suddenly, benches were screeching against the floor, and books were being gathered. Tobias, Gemma, and I all stepped away from the door as everyone walked past, pretending not to be intrigued with Tobias.

"What's your first class?" Gemma asked with a little pep in her voice. Isaiah appeared a second later and tipped his head at Tobias who gave the slightest flick of his chin.

"Modern Lit," I answered for him. "Same."

Tobias shot his gaze down at me. "Did you have Tate put us in the same classes?"

Gemma grinned. "He probably did that on his own. He has a way of subtly being kind."

Tobias chuckled sarcastically. "I guess I didn't get that gene from dear ol' daddy, huh?"

Gemma's smile fell slowly, but Isaiah was quick to swoop in to intertwine their fingers. He brought their hands to his mouth and placed a gentle kiss on hers. "We're gonna be late to class. Journey can show Tobias where class is, yeah?"

My lips closed, and I gave a curt nod. *I need my books.* I flung my hair over my shoulder as I turned around but stopped dead in my tracks as my books were thrust outward with one strong hand holding them tightly. My eyes lingered on the whites of his knuckles and his tight grip.

"Here." The one tiny word was full of something heavy, and it suddenly had me dodging the flicker of guilt inside. I slowly brought my gaze up to Cade as his muscles tightened. His neck was turning red with some emotion he was trying hard to push down, and I couldn't help but wonder if it was anger, betrayal, jealousy, or hurt.

My fingers were trembling as I shot them forward, ready to take my books from him, but another large hand came swooping in like a vulture over dead prey and plucked the books right out of his grasp.

"I've got it," Tobias said, voice rubbing gruffly over Cade's raw emotions. I felt the tension rising like a tide at sunset, so I quickly intervened before I suddenly became the red flag in between two bulls.

"Great," I rushed out, gripping Tobias' arm. "Let's go."

I caught the slight curve of his lip and nearly smacked him outside of the dining hall with the rest of the Rebels at our backs, but instead, I walked us both to class in calming silence.

———

"So," Tobias' apathetic voice was both tired and bored as he slumped down beside me in the library, pressing his back to the stack of Jane Austen books that taunted me in silence. This aisle used to be a place of solace for me. This *school* used to be home. Now, both of those feelings were ruined, and maybe I was a glutton for torture and pain, because I somehow found myself resting across from the books that were an echo of Cade and his hot touches against my skin. "This is St. Mary's..."

My smile was half-hidden behind my worn hardback. "As it lives and breathes."

Tobias was quiet for a moment, our breathing blending in with the loud creaks of the library floor and the flipping of book pages. When he spoke again, he was agitated. "It's better than the only two places I've ever known, but it still fucking sucks."

I snorted, plopping my book down on my bare lap. My plaid skirt had risen up a notch, and if it were any other guy in this aisle with me, I would have pulled it down, but it was Tobias, and he'd seen me in much less clothing before and had never even made a remark.

I'm broken, Journey. And although I can be sharp, I can be dull, too.

And dull was what he always was to me. Just another living, breathing soul to share an empty space with when it all became too much.

"What's so wrong about St. Mary's? Tired of the girls staring and wanting a piece of you?" I shrugged, pulling the book back to my lap. "It wasn't like you had much action at..."

I trailed off, not wanting to say the name of that place.

"The Covens?" Tobias finished for me. "How do you know?"

My brows crowded as I kept my eyes down. "Who'd you sleep with at the Covens?"

Tobias chuckled darkly. "You weren't the only one who could use their body, Journ."

My heart came to a screeching halt at the quick reminder of what I'd done while at the hospital. I was a fool to think that Tobias wasn't aware of my tricks. Just because I never had to use any on him didn't mean he was dense.

"I'm not judging you. Stop making that face."

I quickly unfurrowed my eyebrows, irritated that guilt was catching up to me.

"I feel guilty," I admitted, staring at a page in my book with blurred words.

"For what?" Tobias asked, lowering his voice. "For surviving? Never apologize for surviving. No one is going to save you, Journey. You have to save yourself, and you did."

My chest filled with air, and I let my lungs burn until I couldn't take it any longer. My breath came out so heavily that it flickered the pages in front of me. Tobias and I sat in silence for a little while, both of us reliving things that we should have been shoving away, until he pulled his khaki-clad legs up and rested his forearms along his knees.

"Tate said I have to have a student aide."

I peeked up quickly. "A student aide? What does that mean?"

Tobias angled his head back, showing off his model-like jaw, and sighed irritably. "I failed the entrance exam for this godforsaken school. Tate said the SMC would allow me to attend, as long as I had a student aide who could help me if I fell behind. It's bullshit."

"Who is it?" I asked, scooting up a little taller.

Tobias ran a hand over his face, clearly annoyed. "Snow White."

I laughed. "What? Snow White?"

"I forget her name, but she looks like fucking Snow White."

"How do you even know what Snow White looks like?" I asked, knowing he didn't have an easy childhood full of popcorn and Disney movies. It alarmed me that he had been in that place for so long, kept captive, beaten and broken both physically and emotionally. He'd once told me he'd been at the Covens—underneath where I was *rehomed*—for so long that he'd forgotten the actual number of years. He wasn't sure how old he was, and the days blended with lack of sleep. After learning that Gemma had turned eighteen shortly after Tobias and I had escaped, I knew he'd been there for far longer than he thought.

There was a tiny divot in between Tobias' straight, dark eyebrows. His scar became invisible as he furrowed his forehead. "I don't know. I guess maybe just a memory from my fucked-up childhood that stayed. Probably has something to do with Gemma. Richard would sometimes let her watch movies. Always the ones that he knew I'd hate."

"Why the hate for Snow White?" I asked, half-smiling.

Tobias looked me dead in the eye. "I hate everything."

"That's not true."

He glanced down the darkened aisle full of books and rubbed a hand over his scratchy face. "True. I don't hate Gem, or you." He paused and then grinned like a devil in the dark. "Or pissing off a certain someone who is so easily agitated."

I knew he was referring to Cade. It wasn't my intention to tell Tobias about what had happened between Cade and me —or anyone, really. Every single time I was plopped in a cold metal chair during group therapy, I was asked about my deepest scars, and one of those was Cade. He was kept hidden inside my chest with the thinnest of stitches since that warm night, but my unconscious, sleep-induced state never let those stitches stay intact.

That was how Tobias knew who Cade was. My nightmares betrayed me. A black figure always showed up to take me like a shadow sneaking out of a closet with the things that went bump through the night, and each and every time, I'd yell Cade's name.

I wouldn't admit *why* I yelled his name, but I knew I didn't yell his name because I thought he was the one hurting me, but because I wanted him to be the one to save me.

"Sloane. Her name is Sloane." Tobias snapped his fingers. "Rhymes with moan."

Shaking myself out of the thoughts of the psych hospital, I perked up, ignoring the last part of his sentence. "That's my old roommate."

Tobias grunted, clearly still agitated that he needed an aide.

"At least it isn't Aubrey," I mumbled under my breath, flipping a page in my book to read a few words to silence my beating heart.

"Who's Aubrey and why?"

I shrugged, unable to meet his blue eyes. Tobias was probably the only person I fully trusted at this school, but I still didn't want to open up the locked box of unwanted feelings buried deep in my belly. There were some things I just didn't want to talk about, and Aubrey was one. I felt stupid for feeling jealous—and maybe a bit immature. I'd been through too much over the last year to let myself get worked up over a catty girl who wanted what I had once had.

"She's just some girl that apparently isn't happy I'm back."

I didn't even have to look up at Tobias to see the confusion on his face.

"I guess she and Cade were kind of a thing while I was... away. I don't really know."

A loud, angry heave of breath floated across the aisle and hit me in the face. I peeked up and saw Tobias' face was relaxed and calm, which usually meant he was brewing on the inside. He was difficult to read, but I'd seen him angry before. "Have you found anything out?"

Subject change, thank you.

Shaking my head, I tucked a piece of hair behind my ear, fully closed my book, and pressed harder into the shelf behind me. "No, but even if I did, I wouldn't tell you."

"Why?"

"Because..." I started, knowing it was getting close to curfew. I began to sit up, straightening my skirt over my thighs. "You got out of that place. It's time for you to heal, and I'm not going to weigh you down with my shit."

Tobias stood up beside me and plucked the book out of my hand. His back was to me as he flipped around and pushed it onto the shelf—in the wrong spot—and then said over his shoulder, "I live for death, Journey. Someone tried to kill you, and you think I'm going to let that go?"

My heart clunked to the floor, and my fingers began to get shaky. I glanced over my shoulder and down both ends of the dark aisle. "It wasn't him," I whispered, looking up at Tobias' stoic expression.

He nodded once, trusting my admission.

"He thought I did it to myself."

Tobias dropped his gaze to my arms. "Along with everyone else. Keep me updated, Scar."

I smiled at his nickname for me—the name he'd used before I divulged my real name to him one darkened night when I was prowling the halls of that creepy hospital full of too many secrets. Tobias didn't reciprocate the smile—he never did—and left me in the aisle with my arms wrapped around my middle to hold myself up.

My legs were stuck as I ran my gaze down the spines of each book, trying to calm my erratic breathing from bringing up the one trauma that I wasn't healed from. *Someone tried to kill me.* It was still so strange to think, let alone verbalize. And there was a quiet inkling that was nestled in the back of my mind, like a faded memory that I couldn't quite bring to life, that told me whoever tried to kill me did it for a reason that I wasn't fully aware of. Like something from my past. Something with my parents? Something that had to do with why I was abandoned when I had barely even taken my first breath? That was why I had to start uncovering things that were likely hidden for a reason.

"That's why you were afraid of me?"

A yelp got stuck in my throat as I spun around quickly, almost flinging myself onto the bookshelf behind me. Cade's hand was quick to wrap itself around my lower back, keeping me from banging into it, and my throat closed with the impact. Flutters started low in my belly as my heart picked itself up off the floor, and I found myself staring up at him with surprise.

"Wh..wha..what?" *Get it together, Journey.*

Cade's nostrils flared like a dragon seconds from burning down the world. His warm eyes were hardened as his hand stayed pressed firmly against the small of my back. My covered arm was jerked in between us with his large hand, and I gasped, looking down at my sleeve as he pushed it up higher and higher. The pad of his finger slowly brushed over the raised skin, and the feeling of guilt surrendered to his touch. My breathing picked up, and to anyone else, they'd think I was afraid, but I wasn't.

The fact that he now knew the truth—*some of it*—was liberating, and suddenly, I felt *very* alive.

"Someone fucking did this to you?"

Thump. Thump. Thump. My heart was pounding so hard my ribs ached. When I slowly swung my gaze from his hand gripping my elbow to the look of disbelief against his features, I stayed quiet. I didn't trust myself to speak. I didn't even trust myself to move. My heart was shouting at me to rip my arm away and retire to my room, but my body was burning and twisting, and my feet were glued to the floor.

Shit. Shit. Shit.

The craving and hunger were there, hidden behind guilt and betrayal. I swallowed past the tightness in my throat as

Cade stood eerily still in front of me, still touching me in places that shouldn't have made my knees shake.

"Answer me," he gritted, the hand on my elbow tightening.

I jumped at the sound of an authoritative voice echoing down the long aisle. "Library is closing, and it's almost curfew." It was Mrs. Groves, the librarian who looked like she was near the brink of death. I slid out from Cade's grip, shaking myself out of whatever it was that had just presented itself, and hurried toward her.

"Sorry," I muttered, walking past with Cade still standing in the same spot. I didn't wait around for him to follow me to ask me more questions. I basically ran down the hall, passing by Sloane and Gemma's room, whose door was wide open with Isaiah lounging on Gemma's bed, and slammed my door shut before slumping to the hard floor and placing my head in my hands.

Cade had been listening to my conversation with Tobias, which was a total invasion of my privacy, but instead of feeling angry, I felt ashamed. Now, it was all out there in the open—from being attacked and kept in a psych ward to the dirty details of how I had found my way out.

CHAPTER TEN

JOURNEY

I NEVER PAID much attention to the rumors floating around St. Mary's when I began attending three years prior. In my first year, I kept quiet and blended in with the portraits on the walls, keeping my face impassive and my eyes empty of anything. I'd wondered if that was why Cade picked me out in the very beginning. I wasn't like the other girls here. Being in the spotlight made me antsy and anxious, which was one hundred percent inherited from constantly seeing people's backs turned to you versus their cheery faces. Abandonment and rejection together was like the binding of an unbreakable shield. *Don't draw attention to yourself so you can avoid the disappointment when they leave.*

But then came Cade.

He saw me, and his lips on mine did *nothing* but melt the shield I'd had up.

And now, here we were, months after I'd disappeared from St. Mary's, with rumors crawling up my back and into my ear at every single turn of this school. Everyone followed my movements. Some pretended like they weren't interested and would look away when my gaze would skim past, but others—like Aubrey—made it a point to snicker, and at the very least, talk about me behind my back. It wouldn't matter much, except Sloane was waiting outside my bedroom door this morning, nibbling on her lip in a way that was *not* comforting.

"*I need to warn you.*"

"*About what?*"

Her phone was flipped over in her hand, and I scanned over the big, block lettering from Mary's Murmurs, the gossip blog that I was probably featured on as soon as I was found bleeding in the courtyard.

"*Rumor has it that Journey Smith did not try to kill herself.*"

My heart sank the second I read the first sentence, fear like a knife at my throat. It wasn't that I wanted people to think I was suicidal, but I'd gotten used to the fact that no one knew the truth. Now, it was like my little secret to keep hidden until the right moment. If people knew that someone had attacked me and essentially set me up for death, well... I wasn't sure what would happen. What would Headmaster Ellison do? Would the police get involved? Would the person get a little knife happy and come at me again before they were caught?

I snatched the phone out of Sloane's hand with my trembling fingers and beating heart and read the rest of the headline.

"*From a pretty little source comes an intoxicatingly juicy theory that Journey Smith left eight months ago because of an unplanned pregnancy where she later gave birth at the Clemency Orphanage. And the best part? The father is assumed to be our very own bad boy Rebel: Cade Walker.*"

My face had been pale ever since I gave Sloane her phone back. *It's just a rumor. It's just a rumor. It's just a rumor.* But it was a sick one for nothing less than the fact that *I*, Journey Smith, an orphan of her own, would abandon her baby at the same orphanage that I was left at, just to come back to *this* school.

"Don't worry, Journ. Cade will get it taken down." Sloane placed an apple on my tray and her own, knowing I was too caught up in my unwanted thoughts to do much of anything but stand straight.

I found Cade across the crowded dining hall the very second Sloane said his name. My school blouse felt too tight around my ribcage. My breath held itself hostage as he slammed a closed fist down on the wooden table, showing off the tight muscles along his forearms. Mica, one of the Rebels' friends, was glaring up at Cade, speaking so quickly that I couldn't read his lips. Cade's voice carried, and the closer Sloane and I moved into the dining hall, the more my vision grew fuzzy.

Breathe, Journey.

"Who the fuck put that on there? This isn't a *fucking* game."

Isaiah rounded the table with Gemma close by, looking at Cade, then to me, and then back to Cade. "Cade, relax. No one but the students read the blog. You know this."

Cade turned to Isaiah and shot him a glare. He crossed his arms over his chest, and I lingered on the perfect shade of tan against his forearms. The sun had barely peeked through the trees outside, and Cade already looked disheveled with his loose tie and his sleeves rolled up to his elbows. "And what if someone close to our fathers is keeping tabs? Huh? Ever think about that, Isaiah? If someone thinks that I have a child with her, then..."

Cade's tone was subdued, and not many could hear him, but somehow, I found myself inching closer and closer to their conversation, so I heard every last word until he trailed off. His head snapped over to me, the anger swarming his features lessening slightly as I focused on what he was saying.

It stung.

If someone thinks that I have a child with her, then...

Then what? Did he not want to be associated with me? Was that why he kept me a secret for so long? Was that why he touched me behind the bleachers or took me swimming in the off-limits pool that no one ever used? Is that why I had to sneak around with him?

My heart thudded harder and harder, and confusion began jerking me backward until I ran into someone from behind. Cade's brow furrowed, his perfectly sculpted lips parting with some sorry excuse on the end of his lips.

"So, is it true?"

The person I'd run into came around and blocked my view from Cade, and I nearly snarled when I realized it was Aubrey. *Go away.* Her sleek eyebrows were raised to her hairline, and she looked stunned. She actually didn't look vindictive like the other night at the party. In fact, she was curious. "Did you...? Did you seriously have a baby?"

Is she serious?

I heaved, trying to look past Aubrey's big head full of hair for an escape route. *Everyone* was staring at me. Everyone's eyes shot down to my flat stomach, as if I magically grew skinnier after having a baby. I was pretty sure that wasn't how it worked.

"Does that mean it wasn't true that you cut your wrists?"

I am not answering that.

"I..." Sweat started to coat my back, and the room began to spin. *Everyone is staring.* I began to feel trapped, and the only thing that did was push me into the not-so-distant feeling of being back in that psych ward, locked in a room lacking any color, with random people coming up behind me to jab me with a needle or bear hug me until I stopped trying to claw my way out of there. "I...I..."

I was swept away with shock as my tray clamored to the floor, the apple rolling away with my conscious ability to stay present. My name was shouted as my cardigan sleeve was pulled from my arm swiftly, whirling me around until it was half hanging off my body. I blinked my eyes quickly with the speed of a hummingbird, and the girl who'd pulled my sleeve suddenly looked like Barry from the psych ward, and I was taken back to a place that made my throat raw from screaming.

I HAVE TO GET OUT. I have to get out. I have to get out.

My knees were wet from resting my teary face along them, and if I darted my tongue out, I bet I would taste salt. The bandages on my arms were ripped off, and the stitches were poking out like little needles when I ran my fingers against them. If I were truly suicidal, I could have just ripped them out and allowed myself to bleed like I had just a few short days ago, but I wasn't suicidal, and I didn't want to bleed.

What I wanted was to get out of this place.

"Journey, we need you to tell us the truth. We need you to tell us why you tried to hurt yourself."

I wasn't sure how many different ways I could say the words, "Someone did this to me," until they fully understood. The problem was that they did understand what I was saying. I was speaking English coherently. They just didn't believe me.

"You won't get better if you don't tell us."

"I want to leave," I said, looking up at the man with too-tiny glasses on the end of his nose.

"You can't leave."

I laughed sarcastically, feeling the sadness turn to anger like the flip of a switch. "So, what? You're just going to keep me here until I say that I tried to kill myself? I didn't do it. Someone came up behind me and did it."

"And who would do that?"

I jumped to my feet, the room swaying like a boat over a choppy ocean. My stomach rolled, and nausea hit me like a wave. I hadn't eaten in days, and mixed with the medicine they kept giving me to sleep, I wasn't sure what direction was up and what was down. "I don't know! I kept to myself. No one even knew I was out there that night except—"

"Except who, Journey?"

It couldn't have been Cade. He wouldn't have done this to me.

"Was there a voice that told you to do it?"

"What?" I screeched. "Like a voice from my head? No! I didn't do this to myself!"

The man rubbed a hand over the tired lines along his face and sighed. "We will try again later. Get some rest. I can see that you're becoming agitated."

I scoffed, wanting to cross my arms in the worst way. "That would have nothing to do with the medication you're giving me, though, right? What happens when you give these tiny pills to people who don't need them? Probably messes with their mood a little, right?"

The man stood up and ignored me. Hope crashed and fell like the tiny plastic cup with my pill in it earlier as I threw it across the room. I'd never been a violent person. I'd never even been someone to speak loudly. But he was right. I was agitated.

Someone had tried to kill me, and somehow, I was stuck in a psych ward without a single person coming for me. Not even Sister Mary.

My gaze stayed on the dull, scratchy floor of my new home until I heard the opening of the door and slow shuffling of leather loafers. It was as if I had gotten a push from a ghost as I barreled through the skinny man and landed in the hallway. My drab, gray gown was pulled backward, and I whirled around, my unbrushed hair flying into my eyes as I yelled out. Arms went around my waist next as I *fought and cried out, my arms becoming bloody from the jerking of stitches.*

"Journey, calm down!"

"No! Don't touch me! Let me leave! I don't belong here!"

"GODDAMNIT!"

A scream rushed out of my mouth as my fingers clenched down on two strong forearms. Confusion sliced away at the fogginess in my brain when I saw the shiny, freshly waxed black-and-white-tiled floor below me.

"Breathe, baby. Just breathe."

I gasped at the oxygen filling my lungs, and my head automatically leaned into the warm breath at my ear. Comfort filled me momentarily as emotion stung the backs of my eyes. Chills broke like a waterfall over my one bare arm, and I tightened my entire body when I thought back to a few seconds ago when Aubrey was standing in front of me and my tray fell to the floor.

What the hell just happened?

My entire body was shaking, like I was at the center of an earthquake. I trembled when Cade dropped my legs and spun me around quickly, hoisting me up against the hard wall of the hallway. We were tucked around the corner of the dining hall, and the hallway was quiet. Too quiet. It should have given me some solace or at least some space to calm the erratic winding of my brain, but it didn't.

"I can't breathe," I rushed out, knowing that I *could* breathe. It just felt like someone had punched me in the chest over and over again. Every time I blinked, I saw that place. Every time I inhaled, there were knives in my lungs, cutting me up and hurling me into the oblivion of panic.

"Look at me." I shot my attention to Cade, his angry

browline furrowed with worry lines as he stared into my eyes. "You're here. At St. Mary's. You're safe."

A ragged laugh throttled out of my mouth. "I'm not fucking safe here."

He grabbed my waist harder. "You think I'd let anyone touch you?"

My breathing grew even more frantic. "You already did." I looked away, wincing as I breathed. The oxygen was cold, like I was standing outside in a snowstorm rather than inside the warm hall of St. Mary's.

Cade muttered something as his hands left my midsection, and the panic suddenly grew worse, which should have surprised me, but it didn't. *He abandoned you that night,* the tiny voice whispered in the back of my head. But my heart and body were not in sync. I was unnerved in every single way. I had completely lost it in front of everyone who had already formed an opinion about me that fit pretty damn well, given my reaction to a sleeve being ripped off my arm.

"Journey." Cade's hoarse voice snagged my frantically searching gaze. Our eyes crashed, and my heart thumped painfully hard in my chest when I locked onto the gold in his eyes. "Breathe."

"I can't," I choked, feeling myself crumble in front of him. *Weak. Weak. Weak.* I wanted to grab onto him desperately and feel that safety and warmth that I used to feel. I craved it and could nearly taste the retribution that would come with seeking him out despite it all.

"Then, let me give you air."

CHAPTER ELEVEN

CADE

Her. Her. Her.

Journey's tongue moved over mine in ways that were sinfully hot and all things enthralling. Her kiss was rough as I licked, stealing her mind and giving her something else to think of. I bit her lip, my hands digging into her soft hair, tugging on the strands so she'd open up even more.

A door opened, and in the back of my mind, I knew she was on flatter feet and had returned from her little trip down memory lane, but I didn't care. Our lips stayed together, mixing up our emotions like a one-thousand-piece jigsaw puzzle thrown all over the floor, as I pushed her farther down the hallway and felt for the doorknob behind her back. The hinges creaked as I shoved her into a pitch-black room. My senses were on overdrive, thoughts of the brutal past and guilt being erased with the good parts of *us*, mixing with the hissing of the machines that surrounded our flushed bodies.

Boiler room. The temperature was hot in the dark area, making my already warm skin hotter to the touch. My fingers dug underneath Journey's school blouse, and the second I felt her soft flesh brush against my fingers, I felt her body tremble with something other than the panic she had been feeling seconds before.

Need. I needed her. It wasn't the other way around.

The softest whimper climbed from her mouth as she pulled back, likely searching for me in the dark. My hand crept higher as I pushed her farther away from the door, getting as far away from an escape as possible. *Stay.* I was being selfish *again*, driving that mantra into my head that with selfishness came regret, and regret was something I'd likely feel when this was all said and done. And I was reminded of those pesky little threats tucked underneath the shelf in the linen closet. *But goddamn, I missed her.*

If I allowed my heart to open, just slightly, in this moment, with Journey's heaving ribcage in my hands and her soft scent lingering around me, I would probably weep with the fact that I had her back—if even for a drop of a second.

"Nothing has ever come close," I whispered over her eager mouth. I was greedy for the fact that she wasn't pushing me away and darting for the door. Since she'd been back, it'd been nothing but quick glances full of despair and anger, her echoing footsteps as she walked away from me, and angry little lines covering her flawless skin with my demands of wanting to know what was happening inside that pretty little head of hers.

The only thing I could hear was her frantic breathing and the whirling of the machines. The only thing I could feel was the way Journey's skin was growing warmer beneath my fingertips. The rough pads of my fingers brushed over the softest parts of her, and I grew hard within half a second.

"I think I'm fine now." Her whisper didn't deter me from my one-track mind. We were not finished.

"You're still breathing heavy, Journ." My teeth clamped

onto her earlobe, and I *knew* she liked it. I shivered from having her caught in my grip. Journey was forgetting that I knew all her favorite spots and that I once had her heart in my unworthy hands, making her tick in every sinful way.

Her hands found my waist, and I burned all over. My eyes had adjusted a little bit to the darkness in the room. Tiny, red blinking lights only made the room seem that much more seductive with its reddish tint. We could have been in hell at the current moment, and I would have still kept her trapped in here like it was my own personal lair. Journey didn't know it, and maybe she didn't agree with it, but she was *mine*.

"Is that what we're doing here? Pretending?"

Her fingers clenched tightly onto my tie hanging loosely from my neck in between us. My arm rested above her head as I backed her up farther onto something hard—a large pipe maybe. I wasn't sure, and I didn't care. My hand splayed over it to keep me from pushing my hips into her.

"Pretending what?" I asked, crowding her space a little more. "That you need me to calm you down? Sure."

Her light, sarcastic laugh hit me in the face, and I inhaled her sweet scent like a hound dog on a hunt. My eyes shut as she pulled me closer by my tie. "Pretending that we're the same people we were eight months ago."

My nostrils flared as a sinister smile slithered onto my face. My tongue darted out, and I couldn't fucking help myself. I licked the entire seam of her lips, dipping in for a quick jab as if she summoned me. "You still taste the same."

"Maybe," she whispered, "but I'm not the same on the inside, Cade."

I felt my eyes flare in the dark room. All I saw was her silhouette with small flashes of red tingeing her skin with heat. "Let's find out."

My hands dropped to her hips quickly, and she flinched, pressing herself further onto the large pipe behind her. Her skirt was pulled down and over her hips, little rips of fabric blending in with the sound of shrilling whistles of a nearby machine. I swallowed the gasp on her lips as I reached down and felt her ass in my hands, nearly dying right there with the feel of her in my grasp again.

I've been lost without you. I kissed her senseless, taking her soul and putting it right back where it belonged—even if she didn't want to admit it. Journey didn't understand my motives, and I couldn't imagine what went through her head that night when I didn't show and what she went through when she was taken under the assumption that she was suicidal. I couldn't blame her for being standoffish and hating me, at least on the outside, because right now, she may have hated me, but she also fucking wanted me.

"Spread your legs," I demanded, pulling back and trying to get a glimpse of her half naked in front of me. When she took too long to do what I'd asked, I gripped the inner sides of her thighs, nearly devouring her skin with my greedy fingers, and pushed her legs farther apart. A whimper escaped her mouth, and her hands slammed onto my tightly bunched shoulders.

"Cade." My name was a lingering breath on her wet lips that I wanted to feast on.

"I haven't touched you for so long." A pause was shared, and there was a burn in my chest, like a hot iron-clad rod branding me there in front of her. "I know I don't deserve it," I said, creeping higher up her leg, feeling blood rush to all my favorite parts. If she didn't let me in, I'd fucking die. "Let's pretend. You're still panicking, Journey. Don't you feel your heart racing? I can smell the fear."

"I'm not afraid," she barked, hips tilting to meet me at the border of her panties. My teeth clenched as I tried to go slower.

"Good," I said, pulling her panties to the side. The

machines at our backs hissed louder as I ran my finger down her seam, feeling how wet she was. I smiled against her mouth. "Seems like you're not all that different. I still know what makes you hot."

Her fingers dug into my shoulders as I slinked away from her clit and pushed the very tip of my finger into her tight, wet folds.

"Mmm." Her body shuddered as I pushed in farther, and I saw sparks behind my eyelids.

"You're all wound up," I said, taking my hand from her hip and placing it over her rapidly rising chest. Her hand left my shoulder as I pumped in farther, feeling her soak me from the knuckle down. "Has it been a while?"

Fuck, don't answer that.

Her palm enclosed itself around my wrist, and I looked down, wishing I could see her take charge. She began moving my hand faster, and I leaned in, talking over her mouth. "Tell me, did you think of me at all while you were gone?"

"No." Her hips curved up with the answer that I knew was a lie.

"Don't lie to me." My hand went around her neck, and her pulse was a rampage against my palm.

"Why would I think of someone who left me out to die?" Her teeth sunk into my bottom lip so hard that I tasted the rich, metallic sensation against my tongue. I growled, keeping the truth on lockdown. If she was already fearful over what happened, what the fuck would she think if I told her the truth? That I'd been getting threats months before she was attacked? *I don't deserve her.*

"I thought of you every fucking day," I admitted, letting my confession pour out of my chest even though I knew it wouldn't take away my guilt or the betrayal that she felt. "Every time I turned a corner, every time I saw a fair-skinned girl walk past, every time I *touched* myself. *You.*

Journey. I thought of you every fucking time, even if it hurt."

Her head turned, and she heaved out a sigh that was more seductive than anything. I added another finger, feeling myself grow harder than I'd ever been in my life. I so badly wanted to flip her around, pin her hands on the pipe above her head, and fuck her so hard she forgot about what I'd done to her. But I didn't, because this wasn't about me. It was about *her.* Her walls were beginning to tighten around my fingers as I unbuttoned her school blouse, taking my free hand and dipping inside her shirt to feel for that pebbled nipple that I knew would be there. "Do you like knowing I thought of you when I beat myself off?" My nose skimmed the sensitive part behind her ear as she tried to suppress a moan. Her hips were moving, and my fingers were pushing in and out of her so slowly even I was beginning to feel the pull. "I thought of your perfect little pussy and how it always responded to my touch."

"*Cade.*" Journey was fighting the dirty talk that I knew she loved so much. My sweet little Journey, who was timid and soft, turned into a minx when it was just her and I. Even when I had taken her for the first time, deflowering the perfect little thing that she was, she latched onto the dirty things I'd whispered in her ear. Journey was a girl after her own rebellion. She was a flower with thorns that no one had ever dared touch. *Except me.*

"You do, don't you? You like knowing I thought of your perfect ass when I gripped myself in the shower. You like knowing that I pretended I was fucking your sweet little, eager mouth, huh?"

"Stop it," she rushed out, tightening around my finger like a boa constrictor.

"How can I stop when I know how much you like it?"

Just then, Journey's entire body seized, and she sucked my

fingers so hard I had to bite down on my own lip from sinking my teeth into her perfect skin. *She is mine. I'll never stop wanting her.*

"Ride it out, baby," I said, pushing the back of her head toward mine and closing my mouth over hers. She kissed me fiercely, and even if the kiss only lasted a few seconds, I knew the past had vanished momentarily. Journey kissed me like before. With every bit of passion she had to offer. *She gave me everything, and I fucking let it go.*

Once she pulled away and let go of my wrist, I pulled my finger out slowly, unable to focus on anything other than the way my dick was straining against my pants and begging for her touch. I hated myself for trying to fuck away her memory with the other girls at this school. *Loathed myself.* I loathed myself even more afterward, when I realized that the entire time I was fucking some blonde, I pictured her.

"I've been fucked up since that night," I said, standing there with my hands down by my side, feeling a gust of warm air as she bent down and pulled her skirt back up her shaking legs.

Her gulp was loud, and I knew the moment was lost in the steam that surrounded us.

"You think you've been fucked up?" The icy tone was back, and it cooled my hot blood almost instantly. I stepped away and clenched my fists, hardly able to even focus on the way her sweet wetness coated my finger. I wanted to lick it, but it didn't seem very appropriate at the given time. Things had suddenly shifted, and we were back to our little game of hate and love. "I was stood up by the one person I trusted, assaulted, taken away from the only place I'd ever known happiness, and thrown into a psych ward." Journey stepped forward, and I could finally see her face as one of the tiny red lights to the right clicked to green and stayed. The gloss of her eyes sucked me in, and I was drowning. Fully fucking drowning. "And don't even get me started on what I had to do in that place to find a way out."

She shoulder-checked me on the way past. I turned around to follow after her, having absolutely no idea what I could say to fix what was shattered between us. "Journ–"

She whipped around with the door half cracked, lighting up the small room that we just completely lost all direction in. The broken and tired girl that stood in front of me was a knife to my chest. Her cheeks were flushed from the orgasm I'd given her, but her eyes were dull and full of sadness and maybe a little fear. Journey was lost and confused, and I was half to blame.

"Journey? Where are you?" Journey quickly spun away from me, and I barely caught the door in my hand before it slammed as she rushed out. I traveled down the hall and stopped around the corner when I saw her standing with Gemma.

"I have no idea what happened. I've never done that before."

"You had a panic attack," Gemma said, rubbing her hands down Journey's arms. Her blouse was still unbuttoned, and Brantley caught my eye as he stood behind the girls and Isaiah. His eyebrows raised before rolling his eyes, knowing what Journey and I were doing for the last ten minutes.

Brantley didn't believe in love, and I wasn't sure he ever would, and I envied him for that. If you didn't find love, you could avoid that true, earth-shattering pain when you lost it, and that was exactly what I felt looking at the broken girl in front of me who used to radiate nothing but smiles when we were alone in our own little world.

My arms crossed over my chest as Tobias appeared from the stairway that led to the dorms, stalking past his sister, grabbing onto Journey's arms, and looking over her body like she had been hurt.

"What happened? Gemma texted me and said you flipped out. Was it that Aubrey girl?"

Tobias was still looking over her body as my teeth gritted together like sandpaper. *Aubrey?* Well, she was done for.

"I don't know. Someone pulled my sleeve, and it shot me back to when Barry used to come up behind me and try to catch me."

Our group was silent as we stood in between the stairway and the hall that led to our classes. I saw the narrow hall beginning to fill with students from the dining hall who were pretending not to stare but were fully invested in what the fuck was going on with the group of Rebels. The attention was evasive and annoying, and in the beginning, when our elite group started, we ate it up like a pack of wild animals, but now that we had *real* and dangerous shit going on, it wasn't as appealing.

"Jesus," Tobias muttered, still looking Journey over to assess for damage.

A lingering being stood at the end of the hall as everyone began disappearing into their classrooms, meaning we would need to go, too, which did nothing but irritate me because that meant Journey would be leaving with Tobias, and I wouldn't see her for the rest of the day. I found it uncoincidental that we had zero classes together, but that wasn't why my blood pressure was currently rising. The person at the end of the hall had my muscles tensing. I kept my eyes on him and waited until he shifted his attention from Journey and Tobias, then over to me.

Why the interest, Bain?

My eyebrow flicked as I tightened my tie so roughly I felt like I was halfway to choking. Bain had no intention of moving. His face stayed even, but I could have sworn I saw the smallest tick below his eye.

"Why is your neck red?" Shifting my gaze from Bain, who

still hadn't moved from the end of the hall, I turned and glanced down at Journey's neck.

Tiny splotches of pink were covering her chest and creeping up to her neck, which had a long red streak across it. I shoved my free hand in my pocket, knowing that I had trailed my finger across it, down her chest, and into her shirt.

"Oh, uh..." Journey's voice wavered from the confidence that she had shoved in my face just moments ago, and I stayed completely relaxed as Tobias glared at me.

"Couldn't fucking help yourself, could you?"

My heart whacked harder and harder as I glared back at Tobias, trying to right my vision so I didn't dig myself into an even deeper hole.

"Tobias." Journey tugged on his arm, and I pictured myself lunging forward to rip her hands off him. *Get a fucking hold of yourself.* The possessive part of me wanted to use the hand that still smelled of her and punch him in the fucking face and tell everyone that she was mine, but I knew that there was something more going on in this school that was far beyond my jealousy of Tobias and his sudden protection of Journey. He wasn't here when Journey was attacked, so as much as I hated the fact that he was on better feet when it came to her, I knew he wasn't a danger.

"Let's go to class," she said, still pulling on him.

I silently begged her to look back at me. *Just once.* I wanted to see those cool gray eyes and find the tiniest seed of *her* still in them, but Journey kept herself angled away from me as she and Tobias went the opposite direction.

Tobias, however, glared at me the entire way. I had news for the brooding, fucked-up boy from the Covens. I wouldn't stop trying to protect her, no matter who stood in my goddamn way.

CHAPTER TWELVE

CADE

THE REST of the day passed just as slowly as it did when Journey was gone. Eight months had felt like ten years, and today felt like an entire lifetime. Every time I passed by the boiler room, I stared at the closed door, knowing I'd had her in my hands earlier in the day, kissing her, sucking on her skin, feeling her pulse beat around me like my own pounding heart.

Snow had begun falling from the darkened sky, and I gripped my crosse harder through the numbness in my hands as I craned my neck to the top bleacher where she sat with Sloane, Mercedes, and Gemma.

"It wasn't him." I tore my gaze away as the smallest seed of guilt planted itself inside my burning chest, knowing that I shouldn't have been listening to Journey's conversation with Tobias last night. I came in on the tail end of it. It wasn't fully intentional. I wasn't spying. *Alright, fine.* I knew where she was, but I didn't know that Tobias was sitting with her. I was looking for a new book to read, and I always went to the

library right before curfew so no one could get in my business and wonder why I was reading *particular* books. Particular books meaning Journey's favorites. It was just a fraction of something that held me close to her when I no longer could spend my nights listening to her voice read me rich lines from classic novels. My finger was resting on the spine of a worn paperback when I heard her slight whisper. *"It wasn't him. He thought I did it to myself."*

A knife was lodged into my back, and my guilty conscience dug it in even farther, until the handle was the only thing sticking out.

Journey thought I had attacked her that night.

Journey didn't try to kill herself.

Someone did it to her.

I'd always had an inkling in the back of my head. There was a suspicion that I played off as denial. I wasn't totally ignorant, but Isaiah and I searched the school that night. Nothing stood out. There wasn't even a speck of dirt out of line that told us she wasn't alone.

Self-inflicted wounds. That was what the paramedics said they were. But they weren't. Either someone was lying that night, or someone wasn't as medically savvy as they fucking thought.

A slap to my head had me dropping my crosse. "I will beat the living shit out of you."

Isaiah stood beside Brantley and Shiner, and I watched as the rest of the team walked off the field and toward the locker room. *Is practice over?*

"Yep," Brantley snarled. "You were too busy fucking Journey in your head to even realize practice had ended. Coach blew the whistle and all."

Shiner snickered. "He was replaying what they did earlier."

My eyes narrowed as I latched onto him, and he threw his

hands up in mock surrender. "What? It was obvious. I could smell her arousal down the hall, bro."

My vision turned red, and Isaiah stepped between us. Shiner slammed his lips together and shot me an amused look. "Relax. No one else has a sense of smell like me. I'm like half Edward Cullen and half Jacob Black."

Brantley snapped his head over to him, a cloud of warm breath floating from his mouth. "How do you ever get laid?"

Shiner was completely taken aback. "What? I've fucked more girls than you all put together. It's not hard for me to snag someone."

"That's unlikely," Brantley answered calmly, taking the gloves off his hands.

Shiner began walking off with him, explaining his behavior. "Girls love chatting about romancey movies and shit. It makes for easy access." He nudged him. "Like the other night, I talked Kaya into reenacting the scene between Bella and Edward as they had sex as vampires. It was hot. It got rough —just what I wanted. Plus, she came, like, four times."

"Something is fucking wrong with you."

Isaiah stepped forward as their conversation faded. His jaw was its usual tightness as he bent down and grabbed my lacrosse stick. "Tate wants a word with you. I said I would bring you to his office after practice."

My eye twitched. "What does he want?" The options were honestly endless. Did it have something to do with our fathers? Was dear ol' Daddy calling from prison? Did he know I destroyed his office and that Journey stole something from the top shelf?

"I'm sure it has something to do with her." Isaiah nudged his head to the bleachers, and I followed his gaze, landing on a set of fuzzy boots walking down the icy steps. Sloane had her arm wrapped around Journey's shoulders, whispering something into her ear, followed by a laugh coming from both of them, and Gemma and Mercedes were following closely behind.

"Did you fuck her earlier?"

I didn't look back at my best friend as I answered, "No."

"I know how you work when trying to bring someone out of a panic." *He just can't let it go. I touched Gemma one fucking time.* "I give it a week."

"Shut up," I barked. "She'd only regret it afterward, anyway." She hadn't looked at me once today. Not that there were many chances, but when there were, she made sure to protect herself from me.

"Come on. Tate's waiting, and I know you want to hurry so you can be a fucking creep and sit in the hallway near Journey's door, as if she's going to magically disappear into thin air."

I chuckled dryly, not surprised that he knew where I was. "Why are you complaining? You and Gem can fuck all you want now." I paused, shifting my attention from Journey to someone else who had their eyes on her. "Not that you care if I'm in the room."

Isaiah threw his head back and let out a loud laugh that had a flock of birds flying off an icy tree. His hoarse yell of Gemma's name had the hair on the back of my neck sticking up. "Gemma!" I wasn't sure if she turned around, or if Journey was staring at me, because I was too focused on Bain and how his beetle-like eyes were on my girl. "I love you!"

There was a cluster of girly laughter, and my nostrils flared as Bain kept his hands in his hoodie pocket with his beanie-covered head leaning against the fenced area of the bleachers.

"Isaiah." His name was calm coming from my mouth, but I was raging on the inside. Burning with anger and uncertainties.

"What?" It didn't take Isaiah long to follow my gaze, but

when he did, he sighed loudly. "What is it? Has he done something?"

I turned to Isaiah after I watched Journey and her friends disappear into the side of St. Mary's to likely head to their rooms. "She didn't try to kill herself."

My heart caught on fire, burning a hole straight through my chest and landing on the snowy field. Isaiah's dark brows lowered beneath his black beanie. "What? Did she tell you that?"

"Not exactly," I answered, and I knew I didn't need to explain. We had a way of finding shit out one way or another.

Bain was still sitting up on the top bleacher, looking down at his phone, fully submerged in it now that Journey had gone inside. I tore my gaze away, walking with Isaiah toward the courtyard to get to Tate's office.

"So, someone attacked her?"

"You don't seem surprised," I grit out, watching my shoes tread over the thickening snow. "Did you fucking know?"

"I would have told you if I knew anything concrete."

"So, what?" I asked, moving in front of him. "You just assumed? Even after you told me to let it go all those months ago?" My heart was pounding, racing like it was trying to crawl right up my throat and choke my best friend for his betrayal.

Isaiah's grinding jaw was all I could see as he glanced toward the courtyard. "I hated seeing you so fucked up over something that we had no control over. But I had always suspected Bain in every problem that arose in this school." He turned back toward me. "We all did."

"If he fucking touched her, I will kill him."

Isaiah nodded. "I've been there before, too. In fact, I pointed a goddamn gun at his head. Remember that?"

As if I could forget. Bain had been our enemy from day one —his father, Callum, being the biggest rival of ours. We were tasked with the job of following Bain's every movement, and when he'd fucked Isaiah over in the worst way possible, I thought I was going to have to hide his body. He managed to squeak by in the end, helping get Gemma back to Isaiah, but he had his eyes on Journey, and that put him right back at the top of my shitlist.

"Come on." Isaiah nudged my shoulder, and we began walking to the front of St. Mary's with my blood pressure quickly rising. My mind was reeling with too many negative thoughts of Bain, putting him right there in the center, circling around Journey.

"It could have been him," I said, walking up the steps to the school. "We weren't as cautious with him back then. Things hadn't picked up with your father's paranoia yet."

Isaiah nodded. "You're right, but..."

I slammed the door shut just as he'd opened it. I was certain the headmaster would come see what was going on in a few minutes. "But what?"

Isaiah's jaw shifted again. I could hear his teeth clamoring together. "I found pictures of Journey in Bain's room back when I was searching for shit for my dad."

The white snow that surrounded us began to melt with my anger, but before I could fully explode, Isaiah put a pin in it.

"There were pictures of Gemma, and later, he took pictures of her and I together, which he gave to Richard." His eyes flicked to mine with an intensity that we both suddenly shared. *I remember.* "But there were pictures of Journey, too. And of Ms. Glenburg."

My hand trembled with anger on the door to St. Mary's, and blood rushed to my fingertips. Fast puffs of air left my chest, and I was *seconds* from turning around to find him, but Isaiah snapped his fingers in front of my face. "I'm not done."

"There's more?" I choked out, moving past the fact that he had kept this from me. I would deal with that later.

"They weren't sexual." He glanced away, still seeming troubled by this. "They were just...almost like he was spying on her? Kind of like with Gemma at one point. I don't know. There were none of the two of you. Only of her. There were other pictures in there, of Ms. Glenburg, that were borderline pornographic. But of Journey? They were just...normal."

"There is nothing fucking normal about him secretly taking photos of her." The tone that came from my mouth sounded just like my father's. *Calm, collected, and psychotic.*

"Boys." My hand fell when the heavy door propped open, allowing a gust of warm air to hit us. "Get in here."

Isaiah and I walked through the door together, and I shot him a look that said, *This isn't fucking over,* to which he shot me a look right back that said, *Obviously.* When my anger subdued later on, I would better understand why he didn't inform me of the photos. When Journey was gone, I bristled at her name on anyone's lips. Anger and remorse would fill me to capacity, and I would have to start the climb all over again to find my way out of the deepest, darkest hole, but *fuck.* Right now? I was agitated, and my muscles throbbed with fury.

As soon as the headmaster shut his office door, Isaiah sat lazily in the chair in front of his desk, kicking his long legs out and placing his hands behind his head. I stood back by the bookshelf, picturing Journey's bare leg propped on the edge and remembering the brief second I'd had my hand on her thigh.

"What the hell happened earlier?" Tate sat rather aggressively in his chair and slammed his elbows onto the desk. "Cade? I'm asking you, in particular."

I clicked my tongue, crossing my arms. "What are you referring to?"

"I'm referring to Journey and how she nearly clawed some girl's eyes out."

Oh, so he doesn't know she stole something from his office. Good.

"Well, did you ask *said* girl what happened?"

A ragged sigh flew from his mouth. "Yes, she said Journey was crazy and needed to go back to the psych ward because she attacked her for no reason." He raised an eyebrow as my rage kicked up a notch.

"Surely you don't believe that," Isaiah said, taking the reins because he could likely feel my heart beating from across the room.

The headmaster rolled his eyes. "If I did, you two wouldn't be in here right now. I need the full story, and I don't want to distress Journey and have her thinking she is going to be leaving this school again."

I stepped forward. "I will personally strangle someone if they try to take her away again. She does not belong in a psych ward, Tate."

The headmaster's eyes crinkled at the edges. "Why do you say that?"

"Do you not agree?" I countered.

Isaiah raised his hand like he was in the middle of class. "May I speak?"

Tate and I looked down at his nonchalant expression as he lowered his hand. He cleared his throat, speaking anyway. "Journey did not try to commit suicide. According to Cade, she was attacked, and those were not self-inflicted wounds." The headmaster's brows deepened as he threw his hands up in complete bewilderment. I was pretty sure I heard him mutter a few curse words under his breath, as if he couldn't say them out loud in front of the pair of us. "Now, earlier... there was a rumor, a lot of whispering and shit about Journey and Cade, and a group of girls went up to Journey and started to ask her about the rumor, and one of them pulled her sleeve to see if she had the scars that matched the"—Isaiah paused as he used air quotations—"suicide attempt."

Tate sat back, his chair squeaking beneath him. "Okay... uh... And then what?"

"And she freaked out because she said, for a moment, she thought she was back at the psych ward with someone coming up behind her as she tried to run away."

There was a punch to my tense stomach, as if someone had taken the air from me. A replay of some man coming up behind her to put her back into her *room* while she tried to escape made me sick. Protection ran thick in my veins from watching my father protect Isaiah's father and their legacy. It was all I'd ever known, and when that unyielding protection gracefully moved to Journey instead of what I was taught to protect, everything changed.

I hadn't been the same since.

The headmaster suddenly appeared very fucking tired. He ran his hands roughly through his hair and pulled on the ends, dropping his head low as he leveled his breathing. The room was quiet besides the crackling of the nearby fire, and when he looked up again, his face said it all: *What the fuck?*

"I don't even know what to say," he started, rubbing a hand over his five o'clock shadow. "So, someone attacked her? Are you sure?"

Isaiah peered over his shoulder at me. I cleared my throat and looked down at my lacrosse shoes as they left a puddle of melted snow on the floor of the headmaster's office. "Positive." I ground my teeth together. "She doesn't know who." I didn't want to allow the next confession to come from my mouth, but I did anyway. "She thought it was me who attacked her. Or, at least, she wasn't sure."

Isaiah turned all the way around this time with his heavy browline deepened. "Why would she think that?"

I glanced away at the roaring fire. "Because I was the only

person who knew where she was that night." *Fuck.* Here came the truth, catching up to me as I tried to outrun it. "I told her where to meet me, and then I stood her up. I didn't fucking show." My gaze stayed level with the fire, my eyes burning from the heat floating up to hit me in the face.

"Explain."

Black dots danced in front of my vision as I kept my eyes open, as if blinking was going to keep me from feeling the immense amount of guilt that I'd been pushing away since the moment she left.

"Cade. Fucking speak up."

I snapped on the inside. "Because I had been getting threats for months before she left. Warning me to stay away from her."

Both of their heads dropped in defeat, and mine did, too. I was man enough to admit that it hurt to say it aloud. The guilt that I thought was overpowering was now coming at me tenfold, and I leaned back against the wall, hoping it would hold me up so I didn't completely lose it.

I should have been out there that night.

"And you have no idea who was threatening you?"

I met Isaiah head on and breathed out through my nose in rushed breaths. "No fucking idea. I wasn't sure if it was from our father's shit outside of St. Mary's or someone from here." Pushing off from the wall, I began pacing back and forth, just like the other night when Journey left me alone in this dull office. "I waited, watched. *Nothing.* Except for Bain and how his eyes would follow her every so often. But I didn't understand. He'd never tried to pursue her or touch her. It didn't make sense. That was why I got so pissed about the rumor from earlier. If it *was* someone from our father's business that was targeting me from before, if they got wind of me having a child with her? If they wanted to get back at either of us for fucking the entire business up?" A sarcastic laugh left me as I ended my thoughts, knowing they fully understood.

The headmaster muttered from his desk, "Nothing fucking makes sense. Jesus Christ. It's one thing after another."

He was right. It was. Every time we stood up, another fucking thing knocked us right back down. I never truly thought we'd be in the clear once our fathers were behind bars, but I'll admit, I was hopeful.

Isaiah and I sat in the headmaster's office for far too long —well after curfew—thinking in silence. Isaiah pulled out his phone, likely to send a text to Gemma, and leaned forward, placing his elbows on his knees. "We need to know who attacked her."

I watched the headmaster closely as he leaned back in his squeaky chair and flicked his eyes to the top shelf above the books that Journey was skimming the other night.

Bingo.

"She took it."

His eyes shifted to me. His jawline became sharper, and part of me wanted to smirk that Journey's rebellious streak had come out yet again. She was a quiet rule-breaker, so deceiving with her sweet looks and tender voice. *No one knows her like I do.*

"Took what?" Isaiah asked, shifting his attention back and forth between us.

"The file that held her life inside of it," the headmaster answered. "Fuck."

I shook my head, stopping him before he could get too worked up. "I have that vital piece of information you're worried about. Not her."

His head tilted. "Did you help her break in here? God damn, I need to get those alarms installed! I cannot stand you boys."

Isaiah grumbled. "What the fuck did I do?"

"Plenty."

Ignoring their quarrel, I placed my hands on the desk and leaned in between them. "I followed her in here the other night during the claiming. I found her stealing the file, and the paper that had the information from Sister Mary fell to the floor. She left quickly, without realizing it had fallen."

"So, it was you that destroyed my office?" The headmaster rolled his eyes. "Clean up after yourself next time."

Isaiah snapped his fingers. "I told you it wasn't me."

"As if I would believe you." Tate turned toward me. "So, she doesn't know what the note says."

"Wait, what does the note say?" Isaiah asked.

I sighed. "Her mother, or whoever left her at the orphanage, left a note in her baby blanket that said she was in danger and to protect her."

Isaiah nodded. "So, it's probably someone from *her* past that attacked her. That makes more sense."

At the exact same time, Tate and I said, "Nothing makes sense."

Seconds turned to long, agonizing minutes with my chest growing tighter and tighter. The headmaster dismissed us with a wave of his hand a little while later, knowing he had to get to his house for Jack, Isaiah's little brother that he had custody of.

Isaiah and I walked back to the locker room in silence, changed out of our lacrosse gear, and headed straight for our rooms with a note from the headmaster, excusing us if we were caught walking the halls after curfew.

Before the split in the hall for the dorms, Isaiah stopped and looked at me. "We won't let anything touch her again. We protect what's ours, and she's ours, whether she knows it or not."

I pushed past the anxiety that was caving in on me, not

believing his words. Everyone thought being in the elite group of Rebels was how you became untouchable and protected. You were on the top of the food chain; they called us the righteous kings of the school. But it was a load of fucking bullshit. We brought *nothing* but doom to this goddamn school. Our problems followed us here, and it seemed they followed Journey, too. I was beginning to think that St. Mary's was for the cursed.

"You have to stop hiding shit from us, though," Isaiah said, beginning to walk backward toward our room. I sighed, dropping my head down low as my muscles tightened to stone along my shoulders. "Do what you have to do to make her think she's safe with you, because I can assure you, she isn't safe on her own."

No. No, she fucking isn't.

___

CHAPTER THIRTEEN

___

JOURNEY

CLAIMING parties used to be a type of high for a girl like me. Someone who was timid and shy. Someone who didn't like to put themselves out there to avoid being hurt or let down. I loved the idea of no one knowing who you were. When the lights went out, a blanket of darkness covered the room, and you mysteriously turned into whomever you wanted.

The feeling of someone's hands on you who had no true idea of knowing who you were was intoxicating. The letting go and allowing all your inhibitions to disappear, if only for a moment. *I loved it.*

The first time a pair of large, rough hands found their way to my waist, a rebellious thrill rushed through my body, followed by a million little butterflies. His lips found my neck, and my pulse thundered behind my skin. I didn't know it was Cade the first time, but I had hoped. I didn't know it was Cade the second time, either. But by the third time, I knew. I caught him watching me from across the party, with his hands in his pockets and his tongue dipping out to wet his bottom lip. It was as if my body knew it was him. A burn so hot swooped low in my belly, and I grew uneasy on my feet. Right before those lights went out, Cade winked at me, and the next thing I knew, we were in our rightful spot, tucked away in a corner, with his hands caressing my curves and his teeth tugging at my ear.

But now, claiming parties only reminded me of what I never truly had in the first place. Cade's words were always so pretty—and believable, too. I even let myself believe him when he had his hand between my legs just a few days ago, but I wasn't as gullible as I had been last spring. Spring turned to summer, summer turned to fall, and here we were, in winter, with the lock on my heart frozen shut. *Cade Walker is not allowed in.*

"Bye, Mom." Sloane hung up her phone rather aggressively before throwing it onto her bed as she stood in the middle of her room nearly naked. Her chest filled with air as she shakily let it out before turning around and staring at me, Gemma, and Mercedes.

"You okay?" Gemma asked, putting light-pink lipstick on.

I turned away as Sloane peeked over at me, knowing that she was likely about to skim over her own issues like before. Sloane was a closed book—always had been.

Sloane's light laugh filled the dorm room. "Why do you even bother?"

"What?"

"Isaiah is going to have that lipstick off in literal seconds, Gem. What's the point?"

Mercedes laughed, and I forced a smile, ignoring the siphoned anxiety that was filling me from going over my plans for the night. Cade continued to poke at the outside of my brain, trying to weasel himself in there with his scorching gaze and straight jaw, but I blocked him out, slipping into the

Journey that ruled the halls of the psych hospital to save herself.

I was doing the same thing here—trying to save myself from another meet-cute with a knife.

"I like to look good," Gemma said, running her hands through her hair. "Richard never let me do anything for myself, so I'm trying to fight against that and do whatever the hell I want."

"Fuck yeah," Sloane said through a smile. "I like it when you're a little badass."

I shot my gaze down to Gemma's outfit and lingered on her bare wrists, realizing that I had only seen them once before, in the Covens, when she was placed there for a brief time. Her left hand rubbed against the pink skin, almost as if she were nervous, and I latched onto her in that instant because I understood. I understood her in ways that I could never explain.

"Isaiah wants me to show my wrists tonight," she whispered, glancing down at her nervous fingers moving against the fresh marks. "He said it was up to me, but he said it could be good to show them off and be proud that I survived." She looked over her shoulder at Sloane and Mercedes with a show of emotion in her green eyes. Then, she sliced her attention to me and smiled. "You know, when I first met you, I was envious."

"Envious? Of me?" I crossed my arms over my tight tank hidden beneath my usual leather jacket.

"Yeah," she answered, tucking her hair behind her ears. "Not because you could walk freely in that place, because even if you were moving around the halls late at night, I know now that you weren't free."

A swallow found itself lodged in my throat as my heart skipped a beat. That night was trying to break through, just like Cade was, and I wasn't going to let it. Although, I knew here, in just a few hours, I would be reliving that same night all over again.

Gemma snagged my attention back to her as she took a step forward. "It was because you weren't shy about those scars on your arms. I remember thinking how amazing it would be to be proud of something like that...to not give a shit what anyone thinks or assumes."

A shaky breath was summoned from my mouth with the truth following closely behind it. "I'm not proud."

"You should be," Sloane said, still standing in the same spot. *She knew.* Sloane knew the truth. Well, part of it. I wasn't sure if she believed me when I told her that I didn't create the scars on my arms myself. I hoped she did, though, for a reason that was buried deep below the surface.

"We're survivors, Journey. And I don't know you that well, but I have to say, I'm glad you're alive."

Why did that make my heart dip? I cleared my throat and glanced down at the fuzzy rug beneath my boots. With my heart pounding in my ears, I shrugged my jacket off my shoulders so slowly that the cool leather chilled my skin. It dropped to the floor in a quick whirl, and when I looked back at the three girls who were continuing to include me in their newfound trio, something clicked.

I shrugged, allowing a small amount of warmth to fall into place. "Since everyone is so curious at this school anyway, I guess I'll show them that the rumor of having Cade's baby is incorrect and that I have the scars to match my *suicide attempt*."

Sloane nodded proudly at me, and together, we all headed straight to the claiming.

———

THE CLAIMING WAS in full swing, and I was beginning to think that our allotted time to walk the halls purposefully made us the last to show up because *everyone* was already half-buzzed as their heads lazily turned to us when we walked through the door.

I bit my tongue when I snagged onto Cade first. A wicked string of curse words flirted through as I allowed a surge of hot lust to fly through my veins when his brooding eyes ran down my legs and back. He didn't even stop to look at my bare arms like everyone else in the room. Instead, his eyes latched onto mine, and the tick in his jaw sent a shiver down my spine.

"Hmm," Sloane whispered from in between Mercedes and Gemma. "Looks like someone is pissy that you're looking all hot and shit."

"Good," I said, plain as day, staring right back at him. *Look away. Look away. Look away.*

Mercedes blew out a bundle of warm air. "What is it with you guys and playing with fire? The Rebels have a way of being repulsively entitled to what they want and not caring who gets hurt. Just about everyone in this school knows that Cade has it bad for you, and not many people stand up to the Rebels."

"Except Bain." Just then, I skimmed right over the rest of the Rebels and locked onto the mysterious boy who had been watching me from the very beginning. It wasn't like I didn't notice him staring at me from time to time, and I was pretty sure that Cade's feud with him had something to do with me, but what would I know? Cade was never truthful with me. That part was obvious after learning about the gun-running business that Isaiah was a big part of, meaning that Cade likely was, too.

"Whoa, what?" Sloane stepped in front of me, blocking

out Bain's intent to avoid my stare. *Why does he always watch me when he thinks I'm not looking?*

My sentence cut right to the point. "I need to talk to Bain."

"Why?" Gemma asked. "Answer quickly. Here they come."

I felt the shift of air as everyone made way for Isaiah, Brantley, Shiner, and my *least* favorite, Cade. My skin grew hot, even if there was a slight chill to the air from the basement being surrounded by the hard, frozen ground. "I have to ask him something."

Gemma smiled proudly, and Sloane sighed agitatedly before saying, "You two are so much alike it's scary."

"Be careful and act quick before Cade pulls an Isaiah."

I looked over at Gemma. "What does that mean? *'Pull an Isaiah'?*"

As soon as Isaiah's hand went around Gemma's waist, she laughed. "You'll see."

My brows crowded, wondering what they were referring to when Cade came up right beside me. I kept my gaze level, staring a hole in someone's chest who had wandered up to our group. I swore I could feel Cade's beating heart racing beside me, right there along with mine. His familiar cologne filled my senses, and my body hummed as my eyes moved to the side, glancing at him out of the corner of my eye. Conversations were going on all around us. Something about Tobias not coming to the claiming, which didn't surprise me. Music was thumping, and loud laughter came from a group behind us, but I couldn't hear a single thing. All I could do was *feel*. My blood was rushing, and my fingers twitched by my side to reach out and touch him. I felt the low dip in my stomach as I remembered the way I felt alive with his mouth on mine two days ago. I craved the pause in reality he gave me when we were alone, swept away in each other like he hadn't betrayed me and left me alone to survive in a place that I could only describe as hell.

"Aubrey won't be messing with you anymore." The low rumble of his voice skittered over my skin like a whisper in the dark as he turned his head.

It made me angry. I wanted to turn toward him and shove him so he could stop jumbling up my head and pulling me back to that desperate girl that I was before when I allowed myself to fall for him. I needed to stop that pesky little thought that *this* time would be different, that I wouldn't end up alone and desperate for someone to love me enough to not turn their back on me.

"I don't need you, Cade." I bit back like a small dog off its leash. Our group paused for a moment, and I could have sworn I heard a snigger from someone—probably Shiner if I had to guess.

The air that was at a standstill between us grew warm, and I became flushed, my chest feeling sweaty as my heartrate climbed. The music cut off, and I knew that Cade was looking at me. I felt his burning eyes on the side of my face. Someone over the speakers announced that it was nearing claiming time, and Cade leaned in so close I felt the brush of his skin against my bare arm. There was a catch in my breath, and even the mere touch of him had me in overdrive.

"You may not need me, but you want me."

It was as if he could hear the dirty secrets that lived inside my head that I couldn't even face myself. Before the lights shut off, I snapped my fiery gaze to him and calmly lied right to his face. "Wrong."

Then, I slipped right through his fingers.

CHAPTER FOURTEEN

JOURNEY

PITCH BLACK. Just the way I liked it. I moved through the claiming party quickly, weaving and dodging like I was some sort of warrior princess instead of a wounded girl running from the boy who hurt her. I knew where Bain was, and I hoped that he hadn't moved from the last time I caught a glimpse. There was shuffling going on behind me, which both excited me and worried me.

A cat-and-mouse game. That was Cade's and my game before things became real. He'd watch me, toy with me, let me run away until the very last second when his strong hands would grab my waist, and then he'd spin me around and blindside me with dirty words and his scorching touch. Now, though, I couldn't be caught.

"Bain," I whispered, my hand latching onto something hard. My eyes adjusted quickly, and there was a wide-shouldered black shadow in front of me. *Please be him*. In the worst way, I wanted to look over my shoulder, but I didn't. Cade could have been standing there—or worse, the person who had attempted to kill me.

Or am I standing in front of him?

"Journey?"

I gripped his arm tighter and pulled him quickly behind me, and for some reason, he let me. Bain didn't strike me as a guy who let others drag him around. In fact, I bet he took control in every situation he was ever in—even at these parties with a girl beneath him. *Here goes nothing.*

I shoved us both into the first hidden room on the left, angry at the memory of Cade that popped up almost instantly. *This was ours, once upon a time.*

The lights remained off, and the click on the lock blended in with the pounding in my ears. "I wanted to get you alone," I said, shutting my eyes and pretending I wasn't about to go through with this. Tobias would be so disappointed in me, knowing I was using old tactics from the hospital that I pretended he knew nothing about.

I *always* felt sick afterward. Disgusted with myself even though I knew it had to be done.

"What do you want?" Bain was far away. His voice was distant but sharp like a knife.

Taking a step forward, rubbing my hands down my bumpy arms laced with chills, I asked, "Why do you always stare at me?" I hated the sound of my fake sultry voice. "Do you like me, Bain?"

"I don't know you," he nearly barked, halting my steps toward him. *This is not going as planned.*

"You stare at me enough...surely you know something about me." *Like who tried to kill me.*

He huffed out a laugh. "You've been back for, like, a week. I've hardly noticed."

I swallowed my fear and moved toward the sound of his voice. "Now I know you're lying." There was silence, and I stood in the same spot, staring at the dark figure in front of me. "You used to stare at me before I left, too. Did you think I didn't notice?"

He said nothing. Nothing at all. And with each breath I shakily let out, I tiptoed over to him, ready to chew up the guilt and spit it right back out.

"Why, Bain?"

"Why what?" Even without seeing him, I knew he said the words through gritted teeth. Was he holding himself back? Pretending that he didn't have some abnormal infatuation with me? *He used to stare at me like he was afraid he'd lose me.* I didn't mind, but it was perplexing.

"Do you want me? Is that it? Or is it something else?"

"Like what?"

My eyebrow rose. *He didn't deny it.*

My foot nudged his, and it sounded as if he had swallowed air. "Journey, back up."

No. "Or what?" *Will you try to kill me?* The words were there as they lingered on my tongue. I would have thought that it was fear holding me back, but for some wicked reason that I couldn't even begin to understand, I wasn't afraid.

"Journey, just—"

"Just what?" I asked, my face now an inch from his. "Why do you stare at me? Do you know something about me that I don't?"

Here we go, getting to the fun stuff. I hated myself at this moment, but I also loved myself. The thrill of toying with danger, breaking morals and rules that I'd made for myself to get people to love me like I wanted. Fighting and surviving to stay alive and to find out what the hell happened to me, and why I was so disposable to people.

Bain's rough hands landed on my biceps, and a rush of air whooshed out of my mouth. "*Stop*," he said.

"Stop what? Trying to figure out what your deal is with

me? You know, I couldn't stop thinking about it when I was away. Wondering why you always stared but *never* touched me." I swallowed, slicing away at Cade's seductive words as they floated through my head, making me feel guilty and dirty. *"You're mine, Journ. Always and forever. No one else can touch you."* Except, someone *did* touch me.

"Journey, turn the fuck around, and leave this room. You have no idea what you're doing." His hands tightened on my arms. *This is not how I saw this going.*

"Do you want to touch me, Bain? Is that why you stare? Is that why you follow me around?" My heart boomed, and blood rushed with an anticipating dose of terror that I found myself swimming in.

"Fuck. No! Jesus." Just as he barked out his refusal, the door barged open, the stupid lock flinging off and clamoring to the ground. The light was switched on, and I wasn't surprised to see Cade standing there with a beet-red face and an angry glint to his eye. He glared at me and then to Bain, and before I knew what was happening, I was quickly shoved behind Bain, my back slamming into the wall. *Wait, did he just protect me? From Cade?*

Cade snarled, "You're dead."

I yelped as Bain and Cade rushed toward one another. Both of their hands went around each other's necks, and I stood there, glued to the floor, shocked from watching what was unfolding in front of me. Their beady eyes were set on one another, their hands wrapped around the other's windpipes, crushing them so they couldn't speak.

Cade lacked oxygen as he pulled the words out and directed them toward me. "Did he touch you?"

I caught his burning gaze, and my resolve crashed and fell. The guilt was there, wrecking me as I stood in front of someone who hurt me and someone who didn't want me. A scream bubbled in my belly as I barely held it together.

"No," Bain wheezed. "I didn't fucking touch her."

Cade's brows dropped slightly with confusion, and he and Bain remained steady, clamped onto one another's necks.

I brushed away the hurt and dropped the guilt back on the ground. "Let each other go. This has nothing to do with you, Cade."

Bain's lip curled in satisfaction as he squeezed one last time, causing me to step forward. Then, at the exact same time, they dropped their hands, and Cade was suddenly backed by Brantley who glared directly at *me*.

I dropped my eyes to the ground, and I jumped when I heard Cade bark to everyone, "Out. Now."

I peeked up, heart hammering in my chest, as if I were in trouble. Bain glanced back at me once, but I couldn't tell what was going through his head. There was something tender lingering there, but something angry was brewing, too. It did nothing but cause me to question everything.

Brantley muttered, "It's like fucking Groundhog Day," before shutting the door and leaving me alone with my guilty conscience and Cade.

CHAPTER FIFTEEN

CADE

Journey put on a good front, slipping her mask on right in front of me, as if I didn't fucking see right through it.

I heard the shifting of her feet as she stepped one foot in front of the other as I ran my gaze up her smooth legs. "Nice fucking try," I spat, blocking the door from her sharp gaze.

"Excuse me?" she said with an attitude I craved in every single way. *There she is. My wild girl.* "Get out of my way, Cade."

I tsked, waving my finger in front of her. The same finger that got her off just two days prior. "You're forgetting that I know you *very* well, Journey. I'm not moving an inch until you tell me what that was about. What are you up to?"

Her teeth clamped together, and the echo of it pounded right through my skull. Her dainty chin pulled up high, doing nothing but showing off more of her flushed chest. *Silence. Nice.*

"So," I started, stalking toward her like I was ready to attack. "Did you do that to piss me off? Or was there a reason for your mindless behavior?" Granted, she probably didn't realize how dangerous Bain truly was, but that didn't matter at the moment.

Her lip twitched, and fuck me if I didn't want to smile, too. "There was a reason, but I have no issue killing two birds with one stone."

I laughed. I actually dropped my chin, a single foot away from her, backed against the same wall that I watched Bain push her into, and let out a low chuckle that I felt vibrate throughout my limbs. "And you pretend like I mean nothing to you." My head snapped up as soon as the words left me, and she jumped. Her red lips were glistening from her tongue dipping out unknowingly to wet them, and my pupils dilated so quickly it hurt to look.

"You don't."

I hummed, turning around swiftly, feeling the slippery dust on the concrete floor under my shoes. I could feel her disappointment, as if she thought I was actually going to walk out of this room and leave her be. The question was still trying to dig out of my chest and come from my mouth. *Why Bain?* Why did she seek him out? What did they discuss? And why was he so adamant that he hadn't touched her? He was disgusted when I asked. His body tensed, and his ugly face that most girls *loved* scrunched up. *What the fuck was that?*

My back was ramrod straight as I shook the unease away, feeling myself click into the mischievous Rebel everyone knew me as. I peered over my shoulder, locking onto Journey's flushed cheeks and blank face. Her features may have been easy and relaxed, but the smallest seed of desperation glinted like a piece of flint in her gray eyes. *I'm not going anywhere, baby.*

"You say you don't want me?" I asked, lowering my voice and dropping my eyes to her ribs screaming for air. My hand was steady as I pushed it forward, running my finger down the lone string that was tied to the only light in this dusty little room that I had found my first taste of love in. "How about now?" Darkness spread like the plague as I clicked the light off. The temperature of the room was as hot as the boiler room the other day.

I knew it was wrong—the little game we were about to play like old times.

There was so much shit between us that was covered beneath a million little pieces of debris. Things needed to be said. The truth needed to be told.

Yet, here I was, turning around and staking claim on a girl who I didn't deserve.

"What'll it be, Journey? Do you want Bain? Or do you want me?"

"That depends," she whispered. "What version of you am I getting? The boy who told me he loved me? Or the one who stood me up in the courtyard?"

The game paused for a second as I pulled the flaming fucking arrow out of my chest. *Tell her. Tell her everything.* See, this was the problem with a guy like me, who'd had no real fucking guidance in his life. My morals were skewed. When I should have been learning how to fish in the pond behind my house with my father, I was learning how to hide a body. Telling the truth was never a component of my childhood. Sometimes, the truth made things worse, and lies made things better. I wasn't sure which end of the scale I was supposed to be on. I, Cade Walker, didn't know right from wrong. *Thanks, Tommy Walker. Your fatherly contributions to my life did nothing but fuck me up.*

Coming back to Journey's question, I subtly skated over the heavy shit. "Does it matter?" My hands landed on her waist, and my stomach dipped with need. There was a low throb starting in my groin, and I could already taste her sweetness on my tongue.

Ravage. I wanted to ravage her until she forgave me.

And I hadn't even said sorry.

"Tell me again that you don't want me, Journey. That you never thought of me. That you want someone other than me to do this." I couldn't stop. My hand trailed up her rising chest, pausing at her thundering heartbeat, right over that perky mound that I wanted to smother my face into. I wanted to inhale her scent and never smell anything else again. Emotion crowded in for a second, blending in with the darkness that surrounded us. *I miss her so much it hurts to breathe.* I winced, knowing she couldn't see me, as I finally reached her neck, remembering how she loved it when I touched her there.

"Three," I whispered, nudging my jean-clad knee in between her legs, right below the little mini-skirt that she probably wore just to torture me. "Two," I said, sinking my teeth into her earlobe after running my tongue around her cute little diamond studs. "Last chance." I gripped her hip hard with one hand and began moving her over my knee, wishing like hell it was my dick.

The only sound I heard from her was heavy breathing, and I took that as a green flag. "*Mine,*" I said right over her lips before moving the hand around her neck up to her chin and sealing our mouths together.

Relief. I felt relief that she didn't fight me, and shock sunk my feet right into the floor as things twisted on the inside that were much more powerful than just a physical need. Journey and I were in the gray matter. She was the light, and I was dark. I sucked, and she kissed. I pulled, and she pushed. Her hands went into my hair, and her hips ground over me like I was fucking her with my knee. "Don't you get it..." I said quickly, pulling back to grip her ass. Her legs went around my hips, and my hard-as-a-fucking-rock dick pounded into her slick panties, moving roughly against her. "I'm still just as infatuated with you. Nothing has changed."

Fuck, yes.

But wait. *No. Wait.*

It was hard to let her go. My fingers dug in like they were in the sand on some perfect, sunny, getaway beach. She wiggled once, and then twice, and the second she turned her head and unsealed our mouths, I felt my heart drop to the floor. *Fuck.*

Her feet slammed down, stomping all over my dirty little intentions. "That's where you're wrong, Cade. *Everything* has changed. Especially me."

My mouth opened, but nothing came out. The light was turned on, and there she was, standing below the spotlight like my own personal angel, ready to damn me into hell.

"You don't get to do that."

I locked onto the trembling of her lip, hating that she was trying to make it stop. As if she couldn't show her weaknesses to me.

"Do what?" I asked, backing myself to the wall that she was just plastered against.

"Fuck away the guilt. You aren't telling me something, Cade. You left me out there that night for some fucked-up reason that you can't even admit out loud, and I just... I don't understand." Her face began to crumble, and it was as if I could see the walls shooting up around her. "So, no. You don't get to touch me and pretend like it didn't happen. Because it did, and you think you're messed up over it?" She turned around, taking her hurt with her. "I can't even manage to say no to you. I let you touch me even when I didn't know if you were the one to attack me. It's like I have some death wish when it comes to you."

I sucked in a breath, wanting to reach inside my chest to make the beating muscle stop screaming in agony. *God, I hurt her so bad.*

"I hate you," she said with a cracked voice, putting her

back to me. "I hate you for ruining years of self-preservation. I've been abandoned all my life, Cade. You knew that. And you did the same thing to me that night. And you won't even tell me why."

"Journey." I pushed past the hurt *she* was causing *me*.

Thump. Thump. Thump. My heart had climbed into my ears as I waited for her to turn around. My beats were exploding throughout the room. *Can she hear it? Can she feel my desperation? Can she see how torn I am?*

She slowly turned around, and I latched onto the wet streaks covering her cheeks. My voice suddenly disappeared as I stood there and stared at her. *Fuck.* "What was it?" she asked, hand on the doorknob. "Another girl?"

"What?" I was on the edge of a cliff, my voice growing more frantic with guilt. "No." My feet begged to carry me over to her, to shake her stupid for even asking such a thing, but then I was quickly reminded of the fact that I had lured her out to the courtyard, didn't show, and then she was brutally attacked. Why would she trust me or think anything other than the worst possible thing?

"Did you forget I was out there? Waiting for you? I had the note in my hand. The one that *you* wrote."

I didn't even want to answer her. The words were stuck like glue inside the back of my throat, cutting off oxygen. "I didn't forget." *How could I ever forget you?*

There was the slightest little crease in between her eyebrows that I wanted to smooth out with my finger. "Then...I–I... I don't understand." My eyes shut as the battle continued to go off inside my head. *Do I tell her? Will it make things worse? Will she hate me even more knowing that I knew she was being targeted and that I didn't do anything to stop it?* "Were you in on it?"

If there were a mirror in front of me, I could only imagine

how angry I looked. The instant anger was a bitter taste to swallow. "You really think I would let someone hurt you?"

Her anger reflected mine at that moment. The apples of her cheeks were red, the tears now dried and long forgotten. "How would I know? Maybe they offered something to you that you couldn't refuse."

My head shook back and forth with anger pulling me from every single side. I stalked over to her quickly, but she opened the door and stepped out of it and into the darkened hallway that reeked of booze, sweat, and sex. "The only thing I couldn't refuse would be you. Do I need to prove to you how much I want you? Still? Even knowing that you hate me?"

I caught the shine of hurt in her eye as the light behind me snagged the gray color. Her bottom lip trembled, her bare arms out in the open with scars so deep I felt them myself. Her mouth stayed shut as she disappeared into the dark, and instead of following after her, I stomped back inside the room, slammed the door, and rammed my fist into it so many times it went numb.

CHAPTER SIXTEEN

JOURNEY

I READ the same line ten times, and I still had no idea what it said. The smell of St. Mary's library used to calm me. The feel of the leather-bound books used to ground me. But nothing I did could soothe what had happened the other night. I had been quiet and brooding, two things that Tobias had pointed out to me during dinner last night, which led me to shooting him a knowing look because he was acting the same way—not that it was out of the ordinary. I pondered Bain, what had happened between us, and everything that Cade had said to me, which did nothing but irritate me even more.

"I've read it fifteen times. I don't *fucking* know." I leaned forward, half-smiling for the first time all week as Tobias broke a pencil in half with Sloane glaring at him. Sloane had been following Tobias around like a lost puppy per the SMC's requirement of allowing Tobias to attend our school. She was his student aide, which meant she had to keep him in line and help him with any missteps he encountered with his schoolwork.

"Tobias Richardson!" She slapped her hand down on the table. "The fucked-up lens that you currently have on that says everyone is out to get you needs to be taken off. *You do know.* I'm here to help you. I'm not out to get you."

I blew out a breath as Tobias sent her the chilliest glare I had ever seen. No one could pull off that look like Tobias, and no one other than Sloane could chew it up and spit it back out. She was the perfect choice for being his student aide—something Headmaster Ellison probably already knew.

Slamming the book shut, I started to climb to my feet to head back to my room. Was I hiding in the library, in the farthest aisle away that still had visibility of the doors so I could see who came and went? *Maybe.* I may have been trying to figure out who tried to hurt me, watching everyone as closely as possible, but I wasn't stupid.

Unless it came to Cade.

He makes me so stupid! Just being around him made me act erratically and like some girl who had never been kissed before. But he was like a drug to me, enveloping me in his cool scent, making me feel safe and wanted. He gave me some fake sense of protection, like everything was okay, when, in reality, *nothing* was okay. I had the scars on my arms to prove it.

Right when I went to push *Pride and Prejudice*—my comfort read—back into its rightful spot on the dusty shelf, I stopped with a breath halting in my chest. Two big, honey-colored eyes that were strikingly intense and the very end of my being were staring back at me. Blond hair fell onto his forehead, and everything seemed to crumble around me. *Not again.*

"Stop following me around," I whispered, trying to avoid a scowl from Mrs. Groves, the librarian, who was walking around, trying to catch sneaky teenagers who had nothing better to do than touch inappropriately in the depths of the aisles.

"Well, when you make stupid decisions, I really have no choice, do I?"

Something ticked on the inside, and I bit the inside of my cheek, shoving the book back into the shelf so far it blocked out every part of his face. It wasn't as if I could run away at the first sight of him. I was tucked too far in the back of the library to escape, even with the direct line to the doors. So, instead of running away like the other night, I quickly went back to the feeling I'd had on those lonely, scary nights in the psych hospital and remembered how angry I was at Cade and how confused I felt. I let those feelings fester so I would have no choice but to deny him and put a stop to his words.

When he rounded the corner of the aisle, darkness following him like a thundering cloud, I stood my ground and leveled my chin. *He looks good, of course.* Cade Walker was no match for a girl like me. I wore hand-me-down clothes when I wasn't wearing one of only two uniforms I owned. My sandy hair needed another trim. Sloane had been the last one to cut it in our room with dull scissors that she'd stolen from the kitchen. My face was free of any makeup, and my long-sleeve shirt was two sizes too big, making my already slender frame look malnourished. I'd never been a large person, and I had no idea if that was due to my genes, or if it was because I'd never been full a day in my life. The orphanage fed me, of course, but it wasn't as if we were going to the grocery store every weekend for snacks. Three meals a day, if that, and soup didn't do so much as fill me for the night, let alone give me luscious curves.

"What did you think was going to happen if you didn't barge in the room the other night?" I asked Cade as he slinked down the aisle, holding something tightly in his hand. The only eyes on us were those of fictional characters inside the spines of hundreds of books, and our whispers were hardly audible to each other, let alone anyone else in the library.

He shrugged, standing a foot away from me. "I probably would've ended up arrested with blood on my hands."

My jaw dropped at his brave honesty. *Nothing like scaring me with violence.* I crossed my arms over my chest, ignoring my beating heart. "So, what? No guy can touch me because you once had me?" The devilish girl that only came out to play with Cade was here, and she was feeling feisty in our secretive little corner. "I have news for you. I've been touched since last spring, Cade. *Multiple* times."

The sharp emptiness inside his dark eyes made my scars burn, like he was cutting me with unsaid words and a deadly look. "I'm sick of you twisting the knife, Journ. It's been plunging in a little deeper each fucking day." The papers in his hand crumpled with anger, and small puffs of breath were trying to escape as they filled my chest with an agony that I refused to yield to. "That's the *only* reason I'm giving in. I'm waving the white fucking flag. Hate me or don't; it will do nothing to change the way I feel about you."

I swallowed his honesty whole as he threw a bundle of papers in between us. Each one hit the library floor with a loud slap, echoing in between the bookshelves. "Read them."

My beats grew louder, my pulse thrumming in my ears, but this time, I wasn't feeling that sexual pull between us that was fueled by butterflies and want. This time, there was fear and confusion lingering. Two things that I was very familiar with.

Dropping down slowly to my knees, I gave way to my stubbornness of pushing Cade away as if he were nothing to me. I couldn't resist my need to know what he'd thrown to the floor or why he was so bitterly angry as the papers flew from his fingers. *Hate me or don't.*

I wished I hated him. Then maybe my fingers wouldn't be trembling as I read over each and every last paper that had torn edges and markings that looked as if they'd been rubbed against jagged spikes.

STAY AWAY FROM HER, or you'll regret it.

Where were you last night?

She'll end up hurt, and it'll be your fault.

What will you do when she's gone and you have nothing but a guilty conscience to feed your wants?

Journey does not belong to you or fit into your lifestyle.

She isn't yours.

Stay away.

This is your last warning.

MY EYES BEGAN to blur the more I read until I couldn't see the scribbles any longer. My back thudded against the bookshelf as the papers scattered around me like my thoughts. At some point, Cade had moved closer, his back resting against the same hardness that mine was on. Our elbows were touching, his warm skin mixing with my already rising body temperature.

My mouth opened, but then I shut it. There were muffled sounds around me, and I slowly looked over at Cade who was staring at me leerily, his brown eyes landscaping over every inch of my face.

He mouthed my name, "Journey," and when his hands wrapped around my face, that was when it all came whooshing back to me. "Breathe."

I gulped in air, realizing I had been holding my breath to the point that dots were dancing around his face. That was something I'd adopted from my childhood when I would feel the walls of the orphanage caving in on me. Every time someone passed me up and didn't adopt me, I would hold my breath until I remembered that I needed air to breathe. Cade's hands dropped after I gulped oxygen and turned away, blinking rapidly as I glanced back down to the papers scattered everywhere.

"Wh–what...why? Who?" *Was I punished for being with him? Was that why I was attacked?* No wonder he looked so guilty.

I heard his rough gulp, as if he had swallowed the icicles hanging from the school's roof. The sound of his popping knuckles made me even more nervous than before. "I don't know." He sighed. "This is why I didn't show that night." Cade leaned forward, his knee brushing mine, which we both noticed. I quickly looked down at the paper he was pulling out of his back pocket. It was folded up neatly, and when he opened it, it was as if it had been opened a million times. Each crease was cemented in the paper, and once it landed in my shaky hands, I put my palm to my mouth.

Her death will be on your hands.

My gaze shifted to his, and my throat closed. His warm eyes had glossed over right before he turned away, leaning his head back on the books. "That was the last threat I got. I found it right before I was supposed to meet you."

Pain. Pain. Pain. Pain. That was all I felt. There was a knock in my chest, and I felt every bump as my heart slid down to the floor. "That's why you didn't come?"

"Yes," he gritted out. "But–"

"But I still ended up almost dead." Chills coated me from head to toe, a cold whip stunning me instantly. *What the hell does this mean?* "And you don't know who these were from or where they came from?" There was a sudden pause in my hatred for him, and the feelings of betrayal were slowly disappearing. The protective urge to punch down the feelings I had for him remained unmoving. Things were becoming real —*fast*.

His head sliced over to mine, the truth burning like a fire over his features. "Do you think they'd still be alive if I knew who had hurt you?" He turned away slowly, staring at the shelf in front of him, as if he didn't just proclaim that he'd murder someone. "Isaiah and I searched the school, but..." He shrugged. "No one knew you'd be out there that night from what I was aware of, and even so, the paramedics said they were self-inflicted wounds, Journey. I... I..." His teeth ground together, and his hands flexed over his lap. My belly tugged, and I wanted to reach out and grab his hand, but I didn't. Instead, I stayed still as he finished. "I left you alone, like the fucking threat said to do. I didn't understand, and since you'd left, and we were told that you would be staying with a foster family, I assumed that was for the better. Being near me wasn't doing you any justice."

It was a mess inside my head. We sat in silence, and I replayed his words over and over again until they blended together and grew messier and muddled. Uncertainty and even more confusion filled me, and there was nothing to be said. Nothing came out of my mouth because I was in a complete daze.

So, he didn't abandon you for any of the reasons you thought. But I still didn't understand. Who tried to kill me? And why?

Emotion and the smallest sliver of relief came creeping in, and when I heard Sloane's voice from the end of the aisle, I quickly hopped to my feet and put distance between Cade and me.

Her hands were on her waist, and her hair was pulled into a top knot on the top of her head. "I swear to God, Journey...

I know that you and Tobias have some bond, but he is the *biggest* fucking jerk I have ever met." She peered around my body. "And that's saying something, because I know the Rebels."

I heard Cade mumble something behind my back, but I didn't stop to find out what he'd said. I rushed toward Sloane like she was my life raft in the middle of a hurricane, and I left Cade and the many threats of my life with him.

"Let's go," I said, snagging her by the wrist. The entire way to our dorm rooms, she went on and on about Tobias and how much she hated him, but all I could do was nod and act like I understood.

But the real reason I couldn't speak was because I was still stuck in that library with a boy who didn't deserve most of the hate I was giving him.

CHAPTER SEVENTEEN

CADE

THINGS FELT DIFFERENT. *I* felt different. At least on the outside. Sure, I was still coming off as detached to just about everything going on around me, and everyone knew to keep a safe distance from me and my pensive attitude, but on the inside, something had changed.

It was *her.*

Journey.

Her gray eyes found me a few times this weekend, and I caught the troubled storm brewing even from across the lacrosse field through the thickening flurries. Her pink cheeks grew warmer when she'd eventually tear away from my gaze and go about her conversation with the girls. She watched Bain, and then she'd watch me, like she was trying to figure out the connection between the three of us.

I was trying to figure it out, too.

I rounded the girls' hallway, passing by the linen closet where the threats lived and breathed. There was one paper that Journey didn't see the other night in the library, and I was thankful Sloane tore her away at the last second. I wasn't sure she'd be able to handle any more of the truth than what I had already given her.

I knew Journey. She needed to think things over. She was a planner by nature, a careful person, and that was likely why she was keeping a safe distance from me now.

I understood.

I hated it, but I understood.

A throat cleared behind me, and I rolled my eyes, stopping in the middle of the hall. Isaiah's low grumble of a voice hit my backside. "I'd say you're pathetic, but I'd do the same."

I glanced behind my shoulder at him, standing right outside Gemma's door. "You're likely the only one who understands."

His low chuckle filled the empty hall. "The others will understand eventually."

I thought for a moment. "Not so sure about Brantley. He has a pretty big vendetta against commitment."

Isaiah nodded with a half-shrug, both of us silently agreeing that Brantley was more damaged than the both of us. "Does Journey know you camp out in front of her room?"

Shaking my head, I answered quickly, "No, and even if she did, it's not like she'd invite me inside. She's more guarded than before—which is a good thing."

"If you need something, I'll be in here, watching some stupid fucking girly movie with Gemma and Sloane."

I laughed quietly and headed toward Journey's room, sliding back into my little cubby with my paperback still perched up in the corner for when I needed something to distract my tired eyes.

I began reaching in my pocket for the one piece of paper from Journey's file that held any bit of indication that there was something from her childhood that was a direct line to the threats I'd received, but I paused when I heard the click of her door. I jumped to my feet in record time and pulled my black hood up to blend in better with the darkness. My veins surged with thick, hot blood as anticipation, followed by protection, ran through them, and when I heard her small gasp, I pulled my hood down quickly.

"It's just me."

Her hand went to her heart, and I held back a smile when I saw she was dressed head to toe in black, too. A little tip from me to her when we used to sneak around together. "What the hell are you doing standing here in the dark?"

She didn't say the words, but I knew I had scared her. She was on edge, which I was glad for. Fear made you aware of your surroundings. "Better question is what are you doing in the dark hallway alone?" I stepped closer. "Wearing all black, might I add."

There was a jealous poke to the side of my brain that had me questioning if she was sneaking out to meet someone. *Someone like Bain.*

"Didn't you hear? I'm an emo girl. Black is my color." Her light laugh floated around me, and I wished I could bottle it up. I hadn't heard that sound in so long. "I have the scars to prove it."

I reached my hand out quickly, wrapping it around her covered arm, and pulled her into my *new* room. Her gasp hit me in the face before she said, "What are you doing?"

"Duty teacher," I whispered, walking the few steps to the very back of the small cove. Journey's back hit my front as she turned around, and her long, sweet-smelling hair was a cloud around me. I was instantly in overdrive.

The light of the flashlight swayed back and forth down the hall as Journey and I stayed tucked back into the moonlit area. The window was mainly frosted, and hardly any starry glow filled the small cove, but I could see her just fine. Her head turned to the left as she followed the line of the flashlight, and when she backed herself up to my front, I placed my hands over her hips, steadying her. "Why haven't you told anyone the truth?" I leaned in as close as possible to her ear. Her hair was tucked behind it, showing off the diamond studs that I remembered pulling with my teeth the other night.

Honest to God, I was trying to keep this moment as platonic as possible, knowing that what I'd done the other night was purely driven by a possessiveness that I'd only ever felt for her. It wasn't fair to keep pulling her in only to make her feel worse afterward. It was hard to keep things neutral, though. My fingers burned to dive into her tight, little jeans, and her ass begged to be grabbed as I bent her over. I was salivating at the thought.

I cursed on the inside as I fought the urge to pull her closer as I backed up. My dick had already started its shit, and there was a place and a time, and this wasn't it. Not anymore.

"I did tell someone," she whispered so low I hardly heard her. My eyes traced the curves that her lips made, and I read the words right off of them.

"And?"

The sway of the light was gone, the duty teacher now moving to my hall. The Rebels and I were damn lucky they didn't do nightly bed checks. How would we get anything done? My hands dropped as Journey flipped around, and it was the first time since she'd gotten back that I didn't see blazing anger or fear on her features. My heart sank to the bottom of my stomach, and I rested my head against the cool window behind me.

"No one believed me." She glanced away. "Except Tobias."

My brows felt heavy. "No one at all? No one at the hospital believed you were attacked?"

She shook her head, her tiny jaw clenched tightly. I almost

reached up and smoothed out the flickering muscles on her face. "They just kept dosing me whenever I'd scream that I didn't belong there." A tiny, sarcastic laugh floated out of her mouth. "Granted, most people that were there said they didn't belong."

Anguish like no other fell on my shoulders, and I unknowingly reached up and tucked a piece of her hair behind her ear. Journey peeked up at me slowly, and last spring, I would have known what was going through her head. I would have leaned in and kissed her by now, but too much had happened, and I was on unsteady feet. I didn't know what she was thinking, what she'd been through, or how she must have felt locked away without anyone coming to get her. "If I had known you were there, I would have broken down every last door."

Her eyes glossed over, and she took a step away. The moment was as icy as the window behind me, and I felt the chill in my bones. She was so far away, even as she stood a few inches in front of me. "It doesn't matter anymore." Her back turned toward me, and she peeked out into the hall. My eyes dropped to her ass, and I closed them instantly. *Damn it.*

"Are you going to tell me where you were headed to at ten at night, dressed in all black?"

She lowered herself onto flat feet, coming back into our hiding spot. "Nowhere."

I hummed, halting my hand as it reached out to snag her again. I put both hands in my pockets to keep myself on a short leash. "Are you forgetting that I'm the one who taught you to dress in dark clothing when sneaking around at night?"

Another sarcastic laugh left her. It was more of a scoff, really. "I haven't forgotten anything you taught me, even when I wanted to."

The question was right there, burning at the edge of my lips. *What else did I teach you, baby?* I knew the answer, but just as my fingers brushed over the piece of paper in my pocket, all thoughts of us touching in the dark vanished.

"You left too quickly the other night for me to show you this."

Journey spun around quickly with temptation following closely behind. "Show me what?"

The paper crumpled slightly as I pulled it out of my deep pocket, trapping it between my two fingers. A sudden idea came to mind, and I was thankful that I was raised to be deviant when needed. The second Journey reached up to grab the paper, I pulled it back quickly and caught her glare. "Let me come with you wherever you're going, and I'll give it up."

Her hands flew to her waist, and I had to grind my teeth to keep from smiling.

"Are you serious right now?"

I crowded her space, and it surprised her. Her hands dropped, and her head tipped upward, making her long hair fall behind her back. "Dead." I was inches from her face. I couldn't help it. She was like a magnet. I was drawn to her with every single breath I took. *Mine.* She was mine. She might not admit it, but she was mine, even if she pretended she wasn't.

Her little growl rumbled against my chest. "Fine." Then, she turned around with her hair whooshing between us. "But you better dress warm."

CHAPTER EIGHTEEN

JOURNEY

HE WAS FOLLOWING CLOSELY behind me. I heard every easy stride he took, and with each step, my heart raced faster. The hate had slowly dissolved over the last few days, and it scared me. I had hated Cade for reasons that weren't true. Would anyone else be angry that the person they trusted the most had hidden something from them that was vital to their well-being? *Maybe*. But I couldn't deny that I knew Cade well, and deep down, I knew he hadn't been the one to attack me. Part of me wanted it to be true. If he had hurt me then, then he couldn't hurt me now. He'd be all out of chances, but he stood me up that night because someone had threatened him. He was trying to protect me, not hurt me.

That didn't mean I wasn't irked that he just conned himself into joining me on my escapade. *Let me come with you, and I'll give it up.* Such a Cade thing to do. He was always so sly and devious, slipping in like a villain, using stealthy tactics to get what he wanted. *Typical.*

The crunch of the snow under my boots grew increasingly

louder as I stomped my annoyance out. I was going to have to keep my guard up while at the psych hospital, even more so with Cade lingering in the background like a ghost. *And what does that paper say?* There was a very small, twisted part of me that still lived and breathed, begging me to use my own sly ways. I *could* steal it from him. I pictured myself spinning around, backing him up to the tree, and kissing him so hard he'd be forced to react and put his hands around my waist. My fingers could slip inside his pocket, steal the paper he was holding over my head, and be done with it.

But I couldn't.

There was a fine line that lingered between my morals and ethics, and crossing that to trick Cade felt wrong in such a dirty way. I cared what he thought of me.

"No."

My foot stayed hovered above the snow mid-step as Cade's bark-like refusal hit me from behind. "No, what?" I asked, turning around and seeing him standing in front of our snowy castle-like school like some righteous king. His black hood was pulled up over his head, and his hands were in his front pocket as he stood lazily against the icy iron gate. I was mistaken before: he wasn't standing there like a righteous king; he was standing there like the villain of a fairy tale. All dark and brooding and utterly attractive with a sharp jaw and full lips.

"You're not going there."

I kept my face steady and crossed my arms across my chest, ignoring the way I wanted to shiver from the cool air. I played stupid. "Going where?"

"You are not going back to the Covens, Journey. Nope."

I pulled back, anger fueling my annoyance. I may not have hated him as much as I did two days ago, but he was going to need to learn that I wasn't the same girl he was used to. "You were the one that wanted to come with me. I'm going one way or another, and you won't stop me." I huffed, trying to reel in my irritation. "I don't need your permission, Cade Walker."

The lift of his lip warmed my body. *Ugh.* I spun around, irritated that my breath caught at the sight of his dimples.

He caught up quickly, slowing his pace to walk beside me as the school disappeared behind our backs. "I like this new version of you."

"Lucky me," I said dryly, wanting to keep my head on straight as I traveled along the same path that Tobias and I had used to run away from the very place I was heading back to.

Cade laughed under his breath, and I sliced a fiery gaze over to him. His kissable lips smashed together below the pink tip of his straight nose. A bundle of white breath left his mouth as he turned his head away. "Why are you going back? It's shut down."

The Covenant Psych Hospital had shut down right after Tobias and I ran away. As soon as the Rebels found out that Gemma had been taken there for *punishment*, it was made apparent that the psych hospital was much more than a hospital. It had been turning convicts into black-market killers underneath the main floor—like Tobias. Although, he wasn't a convict; he just got the raw end of a shitty deal. But once the FBI and ATF came to the scene, they swooped in and placed the patients elsewhere, and numerous arrests were made.

But there could still be something there that related to me. A file? Notes? *Something*. There had to be. Why was I kept there on suicide watch for months? Why didn't anyone believe that I had been attacked? And why did Sister Mary tell Headmaster Ellison that I was going to be placed with a foster family after my treatment? There was no treatment. All they did at the hospital was trap me in a room and feed me drugs. Nothing made sense, and I was determined to figure it out, mainly because I was pretty sure my life depended on it.

"Journey." Cade's voice startled me as his warm breath hit the side of my face. We were at a standstill, neither of us taking another step. "Is there something there that you need?"

I stayed quiet, thinking over what I wanted to tell him. His eyes stayed locked on mine, and he blew out another breath that seemed more like a frustrated huff. "You think there's going to be answers there?"

Putting my cold hands in my pockets, I shrugged. "There weren't any here. Not really, anyway. Nothing that I wasn't already aware of. Someone wanted me dead or..."

"Or sent away, at the very least," Cade finished for me.

I nodded, inhaling a gust of cool air.

Cade reached into his pocket and pulled out the paper he had teased in front of me just a little while ago. My heart leapt in my chest, and I almost darted forward to grab it. He flicked his eyes up to me over the brim of the paper and began reading what was written on it. "*Journey Smith - assumed birthdate: 10/18/2004. Arrived at Clemency Orphanage as a newborn on October 18, 2004 (given birthdate) bundled in a pink blanket with a note that read:* In danger - keep safe and do not tru—"

I gasped as I reached forward and snatched the paper from his hand. Our fingers brushed along each other, but I ignored the jolt as I read over the rest of the contents with my hands shaking so hard the paper began to crumple. "What the—" I whispered, lowering my shoulders. My mouth suddenly began to dry out, and I blinked so many times my eyes began to sting.

"I suspect whoever hurt you has nothing to do with you, but something to do with where you came from."

I found his piercing gaze full of concern and worry. "You

think someone tried to kill me because of something with my birth parents?"

He nodded to the shaking note in my hand. "Seems like you were in danger before you were even born." Cade reached out and placed one of his warm hands over mine, pulling the paper out from my tight grasp. "At first, I thought the threats had something to do with my lifestyle. I'd thought that from the very beginning. But now——"

"And what is your lifestyle?" I countered, hating that I wanted his hand back in mine.

Another tight breath left his puffed-up cheeks as he angled his head to the nearly hidden cottage just over the hill. He waited until I took a step beside him, and then, in silence, we walked over to the very edge of the hill. And before I could even attempt to take a step on my own, his arm shot forward, and he stopped me. "Let me go first. Walk in my footprints so you don't fall."

Something warm covered my chilled skin, and I crushed my lips together, giving him a subtle nod. I followed his footsteps, like he wanted, feeling the uptick in my emotions with each second we spent together.

It was just like old times: him and me alone, blanketed in darkness, feeling things deep inside that only people like Jane Austen could describe with words.

Cade's hand found mine just as I stepped over a large stone covered by a thin layer of snow, and he pulled me closer to the quiet cottage. "Are you going to answer my question?"

His shoulders tensed. I could see the muscles tighten through his dark hoodie. "You already know the answer."

I scoffed under my breath, rolling my eyes. "I see you haven't changed at all since I've been gone, then. Tell me, does Aubrey know anything real about you? Or any other girl you've been with? Or is it just me you won't tell the truth to?"

The second I let my guard down and showed my hurt, I

cursed myself. *Shit, why did I say that?* Cade's entire body angled toward mine, his dark eyes squinting at me as if I had just slapped him.

"I'm—"

"No," he said calmly, putting his hands on a dark-green tarp covering something large. "I hope you're not about to apologize. I deserve it."

Wait, what?

The tarp was bundled in his reddened fingers. "And to answer your question, you know more about me than anyone. Just because I shielded you from my fucked-up and unethical upbringing does not mean you don't know me. I'm still the same on the inside."

"You were raised to kill people." *Right?*

His dark gaze was piercing from across the tarp. "No. I was taught to protect people. The only issue is that protecting psychotic people usually leads to killing." He shook his head so angrily his hood fell back, revealing his perfectly messy hair. "I haven't killed anyone, Journey. And my father is in prison with Isaiah's because of the illicit-gun trading *and* what the FBI had uncovered at the psych hospital when you and Tobias snuck out. That isn't really my life anymore."

I stood back with my arms crossed over my chest as he went back to pulling the tarp. "So, why were you so upset about the rumor, then? I heard what you said. You didn't want anyone thinking I'd had your baby."

He laughed, finally pulling off the last of the tarp. "Just because I'm not in the lifestyle of killing or illegal gun selling doesn't mean there aren't people that are. My dad is a piece of shit, and he has a lot of enemies. Not only could his enemies come after me, but Isaiah, Brantley, and I put *our* fathers in prison, and we worked with the feds. A large fraction of our deceitful world is angry." His laughter faded, and he suddenly became serious. "And when those types of criminals get angry, they look for revenge in the worst way possible."

Oh. Okay, then.

Cade quickly changed the subject as he stepped away, revealing a motorcycle behind him. "We can take this. As much as I don't want you going back to that place, it's probably not a bad idea. Because the truth still stands: you're in danger, and we need to figure out why."

So, does this mean we're working together now?

I swallowed, taking a step forward and looking at the gleaming motorcycle. "Is this yours? When did you get a motorcycle, and since when are you allowed to have one on school grounds?"

His lip twitched, and I had to look away so I didn't fully combust at his bad-boy smirk that I'd grown to love in the past. "Now that's something that hasn't changed, Journey. I don't believe in rules." He winked, and butterflies flew all the way up to my throat. "And it's my father's. So, if the cops were to run the plate, we'd have to dip, but my mom left it behind."

"Left it behind? Where did she go?"

He cleared his throat, pulling the helmet off the back. He was avoiding my gaze, and that didn't feel right. "Away from me. That's where." The black helmet was suddenly in between us as he held it out, and I took it, trying to ignore the way my heart was creeping toward his. It wasn't often that I heard melancholy in Cade's voice. In fact, I don't think I had ever heard him sound so sad before. It wasn't the type of sadness that felt desperate, like when he and I had first spoken again. This was different. This was almost in a pensive way. *Finished.*

"Are you coming or what?"

"Yeah." I pulled the helmet over my head, tucking my hair inside so it didn't get in my face. Before Cade hopped on the motorcycle, the tiniest, barely there smile found its way to his mouth as he stepped forward. He towered over me as I tipped my head back, peering up at him.

"Hottest thing I've ever seen," he mumbled, quickly slapping the shield over my eyes.

My cheeks burned at his words, and I already found myself craving more of his whispers in my ear as we stayed hidden away, in the darkness, from everything that surrounded us.

CHAPTER NINETEEN

CADE

THE RIDE to the Covenant Psych Hospital was my favorite type of torture. Journey was behind me on the bike, and at first, she shied away, as if I hadn't finger-fucked her a few days ago. *As if either of us could forget that.* But soon after we began down the hill of St. Mary's and started along the curves of the snowy road, the chill in the air pushed her closer, and by the time we reached the hospital, her hands dove in my front hoodie pocket, and her face was buried in my back.

I would have given many things to stay on the bike. I had a sense that Journey didn't want to get off either. She was tough as nails, always trying to hide her vulnerability—even more so now, after the last several months—but I felt her slight tremble the second I lowered my feet to the ground.

"You ready?" I asked, unable to stop myself from taking my hand from the bike handle and shoving it inside my hoodie pocket. I nearly sighed with relief when my palm hit her skin, relishing in the mere touch of her. *Warm. I feel warm.*

"Yeah," she croaked, slowly taking her hands out from my hoodie and climbing off.

My jaw clenched with our sudden distance, but my wants faded when I saw her standing beside the unlit sign to the psych hospital. Her cheeks were rosy despite being underneath the helmet the entire ride, and her long hair swooped in waves over her shoulders.

I stood back along the bike for a few minutes as she stood unnervingly still, peering up at the ugly building like it held all her answers. I cased the area, scanning for anyone or anything. The Covens, the dark and bleak lower part of this building, was no longer, and I knew for a fact that the psych hospital closed down shortly after. But old habits died hard, and I was on full alert. Maybe it was memories from the last time I found myself at this shithole, or maybe I was just *that* fucking possessive over Journey that I didn't want even a snowflake to fall on her head.

Her footsteps began crunching against the hardened snow, and I followed after her, reaching up the sleeve of my hoodie and unsheathing my knife. I paused for a second, wondering if I should bring it out in front of her, but just a little while ago, she snapped out a remark about me hiding shit before she was stored away in this fucking place. *You want to see the real me? Well, here I am.*

"Stop," I said, catching up to her. Journey's troubled gaze swept over the snow and landed on my face before dropping to my hand. Her lips parted, and a light gasp flew from her. She began backing up slowly, her troubled eyes now wide with fear. Her shaky hands came up in front of her, and I furrowed my brow before I nearly choked on my spit.

"Jesus, Journey," I rushed out, putting my free hand up. "I'm not going to hurt you. I brought a knife in case anyone was here and tried to do something. I'm not..." *Does she think I brought her here to kill her?* By the expression on her face, she did, and it was as if I took the knife in my hand and plunged it into my own stomach.

Her hands fell instantly, and she spun away from me, walking quickly to the door. "I know."

I jogged over to her, the beats in my chest demanding I pay attention to the aching muscle. "Journey." My hand landed on top of hers as it gripped the lever on the door. She peeked at me, but only for a second. "Your vulnerabilities make you *you*. Don't hide your fears from me."

Her mighty chin flew upward, full of confidence. "I'm not afraid."

We both swung the door open, the knife still in my other hand as I gripped its handle. The Fawkes with a D2 blade was a gift from my father years ago that had yet to see blood—something I was certain he was disappointed over. "You are afraid," I said, allowing our hands to fall and the door to shut behind us. The open waiting area was filled with darkness. The only light source was the bright stars shining through the tiny windows at the top of the square room. "But I am, too."

Her tender, soft whisper was the only noise to be heard other than my pounding heart. "Cade Walker, afraid? Of what?"

Of losing you. My mouth opened to say just that, but a noise from down the long, narrowed hall, which was thick with darkness, had me tapping into my instincts and losing all train of thought except one: *Protect*.

Journey was pushed behind me within a millisecond, and the Fawkes felt like slipping into my own bed for the night. My senses were heightened, and my heart slowed to a predator-like speed.

"What was that?"

Journey's hands had clenched onto the cotton of my black hoodie, which sent pride flowing through my veins. "Put my hood up for me," I said in a slinking, low voice. One of her hands unbundled from my hoodie, and she pushed my hood up slowly, her fingers softly sweeping over my neck. I pushed past the tingle her touch left behind and began moving us forward with her lodged at my back. "Do you want me to stay here?" she asked after the first couple of steps.

"You are not leaving my side. You're staying right there."

I wasn't sure if she felt the relief, but I did. Having her close gave me more purpose, and I wouldn't be able to think straight if she wasn't with me.

The noise we'd heard earlier hit my ears again as we began to descend down the long hallway. I was right when we had pulled up earlier: the Covenant Psych Hospital was officially closed down. There was a sign on the front door, and the caution tape was as yellow as ever. Although a poor attempt to keep people out, it was there. *I mean, the fucking door was unlocked.* Which either meant that the city didn't really give a fuck about this place being unsecure, or someone else had busted the lock.

I halted in front of Journey and felt the tips of her boots hit the backs of my shoes. I turned my head to the side, listening for the sound again. *Scratch, scratch, scratch.* My tongue darted out to lick my lips as I slowly reached into my pocket and pulled out my cell phone. "Don't move," I whispered. She stayed quiet behind me, and that was when I clicked the flashlight on with my knife fitting snugly in my palm. The bright light swung around, and when I saw two beady, beetle-like eyes staring back at me, I dropped my shoulders.

"For fuck's sake," I said, kicking my foot out quickly and scaring the little critter away.

"What was it?" Journey asked, removing her tight grip from my hoodie and stepping beside me. She followed the beam of light, and her brows crowded above her eyes. "A mouse?"

I chuckled. "A fucking rat. Probably trying to stay warm."

"Oh." There was the smallest, cutest smile on Journey's face that sent me spiraling back to the past. It was the same pretty grin that had me *almost* falling to my knees at the sight. I remembered the first time I had put a smile on her face—it was a high that I chased every single day. Even when she and I were nothing more than two beings touching in a dark corner, pretending like we didn't know who the other one was. I used to put notes in her backpack during class without signing my name, just to see her unfold the tiny paper and watch her face light up at the compliment. I would purposefully stare at her from across the dining hall and wink when she'd catch me staring, just to watch in awe as the pink spread over her cheeks. It was a sight that concealed the darkness in my life, a brief tourniquet to the tasks and goals that my father pounded into my skull every single day.

"Cade?" I snapped my head up and caught Journey staring at me. The flashlight of my phone was still in my hand, and this time, it was shining directly under her face.

"Yeah?"

"I want one of those." Her eyes dropped to the knife in my hand that I was still holding tightly in my grasp. Her barely noticeable gulp caught my attention, and our gazes collided.

"Then I'll get you one."

And with that, Journey nodded with a hidden smile and turned to walk farther down the hall.

CHAPTER TWENTY

JOURNEY

MY STOMACH TWISTED as I crept farther down the hall with Cade at my back. He was never far behind, even when I sped up to get to the room that I knew held files of the patients here. A breath was stuck in my chest, as if I'd swallowed the key to get into this room. The door handle was locked, and my shoulders dropped.

"Move over; I've got it." I knew I was being delusional and maybe a little bit naïve, but I swore Cade's voice was laced with protection. As if Cade Walker himself would burn this place down for me if I asked him to. I relished it. I relished the way he pulled me behind him when we heard a noise. I became obsessed with the tick of possession in his voice when he told me not to move. When his arm brushed against mine, even through our hoodies, there was a jolt of something buried deep, and instead of being in here, with bad memories and thoughts that made me sick weighing me down, I was totally focused on him.

I wanted him so much that even when he was holding a

knife and I'd had the jutting thought that he brought me here to hurt me, I wasn't as scared as I should have been. As if dying by the hands of Cade Walker wouldn't be so bad anyway.

The lock to the door clicked, Cade's large hand turned the knob, and before I knew it, we were in the room with shelves from floor to ceiling with a ridiculous number of files. The room wasn't completely dark because of the far window on the left, even if there were bars covering it to keep people like *me* inside. A desk was pushed toward the back wall with nothing on it but a name plate that read Doctor Melrose. I walked over to it slowly, and my finger traced the letters engraved in the gold nameplate. Anger started to fester like the start of a bonfire. With each curve of Doctor Melrose's name, my stomach hurt, and my breaths came in fast. There was a shuffling of papers behind me, and I knew that Cade was probably looking for my medical records. But before I turned around to help him, I shoved the anger to my fingertips and swept my hand over the gold nameplate, and it flew across the room, falling to the floor with a loud thud.

The papers stopped shuffling, and I knew that Cade was staring at me—likely curious and maybe concerned. My back was to him as I pushed the hood off my head, letting the cool air of the room hit my hair. "You know, this was one room that I never came in when sneaking around."

"Oh yeah?" he asked.

I turned around slowly, keeping my eye on the nameplate that I'd thrown to the floor.

"Why didn't my little rebel sneak into the doctor's office, huh?"

Suddenly, the anger was replaced with something else. My lips twitched as I found him leaning against the shelf, holding a dark-colored folder in his hand. I began to walk toward him as he held it tighter in his grip. "I knew that Doctor Melrose wasn't easily swayed. He didn't fall for my tricks. I couldn't risk getting caught."

"Your tricks?" The shadows along Cade's face deepened. "What kind of tricks?"

Impending doom swept in the room like a snowstorm, freezing everything in sight. I kept my mouth closed, my secrets tucked behind my closed lips. I reached out with a shaking hand, grabbed the file from Cade, and flicked my eyes to his when I heard the grinding of his teeth like he was some type of machine. "It's missing."

"Missing?" I opened the folder, and my heart sank to the floor. This place was *nothing* but desperation and disappointment plastered to every crack, crevice, and pore. "Where is it?"

I threw the empty folder down, and it landed like a little teepee over the nameplate. I refrained from kicking them both as my anger started to subdue my earlier calmness with Cade by my side.

"Someone could have taken it before this place was shut down," Cade said as he leaned back on the shelf, crossing his arms over his chest. His hood was still pulled up over his head, and even with my heart clashing with anger and disappointment, one look from him put a pause on it all.

I looked at the door, feeling slightly tormented that I was back in this place, even if I wasn't locked inside. "Someone like the person who tried to kill me."

Silence followed me as I walked past Cade, frustrated with the office I was in, knowing that there probably wasn't anything here that was helpful now that I knew my file was empty. *Why did someone want me dead? And as an infant, at that. Did anyone ever come to the orphanage, looking for me? Was it Sister Mary's job to hide me? I need to talk to her.*

As the thoughts began gathering, I somehow found myself walking down the hall and ending up in front of my room. The door was all white and blended in with the wall. Except, at the moment, in the dark, it looked gray. My fingers reached out with something thick sliding through my veins like an illness that never truly existed, chaining me inside that room where I had to do things that made me cringe. The second I opened the door, knowing the automatic locks never really worked as well as the psych hospital had hoped, the scent of *me* hit my face.

I felt Cade behind me, giving me space but not too far that I couldn't feel his warmth. The door shut behind us. I was one of the lucky ones who had a window in their room, although it was fully sealed with bars on the outside of it. There was a gleam of moonlight that fell onto the floor and over my bed that was smack dab in the middle of the room next to a chair that I had sat in more nights than not.

"Is there something in here?" Cade asked, still keeping a short distance away from me.

A soft, sarcastic laugh fell from my lips. "Just my pride and dignity."

"What does that mean?"

My fingers slowly swept over the worn, baby-blue blanket that I cried into for a month straight, walking farther and farther over to the window to stare out into the darkened forest. The trees were snow-covered, and icicles hung from their limbs like fingers. "I did things here that I'm not proud of." My head dropped as my stomach tensed. "Things that make me sick."

He took a step closer, his shoe smacking against the floor that I'd been thrown onto by Barry. "But were they necessary?"

I peeked over my shoulder at him, the moon casting a light right over his mouth. His lips were full, and even though there were things that happened in this room that made me want to destroy every last inch of it, all I could truly focus on was how badly I wanted his hands on me, making me forget it all.

But I couldn't forget it. I *shouldn't* forget it. Because even though there was an ounce of disrespect for myself for the actions I had to endure, there was ten times the amount of pride. I'd been wanting someone to save me all my life, but really, it just came down to me.

"I know the feeling, you know." Cade's shoulder brushed mine as he stood beside me, causing my senses to trip over themselves. "I've done things that I am not proud of. Trust me."

"Like what?"

Out of the corner of my eye, I watched his head drop slightly, as if he didn't want to tell me. Honesty was hard for a guy like him—someone who was guarded and appeared so strong and authoritative on the outside. "I chased Gemma through the forest with Brantley under the assumption that he and I were going to rape her to prove a point to Isaiah's father."

I kept my mouth closed, but I *almost* let my jaw drop.

"We didn't. But she thought we were. She ran for her fucking life. She was so scared that she had a panic attack."

I swallowed every last question, landing on one. "Then what happened?"

Cade looked down at me, and his white teeth sunk into his plump bottom lip. "Do you really want to know?"

I nodded, and he turned away. My favorite little jaw muscle of his ticked again, barely visible from behind his hood. "We seduced her to bring her out of it."

I said nothing because he had no idea how unsurprising that was to me. It seemed Cade and I were more alike than I knew—which, again, was unsurprising.

"Say something," he whispered, placing his knife on the windowsill in front of us. The irony of putting a knife in front of me in the same psych ward I was placed in because everyone thought I cut my wrists was not lost.

"Seducing someone to get a different reaction is my specialty. I would have done the same thing." I paused. "I mean, if the roles were reversed."

Now it was his turn to be silent, and it was as if I could read the question brimming behind his closed mouth. "Don't ask me what happened here." My head dropped, knowing I would probably hate myself if I said it out loud to him. I was torn, feeling slightly sick over the things I did, but even sicker when I buried it deep down. *Maybe I should tell someone.* Maybe I should tell someone that what I did was considered unethical in a way, and the thought of it made my stomach ache, but I was also proud that I saved myself.

Gemma came to mind for a split second, because she saw it first-hand. She saw what I could do when she was here and how I managed to get my way around this place. I cleared my throat, taking his silence for submission. "I–I don't know if I can even say the words."

"Did someone seduce you to make you stop panicking, Journey?" His voice was cold, freezing me there against the window.

I turned toward him, startled. "What? No." I paused, knowing exactly what he was thinking and why. "No one touched me like that without permission." *But they did touch me.*

The confusion lingered as he was trying to piece together the jumbled words coming from my mouth. The thought was there, flashing in front of me like a billboard standing alone on a highway. "I feel like a victim, but at the same time, I don't."

"Have you told anyone what happened here? Anyone at all? Besides Gemma."

"I haven't told Gemma anything. Why do you say that?"

Cade sighed. "I overheard a conversation between you two when you first came back."

So he knows? I blinked a few times, unsure of how I felt. "So you know what I've done? What I had to do?"

"No." He turned toward me with a steely expression. "Gemma didn't tell me anything. She said if you wanted to tell me, you would."

I sucked in a tiny breath because, in a way, I *did* want to tell him. I wanted to tell him that every time I touched another guy to win over their affection so I could use it as trickery, I felt sick because it wasn't him. I wanted to tell him that every time it was over, I'd run into my bathroom and throw up with tears streaming down my face with the taste of someone else. "I don't think I can tell you." I shuddered, looking away. "Not because I think you'll be angry, but because you might lose respect for me."

His tone was low and grumbly as he gripped my chin and pulled my watery gaze to his. "That will never fucking happen." His Adam's apple bobbed, and I hated that I couldn't read his mind. "And if you can't tell me, then why don't you just show me?"

CHAPTER TWENTY-ONE

CADE

THOSE GRAY, stormy eyes flung to mine in an instant. It almost knocked me down with how intense they were. The moon cascaded a glow over her face, catching the glassy look in the little storm clouds, and her mouth parted in exasperation.

"Show you?" she whispered, keeping a hold of my gaze like the brave fighter that she was.

I nodded, heart pounding viciously underneath my hoodie. *What am I doing?* I gripped her chin tighter, and although there were things going through my head that made me want to ram my fist into the window, I knew that this wasn't about me. This was about her and the internal fight she was having with herself. She seemed confused and torn, like she wanted to rid herself of what had happened but also slightly afraid to say the words.

I'd been there.

I'd been there with *her.* I couldn't even manage to hear her name after she left.

"Sometimes, facing your trauma can be therapeutic." I shrugged, lowering my voice even more, as if someone could hear us. "It might show you something about what happened that's currently clouded with judgment."

She sounded out of breath. "What are you? Some psychology guru?"

A deep chuckle left me. "I read a book while you were gone. It said something similar."

There was the smallest flicker of surprise in her stormy gaze. "You read a book?"

"I've read a lot of books since you've left. All of your favorites, actually."

The tight look on Journey's face softened as her eyes bounced back and forth between mine. I wondered if she could feel how wound up I was. My pulse thudded, my heart skipped a beat every few seconds, and my fingers sparked with anticipation to touch her again.

After a painful minute or two, Journey slowly backed away from me, taking my billowing hope in her two hands and crushing it. *Come back.*

My throat began to dry out, and I couldn't seem to swallow enough times to breathe correctly. I was twisted up and confused. Every emotion that I had stowed away since she'd disappeared was back, and they were crashing into my back like a tidal wave. *Worry, fear, hope, jealousy, protection, possession.* I wanted to grab her, lose myself in her kiss, smother her with everything I felt for her, and then demand she understand that she was mine and that she was safe with me.

My breath hitched as the back of Journey's knees hit the bed. My pulse suddenly jumped when she pulled the black hoodie over her head, allowing her light hair to fall in waves over her shoulders. Her tentative gaze found mine, and it was like seeing a ghost. For a single, fleeting second, she was *my*

Journey. The Journey that was innocent and full of life, who wanted a taste of rebellion and held onto me for dear life while surrounded by night.

"What are you doing?" I asked, leaning against the windowsill as she sat down on the bed and swung her legs over top. She looked like fucking Sleeping Beauty with her hair spilled around her, lying still right there for the taking.

"Showing you my ugly scars." Her whisper was soft but poised. "The ones that no one can see."

The only sound in the room was our uneven breathing. My breaths were deep and thundering as she lay completely still.

Too much time had passed, and the only thing it did was speed up my temptation. I waited for her to make a move. I gave her the space she needed, although all I wanted to do was stride over to her and climb on top to make her forget everything that hurt her.

Her voice croaked, almost too low to hear. "At first, when I got here, my behavior was volatile. It's no wonder they kept putting me on medication. I acted erratically, shoving and kicking. I screamed so loud sometimes that I would lose my voice." She huffed out a light laugh. "Which came in handy when it was time for group therapy. At least I didn't have to talk."

There was a long silence after she spoke, and I knew that she didn't need a response. She didn't need me to tell her everything was okay. She just needed to rid herself of the ugly that came with going through some fucked-up shit.

"I realized they weren't going to believe my story after about a month of trying." Journey's head turned to me, and our gazes crashed like two cars going full speed up ahead. "That was when I began to change."

"Change can be good," I said, gripping the edge of the

windowsill that I sat on. *Is she purposefully lying on that bed to taunt me?*

"I started to make friends."

"With the other patients?"

Her response was quick. "No. With the staff."

Fuck, I know where this is going. And I wasn't sure I wanted to hear it, but again, this wasn't about me. This was about her.

"The nurses would come do bed checks, as if they knew the locks on those doors were shitty. They'd make sure we were all tucked inside our rooms, *safe* for the night."

My nostrils flared with unshed anger. "And were you safe?"

She thought for a moment. "Yes. I guess. But..." Her head turned to me again, her soft expression hiding the realness of what she was feeling. "I had to make them think they could trust me."

"Them?" The pounding in my skull gave me a headache, and when Journey started to speak again, I had to dig my nails into the cement block wall to keep myself steady.

"There were a few different male nurses that I had to win over."

I will kill them all.

My face stayed steady as Journey flung her legs back over the side of bed, still hiding her emotions well. Her footsteps were slow and light as she crept over to me, the moon staying in its rightful place, causing her to blend in with the darkness that surrounded us. My dick jumped, ready to show her that she was mine and not theirs, like the possessive fuck that it was. Her breaths were shaky as she stood right in front of me, and even if I wanted to stop myself from gripping her hips and pulling her in close, I wouldn't have.

"Show me."

Journey peeked up at me, her gray eyes smoldering below her long lashes.

"Show me how you won them over. Show me how they *stole* you, and then I want you to watch me steal you right the *fuck* back."

I heard her swallow first, and then I watched her hot little tongue dart out to lick her lips. My possessiveness was not supposed to make an appearance tonight, but I was becoming aware that Journey may have liked my possessiveness. It seemed my shy Journey relished in the fact that I wanted her and that I wanted to break anyone else's hands who touched her.

Angry beats stood between us, my heart thumping like the beat of a drum. Journey's gaze lowered, her teeth sinking into her full lip that I zeroed in on like some psychotic machine. *I want to sink my teeth into that lip, too.*

"It all started with small talk," she started, slinking in closer to me. "It bothered me at first because..."

"Because why?" I interrupted, gripping her hips tighter. My fingers begged to dip underneath her shirt to feel her soft skin.

"Because their small talk didn't interest me. It wasn't you." She gasped when I pulled her in closer, her chest hovering right in front of me for the taking. Part of me wanted to pop up from the windowsill and throw her onto the bed, but I didn't. I stayed right where I was. "I hated that you always slipped in while I was putting on my front. I felt guilty and then angry that I felt that way."

"It's okay that you hated me. You thought I had set you up that night—or, at the very least, that I didn't mean all those things I said to you."

Like that I loved you. I still do.

"Yeah," she breathed out, her sweet breath wafting over the hair that was hanging in my eyes.

"Tell me what happened after the small talk."

Things were suddenly taking a turn. I was in over my

fucking head. My neck was beginning to grow warm. I felt the fire getting higher and higher, spreading against both of our skin. My fingers were on her belly now, and I ground my teeth to stop myself from pulling her onto my lap.

"I think you know."

"Show me," I demanded, peering up at her through the curtain of her hair.

Journey took a step back, and she stole my breath away. My hands fell swiftly from her hips, and I watched in awe as she walked back over to the bed. Her black combat boots were thrown to the floor, and she lay flat on the blue blanket with her hands down by her sides.

I sat up a little taller, gripping the windowsill so hard my fingers were possibly bleeding. The sliver of light from the moon hit her on the chest, and it was rising just as fast as mine. When her hand moved to the brim of her jeans, I stopped breathing. I meant to keep my expression steady, but I felt the narrowing of my eyes.

"The first time Ash walked in here and saw me, he paused right there inside the doorway."

Ash? Sounds like he's about to fucking become ash.

I followed Journey's movement as the button of her jeans popped through the hole, snagging my ears as every single sense was fixated on her. *Fuck.* I wanted her to scoot up so the sliver of moonlight was on her hand instead of the rising of her breaths. I wanted to watch, even as angry as it made me that someone else saw this, too.

"I stopped what I was doing just long enough to see his mouth open. We stared at each other, and although my stomach shrank with unease, I kept going."

My gaze moved from her profile, seeing that her eyes were closed, to her hand, which was dipping underneath her panties. I stared long and hard, knowing that if I didn't get us out of this fucked-up place in the next few minutes, I was going to be touching her, too. *Does she want that?*

"And?" I said, startling her. Journey's eyes flew open, but she kept her stare locked on the ceiling. *Look at me.*

"And he shut the door."

I released a growl. "With him inside the room or out?"

"Inside."

Journey's hand was moving faster, and the room began to tilt. I stood up quickly from the windowsill, biting the inside of my cheek as I gripped the bottom of my hoodie and pulled it up over my head. I had a t-shirt on underneath, but I was still fucking hot. A faint noise left her, and my eyes flared right along with the burning room. "Did he watch you finish?"

"Yes," she answered quickly. "And the next time, he helped."

No. No. No.

My hands dug into my hair. "Scoot up on the bed."

Journey stopped moving. Her entire hand had been underneath her panties, and I was going to suck on every last finger before the night ended.

"What?"

"I want to watch you. Scoot up now. I'll tell you when to stop."

I was out of breath, terrorized by the fact that someone else had watched this. It angered me but turned me on at the same fucking time. Journey's hand came back out of her panties, and I watched as she bundled them in the blanket to pull herself farther up on the bed.

"Stop." My tone was harsher than I meant, but she didn't seem fazed by it. "Go on."

Another swallow moved down her throat, and her hand disappeared again. I traveled down her entire body, stopping at the skin on her belly from her shirt that had been pulled up. Her breathing was growing faster, and I knew she was starting to move past the last time she was in this room, doing this. "What else happened, Journey? Did you let them taste you?"

I shall add cutting someone's tongue out to my list of things to do.

"What part of me?" she countered, and I squeezed my eyes shut for a second.

"Any part is too many."

Her legs began to part, her jeans half on and half off. I took a step closer, fixated on what her body was doing and how I was about to make it mine. The denim was going to be ripped off her fucking legs, her panties torn in half, and my fingers were going to replace hers.

"Sometimes they kissed me. I did more of the tasting than they did, though." *Their dicks will also be cut off.* "I basically had to con my way out of this place."

"Don't get yourself off."

Her head turned toward me, and that was my breaking point. I stormed the rest of the way over to her, and she peered up at me from below, head resting against the pillow like she was purposefully waiting for Prince Charming to kiss her out of her slumber. *No Prince Charming here. Prince Charming doesn't do what I am about to do.*

"I just need to know one thing," I said, leaning down and placing my hands on each side of her head.

Her nod was hesitant.

"Did you think of me while lying here, trying to get yourself off for another guy?"

Her gray eyes sucked me right the fuck in. "Every single time."

CHAPTER TWENTY-TWO

JOURNEY

Cade's sandy hair hung in his eyes as he stared down at me with possessive eyes and parted lips. Butterflies replaced the disease spreading through my belly, remembering the way Ash and the others felt in my mouth.

His rough hands moved from beside my head, and they landed on my open jeans. "Good," he snapped, ripping the denim down my legs in one single whoosh.

My heart raced to my throat as his fingers clamped down on my wrist, pulling my hand out of my wet folds. I was completely out of breath, holding back a moan as he took his other hand and slowly pulled my panties down my legs, throwing them on the floor with my pants. He climbed on top of me, his jeans rubbing over me so harshly I wanted to cry out. He hovered above me, holding himself up with one hand that dug into my wild hair, tugging on the ends to gain my attention. "This," he whispered right over my lips, placing his other hand right at my entrance. I ached and throbbed, and he was right: *reliving this was a good idea.* "Was never theirs." His finger sunk into me, and I arched my back, hitting his solid chest. "And neither were these." Cade's tongue darted out of his mouth as I flew back into the pillow, my hair a parachute as I fell back. He leaned in quickly and traced the curve of my lips with his tongue, and I felt myself go into a frenzy. When he pulled away and stared down at me with that intense, hungry look he'd given me in the past, I suddenly wasn't a girl who had experienced a trauma in this place but a girl who knew what she wanted—and his name was Cade Walker.

Our mouths were sealed again, and his finger plunged back in as my hips spread. A moan left me, and he swallowed it. My hands went underneath his shirt, and I pulled it over his head, running my fingers over the dips and curves of his abs and shoulders. "I missed you," I said, allowing my emotions in for a second. *I missed him so much it hurt*.

"Missing you doesn't come close to what I felt when you were gone. I felt like I couldn't breathe." He took my ear in between his teeth. His breath was hot and seedy, and without even knowing I was doing it, my hand was unbuttoning his jeans, and I was pushing them halfway down his thighs. My hand dug into his boxers, feeling completely out of control with need. *I want to touch him*. I missed his skin against mine. I missed everything.

His mouth was back, his tongue sweeping inside, making my hand move faster as I gripped him. He was hot and hard, and he hissed as he pulled up to look down at me. My hand was in his pants as he hovered, and his was buried in between my legs, both of us completely captivated with the other. Cade's dark eyes were full of something intense beneath his hair. There was a bead of sweat right beside his temple, and something wild came over me as I arched my back, feeling his finger go deeper, just so I could dart my tongue out and taste the salty moisture.

He grunted, dropping his head. "*Fuck.*"

We moved in sync, my hand moving against him, and his moving inside of me. We chased the high. Kissed like we were frantic animals. Teeth clashing, bodies glistening with sweat. "Don't stop." I pulled back, gasping for air, moving beneath him as I chased the high only he could give me.

"I wouldn't dream of it. I know when you're close."

His lips fell to my hammering pulse, and his hips thrust in my hand as I continued to pump him as fast as I felt my orgasm peaking. "God," I muttered, moaning as we both rocked like we were fucking one another instead of each other's hands.

"Stop tormenting me. Come for me, baby."

I gripped his dick as an abyss took me under. My body spilled over the brink of insanity, and I yelled out louder than I ever had in this room.

"That's it," Cade's whisper tickled my ear, and I was alive, burning bright with a glow that not even this place could dim. "That's my girl."

My hand stilled on him, and I caught the untamed look of hunger in his eye before I pulled his fingers out of me, wet with my need, and pushed on his chest. His brows flickered with confusion as a lazy smile curved on my face.

"We're not done," I whispered, crawling out from beneath him. We both stood from the bed, and when I dropped down to my knees, his lips parted. There was an energy brimming around me, and I suddenly felt like I was on top of the world. Like the things that had happened here were nothing more than a survival tactic, and I was allowed to relish in that. Cade snipped the last string that I was balancing on, trying to figure out if what I did in this place was unethical or not. Either way, I made it out alive, and there was something to say for that.

Cade's jeans were still unbuttoned and slightly pulled

down. "You still want me to show you what happened here, right?" I asked, tracing my finger over his abs. His hand caught mine in a fast reflex, and he pulled me to my feet.

"That depends," he started, dropping his gaze down to my bare legs and back. "Is it working? Are you forgetting how their mouths felt on you? Do you understand that even though you had to do certain things, you weren't theirs? You weren't theirs then, and you aren't theirs now."

I nodded slowly, feeling the truth vibrate behind my lips. "I still feel dirty, but..."

Cade's eyes narrowed, ready to tell me that I wasn't, but I stopped him.

"I think I like being dirty, Cade."

His hot gaze locked onto me. "But only for me."

I nodded, enjoying the way my stomach fluttered and how blood rushed to between my legs. "Only for you."

His hands landed on my shoulders, and he pushed me back down to my knees. I breathed out a hungry sigh, peeking up at him as he stared down at me. His jeans fell down in a single swoop, and next came his boxers. When he gripped himself at the base, I licked my lips.

"I've missed those smoky eyes looking up at me like I'm the only one you see."

"You are," I said before taking him in my mouth. His hand shot to the back of my head, his fingers weaving through my hair. I sucked and ran my tongue over his length like I'd perfected in my time away, and Cade's hips flexed, bringing himself close to retribution.

"This is what I pictured," he said, voice hoarse as I continued sucking him and bringing him on my level. "Every time I beat myself off, I pictured those eyes and those lips. You're all I've thought about from that first claiming, Journ. If you disappear again, I will, too."

My throat vibrated as his hand gripped my head harder. I

knew he was close, so I took him deeper, feeling my emotions emerge with the fact that although I came back to St. Mary's under the impression that Cade had hurt me beyond belief, I still felt an undeniable connection with him.

"Fuck, Journey," he grunted, thrusting one last time into my mouth. I had to fight the way my lips wanted to curve as I drank every last drop of him, knowing his eyes were pinned on me down below as I sucked him dry.

As soon as he pulled himself from my mouth, I peered up at him, and his chest was fighting for breath. His hand gripped my chin, and his thumb swiped over my bottom lip, wiping away the last bead of moisture from him.

"I would rather die than hurt you." I swallowed as he pulled me to my feet, wrapping his hands around my face. "I need you to know that. Tell me you hear me."

I didn't know desperation could look so good on a guy like him. The hollow part of his cheeks were reddened from our loss of time, and his eyes were wild and untamed, trapping me there with a fierce need to prove something to me.

"Please," he urged, rubbing the pads of his thumbs over my cheekbones. "No matter what happened in this place or while we were apart, I need you to know that my heart still beat for you." His head dropped with this admission, and he blew out a breath.

There was a slight prickle in the back of my throat as my hands came up and wrapped around his large wrists. "I hear you. I just thought you had abandoned me that night, like everyone else."

"I now know how that feels, and I'm sorry. If I could go back, I never would have left you alone. I never would have written that note to meet up." A harsh chuckle left his throat. "I never should have let you fall for me."

"Falling for you had nothing to do with what happened to me. You read what Sister Mary had said. There's been a threat on my life since I was born." I glanced up at him, seeing the trouble brewing. "Wait, what do you mean you know how it feels to be abandoned?"

He shrugged, dropping his hands from my face. I watched in confusion as he went over to grab my underwear and jeans. I felt a strange tenseness to him that felt too familiar to my own when he bent below me to slip my underwear back up my legs. It was a sweet gesture, and if I weren't so wrapped up in the way his nostrils flared with silent anger, I would have said thank you, but instead, I placed my hands on his, resting right over my hips with him bent below. "You don't get to shut down. Not after what just happened."

We stared at each other like we were opponents in a game. He was on offense, and I was on defense. My eyebrow raised, and he glanced away. His warm breath floated over my bare legs. "I just meant that I can understand, on a certain level, how you feel." Cade began putting my jeans on, slipping my foot inside each rightful hole and sliding them up my legs. "My father is a piece of shit. I get it. I know the things he's done, and my mom is better off without him. But she left me without saying goodbye or leaving a forwarding address. So, I get the feeling of abandonment to an extent."

Ouch. I had always made up some fruitless story in my head that my mom had left me with good intentions. I conjured up some fake fairy tale that she was going to come back for me and save me from my life of poverty, abandonment, and loneliness. It was comforting to think the best of her. I wasn't sure how it would feel to know the truth and for that truth to be nothing good.

"Cade," I whispered, wrapping my arms around his waist. My head went to his chest, and I winced at the hard pounding of his slightly broken heart. "I'm sorry."

For a second, he just let me hug him. His chest didn't rise with breath, and I knew he was holding it. He was holding his emotions in so I couldn't see his pain, but I felt it, and I understood it. "Breathe," I whispered.

He took a hefty gulp of air, and that was when he wrapped his arms around me. I nodded against him, and we stayed like that for what seemed like hours.

CHAPTER TWENTY-THREE

CADE

"We should go," I finally said, pulling away from my one and only comfort. "If Tate knows we're gone, he'll be having an aneurysm by now."

Journey's arms dropped from my waist, and she nodded, seemingly uncaring that the headmaster might be aware that we took a little field trip. She always was a quiet rule-breaker, but she used to be hesitant with our escapades, never truly wanting to get caught, but now, her mind was on other things.

We were both fully dressed, looking less disheveled than a few minutes ago when I drove my cock into her mouth. Again, that was never supposed to happen, but the second she kneeled in front of me, I couldn't fucking help it. How could I have denied those somber gray eyes as she peered up at me with her tongue darting out of her mouth like that? *Fuck. No one can get to me like she can.*

I traveled behind her as she exited the room and stepped into the dark hallway. Instead of going to the front doors that we came in through, she walked in the opposite direction.

Her footsteps were light, and she walked the hall like nothing more than a silent presence. Her finger curved against the side of the wall as she rounded the bend and stopped at a tall, heavy door.

My brows fell as she remained unmoving. I walked beside her, aching to touch her again in even the simplest of ways. There was something about Journey that called to me. It had always been there. Living, breathing, running through my veins like she was made for me and no one else. I sensed her conflict, watched her body tighten with anger.

Sweeping her hair back from her shoulder, I gazed at the side of her face, giving her the space that she needed. When she turned toward me, I was jolted. Locking onto her gaze always seemed to stun me at first. There was an instinctual part of me that wanted to grab her face and shoot breath down her throat to give her life. It was as if I was put on this earth to keep her alive.

It was unnerving.

I felt consumed by her, more so now than ever.

"What are you thinking?" I asked, rubbing the pad of my finger against her soft cheekbone.

Her shallow breath filled the empty space, and the parting of her lips caught on every one of my freshly satisfied nerves. "I'm thinking I want to burn this fucking place to the ground."

She turned away from me and continued to stare at the door in front of us. I had a hunch that it was the door that led to the Covens, where Gemma was kept and punished. Tobias, too. If there was one thing I knew for certain about Journey, it was that she hid her emotions well, too afraid to give them the space they needed to breathe, because deep down, she was afraid.

She was afraid to give anyone or anything the power to hurt her, but just because she kept her emotions locked down on the outside didn't mean they didn't fester on the inside. Hate was brewing, and she smelled like the sweet scent of revenge.

"I have an idea," I said through a half-grin. "Come here."

Our hands joined, and I pulled Journey quickly through the darkened hallway until we met the light of the moon near the front doors. The cool air greeted us as we left the psych hospital, and Journey turned and looked over her shoulder once, as if she were leaving behind a limb.

"What are we doing?" she asked as I pulled her over to the motorcycle.

I spun around quickly, and she jumped with her eyebrows furrowing. "I'm going to light this fucking place on fire, and we're gonna turn it to ash." I stepped in close, tipping her chin up because I truly couldn't help myself. "For you."

The reluctance was lingering as she thought over what I had said. But there was no time for second thoughts. My Journey girl loved the taste of rebellion, and I was lucky enough to be the one to give it to her.

"It needs to be burned to the ground." I opened the small compartment on my father's motorcycle, having the mere thought that maybe I should burn the hunk of metal, too, right along with the Covens. "Let's burn it for you and Gemma." I snatched the small pack of matches that I knew were in there. "And for Tobias."

Pulling us back toward the psych hospital, I stopped in the lobby and peered over at her with an obvious deviant edge to my words. "Where are the medical supplies? We need something flammable."

She raised a hesitant finger and pointed to a door just off the left side of the hall. Journey followed closely behind as I went inside the room, allowing my eyes to adjust to the darkness, and found a line of rubbing alcohol in glass bottles.

Bingo. I snatched one, opened the cap, and poured some onto the floor, hearing it splash below us.

"Let's go," I said, holding the half-full bottle of flammable alcohol in one hand and her palm in the other.

Another second later and we were inside Dr. Melrose's office again with a shelf full of files just waiting to be burned. I snagged onto Journey's wide eyes after placing the rubbing alcohol on the desk and slowly prowled over to her. I lifted up her black hoodie, feeling her warm body heat. There were so many things floating behind her eyes, and all I wanted to do was give her a life raft. "You in?" I asked, gripping the bottom of her thin shirt underneath. My fingers brushed over her soft skin, and I felt the rise of her goosebumps. If I didn't know her well enough, I would have been reluctant to do this, but the slight nod of her chin was all the push I needed.

The ripping of her cotton shirt echoed between us, and each time I pulled the fabric, her supple body would slam into mine. I kept a hold of her torn shirt as I bent down, resting my calves against the backs of my thighs, and I snagged the cotton with my teeth and ripped it the rest of the way.

Journey's hands fell to my shoulders, and before I stood, I placed a quick, soft kiss to her skin, feeling another bout of heat creep up my neck. *Jesus.*

"You're my favorite flavor," I said, hopping back up. Journey's cheeks reddened, and it was a swift punch to my chest. *That's my girl.* She hadn't blushed like that since before she ended up here.

Journey's lips rolled together to keep her soft smile at bay, and I turned around and shoved the torn, bundled fabric into the rubbing alcohol bottle, soaking it on the bottom half and pulling the cotton so it was airtight at the top of the bottle.

"Are we really doing this?" Her tender voice cut through the quiet office.

"Yes," I answered, inspecting the Molotov cocktail that I'd been forced to make many times before.

"This is illegal."

"So is attempted murder and locking an innocent girl away in a fucking psych ward."

Her mouth shut in response, and we stared at each other with the smell of alcohol between us. Another slight nod and a soul-snatching smile, and I was pushing her up against the door so we could make a fast getaway.

A warm surge of heat coated me from the head down when I felt her hand brush mine. The warmth only intensified when I glanced at her, seeing her perfect profile from beside me with the tiniest grin covering her lips.

"Want to do the honors, baby?"

Those gray eyes hit me, and I swore my heart did a double-take. Her fingers swiped over mine, and she took the bottle from me. I pulled out the matches from my pocket, and the flame came to life a second later. We were facing each other now, and neither of us looked away. "On the count of three, throw it."

She nodded, and I began the countdown.

"One." I inched the flame closer to the rag.

"Two." She raised the bottle.

"Three," we said at the exact same time, throwing the burning bottle toward the files along Doctor Melrose's wall and watching it erupt.

The sound of glass shattering caused Journey to dive into my side. It took a few seconds for the flames to climb, and when they did, I glanced down at her, and my knees shook. She was the prettiest thing I had ever laid my eyes on. Her face was cast in red and orange hues, flickering like she was in front of a fireworks show. The bow shape of her lips parted just slightly as she stood and watched with an overpowering fulfillment. "Pretty sight, yeah?" I asked, voice hoarse with something too heavy to name.

Her smile snagged my attention when she turned to me. "Should we make a run for it?"

Everything suddenly felt exciting, and I was back to feeling like I was *me*. Even with the nudge of pain and confusion over my mother leaving me high and dry without a simple, *'Here's where I'll be if you need me,'* and the slight worry of my father planning my demise, I was the Cade Walker that Journey once knew. I was the guy that put the light in her eyes, and the guy who let a girl wrap herself around his finger.

"Hop on," I said, feeling the warmth of the fire against my back. I bent down, and there was the faintest of giggles from her that had my dimples popping out. Journey's legs wrapped around my waist, her hot little middle pushing up against me, and then I was running through the psych hospital with my girl on my back, laughing like we didn't have a care in the world.

———

As soon as we made it back to St. Mary's, our footprints had been covered by a light layer of snow. Together, Journey and I pulled the tarps back over my father's motorcycle, and we began walking back up to the school well after midnight.

"I feel like we should have worn white instead of black," she said, gripping my hand hard as she almost slipped on the stone walkway. I purposefully had us walk around the other side of the school, avoiding the courtyard where I had spent most of my summer nights, just sitting there, wondering how I had let her slip through my fingers.

"Nah," I said, opening the side door to St. Mary's that was propped open with the small rock. *Thank you, Shiner.* "No one is out here looking for us. The real eyes of St. Mary's are on the inside."

Just as I said the words, a foreboding glimpse into the future slid in front of me. My hand gripped Journey's a little tighter, and I glanced over our shoulder, scanning the area for anything. *Like more footprints.*

I was pulled back to reality when Journey's whisper hit me. "Is someone out there?"

Now that we were back at St. Mary's, with our needs in line and our checklist of breaking rules (also known as burning down buildings), reality had set back in. My pulse thrummed, and each beat of my heart thumped with suspicion.

"Cade?" Journey prodded, tugging on my hand a little tighter. I pushed her farther into the school, shutting out the gusting snow flurries.

"Shh," I hushed, moving us through the quiet halls. Every time we'd pass by a nearby closet or empty classroom, I wanted to shove her inside to keep our night of placid fun going. I missed the quiet moments with her where she lay underneath me, touching and feeling and just *being.* I even missed the nights, before any of that happened, where she'd read her classic novels to me in the back of the library after lights out.

After rounding the girls' hall and sliding past the locked dorm rooms, Journey and I ended up right in front of hers with my anxiety still residing nice and heavy on top of my shoulders. She stared up at me, and every so often, the flickering of the candle would cascade over her soft face, and I'd force my hand to stay by my side so I didn't grab her cheek and kiss her. *Where does this leave us?*

There was a sudden noise at the end of the hall when I opened my mouth to say...*anything.* Journey's face was conquered with sudden fear, and I hated to see it, so I quickly undid the lock of her door, turned the knob, and shoved her inside. "You're safe."

I promise.

A stern nod stood between me and her, and then I shut the door and stealthily took three steps back and slid into my favorite little nook of this school. With my shoulders as wide as they were, I still managed to crouch down, feeling for my worn paperback in the corner. I placed my closed fist to my mouth so I didn't breathe too loudly and waited.

Is it the duty teacher? This was a gamble, if there ever was one. I kept myself steady, not even wanting to pull my phone out to ask the other Rebels if they were up and moving about. *Particularly Isaiah.* I was positive most of the faculty knew that he and Gemma slid into each other's rooms on a daily basis, and truthfully, with everything that had been going on lately, I was surprised they didn't start bed checks. But knowing Tate, I bet he would argue that it was unethical or something if the SMC—St. Mary's Committee—even suggested it.

After a few long, painful minutes with nothing but my faint breathing filling the small space, I stood back up, tucked my worn paperback in my hand, silently slid forward, and peered down the long, grim hallway.

Protection pounded through my veins when I saw a dark figure standing outside of Gemma's door. I reached for my knife but paused when I heard Isaiah's voice.

"Did you hear that, too?"

I gripped the handle hard, half-whispering down the hall. "I just about gutted you." *For fuck's sake.*

Isaiah didn't move from Gemma's door. "Why?"

I scoffed. "Oh, I don't know. I thought maybe someone else was here to fuck with Gemma. The girl has some bad luck."

A gruff chuckle left him. "Glad to know she has more than just me as a bodyguard."

"Rebels protect their own. You know this."

"That's a new rule, though," Isaiah countered. "Neither of us were supposed to have someone."

Nothing came from my mouth because he was right. We had made the decision to never get wrapped up in someone, because we refused to bring anyone into our less-than-appealing futures, but here we were.

Isaiah must have realized that I wasn't going to say much of anything, because he opened Gemma's door and slipped inside without saying another word. I pushed past the leeriness that lingered in the empty hall, glancing at Journey's closed door once more, and began to step back into my spot when her door opened.

Her pretty face appeared in the crack, and even though I could only see a small sliver of her, I knew she had changed out of her hoodie and into her sleep shirt. *Fuck, I know what lies beneath that thin lavender tee.*

"You okay?" I asked, keeping my cool even though the hallway suddenly felt stuffy.

Journey's light hair fell forward, sweeping into her face as she looked at the knife in my hand and the book in the other. She peered behind me and landed on the dark alcove that I would be spending the night in. "Have you been sleeping in there?"

"Sleeping? No."

"Then, what are you doing standing outside my door with a knife and a book?"

My chin raised, and I walked closer to her, smelling her sweet scent waft into the hall. "Protecting you."

"I didn't ask for that, Cade."

"I don't care."

Her face fell momentarily, her head going next. But then, I heard the squeaky hinges of her door as she slowly pulled the heavy oak toward her, allowing me to see those bare legs peeking out from her purple shirt.

I didn't move a single inch. I wasn't trying to make it hard on her, but I didn't want to push. This was a conscious move between us. We weren't blinded by raw, surging emotion or the desires of our attraction. We couldn't blame this on being caught up in the moment, fueled by desperation. This was something else entirely.

"Might as well come in here to read if that's your plan for the night. I'm doing the same."

I peeled my eyes from her body and looked at her unmade bed. Her night table had several books propped up on top, one already opened, with her lamp on.

"What are you reading?" I asked, unraveling the tightness in my chest.

Journey's face stayed relaxed as she looked from the book in my hand to my face. But I saw it in her eyes. I saw the glimmer of happiness. "Same as you."

Then, the door was shut, and she and I were back to *us*.

CHAPTER TWENTY-FOUR

JOURNEY

THERE WAS a fluttering in my chest that had replaced the dread weighing me down like a stone was tied to my heart. I purposefully kept my eyes down as I grabbed a small container of syrup for my pancakes. In fact, I didn't even look up at Sloane as she went on and on about Tobias and how he *"incessantly annoyed"* her with his *"bad attitude and shit behavior."*

"I can't really talk about this with Gemma because I know she feels bad that he's giving me such a hard time, but she also feels bad for him because of his life."

Where is Cade? He slipped out of my room early this morning, and I only knew that because I heard the chain on my door and saw his tall frame slip through and into the dark hall. We stayed up most of the night, reading, until I fell asleep, and I knew I'd fallen asleep on him, because my hair held his scent.

My emotions were all over the place, and when it came to Cade, I had a hard time deciphering between my physical needs and my emotional needs. It all sounded very philosophical and mature, but I supposed that was what you got when you were forced to grow up at a young age and thrown into a psych ward where highly educated—or so they said—individuals critiqued your feelings and tried to make sense of your behavior.

An abrupt laugh left me. *I wonder what Doctor Melrose would have said if I had told him I was seducing the staff so I could steal a key card and get to Tobias so we could run away from the tiny pills that haunted me.*

"What are you laughing at?"

I peered up at Sloane as we began moving down the breakfast line full of steaming food. My mouth opened, and I realized that I had totally zoned out while she talked about Tobias.

"Where is Tobias, anyway?" I asked, managing to scan the dining hall briefly before landing on the Rebels' empty table.

"Probably planning another way to torture me." She laughed sarcastically. "I sound like Gemma when she used to tutor Isaiah."

"She tutored Isaiah?"

Sloane rolled her eyes. "I mean, no, but that was their cover while Isaiah snuck out of St. Mary's and went to the Covens to follow Bain."

This time, I snapped to attention. "And why did he follow Bain again?"

"Because of his father's business. Bain's father, Callum, and Isaiah's father were rivals in their gun-running *business*. Didn't yo—" Her voice lowered. "What exactly do you know about the Rebels, Journ?"

Sloane walked with me over to my table as I tried to piece together what I knew and what I'd learned since leaving the psych hospital. "Not enough, apparently."

Sloane rolled her eyes. "I fucking hate him."

Are we back to Tobias again?

"I've been wracking my brain since you told me that you didn't..."—she leaned in close as I placed my tray on my table—"try to kill yourself, and I've been giving you space because I know you're private."

I swallowed, staring down at the syrup as it soaked into my pancake.

"But it has to do with him, doesn't it? That's why he hated to hear your name. That's why he was so fucked up when you left. It had something to do with the shit they were caught up in. He felt guilty because you got hurt."

I couldn't fault her for putting the blame on Cade, but I could fault myself for leaving her in the dark. "You're right when you say I'm private. I like to keep my secrets close." Sloane's hazel eyes bounced back and forth between mine, her perfectly shaped eyebrows lowering as I pulled her in close, whispering, "And I'm sorry for keeping you in the dark. It's just...when I got back here, I didn't trust anyone. Not even you."

She winced at my words, and I hated myself for saying it. Sloane had proven herself over and over again, and deep down, past her cool, airy, *girls-just-want-to-have-fun* attitude, she was fiercely protective and safe beyond measure. She watched people closely, just as I had. "Someone tried to kill me and..." I looked past Sloane's ear as she leaned in closer and locked onto Cade as he walked behind the rest of the Rebels into the dining hall, snagging his attention at once. Butterflies shot to the darkest, quietest parts of my body. "And it had nothing to do with Cade."

"Are you sure? I don't think Cade would ever purposely hurt you—not after seeing how torn up he was when you left, but—"

My hand landed on hers, still holding her tray. "I'm one hundred percent positive. There's been someone after me since I was a baby."

"What?"

I pulled back when I felt the shift in the air. My hair tickled the side of my face, and air whooshed out of my mouth. Cade and the rest of the Rebels, along with Gemma, were standing mere feet away from Sloane and me.

"We're sitting here today."

My mouth opened but then quickly closed as Shiner and Brantley made the first move and pulled out the long dining-hall bench, placing their uniform blazers on top while leaving quickly to go get food. Isaiah pulled Gemma beside him as she gave us a tiny shrug followed by a smile, and then it was just me, Cade, and Sloane.

"What? No *'fuck you'* today, Sloane?" Cade's hands went to his loose tie, and he began tightening it until it fit snuggly below his bobbing Adam's apple. *Why is that so attractive?*

Sloane sighed, placing her tray beside mine. She looked at me, ignoring Cade. "Are you sure?"

"Are you sure, what?" Cade asked, sounding impatient. He growled quietly, and when I moved my attention from Sloane to him, I noticed that he wasn't even looking at us. He was staring toward the far corner of the dining hall—at Bain.

"I'm just making sure you weren't the one who tried to kill her."

Cade's attention flew back to Sloane, and that was when I took over looking at Bain. My stomach dropped when I saw that he was staring *directly* back at me, but if I thought that Cade and the rest of the Rebels were hard to read, Bain was like reading a dead language—even if I wanted to read him, I couldn't.

"I'll kill everyone in this school before I ever let someone touch her again. So, *no,* Sloane. I wasn't the one who tried to kill her."

Sloane sat down, unfazed by Cade's threat. "Not surprised to hear a threat leave your mouth. You probably have a knife or gun on you at all times. Just like the rest of you Rebels. *Fucking psychos.*"

"We sure are," Shiner said with a little skip in his step. His long legs straddled the dining-hall table as he stuffed a breakfast sandwich in his mouth, chewing and swallowing it in record time. "Psychos are better in bed."

"So I've heard." Sloane rolled her eyes and waved her hand at Mercedes so she could join...*our?*...table.

I stood awkwardly, looking at everyone as they sat down at my table that was supposed to have been for me and me only. I wasn't sure how I felt about everyone suddenly coming to sit with me and the fact that the entire dining hall was staring at us. I *knew* Aubrey was probably fuming as she sat with her friends, looking at the Rebels' empty table, but Cade had been correct when he told me that she would be leaving me alone. I hadn't caught a single look from her.

Although, that could have been because I had lost my shit that day when her friend pulled my sleeve. She probably thought I was unstable. And maybe I was.

"Sit." Cade's command did nothing but twist my insides. How could he make such a tiny word sound so inviting? Especially when he was bossing me around?

He tugged on my plaid skirt, his finger brushing over the skin along my thigh. My eyes widened briefly, and I was certain no one else had noticed or felt the uptick in my pulse, but Cade had a way of sensing these things in me. He leaned in close and whispered, "Was last night not enough?"

My cheeks were warm, and I elbowed him as I sat down beside him. "Stop it." One finger-fuck and a blow job, and he suddenly thought we were back to normal.

But are we? This really was no different than before. Sexual innuendos, touching in the dark where no one could see, desperate for each other's attention. *Shit, we are back to normal.*

"That's right..." Isaiah interjected, placing his arms on the table. He leaned in closely, and Gemma gave him a side-eye. "What exactly *did* you two get into last night?"

Cade and I both paused, his leg stopped bouncing beside mine, and I had the sudden urge to scoot away.

"You two were together last night?" Sloane gave me a look that made me backtrack.

"What? No." The refusal to admit anything jutted out like a swift punch. *We were not together. We did not go to the psych hospital. We did not touch. And we did not set a building on fire.*

My face was as red as those flames. I could feel it.

"That's interesting," Isaiah mused, his hand disappearing under the table. Gemma grinned as she tried to busy herself with her oatmeal. "The headmaster pulled me aside this morning and told me something I think you'll all like to hear."

"Spit it out, Rebel. We don't have all day." Sloane sipped on her tea, giving no more than a second of silence.

"I heard that the Covens was set on fire last night."

Shit.

Cade's hand landed on my thigh, and although it was such a subtle movement, my leg kicked in response. Isaiah's mouth curved as he dropped his eyes to Cade's arm that I was certain he knew had moved to my leg.

"Wow. Really?" Cade bemused, grabbing his mug. Black coffee laid inside, and that didn't surprise me at all.

"Wait, what the fuck? Are you serious?" Brantley dropped his fork.

"Yep," Isaiah said, wrapping his arm around Gemma's waist. "They aren't sure who did it, but it looks to be arson."

I swallowed a bite of my pancake to keep my mouth busy. *What were we thinking? What if they trace it back to us? What if they come to take me away again?*

My head was spiraling as Brantley asked questions and

Shiner joked beside him. "Maybe it was your brother, Gem. Or maybe it was Cade and Journey since they look pretty fucking guilty over there."

Cade shrugged. "Wasn't us."

"It wasn't Tobias," Sloane said before shutting her mouth like she had admitted something she shouldn't have. Gemma's eyes flew over to her, but I couldn't pay attention because I was suddenly feeling uneasy and unprotected.

Cade turned his head slightly to me, tapping the inside of my leg. "Breathe."

A burn zipped through me that left a trail of embers behind. Except, it had nothing to do with his hand clamped on my leg. "I want that knife," I whispered, blocking the side of my face with my hair. It was as if Cade and I were in our own little world, tucked away from everyone in St. Mary's.

"I have it."

Our eyes met, and there was no time to waste. "Meet me at my door tonight. After curfew."

I zeroed in on his dimples as he tapped my leg again. "I would have been there regardless."

Then, he turned away, and we joined the conversation as if there wasn't a literal threat hanging over my head and a burnt-down building with our names smeared in the ashes.

CHAPTER TWENTY-FIVE

CADE

I SPUN the knife around and around in my hand as I stood back in my favorite little cubby, waiting for the duty teacher to finally make her way down the hall. My heart was skipping like a child in a candy store with an unlimited amount of money to spend, just knowing that I was seconds from tapping on Journey's door.

Sitting at her table today during breakfast was a mere reaction to seeing Bain looking at her while she huddled with Sloane, whispering about God knew what. His brows were etched with confusion, and if he hadn't seen me walk into the dining hall with my murderous gaze set on him, I had a feeling he would have walked near them to have a listen.

What is his fucking deal?

I couldn't figure it out. He wasn't the one who put a threat on her life—he would have been an infant at the same time she was. Nothing made sense. The only logical thing I could do was corner him and put a knife to his throat until he told me why he was so fucking fascinated with her. He didn't try to fuck her at the claiming, which only confused me further. He hadn't touched her—*yet*. But the second he did... I stopped spinning the knife in my hand, gripping the handle a little too tight.

Calm the fuck down.

The shuffling of feet from the duty teacher slowly faded away, and all thoughts of strangling Bain left as I took a hefty step forward and raised my hand to knock. I rapped my knuckles on Journey's door three times, and she opened it immediately, wearing that same black hoodie from last night. *Oh, are we going on another adventure?*

"Good, get in here," she rushed out, gripping my arm and pulling me inside. Something wicked stirred deep in the pit of my stomach, and I immediately glanced at her bed. "I want to go to the orphanage."

I gripped the knife tighter. My chin tipped as I stared at her determined face, feeling my groin awaken with the fascination I had over her bossy, insistent tone.

"Why?" I asked, leaning against her door so I didn't storm her and throw her onto the bed. All I could think about was how beautiful she had looked with the color of fire licking over her face at the psych hospital last night, and how her lips had torn into mine like I was the only thing she wanted to taste.

"Because," she started, pacing back and forth on bare feet. Her blue-painted toes caught my eye as she continued to stomp. "Someone tried to kill me!"

Are we panicking now?

"I'm aware," I calmly stated, pausing my spinning of the knife that she hadn't even noticed.

She huffed, placing her hands on her hips as she stopped right in front of me. "Do you know how demoralizing it is to not know a single thing about your past? Your family? To get passed up by family after family because they all thought you were too broken to adopt? Then to find out there had been a threat on your life since you were an infant, and you still have no idea *who* would want you dead? Or why they want you dead?" Her words sped up, and I took a step forward, ready to steady her. "And to be attacked from behind? I'm scared, Cade! I know it seems like I'm not, but I am! What if they come back?"

"No." I strode over to her quickly, catching her by surprise. My hand clamped onto her trembling chin tightly. "Even if they do come back, they're dead."

Her fierceness replaced the fear. "I thought you weren't a killer."

I smirked. "When it comes to you? I'll be anything."

There was a knock in my chest, and I knew it was the beating muscle that I kept on lockdown most days, reminding me that it still felt. It breathed Journey in and out, and my words were as truthful as if I were hooked up to a lie detector test. There were many things that I had seen over the years with my so-called father figure that I would never divulge to Journey. I'd seen dead bodies. I'd watched a man bleed to death. And just because I wasn't the one who caused the violence, that didn't mean I wasn't fazed by it. Because I was.

I hated my father. I might've hated him even more now because he was the one that drove my mother away, even without doing so consciously. My own mother was afraid of me. She was afraid I'd turn out like him. I knew, deep down, that was why she left.

"We should go before the duty teacher does her rounds again," I whispered, gazing into Journey's troubled gray eyes. She swallowed before giving me a subtle nod. Before I let her go, I flipped the knife around in my hand and thrust the handle into her small, free palm. Her head dropped, her sandy hair cascading over us.

"Do you know how to use it?" I asked, wanting nothing more than to flip her around, press her tight little ass to my front, and teach her.

"Yes. Tobias taught me at the Covens when I told him what happened." Her whisper floated around us as I kept our hands joined over the handle.

I moved our hands forward, jutting them through the air. "If anyone, and I mean *anyone*, comes at you, and I'm not around, stab the fuck out of them. Act first, ask questions later. I'll handle the rest when I get there, okay?"

She nodded, and I pushed on the sheath that the knife rested in, closing off the sharp edge, and put it in her hoodie pocket. I left my hand inside as I buried my face into her hair, inhaling once before stepping away. "Let's go."

As soon as Journey turned around, she peeked up at me with something unreadable in her expression, and before I knew it, my breath was stolen as she glued herself to my front, wrapping her hands around my waist. Her head hit the center of my chest, and I immediately wrapped my arms around her. "Thank you," she said, voice muffled from the thick cotton of my hoodie.

"Never thank me for keeping you safe," I whispered, kissing the top of her head. Then, I walked us over to her door, and we slipped out into the darkened hallway.

———

THE RIDE to the Clemency Orphanage was just as torturous as riding to the Covens the previous night. But this time, Journey didn't even try to shy away from me. She pressed in close, resting her head on my back as her hands wound around my waist. Even though it was cold as fuck out, I was sweating when she climbed off the back and stood in front of the orphanage with her chin tipped high and her delicate profile in my direction.

The orphanage was similar to St. Mary's in terms of architecture—something I'd noticed the first time I crept out onto the road underneath the burnt-out streetlamp to watch her. I turned back and saw that the tall, looming light was still burnt out, and when I glanced back at Journey, she was staring at me with her hood propped over her head.

"What?" I asked, placing my hand in my pocket, feeling for my trusty knife.

Her lip twitched, and I immediately found myself unable to look away. "Why did you come watch me when I got back?"

I shifted on my feet, seeing a glimmer of hope that she *never* showed. "Why do you think?"

An abrupt laugh left her mouth, followed by a cloud of breath in the cool air. "At first? I wasn't sure. I wasn't sure if you came back to finish the job or..." Her big, gray eyes stunned me for a second with the fact that she truly thought I'd tried to hurt her. "Or maybe you came to make sure I was okay. Although, this is the first time I'm admitting that aloud."

The words flew from my mouth quickly. "It was to make sure you were okay." Then, I shook my head, pulling up my own hood and storming over to her. "I didn't say it enough in the past, and it's obvious since you had the mere thought that I could have been the one to hurt you, but I would rather split open my chest and pull out my own heart than *ever* let someone touch you."

Her eyes widened as she pressed onto my arm wrapped around her lower back. Her chest tipped upward, and her lips parted with...fear? Surprise?

"What are you thinking?" I asked.

She blinked, and her eyes grew glossier by the second. My

heart was humming, and I wanted to pull her up those decaying stairs to the place she grew up in, shove her into the nearest room, and prove to her how truthful my words were.

"I'm thinking I like hearing you say those things, even though I promised I would never, *ever* let my heart get invested again."

I immediately pressed my lips to her forehead to hide the emotion that was clogging my senses. What Journey didn't know was that I knew exactly how she felt. Being *this* infatuated with someone came with consequences. I'd lived with them, and so had she. Abandonment and desertion by those who were supposed to care for you, and had promised to do so, went a long fucking way. We were both jaded when it came to love and stability.

"Your heart doesn't really give you a choice. It wants what it wants, and we want the same thing."

I dropped my head, wanting to do nothing more than pinch the bridge of my nose to stop the burning. But instead, I grabbed onto her hand, looked up at the orphanage, and remembered why we were here.

"Are you going to confront Sister Mary?" I asked, changing the subject. Journey pulled away and glanced up at the same three-story brick building that I was. The windows had tiny, orange flames flickering behind the cloudy glass, and that was the only light that I could see.

Journey's warm hand left mine, and she pulled out a small key from her jeans. "Sister Mary is the only parental figure I have ever had." Her shaky breath puffed out into the air when she took a step forward. I followed closely behind, peeking over our shoulders for the tenth time in the last few minutes. "I know she has kept me safe all these years, but I have a feeling she knows more than she told Headmaster Ellison."

"And if she doesn't?" I asked as we stood in front of the

oak and wrought-iron door with a key dangling from Journey's fingers.

She shot me a sharp look, and my rebellious girl was back in action with her dewy eyes and crescent-like smile. "Then, we start uncovering the secrets that I know she has hidden inside this building."

CHAPTER TWENTY-SIX

JOURNEY

IF I WERE ALONE, I would have been looking over my shoulder every three seconds with my heart tearing through my body. Chills would have covered me from the second I stepped foot in the dark entryway, and I would have prepared myself for Sister Mary to reprimand me for sneaking out of the boarding school to pay her a visit.

But with Cade's hand in mine and his imperious attitude and somehow attractive arrogance, I felt like I could tackle anything. In fact, I felt like the girl I was when I seduced a male nurse at the psych hospital, stole a key card, grabbed onto Tobias' hand, and broke through a window to walk to St. Mary's. *Unstoppable and determined.*

I narrowed my gaze slightly as the door to Sister Mary's office was cracked. I ignored the inkling festering in my belly. Her door was never open. Whether she was inside of it or not, it was shut and usually locked. She didn't keep much in her office, and that remained the same as I stepped inside and saw that it was just as bare as it was the last time I had been in here. One tiny, shitty desk sat in the middle of the room with paintings from the little girls, covered in pretty reds, pinks, and yellows, hanging off the tied string on the front of it. And an old, leather, sage-green chair was propped behind it. File cabinets were placed to the left of the desk, and there was one worn rug underneath two chairs on the opposite side.

"Well, she's not in here," Cade whispered, looking around the office. "Maybe she's asleep?"

I shook my head. "She stays up until one or two most nights, working here or taking care of the babies on the second floor."

Cade's hand fell from mine as I pulled my fingernail up to my mouth and started to nibble on it. His easy strides took him over to the metal file cabinets, but my voice stopped him. "Don't bother. There is nothing useful in there."

He turned back to me, and all I saw was the sharp edge of his jaw. He was outlined by the window behind him, and my mouth grew dry.

"How do you know?"

"Because I was the one to organize them. There is nothing in those file cabinets that will lead anyone to me." I let out a light, sarcastic laugh. "Which kind of makes sense now."

I turned around swiftly, annoyed by the fact that I was so naive before. *Why didn't I have a file? Why didn't anyone know anything about me? Why did every single potential adoptive parent pass me over?*

There was a burning question on the tip of my tongue, making me taste something sour, that only grew stronger as I walked down the long, narrow hallway with worn floors and crumbling walls. *Did Sister Mary make sure no one adopted me on purpose?* I shook my head, ignoring the tightening in my chest, and scanned the hall. This place was in desperate need of repairs, but it was still home to me, as shitty and as heart-wrenching as it was.

I stopped in front of the last door on the left and stood on my tiptoes, peeking inside the scratched-up glass covered in a sheen of dust. Cade, being taller than me, leaned forward, his front gracing my back. His arm curved around my middle, and I immediately grew warm. "Lots of cribs and a few beds," he whispered from behind. I nodded, lowering back to level feet. I peered up at him and saw his dark eyes looking down at me. "This is the early childhood wing. Ages two to eight."

Cade nodded, staying quiet, as we both started for the stairs. I went up first and whispered over my shoulder, "Walk on the same steps I do. Some of them are squeaky."

He nodded, following so closely behind I could feel his body heat mix with mine. When we reached the second floor, I peered down the hall, making sure none of the nuns who did the infant night shifts were wandering about with their quiet, brooding footsteps. There was one piercing infant cry that made me jerk. Cade walked over to the door that was an exact replica of the one downstairs and nudged his head over to it. I slid in front of him quickly, and his arm came around my middle again. I peered inside, focusing on the one nun I saw holding a crying baby. I weaved my attention through the cribs, looking for one in particular. "Sweet baby must have gotten adopted," I whispered, hating that I felt sad.

"Who?" Cade asked, pushing my hair behind my shoulder. My hood had fallen back at some point, and although I wasn't *too* nervous to be walking the halls in the dark, the other nuns weren't as forgiving as Sister Mary.

"Her name was Callie. I had taken care of her for a few nights before coming back to St. Mary's." Warmth slid to my cheeks. "Sister Mary put me on baby duty because, for some reason, Callie only calmed when I held her. Like she felt safe with me or something." I shook my head, feeling stupid. "It's silly. She was probably just afraid of those damn cornettes."

"What the fuck is a cornette?"

I suppressed a laugh. "The hats the nuns wear. I told Sister Mary to lose it, but she scolded me—or what she considered *scolding*."

I sighed, shaking my head. "Let's go see if she's upstairs." *To my floor.*

As soon as we made it to the top, Cade's hand landed on my arm. My stomach tensed, and I immediately began searching the hall for something suspicious. The knife he'd given me was burning a hole in my hoodie pocket, and I *almost* reached for it before his hoarse voice broke through the silence. "It's not silly."

I paused. "What isn't?"

"Callie feeling safe with you. Who wouldn't fall in love with you after just one glimpse?"

My throat began to swell as his finger brushed my cheekbone, causing little chills to roll down my arms. "You have a warm soul, Journey. I couldn't even stay away."

My eyes fell to his lips, and I knew we were on borrowed time, creeping through the halls of a quiet and sleepy orphanage without having permission to do so. The orphanage was locked, yes, but even having a key, I wasn't supposed to be here. It didn't matter if I was legally an adult. Sister Mary didn't allow people to roam the halls at night. And she, along with the other nuns who had watched me grow up, would likely have a heart attack if they caught me with a boy like Cade.

"Come on," Cade finally said, dropping his hand. "Is this the last floor?"

My voice cracked at first. "Um, yeah. Sister Mary sleeps on the first floor, but her door was open when we walked past, so she's not in there. If she isn't up here, then I don't know where she is." I grabbed my knife with the thought. *Where could she be?* Sister Mary never left the orphanage—and especially not at night.

The door to the final sleeping quarters, the one that I'd been placed in since I turned of age, was open. That wasn't surprising at all. I was the only older orphan that Sister Mary ever housed, which meant that I had the entire top floor to myself.

Most girls would probably love that. I didn't. It only reminded me that I was alone and not worthy of what the younger girls had—potential for adoption.

"Doesn't look like anyone is in here."

Slowly, I felt dread slide down my spine like thick mud. *Where is Sister Mary?* My slow footsteps took me over to my bed, which was neatly made, just like I'd left it. Chips of yellow paint flicked off the headboard as I ran my finger along it. "This isn't right," I said, turning around and seeing Cade watch me from across the rectangular room. There were at least ten beds in here, all in a single row, but only one had ever been used. *Mine.*

"What isn't?" he asked, raising his chin, making the honed lines look sharper—as if he needed to look any hotter from across the room.

"She never leaves the orphanage."

I dropped my head down to my bed with an evident crease in between my eyebrows. *Where is she?*

Cade began walking over to me. "Then, let's wait for her."

I sighed, feeling frustrated. "But what if she doesn't come back tonight? We can't stay here all night. We *do* have school tomorrow."

"Take a breath." Cade's hands fell to my shoulders, and he gave me a light squeeze. "We have some time. The Rebels will let me know if something is off, or if Tate somehow finds out that we left."

I inhaled and then blew out a breath, which landed right on Cade's chest. "Okay," I whispered, taking a seat on my bed. Cade walked over to the window directly behind the bed and rested his shoulder against it. The candle wasn't lit, and I kind of liked it like that. If we were in the dark, then no one from the outside knew we were in here.

And there was potential that someone could have been watching, which was probably what Cade was thinking as he peered down to the darkened road. My hand found the sheathed knife in my pocket again, and I ran my fingers over the worn leather, wondering where Cade got it from. Was it his? Who gave it to him? His dad? His mom? Did he get it specifically for me? I liked the idea of having a way to protect myself, considering the fact that, every so often, I would be reminded of that dreadful night where someone came from behind and hit me out of nowhere. Even if I could have fought back, I didn't have a way to do so other than with my fists. Having this knife felt comforting, but I couldn't deny that Cade looked really, *really* good standing behind me, peering down through the window, ready to stop anyone from hurting me.

I liked it. I liked it a lot.

TOO MUCH TIME HAD PASSED. I knew it when I felt a dip in my bed. I was confused and disoriented, and when I found my hand sweaty from holding onto something, my eyes flew open, and I unsheathed my knife and rounded on the person who had slipped beside me.

The silver blade was to their throat, and my legs clamped over their hips with my heart no more than a nuisance in my chest.

Cade's hand clamped onto my wrist so hard I held back a

yelp. When I saw his fierce glare from down below, I gasped and immediately let go of the knife handle, allowing it to slide down his neck and onto the spot on my bed that I was lying on.

"Oh my God," I rushed out, trying to climb off his lap. His other hand slapped down onto my hip to keep me there. "I'm...I'm sorry," I said, putting my shaking hand to my mouth. My eyes immediately went to his neck, which had the thinnest line of blood trailing from it. "Holy shit, I cut you."

"Good." His voice was hoarse, and it rubbed at parts of me that were fueled by adrenaline and excitement. "You weren't kidding when you said Tobias taught you how to use a knife."

I slowly rested my legs and sank down onto Cade's middle. His hand on my leg didn't loosen, and neither did the one on my wrist. His eyes looked even darker in the room, especially given that mine hadn't adjusted from my accidental sleep.

"He is a scary-good fighter. He was trained to—"

"*Kill*. A black-market killer. Yes, I was, too—in a way." A dark chuckle left him.

I nodded, glancing at the window behind the bed. I couldn't imagine what Cade had been taught over the years from his father. Someone who dealt in illegal firearms and had a hand in the Covens, an elusive place for creating black-market killers...it had to be terrorizing.

The moon had moved, and I could no longer see it in between the stars. "We should go, right? How long have I been asleep?"

"We can stay a little while longer. It's been pretty quiet out there," he said, finally dropping my hand. His heart was a thundering clap against my palm that I couldn't stop focusing on.

Silence passed between us as I ran over scenarios

involving Sister Mary and her whereabouts when Cade spoke again. "What else did Tobias teach you? Besides knifing someone in your sleep."

Both of my hands rested against his chest now, and I zeroed in on the tiny trickle of blood running down his neck. *I seriously cut him.* "What do you mean?" I asked, reaching up slowly to wipe at the dribble. Cade's chin moved to the side, giving way to his wounded neck, showing off his strong features and bobbing Adam's apple.

"Did you two fuck?"

I paused, my finger pressing gently over the wound. There was a strange part of me that wanted to reach down and press my lips to it, like I used to do with the little girls when they'd bang up their knees from running too fast over the chipped sidewalk out front.

"Would it make you angry if I said yes?" I wasn't sure why I was toying with him. We were in uneasy times and physically in a place that we shouldn't even have been in, and here I was, prodding him to react. The truth was, I *liked* it when he got jealous. I *liked* it when he proclaimed that I was *his.* I *liked* being wanted by him.

"No."

Immediately, the room grew quieter, and as soon as I wiped the blood from his neck with my thumb, he grabbed onto my hand with my red-stained finger in between us. I was aware of what I was pressing down on with my middle and was completely and utterly exhilarated.

"No?" I asked, tilting my head so my hair fell in between us. *What the hell are we doing?* If one of the nuns heard us or *saw* this...they'd drop dead.

His head shook slowly, almost in a predatory way. "No." Cade shifted beneath me, and I felt the hard nudge, even through my jeans. Something tightened, and I held my breath, wanting nothing more than to move over him. "It would just give me an excuse to prove to you that you're mine and not his."

There it is. That unyielding spark deep inside that clung to his words like they were a lifeline. *Do it. Prove it to me, Cade.*

"You'd like that, wouldn't you?" he asked, pushing my bloody thumb up to my mouth, pressing it ever so gently against my lips.

"Why do you say that?" My voice was breathy and dropped so low that I wasn't even sure he heard me.

"You've got that look." His eyes scanned over my face, and my core twisted in delicious agony. Cade and I had been in this exact position many times before: me straddling him with that glint of pure rebellion in his eye. But this time felt different. It was as if we were balancing over jagged spikes, ready to fall to our demise with one wrong move. There was a lot of baggage between us and open wounds that had yet to be closed, which made any moment with him seem like the last. We'd lost each other before, and it was, without a doubt, what fueled this moment right here.

Cade's other hand fell to my hip, his fingers resting over the spot where my groin was, lighting a torch right there in the middle. "Your eyes are hooded, and you've got that lust blazing inside them that I've lost myself in too many times to count. Your pussy is warm, so warm that I can feel it through both of our jeans." He pressed my thumb harder onto my bottom lip, and I had to force myself to keep my tongue inside my mouth. "Your lips are begging me for a kiss, and it is taking everything in me not to give it to you right this second."

I said nothing, but I felt his words wracking inside my body, hitting every intimate part that wanted him. "Am I right?" he asked, peering up at me in a devilish way. "Do you want me to prove it to you?"

"Tobias and I were nothing more than friends," I admitted, moving my hips over him and breaking the hold I had on myself between right and wrong. There wasn't even a slight misstep in my brain that told me doing this with him was wrong, even if we were hiding out in the place I grew up in with holy nuns wandering the halls down below.

A ragged breath left him, and his teeth sunk into his bottom lip. "Good." Suddenly, my thumb was in my mouth, the taste of his tangy, metallic blood hitting my taste buds with surprise. He lowered his chin, looking dangerous from below. "Now *suck*."

I wasted no time. There were no thoughts about *us* or what we were doing in the orphanage on top of my shitty, half-painted twin bed. All I focused on was the burning intensity burrowing deep inside and the look of carnal need on Cade's face. His grip on my wrist tightened as I sucked my thumb, licking my lips after the blood had disappeared. My hand slowly fell to his chest as he moved his deft fingers to the button of my jeans, popping it through the hole and then yanking the zipper down in one fluid motion.

"Lift." It was a single demand, and although his voice was rough and hoarse, I did exactly what he wanted.

My hands fell to the headboard behind him, and I lifted my hips, hovering *very* closely to his mouth as he pulled the denim from my legs. I was left in a thin black hoodie and my panties that Cade suddenly hooked his fingers into and peeled away just as slowly as he did my jeans. His strong hands gripped my waist, keeping me in place. "*Sit.*"

My brows crowded, pausing on the word. "Sit?" I tried to back my hips up, but his fingers dug into my skin, biting me with pleasure.

"Yes. Sit." I dropped my gaze to his, and that famous, *can-make-a-girl-do-anything* grin was staring back at me.

"Right...right here?"

"Do you know how many times I've thought about you

sitting on my fucking face? You're all I've wanted to taste since you've been back."

My breasts suddenly felt heavy, and the tightening of my nipples brought everything to life. Cade's nose trailed up the side of my thigh, and my legs quivered. He pushed my hips down as I kept my hands tightened on the headboard, feeling the yellow chips of paint fall to the floor. The *second* his mouth was on me, I threw my head back, sagging further onto him.

He was warm and wet, and it stole my breath. His teeth snagged on my delicate skin, and I moved over him, letting him feast on me like I was his favorite meal.

"Cade," I moaned, not caring at all that I needed to be quiet. In fact, I wasn't even sure where I was at the moment.

He pulled away for a quick second, only to say, "This is the hottest thing I have ever done and the best goddamn thing I have ever tasted." Then, his tongue was back, and his fingers were digging further into my hips, rocking me back and forth.

I felt myself moving above him, knowing that I was chasing a high that only he could give me. Sweat began to coat my breasts, and my hands begged to slip from the headboard. When I peeked down at him, watching him move his face beneath me, tasting me and sucking with skill, I tightened in all the right places. A soft moan bellowed from my mouth, but he pulled away at the last second. I was frantic, snapping my head down, wondering where he went. "Not yet." His sexy smirk was gone and replaced by parted lips and a fierce gaze. "I want you coming on my dick."

As soon as he slipped out from under me and climbed off the bed, he pulled his jeans down, revealing his hardened length. My stomach fluttered, and my core twisted, but that all came to a stop when I heard the creaking of stairs. *Oh my God.* I gasped, flipping around onto my back, letting my hands fall from the headboard. Cade's hand was wrapped around himself as he slowly turned his head to the door, cursing whoever was walking up the stairs. I would have told him that cursing a nun was probably terrible luck, but I didn't have time as he scooped up our belongings and pulled on my hand, racing us to the tall armoire that pressed against the wall.

It was the same expansive, tall, vintage armoire that sat in each of the dorm wings—so big it could hold every orphan's clothing. Except, this one was completely empty. The door opened with Cade's large hand, and we were both snuggled inside with our erratic breathing and my wet thighs. Our view to the long room was only partially visible through the tiny, woven holes in the cane-webbing material of the armoire as I peered out, waiting for whoever was coming upstairs.

"Shit," I whispered, coming back to reality that I was literally just *riding* Cade's face in my childhood room at an all-girls orphanage.

Cade's hand slithered up the front of me, his chest pressing firmly against my back as he covered my mouth with his hand. "Shh." His whisper tickled the inside of my ear, and the only thing that did was make me burn hotter. Cade was wearing nothing but his hoodie and boxers, our clothes *and* my knife in a heaping pile underneath our feet. The scratchy hair on his leg nestled in between mine, and I throbbed from the theft of my high. My body was still curving and twisting in unimaginable ways, and although I knew it was wrong on every level, I wanted him to finish me off so I could breathe again.

The black veil of Sister Elizabeth caught my eye as she weaved in between the beds, pausing on mine with the rumpled pillow. Cade's hand tightened over my mouth as my breathing picked up. I saw the large crucifix tied around Sister Elizabeth's neck swing low as she bent forward, straightening the blankets, when Cade's seedy breath hit over the sensitive part of my ear. "Should I finish you off with her in the room?"

He wouldn't!

"Oh, I would, baby." His quiet growl rumbled against my back, and my mouth opened, wondering how he read my mind. "I swore that if I ever got you back in my hands, I would stop at nothing."

I wanted to slap Cade for turning me on even more while we were hiding away in this holy fucking Catholic orphanage with a nun in plain sight. Sure, she was several yards away, standing over my bed, but the devil had to have been enjoying this on every satanic level. Sister Elizabeth slowly crept over to the window that Cade was leaning on a little while ago, staring down onto the silent street, when my core jolted.

Cade's hand left my mouth, and he placed it on the inner part of my thigh, which was still wet from his mouth. "Mmm," he whispered. His finger brushed over my swollen clit, and my head flung back onto his hard shoulder. "Still wet? I'll take that as a yes, then."

His finger moved back to my slick entrance, and he nudged my legs apart, clamping onto my ear with his teeth. I was completely frantic on the inside. Something wild was carving through my bones, and even though I kept my eyes on Sister Elizabeth, in all of her black glory, I was focused on pressing myself against the front of Cade.

His boxers had somehow disappeared without even making a noise, and when he placed himself at my center from behind, I desperately looked for something to hang onto. The armoire we were hiding in was bigger than your usual armoire. Cade and I were in tight quarters, but we could still fit as long as he bent down an inch. It was sturdy, too. I remembered when Sister Mary had them custom-made by an

Amish man years ago, but *surely*, the rod above my head would snap if I pulled it.

Cade inched in slowly, cursing quietly at how wet I was. His forearm rested below my hoodie, holding me up, and then he took my hands and placed them on the same rod I was afraid would break. I bravely wrapped my hands around it, and when he entered me all the way, filling me up as much as he possibly could, my fingers tightened, and I leaned farther forward for a better angle.

"That's it," he whispered.

I snapped my eyes back through the woven material on the armoire door and nearly snagged in relief as Sister Elizabeth walked to the door and disappeared from the room. I knew we weren't in the clear yet and so did Cade, because his thrusts were slow and deep, hardly making any noise or sharp movements at all.

"Good girl keeping quiet," he coaxed. His hand grabbed onto my chin, and he turned my head back so he could kiss me deeply. My eyes shut, and my hands pulled on the rod above us. He knew his dirty words always gave me that extra push, and all the times I had touched myself in the last several months were *nothing* compared to this moment right here. In fact, nothing at all topped this. I was pushing back against him every time he dove in a little deeper, and our tongues mixed together like two snakes tangling in the wild.

"I'm going to make you come twice, baby. Are you ready for the first?"

Wait, what?

His thrusting grew harder and faster, and my head spun with the tightening of every muscle I had. His hand landed over my mouth to keep me quiet, and he pressed a hot kiss to my neck, right over my pulse. "Let go," he said right before he pressed his fingers onto my needy clit, and just like that, my body yielded to his demand. Stars coated my vision, mixing with the darkness, and I couldn't even catch my breath as Cade's fingers began touching me over and over again, circling me, rubbing me, lightly brushing over the sensitive bud before he pushed me forward, giving me a new angle.

"Cade, I...I—" A frenzy fueled the intense, mind-numbing pleasure, and I was truly incapable of making words.

"Fuck, I missed this. I missed *you*. Are you ready for round two?"

One of his hands cupped my waist, and the other gripped my hair. We were in tight quarters, and at some point, we'd moved around so I was no longer facing the doors.

"Nothing..." he said, brushing over my clit again, bringing me to insanity. He pumped in short strokes, itching the need I had to the point that tears gathered in my eyes. "Will ever replace you, Journey. This right here?" He moved in and out, and I froze, completely at a standstill with how emotionally and physically connected I was. "Is me *showing* you how much I love you. Do you feel it? Do you feel me burying myself inside you? Filling you up with everything I have? It might not be much, but it's all of me."

Yes. Yes. Yes.

Just then, I came in hard, crashing waves, biting onto my lip so I would keep quiet. Cade pulled out of me a second later, and I felt his hot liquid hit the back of my thigh and burn me all the way down to my ankle.

I snapped my head back to him, still out of breath. Our dark gazes met instantly, and it was then that I knew I wasn't trying to outlive the *threat* on my life for me, but I was doing it for him.

CHAPTER TWENTY-SEVEN

CADE

IF THERE WAS A GOD, he was ready to throw Journey and me both down to hell for what we just did. I knew she made me lose control—I had never denied that—but it wasn't my intention to take her from behind with a fucking nun in the room.

As soon as we cleaned up and got dressed, with her sneaking glances at me with those pink-tinted cheeks, she crossed her arms and sunk her teeth into her lip. Her expression was tender and slightly naughty, which sent a heavy punch of pride straight into my chest. *She's back.* I almost stormed over to her to press my lips to hers with the undeniable relief I had, but her head turned at the last second, and her jaw dropped.

"Journey? What's wrong?"

"Cops."

My pulse flew as the word fell from her mouth. "What?"

I rushed past her and peered down onto the street below. There were two police cars, both coloring the street with their red and blue hues. Two men in black, with guns strapped to their sides, were on the icy stoop, talking to one of the nuns. Journey's warm body pressed up against mine, and she looked down below.

"That's Sister Elizabeth. That's probably why she left the room so quickly." There was a line of worry on her forehead. "Where is Sister Mary? She would be out there if she was here."

I shifted my jaw back and forth, grinding my teeth. The surge of endorphins from burying myself inside Journey was long gone, and now I was agitated. "Better question is why the police are here. We need to leave."

I kept my suspicions to myself because they could have been off, but I knew not to trust a man just because he wore a uniform with a shiny badge on the front. They could have been on Callum's payroll for all I knew, or another one of our enemies' payroll. And if so, then one glimpse of me and the mention of my last name, and they'd be slapping me in handcuffs and throwing me in a cell with my father.

"I have a way out," Journey said, her voice still on the brink of panic and worry. She turned on her heel and popped her thin black hood up on her head. I didn't even hide my smirk when I did the same and followed closely behind. She froze a second later, and I ran right into her back.

"Cade." She spun around, ignoring how I just trampled her over. "What if they know we burnt the hospital down? What if they're here to take me away?"

I shook my head, driving my own blazing determination into her. "I wouldn't let that happen, and they aren't here to take us anywhere. No one knows we are up here." I grabbed onto her face, brushing my thumbs over her hot cheeks. "Now, let's go."

One stern nod, and we were striding through the orphanage with quiet footsteps and leveled breathing. Once we descended down the first flight of stairs, Journey stopped at the end of the long hallway and bounced her eyes back and forth between the doors, seemingly looking for a certain one.

"Third one on the left. It's the laundry shoot."

I snapped my head to her. "The laundry shoot?"

She grabbed onto my hand. "Yeah, we're gonna go down it, and we will be in the basement, which leads to the side alley. Let's go."

I held back my question of wondering how many times she'd used this plan of escape and let her lead me through the dark hall until we both froze at the sound of footsteps. I hurriedly pushed her behind me, backing her up to the door so she could slip in, but then she darted out from under my arm and bristled at the tiny little human standing near the stairs.

"*Emerson Lynn.* What are you doing out of bed?"

The look of sleep on the little girl's face was suddenly washed away by excitement. Journey bent down low when she took off on tiny feet and wrapped her arms around Journey's neck. "Jonry! I mish you!"

There was a hand clenched around my heart, squeezing it as I stood and looked down at Journey and the little girl in their embrace. Something warm rained over me, followed by a wake of chills. *I want that,* a slippery voice said from the back of my brain, buried under uncertainty and fear. I wanted to see Journey's face light up at the sight of a little girl beaming up at her with nothing but pure love in her wide, curious eyes. I wanted to witness the moment that her guard dropped, like it just did for this little girl, and never let her put it up again.

"I miss you, too, sweetie, but you have to go back to bed, and I have to go back to school."

The softest whimper left the little girl, and I had *no* fucking idea how to be a parent, but there was an undeniable snapping in my chest that made me want to steal her from the orphanage and bring her back to St. Mary's with us.

"Can I come, pwease?"

Journey rested on the backs of her heels, wiping the little girl's face as I stood behind, unable to breathe. "No, sweetie. You have to stay, but guess what?"

The little girl hiccupped, holding her tiny teddy bear with a tight fist. "What?"

"I know that, someday soon, an amazing family is going to adopt you and spoil you rotten."

She smiled. "Can you adopt me?"

Journey let out a little laugh. "No. I'm not old enough, Emerson."

Emerson peeled her watery gaze from Journey and locked onto me. I almost stumbled backward, not wanting her glossy eyes set in my direction. I felt weird and, strangely enough, *upset?* I rubbed at my chest, trying to make the burning go away when she sniffed and said, "He looks old enough. Can't you both just take me with you?"

Thankfully, Journey stole Emerson's attention back and pleaded with her to go back to bed with fake promises that she'd come back soon. The little girl agreed, rubbing her tired eyes, and began to walk away.

"Emerson, have you seen Sister Mary?"

Emerson turned back around for a second, her face falling. "Nowpe. She has been away for a couple of dawys."

"Do you know where?"

"Nowpe. Sister Elizabef is worried."

Fuck.

Journey stood up quickly. "Okay, sweetie. Go back to bed. I love you. And don't tell anyone we were here, okay?"

She nodded. "I wove you, bye." Her tiny hand, the one that wasn't holding the teddy bear, gave me a little wave, and a smile fell to my mouth. I waved back, and when Journey turned and looked at me, a soft laugh left her.

"She's cute, isn't she?"

I blinked, confused over what the fuck just happened. There wasn't a word in the dictionary that fit what I was feeling, so all I did was nod and follow her through the door to the laundry shoot.

The room was dark and smelled of cleaning supplies. I pulled my phone out, seeing the text I had from Gemma from an hour ago that said to '*be careful wherever you two are going,*' and turned the flashlight on. Journey was bent down low, sitting on her knees in front of a square hole in the floor.

I gave her a look. "You think I'm gonna fit through that?"

She peeked up at me. "You have to. It's the only way out."

Okay, then. I guess I'm going down.

She began slipping her legs out from underneath her before I stepped forward. "Not a chance. I'm going first. I'll catch you."

I didn't give her even a brief moment to argue as I quickly bent down beside her and braced my hands on both sides of the square cutout. "As soon as you hear me land, you jump." I leaned forward, pecked her on the lips, and then squeezed my shoulders in as tightly as I could, scraping them along the wood.

My feet hit the hard floor with a loud thud, and jolting pain climbed up my spine before I shined the flashlight up the shoot, waiting for Journey. I braced myself quickly, and another second later, she was in my arms.

An exhilarated breath left her, hitting me square in the jaw. "That's so much better when someone catches you."

I chuckled, placing her on her feet, and then we were through the dark basement, passing by two washing machines, out the side door, and into the cold winter air. The cops were already gone by the time we made it to the side alley, so we nearly ran to my father's motorcycle. Journey was putting the helmet on her head when my phone buzzed.

Isaiah: Get back.

Isaiah: Now.

I typed a text back and ignored the dread sitting nice and still in my stomach.

Me: On our way. What's wrong?

I climbed onto the bike, and Journey scrambled on a second later. Before I took off and tore through the street, thankful that there was enough loose embers and gravel on the road to prevent it from being too icy, Isaiah texted me.

Isaiah: Cops are here.

"Fuck," I snapped.

I didn't answer Journey's question as I kicked us forward, and we were off to St. Mary's.

I SHUT the bike off at the gate and pushed it up against the iron rods, not even bothering to try to take it to the old cottage to push it under the tarp. We didn't have time for bullshit like that. Our footsteps were quiet as we trudged through the hard snow, trying to walk as closely to the winding lane that led to the school as we could without being in a direct line of the front doors. Journey stopped dead in her tracks as soon as we got over the billowing hill. The red and blue lights were a caution if I'd ever seen one.

"Cade." My name coming from her mouth sliced through the cool air like a whip.

"I know," I said. "Isaiah texted me."

Her wide eyes flung to mine, catching the shine of the night sky. "They're here for me."

The fear in her voice almost took me down to my knees. I felt sick, and I immediately stole my gaze from her and peered over her head at the courtyard that she had been brutally attacked in. My hands rounded in on her cheeks, her tangled hair getting caught in my fingers. "I would kill them all if they tried to take you. No one is here to get you. I promise."

Her voice was shaky, on the brink of panic. "But what if they know we burnt down the psych hospital? What if they're here to take me back to a psych ward because they think I'm actually mentally ill? What if they think I'm unstable? These are all things they have thought before. Not only did I sneak out of the place, causing a whole domino effect between everyone, but I *burnt the fucking place down!*" Her hand moved to slap against her forehead, but I caught it before it made an impact.

"Look at me." *Fucking look at me, baby.*

Her troubled gray eyes flung to mine, both glossy and fearful. "You're going to go up to your room. Shiner will walk with you. He's already waiting by the side door. I'm going to go listen to what the police want. If anything, I'll tell them I was the one to do it. So, stop worrying, okay? Please." *Because it fucking kills me to see you like this.*

Her face fell. "You can't take the blame. I was there, too."

I laughed. "I can do whatever the fuck I want. Now go."

"Cade."

My forehead fell to hers, and I breathed her in. "Go."

I could tell she wanted to protest, and I wasn't sure what went through her head, but when she heard Shiner hooting from the side door, like an owl nonetheless, she let out a shaky sigh and trudged the rest of the way up the snowy bank.

I walked the rest of the way to the front doors, passing by the bright red and blue lights flickering against the white snow, and put my cold hands in my pockets. The door was slightly ajar, and I could see that Tate had taken the police into his office, probably annoyed beyond belief that they'd shown up so late.

Most of the time, Headmaster Ellison lived in his office. Stale coffee rested in his many mugs, and he appeared disheveled nine times out of ten. He was a hard worker—I'd give him that—and he was probably closer to a father figure to me than my own felon father. But now that he had custody of Isaiah's little brother, Jack, he wasn't here as much as before. He was still packed full of shit to do, but it involved not only St. Mary's but also his family. He'd taken in a child who wasn't biologically related to him and gained two of his own children that he wasn't aware that he'd had. *Dude has his plate full.*

As soon as I crept through the door of St. Mary's, I sat on the bench out in front of his office and could hear the loud voices as if I were inside with them.

My phone buzzed, and I hoped it was Shiner, letting me know that he had gotten Journey back to her room okay, because that was one worry that wasn't far away.

Isaiah: Are you at least going to blend in so they don't see you sitting on the bench, listening to their conversation?

I gazed around the quiet entry hall, wondering where he was.

Me: Just taking a page out of your handbook. Zero fucks are given.

His chuckle echoed, and I placed my head back on the hard wall, straining my ear. Tate's voice was easy to decipher because he was near hysterics.

"You want me to wake up a teenage girl at eleven at night, hours after curfew, for what reason? This couldn't have waited until the morning? I have a child, you know. I'm a single father. He's up at the house by himself." His scoff was so loud it was as if I was beside him.

"This is a pressing issue."

Pressing issue?

"We couldn't risk waiting until the morning."

The creaking of Tate's chair echoed, and my phone buzzed again.

Shiner: Your girl just pulled a fucking knife on me because I told her she had to go back to her room. Why do you and Isaiah both have such bossy girls? Jesus.

A second later.

Shiner: It was kinda hot, though.

My fingers moved quickly.

Me: Where the fuck is she?

The tapping of my leg was quiet, but a nervous jitter was tingling all my limbs. *Journey. Journey. Journey.* Maybe I should punish her later. My dick jumped, but my mind quickly climbed itself out of the gutter when I spotted her slinking down the hallway, dressed in her usual black get-up.

My head shook, and I ignored the text that I was sure was from Isaiah as Journey came and sat down beside me. Isaiah popped out of the shadows a second later.

"Go back to your room," I whisper-seethed.

"I'm not letting you take the blame for it."

Tate's voice rose, and Isaiah bent down in front of Journey's face. "We have pull; you don't. Listen to Cade and go back to your room."

"No."

He rolled his eyes. "Goddamnit. You *are* just like Gemma."

"I take that as a compliment, thank you."

We all fell silent when a deep voice—one I hadn't heard yet—clamored through the room. "We just need to ask her some questions!"

Tate's chair squeaked. "Again, at eleven on a school night?

I don't think so. Not unless you give me a good enough reason. The girl has been through a lot lately."

Journey shifted beside me. My hand fell to her thigh, and her palm fell on top.

"Jesus, just tell him, Mark. It's not like it's a secret. Enough with the fucking power play." There was a beat of silence, but then the same man spoke up again. "We're here to question her about Sister Mary. She runs the—"

"The orphanage. Yes, I know who she is."

Journey's hand tightened on mine, and I flicked my eyes to Isaiah who was staring at me. There was a quick dooming feeling deep in my gut, and over the years, I'd learned to listen to it. Something wasn't right.

"You're familiar with her? When was the last time you've spoken to her?"

"Just a few weeks ago, when Journey started attending our school again. Why? Is something wrong?"

I held my breath, angling my head toward the door for a better listen.

"Yes. She is missing."

Already suspected that.

"And you think Journey knows where she is? Why do you think that?"

"The other nuns led us here. They said Journey and Sister Mary were close. We're hoping she can lead us in the right direction. There was blood at the scene. We believe that Sister Mary is in grave danger, and the Catholic Church is very, *very* concerned." There was a long, heavy pause, and then, before I knew it, Journey was flying past me and running into Headmaster Ellison's office with Isaiah and me trailing closely behind.

CHAPTER TWENTY-EIGHT

JOURNEY

THERE WAS *blood at the scene.*

Blood. Blood. Blood. The last thing I remembered was glancing down to my covered arms, seeing the blood of my cut skin as if I had been transferred back in time, but then somehow, I was standing in the middle of Headmaster Ellison's office with two police officers staring at me with stunned expressions.

"Journey?" Headmaster Ellison flew from his chair, but I was too blinded by my impulsiveness to say anything. *Why did I run in here?!* There were two tall, warm figures beside me, and I knew that Cade and Isaiah had followed me through the door.

Isaiah cleared his throat as Cade moved in closer to me. "I went and fetched Journey for you, Headmaster Ellison." He looked at the officers, and then he sighed impatiently, as if they were stupid. "I have student duty tonight—being head boy and all." *Head boy? What the hell does that mean?* Isaiah lazily took a seat in one of the empty chairs that neither officer sat in.

Headmaster Ellison slowly sank down in his old, creaky chair and smoothed out his features. "Oh, yes. Thank you, Isaiah." Then, he waved his hand out to the officers. "Here is Journey. Ask her what you need so she can get back to bed." My cheeks flamed as all three men took in my appearance and then moved to Cade's.

What? Maybe I like to sleep in black skinny jeans and a black hoodie. Whatever.

As soon as the taller of the two flipped open his little spiral notebook, I was suddenly back to what I'd just heard come from his mouth a second ago. *Blood.* "When was the last time you have seen or spoken to Sister Mary, Journey?"

I swallowed, crossing my arms over my chest in an unconscious way to protect myself.

"The last day I spoke to her was the day I came here. I don't have a cell phone, so I can't call her or anything." *What happened to her? Where is she?*

I knew, deep down, it had something to do with me.

My throat began to close, and the room started to dance in front of my eyes. A hefty breath squeezed past the tightening of my neck, and I felt Cade's shoulder brush over mine. *I'm here.* That was his way of telling me I wasn't alone.

"I heard what you said a few minutes ago," I started, not caring that they were supposed to be asking me questions and not the other way around. "Where did you find blood? Do you have any leads at all?"

The other officer leaned forward with a crease in between his wrinkled brows. "Are you sure you haven't spoken to her? I find it strange that the other nuns told us to talk to you. Do you know about something that Sister Mary was involved in?"

Only to keep me safe. My stomach was heavy, like I'd swallowed an anchor. My hair fell forward, and I had to keep my attention plastered to my boots so I didn't let the tears slip over my cheeks. *There was blood.* I pictured Sister Mary's warm smile and rosy cheeks. Would she have given up her life to protect me? My wobbling chin slowly raised. I looked at Headmaster Ellison, and as my mouth opened, his eyes widened. It wasn't *that* noticeable, but I saw the most subtle shake of his head, and I paused.

That was when Isaiah stepped forward, and Cade pulled me back by my hand.

"She knows nothing. She's been at a psych ward for months, and now she's here without a way to even communicate with Sister Mary. Sister Mary, as far as Journey or any of us know, wasn't involved in anything suspicious."

"Are you her spokesperson now?" the officer asked, crossing his arms. My eyes flew down to his black pistol, and the room was beginning to close in on us. My guard had dropped slightly since coming back to St. Mary's. Cade was like a fine layer of protection, and my jaded trust had been slightly repaired with his warm touches and comforting words. But standing here, looking at two men who weren't believing a word we said, pushed me right back into my untrusting self as if I were back at the Covenant Psych Hospital.

Headmaster Ellison stood up from his desk, causing the attention to shift to him. "Listen, if we hear of anything or Sister Mary contacts Journey, we will give you guys a call. Yes? Does that work?"

Silence filled the room, and all I could hear was the repetition of the word *blood* in my head. What if they cut her wrists, too? What if they killed her? And who the hell were *they*?

"Breathe," Cade whispered as he turned his head. He pulled me farther to the door, and the last thing I saw was the officer putting his notebook away, and then I somehow ended up in my room with Cade peeling my clothes off me and pulling my purple sleep shirt over my head.

His lips gracefully touched the tip of my nose, and he pulled me over to my bed. "Come on, let's get some rest."

Cade's boots were kicked off, and the next thing I knew, I was wrapped up in his warm embrace with my head resting over his steady heartbeat. Goosebumps rushed to the surface as the pad of his finger brushed over the long scar on my arm.

"Just breathe," he whispered, and I did. I took several gulps of air, trying to allow my throat to open for oxygen.

"Cade?" I asked, several minutes later.

"Yeah?" His voice was hoarse, like he had been sleeping.

"Why did you and Isaiah step forward when they asked if I knew anything? Does Isaiah know that someone attacked me?" I paused, replaying the whole thing over in my head. "Does the headmaster?"

His tight chest expanded, and I turned my head and looked up at him. His full lips were flattened, and I had my answer.

"Do you guys know something that I don't?"

I was almost too afraid to know the answer, but Cade's stormy gaze flew down to mine.

"No, and that's why we're all on edge. I don't trust many people, and I take my leads from Isaiah. He didn't trust them either."

I snuggled back into Cade's chest and wrapped my leg over his. I hated that the world was such a corrupt place. I hated that I had been sheltered at the orphanage, not knowing that there was a threat on my life, and all I wanted was to be adopted to get away from it. Regret was a heavy dose of reality, and I was ashamed. But most of all, I hated that I didn't know what safety was until it was ripped away from me.

THE DAYS PASSED without any news of Sister Mary, and more snow had come, seeming to close down everything. The lacrosse game was rescheduled, and most of the student body was out on the field, having snowball fights, building snowmen, and sledding on whatever they could get their hands on. But instead of having fun out on the field, I found myself in the common room with the Rebels, Tobias—who would rather chop his arm off than place himself in such a group— and the only few girls that I trusted.

Sloane's legs were resting on my lap as I buried my nose in a book, sneaking glances at Cade as he stood near the bookshelf with Isaiah and Brantley, all three looking more secretive than usual.

Cade and I had fallen into a good routine since our midnight adventure. We'd spend time in the library in the evenings after he had practice, in my favorite aisle, pretending the subtle touches of his fingers brushing over my hand didn't actually send blood rushing to both of our hearts. Then, after lights went out and he saw me to my room safely, he'd sneak back in, and from there, we'd pretend that the past was nothing more than the past and that I wasn't walking around with a target on my back. Things *felt* normal, but they were anything but.

"I have an idea for tonight," Sloane mused, crossing her legs at the ankle over my lap. I peered over at her and tucked my hair behind my ear. Gemma and Tobias were both sitting on the floor, talking about something secretive, but she still took the bait.

"For the claiming?" she asked, looking up at Sloane.

Sloane nodded, and the smile on her face was mischievous. "Let's kick it up a notch." She sat up a little taller. "Hey, Rebels. Get over here."

Isaiah's eyes fell to Gemma automatically and Cade's to mine. Brantley rolled his eyes, and Shiner popped out from behind the other bookshelf, looking flushed in the cheeks. I dropped my eyes and saw the tips of two Converse hiding behind the shelf and glanced around to see if anyone else had noticed that there was a girl back there with him. Either no one noticed, or they didn't care.

"What do you want, Sloane?" Brantley always seemed so bored with life. Irritation flickered over his sharp features.

There was a faint growl from below that I'd heard a time or two before, and my jaw almost fell when I saw Tobias, the boy who showed *zero* emotion, glaring up at Brantley like he was ready to snap his neck. *What is that all about?*

Sloane ignored Brantley, completely unfazed by his attitude. "I have an idea for tonight's claiming. What if we play the color game?"

"What the fuck is the color game?"

A faint laugh escaped my mouth, and everyone looked over at me, making my cheeks flame. Why did feeling even a sliver of happiness make me feel guilty? I knew the answer. It was because Sister Mary was missing. It was because I was supposed to come back to St. Mary's and push everyone away until I found out who had tried to kill me. I was supposed to be a one-woman show, and here I was, surrounded by the same group of friends I had been torn away from with my heart beating wildly for the boy who was grinning down at me.

"Um..." I started, letting my smile fall. "If it's anything like the game we used to play before I...left...it's where you're basically matched with the person who is wearing the same color as you."

"Wait, what?" Cade asked, brows crowding as he looked down at me.

Sloane laughed under her breath as I cringed inwardly.

"The first time you and I..." *Why is it so quiet in here?* "At the claiming..."

"Did you only want me to claim you because we were wearing the same...color? Did you know it was me that first time?"

Gemma laughed quietly under her breath, and I was suddenly sweating.

Shiner threw his head back and laughed. "Aw, our poor Cade-boy thought Journey wanted him to fuck her because of love at first sight."

There was a sudden grunt followed by choppy laughter from Shiner as Cade punched him in the stomach.

"Okay, so let me get this straight." Everyone but Sloane turned to Tobias, who rarely ever spoke. Her entire body tensed, and she looked in the complete opposite direction of him. "First off, Gemma better not have been involved in this slutty game because fuck."

She rolled her eyes and smacked his shoulder. "Shut up."

"Secondly, you two and the other one...the car girl..."

"You mean Mercedes?" I asked, and Tobias nodded. *Wait, where is Mercedes?* I subtly moved my gaze from Tobias and stared at Shiner, who had a blank expression. *And I now know who those shoes belong to.*

"Yeah, so you three decided one time that you were going to play the color game, and whatever guy matched the color you were wearing, without even knowing it, was who you were going to get to fuck you?"

"What's it to you, Tobias?" Sloane's cheery voice was long gone. "Jealous?"

"Of your slutty behavior? No."

"Tobias!" Gemma smacked her brother's chest again, which didn't even gain a look from him. He was in total lock-down with Sloane, and I made a mental note to ask him what was going on there. There weren't many things that got a rise out of Tobias. I'd been so wrapped up in my own shit that I didn't even think to ask him what was going on with him, and I knew better than to ask Sloane. She kept her secrets to herself. That was why she seemed to understand me the most.

"Anywaaay," Sloane said, dragging out the word. "Are you guys up for it? Where's Mica? Can he send out a mass text about the rules for tonight?"

"Hell yeah. I'll give him the deets." Shiner clapped his hands excitedly and rushed off through the common-room door.

"So," Cade mused as he took a seat beside me. Sloane's feet were on both of our laps now, which she didn't even seem to notice. "What color are you wearing?"

The guilt was back just thinking about going to the claiming tonight to *have fun*. My chest ached with regret, and the uncertainties of Sister Mary missing made my throat close. *Is it my fault?*

"Don't do that," he whispered, bringing his face closer to mine. His arm rested behind my head, and his fingers fell to my hair. "There is nothing you can do."

"It doesn't feel right to just..."

"To what?" he asked, interrupting me. "Not stay in your room all night with your bodyguard?"

A laugh slipped from me. "Is that what you're calling yourself now? My bodyguard?"

His dimple appeared, and I locked onto it, feeling the cold make way for the warmth.

"Listen," he suddenly grew serious. "Isaiah is calling in a favor to his older brother, who's in the FBI. He's gonna look into Sister Mary and try to connect some dots for you. He's going to see if he can find anything out about you."

I perked up a little. "How? My identity is...vacant. I'm Journey Smith. That's all anyone knows."

Cade's hand fell to the back of my head, and he brought

our foreheads together, and it was as if he and I were the only two that existed. St. Mary's no longer breathed, there was no one else in the room, and neither the past nor the future broke through the moment. It was *just* us. "There is *nothing* either of us can do right now other than just *be*."

A shaky breath left me, and I nodded against him only to pull back at the sound of Tobias' scoff from his sister's question. "It doesn't matter what color I'm wearing. No one here is worth my time."

Sloane grumbled under her breath. "As if anyone would want to crawl in bed with you." Then, she turned on her lively voice. "I'm gonna wear black. I'm feeling a little *edgy* tonight."

"Oh, shit!" Shiner bellowed as he walked back in the room. "It's on, baby!"

Everyone laughed as I snuggled into Cade's side, still wondering where Sister Mary was.

CHAPTER TWENTY-NINE

JOURNEY

"I SWEAR, they make us come to the party last every time. Do you guys realize that?" Mercedes laughed under her breath, fluffing up her hair. Sloane, Gemma, Mercedes, and I all squeezed into Gemma and Sloane's room to get ready for the party. Sloane and I were both wearing black, but our outfits couldn't have been more different.

I had on my black skinny jeans, my old Converse, and a black tank that Sloane threw at me after I showed up in my hoodie—the usual. She was showing off more skin by wearing a short black dress and some black Doc Martens. Her makeup was sleek and dark, and it made her a total smoke show. I wasn't sure who she had her eye on, but whoever it was, was in for it.

"Rainbow?" Sloane asked, glancing at Gemma. "Why so many colors?"

Gemma laughed, tightening her ponytail. "Because Isaiah and I didn't discuss what color we were wearing. I just told him he better match me, so I wore every color."

"You guys are so cute it's annoying." That was from Mercedes. She was wearing a light-blue crop top with a leather skirt, which looked pretty against her tan skin and unruly dark hair. I would bet my life on it that Shiner showed up wearing light blue, too.

We all stopped talking as we descended down the stairs one by one, each of us grabbing onto the intricate handrail. It was quiet, and my heart started to skip with the reality that I continued to push away for the night.

I paused, one foot on the step in front of me. "Oh, shit," I rushed out. *My knife.* My anxiety kicked up a notch as I glanced at the scars on my arms.

"What's wrong?" Sloane asked. Gemma was right beside her, looking hesitant.

"Um..." *I can't tell them that I carry a knife around, can I?* "I forgot something in my room. You guys go ahead. I'll catch up."

"Are you sure?" Sloane asked, knowing more than the rest of the girls. Her eyes squinted, and her black, winged eyeliner momentarily disappeared. "We can wait."

"And risk getting caught by the duty teacher?" I shook my head. "I'll be fine. I promise. Trust me, I know how to sneak around. I did it plenty at the psych ward."

There was a strange sort of silence that fell upon the four of us. If I listened hard enough, I bet I could hear the snowflakes hitting the icy ground outside the windows of St. Mary's. There were times where I thought we all forgot that I had been stripped away from this place and thrown into a psychiatric unit and that there were *still* rumors floating around about me that were no more than saying that I belonged in a padded room.

But the truth was, time had passed. We were all different, and we all had secrets.

"Okay, only if you're sure." That was from Gemma, and I

gave her a quick nod, turned around, and began walking quickly to my room to snag my knife. I didn't necessarily think I needed it right this moment, but I also hadn't thought someone would try to kill me out in the courtyard several months ago, so there was that.

As soon as the blade hit my palm, I breathed out a sigh of relief. I felt powerful again, and a little less on edge. There was always an inkling within reach as I moved around quietly, rounding corners and peering in the dark crevices that only housed spiders and their webs, but that inkling didn't feel as eerie with a sharp knife in my hand. I felt like I was a little more invisible than before—although, I knew that wasn't true.

No more than a second after I shoved the knife in my back pocket and turned the corner of the last hall, chills raced down my spine, clinging to every curved bone. My arms grew cold, and my scars tingled. I had my eyes set on the heavy door that led to the bottom of St. Mary's, but it suddenly looked *very* far away.

When I took a step forward, I knew I should have listened to my intuition. A hand snaked around my waist, and I gasped, flinging around quickly in his grasp. *Please be Cade.*

"Well, if it isn't my lucky day," the voice said, deep and grumbly, muffled by the thick cotton covering his face.

Not again.

My only reaction should have been to fight him. I should have reached in my pocket, grabbed the handle of the knife that Cade gave me, and stabbed the fuck out of him like Tobias taught me to do, but instead, I felt my brows dip and my rationality slip away. "Who are you?" I asked. "Are you the one who tried to kill me?"

I wiggled, pushing down on his strong arms that had multiple tiny scars on them, as if he'd been hit with exploding pieces of glass at some point. "Kill you? I'm here to take you."

My heart hammered, and I began to gasp like I was drowning as the reality of the situation I was in made its way to the forefront of my brain. *Run.* The scream that was lodged in my chest finally tore out of my throat like a wolf howling in the night. His grip tightened, and one hand flew to my mouth as my nails dug into his skin, tearing at his flesh. The hallway was dark, but I still wanted nothing more than to rip his mask off. I didn't, though, because I knew that if I didn't act quickly and use the element of surprise, he'd win. Men were bigger than me—it was as plain and simple as that—and this was *definitely* a man. His voice was deep, and his hands had been worked and worked over the years. Scars littered his skin, and he was taller than most.

You have to strike fast and use your specific skills, Journey. You're tiny and quick. Use that. Tobias' hushed voice lingered in the air around me as I was thrust back into reality with my head spinning from the lack of oxygen that the man was stealing. His elbow dug into my windpipe as his hand covered my last scream.

No.

"I should have known you'd fight back. After all, you are half of her."

Anger festered in my core. I knew that he was referring to my mother, and it had my knee swinging upward, colliding with his groin. His head came down swiftly and knocked my lip into my teeth, coating my mouth with blood. *Get to the basement, get to the basement, get to the basement.* My hand dug into my jeans as the man groaned, and I gripped the knife tightly, pulling it in its sheath out from the denim. He was quick, but he *was* surprised that I had fought back. *If I can just get out of his grasp, I can make it.*

Curse words littered from his mouth as he recovered, and

he quickly joined my hands in one of his, and then something strong and painful bit into my wrists. *He can't see the knife.* Since my hands were bundled together in what I thought was a zip tie, my knife was camouflaged in between both palms. I kept my head level and fought the panic as his two strong hands squeezed my bare arms so tightly I screamed out again. *Where is the duty teacher?* I peered behind the man as he swayed in front of me, showing me that my vision was a little muddled from either panic or from the blow of his head onto mine. It didn't deter me from wiggling the knife between my palms and letting the sheath fall to the floor, though. My hand stung as the sharp blade wiggled the rest of the way down, but as soon as I saw the sheen of metal, I planted my feet as firmly as I could, only letting him drag me a little farther. When he turned around, I didn't give him a chance to say anything. I jammed the knife into his belly and watched as shock hindered his movements.

His hands fell, and my knife came next. It clamored to the ground, sounding as if the metal had shattered against the black-and-white tile. I wasted no time turning around and running straight for the basement. I wanted to yell for help, but I kept my mouth shut because I was too afraid I'd lead him right to me.

"Fuck, fuck, fuck," I cried out in a whisper, feeling the hot tears streaming down my cheeks. It didn't matter how mentally prepared you were for something like this to happen, it still shocked you to the core. My hands were shaking, and I smashed my lips together to keep a sob inside as my bloody hands slipped on the doorknob. I used both of them, grasping it as tightly as I could, even if my wrists were raw, and my hand was burning.

The second the latch popped, I felt the relief hit me from behind that kept my feet plowing through the cool, damp puddles beneath my shoes. It was dark in the passageway, and

I bumped into the wall a few times, my shoulder instantly feeling bruised. Choppy sobs echoed around me as I realized I no longer felt safe, and I no longer felt confident enough to deal with this on my own. I had to stop pretending that I could. There was nothing quite like being attacked again to bring up old memories and hidden vulnerabilities.

The second the door for the claiming party was in front of my face, I ran right for it. There was no music thumping on the other side like usual, and my hands slipped on the doorknob before it was suddenly whipped open, and I fell to my knees.

A scream of pain left me, and the room went silent.

CHAPTER THIRTY

CADE

"WHAT DO you mean she went back to her room?" I was stunned in disbelief as my mind raced. My back was against the wall seconds ago as I watched Shiner guzzle three shots, and then, suddenly, I was up in the girls' faces like a rabid animal, looking for Journey.

I snapped my attention to the far corner of the room, knowing that Bain usually took that spot at these parties, and although he was there, surrounded by a few of his friends, I still didn't feel relieved.

I don't like that she's alone. Why wouldn't she take someone with her?

"She was pretty persistent that we didn't go with her. Is there something going on that we should know?" Gemma asked, shooting Isaiah a harsh glare. "Secrets get people hurt. You guys know this!"

"You know what we know, babe. And look"—Isaiah nodded his head to where Bain was standing—"Bain is right there."

"Why didn't you go with her anyway?" I asked, voice slowly rising to panic mode.

Gemma gasped in frustration, crossing her arms over her bright shirt. "What did you want me to say? Oh, hey, I know that there is a threat on your life and that someone tried to kill you, but I'm not really supposed to know that, but I do, so..." She threw her hands up. "She already has trust issues! I didn't want to cause any problems."

"This isn't Gemma's fault, Cade. Back the fuck off."

Tobias lazily stepped forward, pushing past a quiet Sloane. "I've taught her how to stab someone. She'll be okay if it comes down to it. Trust me."

Yeah, I fucking know. She almost stabbed me.

I ran my hands through my messy hair. "You're right. It's not Gemma's fault. It's mine." If it were up to me, I would have been with Journey every second of every single day, but I knew that I needed to give her space, too. Journey had been on her own for all of her life, and I knew, deep down, she was a fighter by nature and as independent as they came. Being overbearing wasn't something I wanted to become to her, but standing here, looking around the room full of my peers and not seeing her face, only set my heart racing—and not in the fucking good way.

I was about to become Journey's fucking shadow, whether she liked it or not.

Make stupid choices, like walking alone in the place that you had once gotten attacked, and you get the consequences.

The music had been cut off as the Rebels grew alert, sensing that something was wrong. My teeth were grinding together as I passed by a group of girls who eyed me like I wasn't going to be spending the party with Journey. I ignored every last one of them and pulled heavily on the door.

I leaned forward until I saw a flash of black whoosh in

front of my eyes, landing in a heaping pile at my feet. I knew it was her without even looking down.

"Journey." The word came out as a hoarse whisper, my breath sucked right out of my fucking lungs.

My knees hit the dirty floor, and her wet, gray eyes peered up at me from below, sending my soul straight to hell. *They are fucking dead.*

"I didn't try to kill myself! I didn't cut myself! Cade, do not let anyone twist this like last time! I didn't do it! I promise. I didn't do it!"

My shaky hands clamped down over her wet cheeks, feeling her chin wobble with rattling fear. I zeroed in on the blood on her mouth, coating those perfect bow-shaped lips. I convulsed on the inside, a raging need to kill someone sending me into blind action. "Where are you hurt?"

Her head shook, and her eyes squeezed shut. That was when I glanced down and saw the red, sticky blood all over her hands and wrists. The white zip tie was stained pink, and I had to focus to keep myself level with the raging beat of my heart on the inside. *Dead. Dead. Dead.*

"Jesus." I looked over my shoulder, and all three Rebels were standing behind me, eyes narrowed and jaws clenched. The girls were bent down beside me, and I had no idea how or when they'd gotten there.

Then, a knife was flicked out, and Tobias gathered Journey's hands in his and cut the zip tie, making her cry out. Her head hit my chest, and a sob erupted. The whispers around us cut through her cry, sounding like the pages of a book flipping in every corner of this room.

"Where else are you hurt?"

"It's mostly his," she choked, pulling back from my chest. "I stabbed him."

"So, it's a him?"

My head nearly fell off my shoulders as I snapped my

attention to the one voice that completely had me unraveling. "Did you have something to do with this?" I asked, focusing on not squeezing Journey's face with my anger for Bain. His jaw was steely, but it would look a fuck-ton better with my fist slamming into it.

"No." He was quiet, looking down at Journey. "We need a description, Journey. Was he tall? Big? Did you see his face? Anything?"

Brantley's tone was edged with anger. "What the fuck is going on? Now you're working *with* us?"

I stayed silent as Isaiah barked out orders. "It doesn't fucking matter. Shiner, take the girls to Tate's. Everyone else stays here until we say so. This is Rebel business, and if any of you go tell your parents or the faculty about this, consider yourself kicked out of this school. You all know the rumors. Consider them true. This is not something to fuck around with."

I couldn't leave Journey, but at the same time, this needed to be dealt with, and I would stop at *nothing* to hunt down the person who did this to her. Killing was the one crime I never wanted to commit, because it was the one crime I was *supposed* to commit, but seeing Journey like this? I was ready to be what dear ol' Daddy wanted.

"Baby." I grabbed onto her face and brought our foreheads together. She had stopped crying, but she was still sitting in the exact spot on the dirty floor with her knees tucked under her and her bloody hands bundled in her lap. "Stay with the girls and do what Shiner says. We're searching the school."

"I stabbed him in the stomach," she said, bouncing her glossy and suddenly tired eyes back and forth between mine. Then, she glanced up to Bain. "He was tall, broad-shouldered, wearing all black. He had a mask." I felt the wind of Gemma's head moving up to look at Bain. I knew why she was looking up at him. She remembered someone wearing a mask back when she was at the Covens. "His voice was deep. Scars on his arms."

"What kind of scars?" I asked, blood pumping through my body like the rapids. My skin felt hot and sticky.

"Small knicks. Like glass had hit him or something. I don't know. He said he wasn't here to kill me, but he was here to take me."

"Take you?" The thought of someone taking her from me pulled me to my feet. I spun around, not even bothering to mind that Bain was interested in helping, and pinched the bridge of my nose.

The girls were helping Journey to her feet, and Shiner had taken the lead with the four of them. Before they walked through the door, I turned around and said her name. She peered over her shoulder at me as I began walking toward her, and I grabbed onto her arm, quickly twisting her body to mine. I gave her a kiss right on her blood-stained mouth. It wasn't a normal kiss. This was a kiss that was filled with an unyielding amount of emotion. A kiss that ripped from my soul and had silent words attached to it. When she pulled back, I swore the room had emptied. I wiped her blood from my mouth, tasting her sweetness filled with the tang of metallic. "I love you," I said, feeling the burn as my heart caught on fire.

Journey's chin wobbled again, and she nodded, a croak of a whisper leaving her. "I love you, too."

And then, she was through the door, and I was turning around with a sick feeling in my gut. "Let's go."

———

THE SCHOOL WAS as quiet as it usually was. It breathed in the dark like it was its only source of oxygen and breathed out a sinister feeling that crept behind my back with every turn I took. The Rebels, along with Tobias, split up, but Bain wasn't far from my eyesight because I didn't trust him.

The pair of us stood inches away from the spot that Journey was attacked in, and we knew this because there was blood on the floor and a trail that had mysteriously stopped halfway through the entryway.

Isaiah's voice echoed through the expansive hall as he talked to the headmaster on the phone. The Rebels and I were jaded when it came to the authorities, so the police were a no-go. We only trusted a select few. We'd learned long ago that some officers were easily paid off, and their handlers weren't on the right side of the line between morally ethical and downright immoral—our fathers being a few of them. I checked out of the conversation when they began talking about the security system Headmaster Ellison was trying to get approved by the SMC.

"You gonna tell me why you're obsessed with my girl?" I kept my head down, staring at the dark-red blood on the floor, inches from my black Vans.

"Not obsessed," Bain answered in a short tone, his words clipped with irritation.

I huffed out a sarcastic laugh. "Oh. My mistake. Someone who takes photos of a girl without her knowledge, stares at her every second of the day, suddenly volunteers to find the person who attacked her—even though he has never once lifted a finger for the right cause before—doesn't indicate that at all, does it?"

"Mind your own fucking business," he said, bending down to inspect the blood, as if he could test the fucking DNA with his fingers.

My foot ached to kick him right in the stomach, but at the last second, he stood up, and we stared at each other as if we were about to throw down. "She is my business, so stay away from her, Bain. I don't know your fucking angle, but I don't like it."

"Calm the fuck down. If you're worried about me stealing your girl, I won't."

"And I bet you didn't give me all those threats before she was taken last time, did you?"

I watched him very closely. His body language. His face. His words ran a circle through my head as I inspected every last syllable. There was the smallest flicker of annoyance there, resting over his blank face. *It was him, wasn't it?*

My foot stepped forward, my eyes flaring. "Did you do it?"

"Did I do what?"

I don't have time for these fucking games.

"Are you trying to protect Journey or get rid of her like you tried to do with Gemma?"

He laughed, a sick smile sliding onto his face. My fist clenched by my side. "Why don't you just worry about protecting her yourself, and then the rest won't matter, right?" He shrugged. "I mean, you didn't protect her last time, or while she was stuck inside a psych ward with men like Richard Stallard, but third time's a charm, yeah?"

My hand was around his neck, but he didn't fight back. His smile grew wider, and the thing with men like Bain? They had nothing to live for. They had nothing to fight for. There was no heavy desperation laying behind every move they made, causing them to act irrationally and out of instinct. Men like Bain weren't driven by self-sacrifice or noble character. They didn't become devoted to another person like I was to Journey, and that made them unpredictable and untrustworthy.

"Cade," Brantley's gruff voice hit the back of my skull, but I squeezed Bain's throat tighter.

"I will fucking kill you if I find out you did something to

her." My hand dropped, and he gasped, the sick smile still on his face.

"We'll see," he said before walking past Brantley and me with red marks around his neck. I glowered as he walked to the stairs and disappeared up them, heading to the dorms. I would have followed him if Journey was up there, but I knew she was with Shiner and the rest of the girls at the headmaster's house.

"School is clear," Brantley said, ignoring my furious gaze that was still glued to the stairs. "Whoever it was left on foot."

I finally looked over at him. "Are there footprints in the snow?"

Just as I asked the question, Tobias walked in with snow-covered shoes with Isaiah walking closely behind, still on the phone with Tate.

"They disappeared. There were tire tracks down by the bottom of the gate. They're gone for the night."

For the night.

"I got it," Isaiah said into the phone before finishing with, "By the way, whoever has duty tonight fucking sucks at their job. An actual assault happened, and they're nowhere to be found."

Then, he clicked end on the call and pushed his cell phone into his pocket.

"Come on, let's go get our girls. I'll fill you in on what Jacobi has found out, too."

I nodded and followed after him with my hope low and my suspicions high.

CHAPTER THIRTY-ONE

JOURNEY

THE HEADMASTER'S house was nothing like I'd imagined and everything that I'd hoped for when I was a young child. It was bigger than I had suspected, with a long hall on the second floor that housed the bedrooms and two bathrooms. Every door was shut, but I saw a blue light shining underneath one of them, and I assumed that was Jack's bedroom.

Jack was Isaiah's little brother, and although the headmaster and Isaiah weren't related, they had grown up thinking he was their uncle. Jack had no one else to live with when Isaiah's father went to prison, thus ending up here, and I had to say it: the kid lucked out.

"Girls," the headmaster started, looking more weary than usual. He was wearing dark-gray athletic sweats with a black t-shirt, making him appear so much younger than I had always thought him to be. There was no loose tie around his neck or coffee-stained mug in his hand. He wasn't perched behind his messy desk in his half-lit office. Instead, he looked youthful and spoke warmly. He was concerned about my injuries as

Gemma kept a warm rag pressed to my busted lip. There was another wet rag wrapped around my hand that he kept looking down at, and I was afraid that he thought I had made it up like the last time I was attacked. *Does he think I'm lying?*

Before he could say anything else, the panic got the best of me. "I didn't do this, Headmaster Ellison."

He was taken aback, shock flickering over the shadows of his face. He walked toward me as I sat on the edge of the chest propped at the end of the full-size bed of what I assumed was a guest room. "Journey," he whispered, bending down low and placing his forearms over his bent knees. "I know. You're safe here, okay?"

I wasn't sure what I was more worried about: someone trying to kidnap me or Headmaster Ellison thinking I tried to hurt myself again and sending me away. Cade's face popped into my head, and my heart squeezed. Would I be feeling so worried about leaving here if it weren't for him? To think, I came back to St. Mary's after running away from a corrupt psych ward with a vendetta against everyone, not trusting a single soul, and now I was surrounded by a kind man who was obviously worried about me, friends who were trying to tend to my wounds, and the Rebels who were currently out for blood.

Maybe *I* was the lucky one here.

"I do have a favor to ask," the headmaster said, slowly standing up and backing away from me. Gemma moved in closer and peeked at my hand, which was still bleeding a little. "I don't want you telling anyone what happened."

Sloane stepped forward. "Headmaster Elllison, I think that ship has sailed. Just about every student saw Journey."

His eyebrow flicked upward. "And what exactly were you all doing together after curfew?" His attention bounced to each of our outfits, landing on Gemma in particular.

"Don't pretend that you don't know we have the occasional get-together after curfew, Dad."

The surprise on Headmaster Ellison's face was plain as day. His mouth opened, his jaw slacked, and then he clenched it back shut and crossed his arms. "You only called me Dad to sweeten me up, didn't you?"

A small smile, that wasn't anywhere close to being fake, crept onto Gemma's face. "Yes *and* no. Don't make a big deal out of it." Her cheeks blushed. "Or else I won't call you Dad again."

There was something so light and airy about their conversation that I had forgotten that I had just been attacked.

"But also, guess what? Tobias came."

"He did?" The headmaster leaned back on the wall beside the door, peeking out into the hall for a second. "That's a first, right? I knew that having Sloane be his student aide would be a good idea."

Sloane crossed her arms over her skimpy outfit. "What does this have to do with me?"

There were a few sounds from somewhere in the house that had me climbing to my feet quickly, reaching for my knife, which was no longer with me. *I dropped it.* There was an emotional kick to my stomach, and I suddenly felt stupid. *Why do I want to cry?*

The metallic taste from earlier, that had since left, was back as I tried to right my vision.

"It's just Isaiah and Cade," Gemma whispered, looking at my tense stance. Just as my shoulders dropped and Mercedes squeezed my uninjured hand, a clomping of heavy footsteps grew louder, and then my heart picked itself up off the floor when I stared into a pair of warm yet worried eyes.

"Hey," Cade said, moving past the headmaster and bending down to be level with me. My legs spread open to let him in closer, and a wave of exhaustion hit me like a ton of bricks. "You okay?"

No. "Yeah."

"No, idiot. She isn't okay." That came from Sloane, but Cade didn't even bat an eyelash.

Headmaster Ellison cleared his throat. "Okay, listen. I don't want this spreading around the school. The SMC is already on edge about Journey being back, and if they get wind that someone from the outside came in and attacked her? They will do one of two things."

My body tensed, waiting for the worst of it.

"They'll either send her away, claiming that the rest of the students aren't safe with her being here, or they'll shut down the school."

"Shut down the school?" Mercedes asked.

"That's if they even believe that I was attacked," I whispered, feeling the vulnerability cover me like a heavy blanket.

I heard the grinding of Cade's jaw without even looking up. The headmaster pushed off the wall and crossed his arms. "Isaiah, I want you threatening everyone that saw Journey, and tell them that I will personally tell each of their parents that they were caught after curfew—at a sex party, nonetheless."

Isaiah laughed, and Gemma smacked his stomach. "Hearing you say that is hilarious. But you've got it. We've already threatened them. No one will risk getting in trouble. The SMC has been a little bitch lately, huh?" He glanced at Mercedes. "No offense. I know your parents are on the committee."

She shrugged. "None taken."

Just as the headmaster explained that everyone needed to get back to the school so word didn't get around that a bunch of students were hanging out at his house after curfew, Shiner walked back into the room holding an entire bag of chips in his hand.

"Did you guys find anyone?" he asked, acting like he owned the place. "There was nothing suspicious when I walked the girls up here. I did a perimeter check of the house, too. Nothing out of the ordinary."

The headmaster stole the bag of chips from Shiner's hand, and he huffed, licking his fingers.

"Alright, everyone out, except for Journey. I would like a word alone with her."

Just as everyone began to shuffle toward the door, I surprised myself. "No."

"No?" Cade repeated, looking down at me. His head tilted, wanting me to explain.

I shrugged, squeezing my hand tight around the wet rag. "If you are all risking your lives by searching the school and escorting me through freezing temperatures, I think it's okay for you to know what's really going on."

Silence followed my profound words that felt confident coming from my mouth, but after looking at everyone's faces, I dropped my shoulders. "You guys already know, don't you?"

"Not everything," Gemma was quick to say. "But we do know that you're in danger, and trust me when I say, I've been there."

The headmaster waited a few seconds before rubbing a hand over his scruffy face. "All I really wanted to do was say I was sorry."

"Sorry?" Cade asked. "For?"

The headmaster didn't stop staring at me. "I told you that you were safe here, and you aren't."

It wasn't a surprise. I knew I wasn't safe. I had been attacked here once and now attacked again.

"Maybe not," I whispered. "But I'm probably safer here than anywhere else, right?"

The Rebels all answered at the same time. "Right."

That was the last thing said as we all piled out of the headmaster's house together and headed back down to the school.

———

As soon as Brantley gave us the go-ahead, we all went back into our rightful dorm rooms—with the exception of Isaiah and Gemma going back to his room, and Cade coming into mine. Sloane rolled her eyes at us and said, "This school should come with a warning label. *Warning: your daughters will end up spending the night with boys who have smart mouths and a penchant for rule-breaking.*"

Shiner threw his head back and laughed. "No, it should say, *Warning: the girls will corrupt your sons and beg them to sneak into their rooms late at night for a good time, only to pretend they don't want them the next day.*"

Mercedes scoffed before shutting her door, and Sloane's eyes narrowed. "Are you fucking around with Mercedes?"

"Come on," Cade said, pulling me back gently and shutting my door. His hands rested on my hips as I stared at the oak wood, and he slowly spun me around and stared down into my eyes. "Are you okay?"

"You already asked me that," I countered, avoiding answering him.

"And you lied to me."

"I didn't lie. Compared to a little while ago, I *am* okay."

His hands left my hips, and he cupped my cheeks, keeping his face nice and smooth while I fought to keep my chin from wobbling. *I was attacked. I was almost taken.* The fear and anxiety that I had been pushing away was making itself present, and I didn't like it. There was something buried deep within that told me I couldn't show my real feelings. It might have been PTSD from the psych ward where they begged me to tell them how I was feeling, and when I did, they invalidated my response and told me I was lying. Maybe I was wounded from that. Jaded from my time away where I acted stronger than I really was.

"You know, you don't have to pretend around me," Cade whispered, rubbing the pads of his thumbs over my cheeks in a comforting way. I wanted to fall into his arms and stay there forever, because the truth was, I didn't feel safe on my own. I was confused and frustrated, but most of all, I was terrified.

"I know." I sniffed. Dropping my gaze to the floor, it grew blurry, and the area behind my eyes pricked like little needles stabbing them.

"Let's go get a shower and wash this blood off you, yeah?"

I nodded as Cade dropped his hands, leaving our conversation unfinished. Cade had a way of knowing exactly what I needed at exactly the right time. Although I was secretive, and sometimes I felt like I didn't even know myself, it seemed he knew me down to my core.

The water was turned on after Cade dragged me through the open door, and I stood in the middle of my small, tiled bathroom, staring down at the marks on my wrists with flakes of dried blood still covering parts of them. They were red and had a couple of thin slices, but they weren't nearly as deep as the cut on my hand from my knife. My heart went into triple speed, my stomach falling to the floor.

"My knife," I croaked out, suddenly feeling overly emotional and stupid. *It's just a knife.* "I dropped it after I stabbed him. Did you find it? Did he take it? I was too afraid to bend down to grab it. Once he let me go, I took off."

Cade's hands fell to my arms, and his eyes bounced back and forth between mine with panic slowly filling them. "Breathe, baby. Take a breath."

Oxygen dove into my lungs, and I pushed it out quickly,

feeling myself shake like I was standing outside in the snow-storm instead of inside my bathroom with steam slowly filling the small area. "I got your knife, but let's just get in the shower and take some breaths, okay? I need you to calm down."

Everything suddenly grew hot, and I felt something warm sliding down my cheeks. Cade's fingers fumbled with the bottom of my shirt, and he pulled it up and over my head, being careful with my injured wrists and hand. My chest rocked as I suppressed a sob, and I *hated* that I was crying because I couldn't seem to stop myself.

"I don't know why I'm crying. It's not like it's the first time someone has attacked me," I finally said as he began pulling my jeans down my legs. I stood in nothing but my underwear and bra when he finally glanced back at my face. His steely expression had been replaced with something painful, a small crease in between his eyebrows with a single, sandy-colored piece of hair hanging in his eyes.

"You're in shock," he whispered, like he didn't want to explain my behavior. He unclipped the back of my bra and pulled my straps down my arms before dropping the small garment to the floor. I turned my gaze away, frustrated that the tears wouldn't stop falling and that everything was suddenly exploding. It was like standing in the middle of a highway with headlights headed straight for me.

Sister Mary.

The police.

The threats.

I felt lost. I was drowning and had no idea how to reach the top.

"What am I supposed to do?" I choked out, placing my shaking hands over my eyes. *Stop crying!* I hardly ever cried. I had stopped that long ago when I had been passed over too many times at the orphanage. Crying didn't make things better. In fact, it made them worse. But here I was, unable to stop.

Cade pulled me into the shower next, and I was thankful because at least the tears would blend in with the water. I may have had a tight burning knot stuck in the back of my throat, but at least I was the only one aware of it. I breathed in choppy, painful breaths, turning my back to Cade as the water pelted me from above.

"Nothing that I can't do for you," he said, turning me around to face him. I opened my eyes, tipping my head back and letting the water run over my long hair. My eyes dropped, and I realized that Cade's strong chest was on display, his tanned body covered in tiny droplets from the water, cascading down to the floor. "I want you to feel this," he said, cupping my wrist right above the sore part and placing my palm on his wet chest. The thumping was palpable and undeniably persistent against my hand. His heart was beating so hard I felt it all over. I snapped my watery gaze to his, and what I saw rendered me speechless. His eyes were red-rimmed and locked intensely onto mine. "Do you feel that?"

I nodded hesitantly, too much in a trance to say anything. There was a tugging on my heart, nearly causing me to bow at his feet. *I am his.* He didn't have to ask me, or tell me, or persuade me that I could trust him. My body told me exactly what I needed to know. My intuitions were spot on.

"This is what happens to me when I think about someone hurting you."

My stomach tensed when he cast his dark gaze to my right shoulder, where I had bumped into the stone casing on my way to him. His jaw tensed, and the beating against my hand grew harder as he looked at my other arm, near my elbow. The pain was there, too, but hardly noticeable with him surveying all my marks.

"My dad raised me to kill," he whispered, stepping in a

little closer to me. The water ran over both of us, warming our already heated bodies. "And it made me sick to think that I would have to follow in his footsteps one day. That was why I always kept you hidden. I was afraid that someone, *anyone*, from my real life would see you and hurt you to get to me. Maybe not right away, but in the future...that would have happened. It still could." His gulp was loud, even with the whooshing sound of the shower. "It happened to Isaiah's mom." Cade's bare leg went in between my legs, and the front of our bodies were almost touching. "I guess I can't really blame my mother for disappearing on me, right? Except, I do. It hurts."

I swear I just felt his heart skip a beat.

My chin tipped, and his lowered. His next words brushed over me softly. "I never thought I'd need anyone like I need you."

I crashed and fell right there in front of him. My legs buckled, and Cade's strong arms wrapped around my bare back, colliding our bodies together in a sinful embrace. We couldn't have gotten closer if we tried.

"Don't you dare disappear on me again, Journey. Because I won't fucking make it if you do, and before you came back, I would have never admitted that to anyone."

My lip wobbled, but this time, I didn't try to hide my vulnerabilities or pretend that I didn't want him to want me in the way that I had craved my entire life. I could survive on my own. I'd done it before. But I knew now that admitting I didn't want to be alone didn't make me weak. It made me human. "I promise not to disappear if you promise not to abandon me."

Before he backed me up against the slick, steamy tiles and grabbed my waist, he whispered against my lips, "Never."

CHAPTER THIRTY-TWO

CADE

REAL.

This was real.

This was as real as it came.

I was as real as I had ever been with anyone.

My heart rammed itself against my chest with her sweet, soft lips moving against mine with the water pelting me on my back. Her waist fit so well in my hands that I wanted to freeze time and stay here forever with our truthful words slipping to the wet floor. She and I had finally figured it out. We needed each other, *wanted* each other, despite the things that pulled us back as individuals. The quiet scars on the inside, that most men didn't want to admit were there, rushed out quickly as I confessed that my upbringing had affected me in ways that I hadn't admitted to anyone. It was freeing to admit to her that my mother leaving me without a single word hurt in ways that I was too stubborn to accept. And all I wanted to do after letting go was show her how much she meant to me. I wanted to show her that I would do anything for her because Journey Smith, the girl who didn't know where she came from or about any aspect of her past, was the *only* fucking person on this earth that knew me from the inside out.

"There is nothing that could come between us. You know that, right?"

Journey jumped up, and I caught her, my hands slapping onto her wet skin. Her legs wrapped around my waist, her hands around my neck. "If nothing has come between us yet, I don't think anything will." She pressed her lips to mine, stealing the words off my tongue. She spread her legs, and I was already nudging inside her, burying myself physically and emotionally. I swallowed her hot, little gasp and pulled out slowly, looking her dead in the eye every single time I pushed in.

Feel this. Feel every bit of me take every bit of you.

Journey threw her head back, pushing her perfect mounds in my face for the taking. Water slipped down to her belly button, and when I caught a glimpse of our joined bodies, I made myself savor it. *Perfect.*

"You and I, Journey. You and I."

She began to squeeze around me, gasping louder and louder. I pumped in harder and faster, taking my hand and bringing her face back down to mine. "I wanna see you when I bring you to the edge."

My finger brushed over her bottom lip, taking it from her teeth. My fingers were plunged into the skin of her ass, and she pressed down on me, both of us bringing each other to oblivion. Her eyes grew hooded, and in between a thrust, I said, "Eyes on me. Watch us come undone for each other."

She moaned, her pretty gray eyes trying desperately to roll in the back of her head. Her pussy tightened, and I almost fell from the way she sucked me. "Fuck, Journey." A tingle shot up from my heels all the way to my spine, and I pushed her back harder against the tile to go in deeper. *Forever. Mine.* A second later, we dove for each other, kissing and sucking as I quickly pulled out of her, coming down the front of her belly. I kept ahold of her as I crashed and burned, only to rise from the embers seconds later.

For the first time, Journey and I were as raw as we had ever been with the truth out in the open and our vulnerabilities somewhere in the past.

We stared at one another as we tried to regain our breathing. My arm rested against her lower back, and I gave her zero space as I crowded her even further. My palm wove into her wet hair as my thumb brushed over her swollen lip, and we stayed like that until the water grew cold.

With the shock washed away, Journey's breathing eventually slowed, and we climbed out of the shower. Neither one of us said a word as I draped us both in towels and pulled her over to the bed. Nothing but the sound of me brushing her hair and our breathing filled the room, and even as we crawled underneath her covers, fully dried from the shower, it was a comforting quiet.

The thinnest sliver of light shined through the window, but I could still see every bare inch of her that was visible from the blankets. Her arm was draped over my chest with her head nestled onto my shoulder, her damp hair a blanket of its own over my skin.

"Let me see your palm." Her whisper cut through the darkness like a light I didn't realize I was searching for.

I shifted under her, glancing down to her plump lips as a small smile crested itself there. "My palm? Why?"

Her voice was airy, like our earlier moment broke through, and she was *finally* here. "I hated most of my time at the hospital." A soft noise left her. "I mean, who could blame me? But there were some good parts about it."

"Oh, yeah?" I asked, fully invested. "Like what?"

The warmth of her body settled in even deeper as she dove under the blankets and pulled my other arm out, gripping onto my wrist. "Well, I wouldn't have survived without Tobias. That's for sure. He taught me how to be strong when I didn't want to be." I stayed silent as she turned my hand over and began running her fingers over the thin lines along my palm. "And I met some really quirky people that filled up my time in between my scheming."

"Like who?"

"Athena would be at the top of that list." My stomach did a flip at the sound of hidden happiness in Journey's voice. I wasn't even sure she knew she was smiling, but the more she talked, the more her cheeks curved. "She was an older woman. She always told me she was celebrating her thirtieth birthday, but I think she was in her sixties. Her hair was fully gray and went down to the backs of her thighs. She used to make her granddaughter braid it every time she'd come to visit."

Journey's light touches on my palm began to send warm signals to parts of my body, so I tried to break up the heat by asking, "What was so special about Athena?"

"She taught me how to read palms."

I paused, my eyebrows shooting upward. "Read palms? Like...magic?"

Her laugh was cute. "Oh, yeah. She claimed she had magic running through her veins." She laughed again, and I swore I fell even harder for her—as if that were possible. "She made me laugh when I was seconds from losing it, always pulling my palm into her lap and running her fingers over the lines, inspecting my hand an inch from her eyes. It was sort of calming."

I shifted underneath Journey, watching her look at my palm like she was going to do the same thing as Athena. "So, could she really read palms? What do you think?"

Journey's bruised shoulder lifted slightly, and I felt her smile along my bare chest. "Maybe. She predicted one thing right, so it's possible."

"And what was that? Did she predict you'd be released from the psych hospital? Because that surely came true." I grinned as I squeezed the top of her knee, making her entire body jolt and causing laughter to fly from her mouth.

She relaxed her leg against me again as her laughter faded. "She predicted my broken heart would mend, and the one who broke it would be the one to fix it."

I burned on the inside with guilt, but it was quickly soothed with relief seconds later. Journey snuggled up closer, quickly moving past the revelation, and pulled my palm closer to her warmth.

A few seconds passed by, and her dainty, soft fingers skimmed the lines over and over again, causing me to suck in a breath. "Well, what do you see?" I finally asked, peering down at her with hooded eyes and a core on fucking fire.

"I'm not sure," Journey answered, grinning like the girl I knew before everything fell apart. Her leg hooked tighter over mine, and I knew right then what the future was. Another shift from Journey and my arm was pulled out from underneath her, making her fall back onto the soft pillow with both of my hands landing beside her face. Her misty eyes were wide, her pouty lips open in surprise.

"I don't need someone to read my palm to tell me what my future holds."

A tiny crease etched in between her brows as I lowered my mouth a breath from hers.

Journey's chin tilted, brushing our lips against one another just to torture me. "You don't?"

My forehead rested against hers, her sweet breath filling my senses and making me downright delirious with need. "You, Journey Smith. You are my future."

Journey's legs parted in a silent agreement, and her hands landed on my flexed biceps. I was still holding myself up, but soon, I'd be buried inside of her, proving to her that my words didn't need to be validated by some palm reading.

I was at her entrance as our mouths teased one another, and my eyes shut on their own when I realized my girl was already wet and waiting for me.

"Am I still your future even though someone is after me?"

I answered her with a thrust, pushing in and feeling us connect in ways that words could never do justice. "Yes," I grit out before taking her body and heart.

———

SHE WAS NEVER TOO FAR out of my sight. That sandy-colored hair always caught my eye, and I'd finally relax again. If I could tie Journey to me without seeming absolutely fucking nuts, I would. Each morning, I'd slip out from her room and go back to mine to get ready for the day, only to search for her every second until she'd walk into the dining hall with her friends, or sometimes with Tobias.

It had been only a few days since she'd been attacked, and although the bruises on her shoulders had faded to an ugly yellow, everyone was still on edge—even Headmaster Ellison. Although, he *did* get the security system installed, but unfortunately, it didn't make anyone feel better.

The Rebels and I knew that any security system, even a top-of-the-line one, could still be disabled. Whoever came to get Journey could be a computer whiz for all we knew.

And that was the thing: we knew nothing—up until a few seconds ago, at least.

Isaiah's phone was still in my hand as I sat on the dining-hall bench, waiting for Journey to walk through the doors. My grip tightened when I reread what his brother, Jacobi, an FBI agent, had sent him.

JACOBI: *There's still not much info to give. The streets have been quiet, but an informant that was working closely with your father gave up a name that could be related. The name is Slave.*

HE TEXTED AGAIN SECONDS LATER.

JACOBI: *That's the end of me owing you, brother. Now please go fuck off. I have an actual case file on my desk.*

IT BUZZED AGAIN.

JACOBI: *Oh, and I'm coming to Uncle Tate's to visit for spring break, so get your insults ready.*

I SNAPPED my attention to Isaiah, who had the same tight jaw that I had. We ignored the last two messages as Brantley pulled Isaiah's phone out of my hand, and Shiner, who was well informed of our past and future dealings with the illicit gun-running business and the Covens, leaned forward to read.

"You know we should follow up," Isaiah admitted, just as on edge as I was.

I sliced past him and landed on Bain across the dining hall, feeling rage burn me from the inside out. I wanted very few things in my life, and one of those things was to never fucking talk to my father again. But I knew by the scowl on Isaiah's face that he was referencing just that. The dining-hall bench was scooted out, and I easily swung my legs over it and walked directly to Bain. I heard Isaiah calling my name, but I ignored him as I crowded Bain's space.

He didn't move an inch, and although he had helped search the school the other night for whoever had attacked Journey and helped get Gemma back when she'd been taken, I wanted to wrap my fingers around his neck and body slam him to the fucking table.

"Can I help you?" His tone was insolent, which only fueled my irrational behavior.

"Who the fuck is Slave?" I asked, leveling my voice and locking down my anger. *Throwing punches will get you nowhere until it's the right time to strike.* I bristled at my father's advice as he taught me how to protect and kill. *Fucker.*

Bain threw down his breakfast sandwich, crossed his arms over his loose tie, and peered up at me as I leaned forward on the table.

"Never heard of him."

I shut my eyes, blocking out the red that was beginning to coat my vision. *Stay calm.* My fingers tingled, and something tore through my chest that I wanted so badly to give an outlet to, but instead, I opened my eyes yet again and saw that Bain was looking at me with a leery gaze. He was waiting for me to strike, but I wouldn't.

"I'll ask you again. Who the fuck is Slave?"

He was good, I'd give him that. Bain knew how to react nine times out of ten. He was raised the same as we were—thrown into a multi-million-dollar business of illegal gun selling, amongst other things. Bain could keep a poker face, just like me. But this time? He stayed silent, and his jaw angled in that haughty way of his.

"The fact that you didn't respond tells me you've heard the name."

His temples flexed as I leaned away and glanced at the opening dining-hall doors. I stepped away, putting space between us, and that was when he said, "Rule number one of the business, Cade—which I'm surprised to learn you've already forgotten with Daddy locked up—don't poke around in shit that doesn't concern you, because chances are, you'll be putting a target on your back, too."

I laughed in a menacing way as I dropped my head. "Everything about Journey concerns me, and if there's something there, I'm going to put myself right in the fucking middle."

Our steely gazes crashed, and there was something hidden there. There was a heeding intuition that wanted to pull me closer and extract information out of his fucked-up brain, but instead, I turned around and spotted Journey walking to our table with her pretty eyes set on me with questions I knew she wanted answered.

____

CHAPTER THIRTY-THREE

____

JOURNEY

"THERE IS AN ALARM SYSTEM NOW. Will you please take a breath?" I wrapped my hands around Cade's face, trying to pretend that I was totally relaxed and not at all on edge, even though I was. Cade was tense, which meant I was tense.

"She'll be fine. The girls are going to stay with her, and Tobias is glued to Gemma's side. Shiner is here, too."

Cade pulled his attention away from Isaiah without saying a word. He stayed propped against the library bookshelf, waiting for Cade to tear himself away from me.

"We gotta go if we want to make it before visiting hours are over."

There was still nothing coming from Cade, but I could see everything racing behind his eyes. His cut jaw was tight underneath my palms, and I wanted to massage the little muscles kicking back and forth along his temples.

"What's going on?" I asked, bringing his attention to me. Isaiah sighed heavily and walked away, giving us some privacy.

"What do you mean?" he finally asked, trying his hardest to close off the nerves that may not have been evident to anyone else, but they were to me.

I bet if I were to move my hand to his chest, his heart would be thumping so hard it would hurt my palm. "Is there something you're not telling me?"

"No," he was quick to answer, and it made me pause. "I promise."

I stared at him for one long second, and deep down, I didn't think he was lying. He and I were past the untrusting phase. I read the text messages from Jacobi, who I had briefly met after leaving the psych hospital months ago, and I knew that Cade, along with Brantley and Isaiah, were going to the prison that their fathers were at, awaiting trial, to ask them about this *Slave* person. I knew that the police had absolutely zero leads on Sister Mary—at least that was what they'd been telling Headmaster Ellison every day since they'd *'pulled me out of bed'* to talk.

"You're not telling me something." I paused, feeling my eyes soften at the tormented look on his face. The easygoing version of Cade that was in my room every night, where we were tucked away from everything and everyone, wasn't the same Cade I was looking at. He was troubled, a storm brewing in the depths of those dark eyes that typically reminded me of honey. The realization hit me a second later. "It's because you're going to see your father, isn't it?"

Only someone who didn't have parents could let something like that slip by until it smacked them square in the face. *He's seeing his father. His father who is in prison. His father who scared his mother so much that she left without even saying goodbye to her son.*

"No." The word ran out of his mouth so quickly I barely caught it. When I peered up at him, he was staring blankly at a book above my head.

My hands left his tense cheeks when he ran his fingers through his hair, breathing in short, quick breaths. My heart flinched as I saw this perfect guy standing in front me, fighting back and forth with something on the inside. I stayed quiet as he worked through it, his jaw clenching and unclenching, his eyes narrowing and un-narrowing.

"Fine," he whispered, breaking through the wall like I knew he would. "You're right. I fucking hate him, and I'll hate him until I take my last breath."

There was a simple solution to this. "Then, don't go."

He looked like I had slapped him, so I quickly added, "It's just... It's not worth it. It's not worth making you feel this way."

His sarcastic laugh hit my face just as his hand wrapped around my chin, tilting my head so those storm-brewing eyes could pin me to the bookshelf. "Oh, I'm fucking going. Anything that can bring us closer to figuring out who the fuck is trying to *take* you is worth it to me. And I will not let Tommy Walker stand in the way of that."

The edge in his voice when he said his father's name struck something inside of me. There was pain there, and resentment, and those were two things that I *could* understand. I'd felt them a million times over when I'd let myself run with the idea that my parents had given me up because they didn't want me, or that there was something worth more than having *me* as a daughter. The resentment went down to my bones, and I latched onto exactly what Cade was feeling. Anger started to coil in my belly that someone—his father, of all people—could make Cade, who was selfless beyond belief, feel so much bitter resentment and animosity. That anger drove me straight down the back of the library with Cade's wrist locked in my hand, passing by several aisles of books, until we got to the ancient history section.

"What are you doing? You're not stopping me from going

no matter how guilty or bad you feel that I'm doing it for you."

"Then you better be quick," I said, reaching up on my tiptoes and planting a kiss on his lips. Something delicious whirled around my stomach that replaced the pungent taste of indignation when I landed on level feet again. Cade's formally stormy eyes were hooded with something else entirely.

"What are you doing?"

"Something to calm you down for the road?" I asked, placing my hands on the button of his dark jeans.

His hand dove into my hair, cupping the side of my face. "Journey Smith, what am I going to do with you?"

I shrugged, looking away for a second. "I *hate* knowing that your father hurt you."

"Tommy Walker didn't hurt me," he was quick to say. "But even the thought of him makes me fucking angry."

I licked my lips as I pushed his pants down and pressed up against his boxer briefs that were already sporting something hard. "Fine. I hate seeing you angry, then." My fingers were inside his boxers, and his hand tightened in my hair. "And when you get back and you get the information you're determined to find, you can work out the rest of your anger... on me."

"Hmm," he hummed, licking his lips.

"Deal?" I asked, ready to drop down to make Cade focus on me instead of this demented father that he was about to come face to face with after getting him thrown in jail. There was something deep in my stomach that pulled my heart lower, feeling guilty that Cade was going through something that dealt with me, but I also knew that Cade was as determined as they came, and no matter what I said to him, he would be going, and he'd be having words with likely the only person he feared.

"Are you trying to distract me?" he asked.

"Maybe," I answered. "And maybe I'm giving you something to look forward to when you get back."

Our eyes snagged, and that was when I dropped down to my knees, feeling the soft carpet of the library brushing over my bare skin.

"Jesus Christ, Journ." He hissed as I licked his tip before gripping him at the base. An evil smile slid onto my face, and I had forgotten how good it felt to do this when your heart was actually involved. I wasn't doing this for me. I was doing this for him. "When did you get so good at this? You know what, don't answer that. I fucking love it."

I wasn't proud of what had happened at the psych ward, which he was well aware of, but before I'd been taken there, Cade *always* took charge. I was naive, innocent, and inexperienced last year. That wasn't who I was anymore, and I felt safe enough with Cade to explore a little further and blur every line that was there before.

"Good," I said, plunging him into my mouth, sucking and moving over him to bring him to insanity. There was something so powerful in making a guy wither from pleasure because of *you*. I felt wanted, and I chased the high just as quickly as he was.

Cade's hand fell to the back of my head as I sucked him deeper. There was something salty that hit my tongue, which only propelled me to work harder.

"Eyes on me." His hoarse whisper made me ache, and when I peeked up at him, I licked the tip of him, tasting him even more. "Fuck," he grit out, shutting his eyes for a brief second. I took him in my mouth again, and his hand tightened around my head. "Why are you so fucking hot on your knees?"

I wanted to smile, enjoying the way I was making him lose himself, but instead, I took him in farther, hitting the back of my throat. I closed my eyes and enjoyed his hand pulling my hair. *Why do I love making him lose himself to me?* It was a delicious high—a high more powerful than when he was bringing me to the edge, if I was being honest. I *loved* that he was out of control. I *loved* that he pumped into my mouth without holding back. And I *loved* swallowing every bit of him as his body shook in ways that only I could summon. When I was done and his hand had untangled from my hair, I wiped my swollen lips and smiled up at him, climbing to my feet.

Cade's eyes were blazing. The hungry, untamed look in them had my smile dropping as he gripped my hips and slammed our bodies together in a frenzy. My leg was suddenly wrapped around his hip, my plaid skirt flying up, allowing his fingers to grip my bare thigh. "I fucking love you," he said, biting onto my earlobe, which was something he knew I liked.

A small moan left me, and when Cade's fingers found my wet panties, he sucked on the skin below where he'd just snagged with his teeth. "Does it turn you on when you suck me off, Journey?" He huffed out a laugh. "Who would have known that innocent Journey, who I deflowered on the lacrosse field all those months ago, would turn into *this?*"

He pulled his hand out from under my skirt, his other hand still gripping my thigh tightly, and inspected his fingers. They were wet, and months ago, that would have made me blush, but now I felt just as wild as he did.

Isaiah's voice called down the aisle, and Cade's devilish stare froze on me. "Stop fucking. We have to go. The car's out front."

"Damn," Cade said. "Looks like we'll have to finish later, yeah?"

I was too worked up to nod, and I had forgotten all about the fact that he was about to go meet his father. I hoped that he had forgotten for a little while, too.

Just as Cade lowered my leg to the ground, he plopped his two fingers into his mouth, sucking me off his fingers with a wickedly sinful glint in his honey-colored eyes. The light was back in them, and it was burning me to my core.

"Mmm," he moaned, pecking me hard on the lips. "My favorite flavor."

He buttoned his jeans as I stood back against the bookshelf, feeling a skip in my chest. I could still taste him on my tongue as he bent down low to whisper over my ear. "Thank you." Then, he turned around and began walking toward where Isaiah had yelled from.

"Don't do anything reckless, Journey. I expect you to be smart and to stay safe. That means no fucking sneaking out."

I grinned. "Yes, sir."

———

"HAVE YOU HEARD FROM THEM?" It was a question I'd been holding in since Gemma came into my room an hour ago. We'd never really hung out alone, but surprisingly enough, it was comforting to have her near. Sloane wasn't there as a buffer because she was in the library, helping Tobias with something he was struggling with in class. Mercedes had said she was studying in her room for the night, but I had my suspicions on that. So, Gemma and I sat inside my room in soothing silence as we both finished our homework.

Gemma put her pencil down and peered up at me from her position, lying on my bed. "Not since Isaiah had said that they arrived. I don't think they can have cell phones in there, so he hasn't texted me back."

I nodded, looking back at my laptop. The nerves that I had erased earlier when Cade and I were in the library were beginning to show, and they were crawling up my back like a million little ants. I felt trapped, like I was back at the psych hospital, not knowing what was going on in the outside world.

I shifted my attention past my essay on the screen and looked at the shelf on my desk that held the file I'd stolen from the headmaster's office. My stomach tightened further as I pulled out the paper that Cade had given to me, with Sister Mary's warning that I had been in danger since the moment I was born.

Keep her safe.

There was a notch on the inside, like a little burrowing hole of invisible information that I didn't have but needed in the worst way. Sister Mary crossed my mind multiple times a day, and I'd caught myself wanting to leave St. Mary's altogether to make sure that the girls at the orphanage were okay without her guidance, but I knew that was a stupid decision. Headmaster Ellison was always quick to remind me that I needed to stay away, desperation always hinting at his words.

The paper floated down to my desk as I peeked over at Gemma who was staring at me. I wasn't surprised that she didn't ask to read what was in my hand or question my silence. She'd always been good at letting information come to her, instead of fishing for it, like everyone else.

"Do you think that their fathers will even tell them anything?"

Gemma closed her book and slowly sat up on my bed. Her brown hair was up in a high pony, and when she reached up to tighten it, she brought her knees to her chin. "Honestly? Not unless they threaten them."

My brows furrowed. "Threaten their fathers? How? They're already in prison for life, right?"

"The trials haven't started yet. It's hard to know what they'll be charged with and what their lawyers will be able to get taken off."

I swallowed back the terror that I suddenly felt, knowing

that there was a chance that Cade's father could be out of prison at some point. I wondered what kind of terror Cade felt.

"I still say they should have separated them. Throw them in separate prisons and make them turn on one another." Gemma sighed. "But from what I knew about Cade, Brantley, and Isaiah was that they were loyal down to their bones. They got that from their fathers."

"Cade surely didn't get it from his mother."

"What do you mean?" Gemma asked, giving me a strange look. *Does she not know?*

I turned fully toward her and sat cross-legged on my chair. "Cade's mom left after his father got arrested."

"Yeah, I knew that. Isaiah told me."

"She didn't even say goodbye to Cade. He has no idea where she went."

Gemma looked confused. "Wait, what? I thought he and his mom had a somewhat decent relationship." Her gaze bounced all around the room. "I don't think Isaiah knows this." The tenseness of her shoulders dropped. "That explains Cade's behavior even more after everything."

"His behavior?"

Gemma half-heartedly smiled. "Cade was *in* his feelings, Journey. After everything that happened with his father and learning that you were kept at the psych hospital the whole time, he was completely closed off. I can't pretend that I knew the Cade that you knew before you left, but the only time I ever saw much emotion from him was when someone brought you up. When you came back, it was like you put the hope back in him or something. He woke up."

I laughed, brushing her off. "That can't be true. I told him I hated him."

Gemma smiled. "That only made him more hopeful. Those Rebels are determined as hell. You know this."

We both laughed, and suddenly, the room grew relaxed again. I turned away and pulled the file down to place the paper back inside. My computer dinged with an incoming message. I still held onto the file as I slowly clicked on my school email, wondering who was emailing me after school hours, and that was when my stomach lurched. The email address in the "From" section caused me to fly up out of my seat with my chair knocking to the ground. *Sister Mary?*

Gemma was off my bed within a second. "Journey? What's wrong?"

IF YOU WANT *answers and to save the nun, follow the instructions.* **4616 Western Blvd, Building C. Be there tonight, 9pm. And don't bring the snitches.**

CHILLS COATED MY ARMS, and I knew whoever had emailed me from Sister Mary's email did so knowing that Cade was two hundred miles away.

"I..." My hands were shaking as I stared at the screen. The file in my hand fell to the ground, and the faded papers scattered around like my thoughts.

"Journey." Gemma's hands landed on my shaking ones, and when I caught her worried gaze, I laid it out in the open.

"Read it."

She bent down and began scanning the computer. It felt like hours had passed, but I knew it was only seconds. And like a harrowing moment in a horror film, eerie silence filled the room as we stared at one another. I knew that it could have been a trap, but in the same thought, Sister Mary's life was quite literally dangling in front of me.

"Don't bring the snitches," Gemma whispered, repeating

what the email had said. "That means they know about the Rebels and how they threw their fathers into prison."

My heart was a deafening drum inside my ears. Each beat shot pain into my ribs. "Gemma." I looked up at her soft-green eyes, and she knew, without me even saying it, that I was going after Sister Mary. I had to. There was no hesitation between what was right and what was wrong. I would *not* abandon the one person who had kept me safe and protected me like I was her own. Because, without a doubt, I knew she had stopped many, *many* adoptions to save me. She kept me close for a reason.

"It only says not to bring the snitches. So, I'm coming, too."

I shot her a look. "Isaiah will kill you."

"Then, we can die together because Cade will kill you, too."

She stood in the middle of my room as I quickly tore a piece of paper from my notebook and scribbled the address down. It was pretty much an invitation to my own death, but we silently agreed that we were going one way or another. There was no time to think about my decision before we tore out of my room. Cade was right there, screaming at me over my shoulder in the outskirts of my brain, telling me not to go, but I couldn't listen because I knew that I wouldn't be able to live with myself if I ignored it.

I wouldn't abandon Sister Mary.

I wouldn't abandon her like someone abandoned me.

CHAPTER THIRTY-FOUR

CADE

Gravel crunched under my shoes as we walked through the prison gates. It was a chorus of determined, pounding footsteps that followed Isaiah, Brantley, and me. We didn't say much on the ride over, which wasn't necessarily unusual without Shiner around. We'd asked him if he wanted to go, knowing his father was locked behind bars here as well and had been for many, many years, but he refused before storming off, which only solidified the fact that Shiner had a lot more under the surface than faceless jokes and fucking girls.

"Are we ready for this?" Isaiah asked, leaning back in the chair.

We were in a single horizontal line, each of us facing a smudged plastic window that looked into the other side of the prison. We weren't the only ones in the room, which surprised me because we were nearing the end of visiting hours.

One woman was three spots down, crying hysterically as

her mobster-looking boyfriend sat stoically on the other side with his hands face-down on the table in front of him. She was blubbering about cheating on him, and if his dark glare said anything at all, it was that he wanted to strangle her.

Then, to my right, past Isaiah and Brantley, there was another woman, but she wasn't crying. She was speaking in Spanish, and if I had to guess, she was fucking pissed about something.

My pulse hammered behind my skin, and although my face was smooth and my gaze was level—because I refused to flinch when I saw him—I felt fucked on the inside.

There was something raw about seeing the man who you were eager to please as a child, only to grow to hate him as an adult, behind a single sheet of plastic. I wasn't afraid of my father, not in the sense that most children were afraid of their abusers, but I was angry and disappointed that *this* was the man who I had been raised by. *This* was the man that I could have turned out like. And worst of all, this was the man that made my own mother reject me and leave me stranded at a boarding school to fend for myself.

The doors opened, and my chest grew tight. *I wish Journey was here.* If she were here, it would only take one touch of her hand on mine to give me the resilience I needed to keep my shoulders level and my fists untighened.

Instead, that was exactly what they did. My fingers dug into my palms, turning white at the knuckles like there was no blood left in them. One by one, our fathers walked through the door in handcuffs, looking smug and airy, as if they weren't locked away in a federal prison, awaiting a multitude of charges that could very possibly leave them behind bars for the rest of their lives.

Arrogance was their backbone, and as they sat down in their chairs in front of us. Isaiah, Brantley, and I all leaned back in ours, seemingly even more arrogant than them. The only difference was that we were the free ones here, and they weren't.

My father was the first to speak. "What? Not gonna talk? Did you boys just come here to stare at your old men, knowing we can't wrap our fucking fingers around your necks to kill you for setting us up?"

I ignored my father, dipping my eyes down to his neck. Faded black ink peeked from under his orange jumpsuit collar, and I knew it was the serpent he'd had tatted there when I was seven. *What I would do to wrap my hands around your neck, Pops.*

"We want to know what you know about someone named Slave."

Isaiah's father chuckled, looking more disheveled than ever before. I'd seen him with blood splattered across his face, but right now, he looked rough. Dark circles laid beneath his eyes, and his black hair was no longer slicked back like usual. It was messy and long, and the snarl of his teeth made him seem like a rabid animal.

My father was looking at his ringleader, and so was Brantley's. When I looked at Isaiah, I had to keep my face steady because the grin slowly slithering on his cheeks made me want to laugh in the worst way. I wasn't going to lie; it was a fucking nice change of pace to be the ones on top versus the other way around.

Carlisle, Isaiah's father, nearly growled. "You punks think you can come in here, after turning us into the feds, and demand information? I hope Slave fucking guts you all."

My ears perked. "So, you do know him?"

His eyes never left Isaiah's. I could feel the burning gaze of my own father, but for once, I didn't *have* to look at him. There was nothing he could do to me or my mother if I didn't submit like a little bitch at his feet.

"What?" Brantley's father finally spoke. "Want to throw Slave in here, too? Good luck with that."

Isaiah's hands were planted firmly on the table in front of him, and he leaned in real close to the see-through plastic in front of his father. "Did you know that I have to give a formal statement soon? That I have to sit down with the DA and tell them *everything* I know about you and your little scheming gun-running business and give them the names of every last person you've killed or had a hand in killing?" He shifted his attention to my father and Brantley's. "And your sons will be doing the same shortly after."

If we were on the other side of that plastic, I bet I could have heard the grinding of each of their teeth. It surely shut them up, and that was something we had never been able to do before.

"So, you're here to make a deal?"

Isaiah shrugged. "Depends on the information you give me."

The haughty laugh was chilling and boisterous all in one. "You think I'm going to trust you? You may have my blood running through your veins, but you, my son, are fucking dead to me. I'm not telling you shit."

"Okay," Isaiah said, staying calm even though I could see the constant tapping of his foot beneath the table. *Same, Isaiah. Fucking same.* "That's fine. Have fun getting the death penalty, then." A laugh left him. "All it takes is for me to give them a few more names, and *boom,* you'll have multiple murders under your belt."

"All of you will," I added, seeing my father looking at me with heavy betrayal over every wrinkled line of his face.

"So, let me ask you again," Isaiah said. "Tell me everything you know about Slave, and maybe I'll knock off a few horrendous acts that you've committed in my presence."

There was silence between us. The crying woman was still

wailing, irking me like no other. The Spanish woman had stormed away moments ago, her fury still intact. I knew that visiting hours would soon be over, so if they didn't start talking soon, then we'd be out of fucking luck, and I was determined to find out who was after my girl.

"Fuck you. I could easily order to have you three killed, even from here." Carlisle's smile was menacing, and there was a hollowing in my stomach. "I'm just buying my time so that when I get out of this shithole, I can do it myself."

Isaiah kept his voice smooth. "Remember Patricia Petrov?"

Carlisle's smile quickly dropped as he leaned back in his seat.

Isaiah tapped his fingers on his chin. "The Russian wife of that mobster, way back when?" He shrugged. "You probably forgot all about her. I mean, after all, how many women did you rape after you shot their husband in the head? And then ordered one of these two fucks to kill her?" Isaiah nodded to my father and Brantley's, and from the moment he said Patricia's name, I knew exactly where this was headed.

"So what?" Frank spat, glaring at his son. Brantley remained unmoving, but I was certain there were many things firing off in his brain.

Isaiah laughed out loud. "There was a witness, you *fucking* idiots. All it takes is one word from us, and she'll be spilling the dirty truth."

Silence rendered them speechless. Frank's nostrils flared, and when I glanced at Brantley, I saw the muscles along his temples ticking. That night was one of the worst nights of Brantley's life. It was the first time he had to witness how much of a monster his father was.

"Clock's ticking," I seethed, glaring at my father. The anger was there, present as it always was. I half-expected him to bang his hands against the plastic as a way to intimidate me. He was always the more physical of the three of them. Isaiah's father was the silent type, shooting people when they least expected, and Brantley's father simmered on his anger, letting it build up within his silence before lashing out. And my father was damn near unpredictable. The three of them together were deadly.

Carlisle leaned back as far as he could in his seat and snarled. "Why would I believe you three?"

This time, Brantley spoke. "Because you can't fucking risk it."

Carlisle cracked his neck, showing his teeth like he was ready to bite someone, before finally spilling. "We've only crossed Slave a few times." *Bingo. Thank fuck.* "We never sold guns to him."

"That's because he was Callum's client," Brantley guessed.

So, Bain *was* involved, but how? My nostrils flared, and I bit the inside of my cheek to keep myself from flipping out of my seat and losing control.

Carlisle ignored Brantley without confirming, but he didn't need to. We had already gotten the gist. "Technically, Slave was our top enemy. He's in charge of Callum."

"I thought Bain's father was the ringleader of their gun trade. He's been working for someone?" Dread began to settle on my shoulders.

Isaiah's father sighed irritatingly. "He owed Slave a shit-ton of money, a debt, so Slave started gaining a profit off their income from gun-selling to rectify the loss."

Which explained why Callum had started stealing our clients months ago.

"Why did he owe him money?"

Fuck, fuck, fuck. I already knew. Deep down, I already *fucking* knew, and when the words left his mouth, my vision blurred, and the room grew dark.

"He sold him a girl or some shit but never handed her over."

He sold him a girl.
He sold him a girl.
He sold him a girl.

My hand slapped down on the metal table, causing the guard to step forward. Isaiah raised his hand in an attempt to signal that we were okay, and when I glanced back at my father, he was smiling wildly, as if he enjoyed seeing me lose it.

"Are you done with your little bitch fit?" Carlisle asked, keeping his gaze level with his son's. He didn't give me a chance to answer—not that I would have—and continued, "This was years ago. Callum gave up part of the company to pay back his *debt.* He and Slave made a deal in order to save his life, because once you cross Slave, you're usually done for."

Brantley cursed. "Why did he sell him a girl?"

Although I needed to hear more, I didn't want to. My stomach burned, and my throat closed. *Journey was fucking sold like cattle.*

"Callum's wife had cheated on him, so he sold the baby to Slave as a way to get back at her. This was before they had Bain."

Brantley's father spoke up beside him in his rough voice. "Probably for sex trade, or maybe to keep her for himself when she became of age. Or maybe Slave's girl wanted a baby. He got married at some point, but she's dead."

"Because he killed her." My father laughed at this, as if it were funny. *Fucking psycho.* It was like old times—the three of us on one side, and the three of them on the other as they talked "shop".

"I fucking hate you." The four words came out quickly, and I didn't even flinch when I realized *I'd* been the one to say them. My father turned his freshly shaved head and glared at me straight on, as if he could do something. "I do," I reiterated. "I hate you, and Mom hates you, too. Did you know that? She tried to run away with me so many times when I was younger I'd lost count, but we always came back because she was afraid you'd never stop looking and that you'd end up killing her or me."

There was silence on his end, and I knew all eyes were on us. I wanted to bang my fist onto the plastic as many times as it took until it cracked and I could reach inside and choke him. With my mother leaving me, him being who he was, and the fact that Journey, the only person on this earth that I was irrevocably attached to, had been fucking sold to some piece of shit... I was rioting on the inside.

"Let's go." I pulled my glare from my father and saw Isaiah standing beside me on the right and Brantley standing beside me on the left. Brantley's jaw was flexing as his nostrils flared, shifting his steely gaze from my father, to Isaiah's, and then to his. The guards came up behind our fathers as we began walking away, and that was when Carlisle called out, "You better keep your end of the deal, son. I can give the order now, if need be."

Isaiah grinned. "Fuck you."

Carlisle's fist banged onto the plastic, and it was the last thing we saw as we turned our backs and walked out of the prison.

It didn't take long for us to climb back into the SUV and for Isaiah to break the silence. "You know what this means, right?"

My leg shook the entire car as we flew down the freeway. Isaiah had been buried in his phone, checking it every few minutes as Brantley drove.

"Which part?" Brantley asked.

My stomach was heavy, and my lungs were tight. I'd

gnawed off part of my fucking cheek, trying to sort through everything.

"Cade. Did you hear me? You know what this means, right?"

I snapped my head up to Isaiah, hardly seeing him in the dark interior of the car. "That Journey was fucking sold like some fucking toy? Yeah, I heard him."

"No," Isaiah snapped. "It means that Bain and Journey are half-brother and sister."

My face fell, and my shoulders were next. I ran over the information that Carlisle had given to us. *Callum's wife had cheated on him, so he sold the baby.* Callum's wife = Bain's mother.

"That explains a fuck-ton," Brantley said before flipping Isaiah's phone out of his hand. "You're fucking stressing me out. Why do you keep looking at your phone? What? Is Gemma sexting you or something?"

Isaiah bent down and picked it up off the floor, clearly agitated. "She isn't answering my texts."

Like a racehorse, my heart flew right the fuck out of my chest. "What do you mean she isn't answering you? Is her location on?"

"Yeah, it says she's at St. Mary's. Last text from her was right before we went into the prison. She said she was hanging out in Journey's room."

"For fuck's sake." Brantley hit Shiner's name on the touch-screen of the SUV, and the ringtone came over the speakers.

This is why Journey needs a phone. Part of me wanted to put a goddamn tracking device on her.

Shiner's phone rang and rang, and Brantley's hand tight-ened on the wheel so hard I heard his knuckles crack.

"Isaiah." The calmness in my voice should have alarmed everyone in the car. "If she isn't at the fucking school when we get there, I will tear the goddamn world apart."

He looked over at me and nodded. "And we'll help you."

CHAPTER THIRTY-FIVE

JOURNEY

GIVING yourself up for someone else wasn't the worst thing you could do in your life. In fact, it was selfless to put someone else before you. So, why did I feel so guilty with every step I took down the darkened hallway of St. Mary's? Gemma's footsteps were as quiet as mine, both of us stealthy as could be.

I paused in the middle of the hallway. "Gemma."

"Don't," she whispered. "Let's go."

I turned toward her and grabbed onto her scarred wrists. The skin was bumpy beneath my hand, but that didn't deter me from squeezing tightly so she would meet my gaze. "I want to go alone."

Her dainty wrists were pulled out of my grasp. "Absolutely not."

My words were more of a plea. "You've been through enough. I'm not dragging you into...*this*." *Whatever the hell this is.*

"And so have you. We're going. The two of us. Together."

I shook my head. "Tobias just got you back."

"And he will still have me when this is all said and done." Her sentence was final, as if we were done with the conversation. "Do you have your knife?"

I pulled it out of my pocket, nearly sagging in relief when I'd found it on my bedside table after Cade had left my room early one morning. "Yeah. Do you?"

"Yep."

We walked a little farther down the hall, but this time, she stopped and grabbed onto my arms. "Just you and me, right? No one else." Sloane popped in my head, and Tobias, too. And I didn't want to admit it, but Bain was lingering in the background also. *Could we trust him?*

"We're on the same page," I said, swallowing back the lump of fear, and guilt, and everything in between.

She dropped my arms as I put my knife back in my pocket, clenching the piece of paper in my hand. Once we got to the end of the hallway, we listened for any movement of the duty teacher, and that was when I felt hesitation on my part. *Cade.* He would be furious. Isaiah, too. And Tobias?

What are we going to walk into?

"Gemma—" I paused mid-sentence when a tall shadow appeared in the boys' hall, getting closer and closer until stopping mere feet in front of us. Bain's shoulders came close to fitting the width of the opening of the hall, and his determined eyes were set on us like a cat catching a mouse in its trap.

"Bain, how interesting to see you." Gemma crossed her arms and smirked. "It's like deja vu."

His attention shifted from Gemma to me and then down to my hand where the address still sat crumpled in between my sweaty fingers. His ambling pace made my heart drop, and before I could react, the paper was ripped from my fingers, and he was scanning the black ink quickly.

There were too many things on the tip of my tongue, but nothing came out. I just stood there, beside Gemma, dumbfounded at the situation I had found myself in.

Bain folded the piece of paper neatly and held it out with two fingers. I slowly raised my hand and snatched it back, as if it had my entire life written in code underneath the black smudges. *And maybe it does.*

He took a step back and threw his arm out, as if he was giving us permission.

"You're not gonna try to stop us?" I asked, spinning around and staring at him after we walked a few paces forward. Gemma stopped right beside me, and her face showed nothing. There was no disgust like there had always been on Isaiah's and Cade's faces when he was near. She didn't seem to hate Bain or fear him, even though *he* was the one that had propelled her into the Covens months ago.

"And why would I do such a thing?" he asked, standing nonchalantly with his back pressed against the intricate wood along the wall. "Because every guy you two seem to come into contact with thinks they need to save you? As if you two are damsels in distress?" He chuckled, and Gemma and I shared a fleeting look with one another.

"Journey," Bain said, snapping himself out of his laughter. "You don't give yourself enough credit. You've been on your own since you were barely old enough to open your eyes. If you think you need someone now, you're wrong."

I turned toward the direction of a faint sound coming from the boys' hall, and I was certain it was the duty teacher. *What will Headmaster Ellison do if he catches his daughter sneaking out of the school with me?*

"Go," Bain snapped. "Now. Before you miss your chance."

I hesitated, but Gemma grabbed onto my arm, pulling me toward the stairs. I got one last look at Bain, and although his voice was low, I still heard it plain as day. "I don't ask this often, but I need you to trust me on this. Just go. Go to the address."

The stairs were never-ending, and I swore, all coherent thoughts were left on the landing with Bain distracting the duty teacher for Gemma and me.

"I don't know what to think," I said to Gemma, darting after her as we rushed down the unlit hall to the side door of St. Mary's. Her phone was pulled out, and I saw that Isaiah had texted her multiple times, his name popping up at the top over and over again.

My throat began to prickle with anxiety, but then I thought of Sister Mary, and suddenly, I felt like I was in the middle of a war, not knowing which side my opponent was on. I was being pulled in two different directions.

"I don't know," Gemma said. "But...there's a really twisted part of me that trusts Bain. Even after everything. At least when it comes to you."

"Why me? Because he has some strange infatuation with me? I still don't understand it."

Gemma pulled up her map, pushing away another text from Isaiah, which only fed into my anxiety. *Where is the fierce girl that Bain was talking about?* I knew she was buried inside of me somewhere. I just needed to let her out.

Fresh air pelted into my lungs, and I gulped it in, coming to the realization that Bain was wrong. It wasn't that I thought I needed Cade to fight my battles for me, or that he was the only one to save me. It was that I was afraid I would lose the battle and then lose him, too.

"I don't know," Gemma began answering my question as we walked over the snowy ground. "He once made a comment about you that told me he would do anything to keep you safe. I just don't know why."

I stopped walking, my shoes plowing into the snow. "He did?"

Gemma's soft face turned back, and she peered over her shoulder. "He threatened to kill someone if they ever hurt you, and I can assure you that he follows through with his threats."

My forehead suddenly felt sticky.

It wasn't the first time someone had said they'd do anything to protect me, but the thing was, I wasn't sure either of them would get the chance.

———

GEMMA DROVE us to the location that was written on the paper in her father's car that had been parked down near his old quarters, only a few yards from the motorcycle that I'd ridden with Cade the first time we'd snuck out.

"Sorry, I'm still not that good at driving," she said, shutting the headlights off and creeping down the last street until we reached our destination. Isaiah had called a few more times, and Shiner had called once, too. Every time it rang, Gemma would let it go, and the last text that came from Isaiah had both of our heads dropping.

Isaiah: I swear to God, you are going to kill me one day. Where the fuck are you? And we know Journey is with you. Tell us you're okay, baby.

"Maybe you should go back," I squeaked. "Just drop me off and go back, please." I felt terrible. My emotions were all over the place. I teetered over the edge between guilt and resilience, determination and reluctance.

"I'm not leaving you here, and we're not going back. Bain was right. You and I are a special kind of breed. We can love those boys, and they can love us back, but we cannot let them fight every one of our battles. We aren't damsels in distress, Journ. We never were." A heavy sigh left her, and she pulled her phone to her lap and typed a quick text.

Gemma: We're okay. Try not to worry.
Isaiah: Why are you near town?

"Wait, how does he know where we are?" My heart began stuttering, and I looked out my window at the tall, looming building that was just as diabolical as the Covenant Psych Hospital.

Her phone clicked off, and her hand fell to the door handle. "My phone has tracking on it. They'll be here soon. I'm sure of it. So, let's hurry up and get this over with."

"What are we getting ourselves into?" I asked, opening my door.

She shrugged. "This isn't the first time I've blindly stepped into a fucked-up situation. We'll be fine."

Her phone buzzed again, and this time, it was Tobias. We both froze.

Tobias: You and Journey better have a damn good explanation, Sis.
Isaiah: Why is Bain missing? Is he with you?

I tried to embrace the rising guilt following closely behind the impending dread. "We should have waited for them," I said, knowing that, even if Bain was right, Gemma and I had *no* idea what was inside that building. None at all. The only comfort I had was the fact that whoever had tried to take me, just a few nights ago, wasn't trying to kill me.

"There wasn't time," Gemma said, showing the time on her phone. Three minutes to nine.

Shit. Our hands clasped together, my other one near my pocket, protecting the knife that I had grown attached to. What I wouldn't give to be that clueless girl from last year, crushing on one of the Rebels, instead of this girl who was leaving a trail of fire behind as she walked to a ruined building, not only feeling guilty for leaving Cade but also slight satisfaction for not falling into the easy road of deserting a woman like Sister Mary, who I was pretty certain had dedicated her life to protecting me. It wasn't even about finding out answers anymore. This went way further than knowing who my mother was or why I was left at an orphanage. There was a present slicing in my chest at the thought of Sister Mary, and hope was the balm that soothed it. *She has to be okay.*

I pulled on Gemma's hand as we stood outside the tall building. It looked empty, and the glass had been shattered on the front of it. There weren't any cars around, which was alarming and even more eerie. "What if she isn't alive?" I croaked, pushing away everything but my determination. *What if they've killed Sister Mary? What if they know she was hiding me from whoever it is that wants me? What if it is my real mother and father?*

"Then, we fucking run."

I nodded before we both pulled our chins up higher and walked into a building with icy, broken glass crunching underneath our shoes.

CHAPTER THIRTY-SIX

CADE

My body temperature was well above normal. The hot blood cut through my veins as Brantley sped past the school and continued on to where the GPS was taking us. There was no time to call anyone. There was no other thought in any of our minds other than following the little red dot on Isaiah's phone that was leading us right to Journey and Gemma.

"What were they thinking?" Brantley asked, smacking his hand onto the wheel. My teeth had left marks on my fist from digging them into my flesh, which was the only thing keeping me from completely raging out in the backseat. All I felt was fear—unbending, panicky *fear*. The same fucking fear I felt that night Isaiah was holding Journey's bloody, lifeless body in his arms.

"I don't know," Isaiah confessed. "If they were leaving, for any reason at all, why wouldn't they fucking take someone?"

"And who the fuck locked Shiner in his room?"

We all knew the answer, and we were all so fucking sick of saying it.

Bain.

Like a beacon in the dark, there was Headmaster Ellison's car parked crookedly on the side of the abandoned road. This part of town housed the homeless. Most of the buildings were vacant and without power or windows. Piss and trash laid near the plowed road, and not a single fucking streetlamp worked.

"Wait, is that Gemma?"

Isaiah was out of the car before Brantley put it in park. His door was left open, and he jogged across the road with his black hoodie pulled up over his head. Gemma dove into his arms, and my heart sunk lower and lower as I searched the area around her.

Where is Journey?

"Stay calm, Cade. Getting overworked means you lose your ability to think clearly. Let's go see what's going on before you fucking lose it."

I didn't tell Brantley, but it was too late for that. My heart hammered, my pulse thrummed, my blood rushed, and my mind spun in directions I didn't want to head toward.

"Cade." Gemma pulled out of Isaiah's arms, and I paused when I saw the tears rushing down her cheeks. She was holding Journey's knife, and my insides burned. *No.* "They took her."

"Who?" The edge in my tone sounded like my father's, but I couldn't focus on that.

"I don't know. But Bain came shortly after we got here. It was a man who wasn't happy to see him. I think it was his father." She grabbed onto my shirt, and her frantic eyes were just as fearful as mine. "Check the tracking on my phone. I slipped it into Bain's hand before he went with them. She had no choice, Cade. The address in the email was just a meeting spot. Sister Mary isn't here."

"Sister Mary?" I asked, backing away and heading for the car.

"What email?" Brantley asked.

"She got an email from Sister Mary's email address that said if she wanted to keep Sister Mary alive, then she had to come here without you guys. I told her I was coming with her because it wasn't safe."

Fucking shit. My determined, kind-hearted, selfless girl going straight into fucking danger to save someone else.

"Cade?"

I turned back as I continued to jog toward the car.

"Bain was with her, so try not to worry. I don't think he is who he says he is."

Oh, I already fucking know that.

———

THE WINDING ROADS blurred as my hands tightened on the wheel, and my stomach turned and flipped with every curve of asphalt. Journey's location had stopped, and I was both thankful and fearful. If it had stopped, what were they doing to her? What did they plan? Was Slave there?

The questions continued to pound through my head, and a breath was lodged in the very pit of my chest. For some reason, my mother's face popped up as I sped the car up to ninety, praying to God there wasn't a patrolman hiding somewhere with his finicky speed radar.

My mother thought I was a replica of my father. She feared that my heart would harden and I'd become just as corrupt as he was. But she was wrong, and I didn't quite understand how she couldn't see it. Would my father race toward her if she were taken? Would my father run through every fucked-up scenario in his head that he was sure to face, trying to figure out how to save everyone involved *except* for the ones responsible? My father preached, day after day, that becoming selfless to another person was the moral of life—it just had to be for the right person.

But he chose wrong.

I was choosing right, and even if my mother thought the worst of me, I wasn't going to let that poisonous betrayal make me hate her. After all, she was the only one in my life that tried to redeem the shit my father would whisper to me in the bleak night, standing over a dead body. I couldn't hate her, even if she hated me.

Pulling up to another abandoned building, way on the outskirts of town, I parked the car and jumped out a second later. I knew what this place was. I'd been here with my father. It was a meeting spot for a gun exchange. The county line was only a few blocks ahead, and the closer I got to the caution-taped door with the yellow tape flying through the wintry wind like a loose ribbon, I cracked my knuckles and felt for my knife.

"He will be here soon, and this will be over."

"And then what?" *That's Bain.* "You'll kill your own son for keeping her from you? Mom kept her from you from the moment she was born, and I've been keeping her from you for the last several years. It's taken you this long to find her?"

My heart stalled when I heard her voice, that sweet sound of desperation hidden behind the fiery girl she was when she told me she hated me a month ago. "Where is Sister Mary? I won't go until you let her go."

"You think you have a choice? Your mother always did, too."

My hand squeezed the handle of my knife as I righted my vision. There was nothing more compelling than me hearing someone talk to her in a demeaning way to drag me into that building within seconds, but I'd been taught too many times that you had to scope out the perimeter and see what you were up against. Otherwise, people got hurt, and I wouldn't risk it. Not with her involved.

Except, when I took my first step to the left to search for exits, I found a blade at my neck with my knife falling to the snow. *Fuck*.

"And what do we have here?"

CHAPTER THIRTY-SEVEN

JOURNEY

I HAD ALWAYS BEEN good at pretending like I wasn't afraid. Each time a couple would come to the orphanage to look at potential girls for adoption, I had always felt a small sliver of fear. My stomach would twist, my little hands would shake, and my eyes would fall to the floor if they even dared to look at me.

So, over the years, I became skilled in not showing my fear and not allowing disappointment to wash me away.

But I was afraid right now.

My stomach was in knots, and my legs trembled. I was on a cold, wooden floor, wishing that the planks below me would snap and I could crash to the dirt-covered ground and somehow escape. *Sister Mary isn't here.* I'd had my suspicions, of course. I wasn't completely stupid. But what else could I do?

"Where is Sister Mary? I won't go until you let her go."

The man, who I realized was Bain's father, glared at me

from across the room. "You think you have a choice? Your mother always did too."

The question was choking me. *He knows my mom?* I shifted my attention to Bain who was staring at his father with a bored expression, as if he didn't scare him in the slightest. There were too many things going on for me to focus on just one, but Bain had something to do with my past, and this man did, too.

'Mom kept her from you from the moment she was born.'

They knew my mother, and although I'd been searching most of my life for someone to tell me who my mother was, or why I was an orphan, I didn't feel the least bit comforted at the moment.

My head was resting on my bent knees as I tried to silently work through what was unfolding in front of me, and then I caught the slight flicker of surprise on Bain's face. Two tall figures walked through the squeaky door, letting in a gust of cold air, and I suddenly jumped to my feet.

The glint of the knife against Cade's throat blinded me as dread scratched at my tight throat. My hand flew to my mouth, and right then was the moment that fear took over. A reaction came from me that had been simmering from the moment I had to leave Gemma. My fight-or-flight response was completely obliterated, and my actions were driven from something deep in my soul.

I'd give up everything for him.

Our eyes caught, and he was clearly panicked seeing me across the room.

"Don't." Suddenly, a gun was pointed in my direction, and I froze mid-step. There was a faint growl from Bain, who was only a few yards away from me, and the man who had Cade at knifepoint sighed agitatedly.

"Do you think it's in your best interest to point a gun at her? In my presence?"

A sickly feeling slithered down my spine, and my legs trembled again. *In my presence?*

Bain's father immediately lowered the gun and ran a hand over his cropped head of hair. There was something in his eye that caught my attention. *Is he afraid of this man?* He was the one who had a gun, and I knew that a gun would always win in a knife fight, yet he submitted.

"So, this is her." My head spun as I slowly wound my gaze past Cade, who hadn't taken his eyes off me, and landed on the man who had him locked against his chest with a knife to his throat. I knew, without a doubt, that I'd be leaving this abandoned building with him if it had anything to do with saving Cade. I knew it.

"Yes," Bain's father answered. "I found her."

"I thought she was dead." His eyes ran down my body slowly, like he was sizing up an appetizer. In the worst way, I wanted to take a step back to get farther away from him, but instead, I stayed right where my feet were planted.

"She looks alive and well to me," Bain's father said with an airy tone, as if he were proud that he was handing over an eighteen-year-old girl to some psycho who had a knife pressed to someone's throat.

"Yes, she does. She looks a lot better than I imagined eighteen years ago."

The edge of my voice ran through the room like I had all the confidence in the world. My arms crossed over my chest as my chin lifted. "Is someone going to fill me in on what we're doing here, and why someone has tried to kill me and later abduct me?"

"Someone tried to kill you?" the man asked, suddenly seeming concerned. *So, it wasn't him.* "Don't you worry. Once I find out who tried to kill you, I'll kill them." He winked at me, and my face fell. "Once people learn that you're my property, you won't be touched again."

A choppy laugh left Cade, and my heart dropped. His words were somewhat muffled as the knife was pressed against his windpipe. "You think she's yours, Slave?"

Slave.

"I have a fucking contract to prove it, and I paid a shit-ton of money, so yeah, she's mine." He tightened his hold on Cade, and I watched as his jaw grew sharper against the knife. "And who the fuck are you to talk back to me?"

Bain's father smirked, and my eyes began to grow fuzzy. I briefly saw Bain standing back with his nostrils flared and his fists clenched, staring at him, too. "That's Tommy Walker's son," he said, driving the sick smile further.

Slave's empty eyes narrowed. "Tommy is in prison with Carlisle and Frank. Are their sons taking back what was once theirs?" He angled his head toward Cade's throat like he was going to bite into his jugular. "Is that why you're here? You want the clients back?"

Cade's face remained motionless as his worried stare drove into me. I saw the flickering of Slave's muscles playing back and forth, as if he were teetering with the idea of cutting his throat. *I would never recover.* Nothing at that moment mattered other than putting this to a stop and getting that knife away from the only person I ever loved.

"So, you sold me to him." I looked at Bain's father, latching onto his beetle-like eyes, trying like hell to distract him from hurting Cade. My heart beat in my eardrums so loudly I could hardly hear his answer.

"That's right. Except, up until recently, I thought you were dead. Your dumb fucking mother hid you from me because she was forced to sign you over to save her own life. She tried to save yours, too."

"And then when she died, that responsibility came to me." My gaze crossed the room like a cutting jab toward Bain, feeling the confusion sweep me off my feet.

Slave seethed. "So, you've been hiding her all these years?"

It felt wrong to wish danger on someone else, but in the moment, the fleeting thought of Slave letting Cade go to get to Bain made my heart skip.

"Don't you worry, Slave. I'll take care of the betraying little fuck. That must be his mama coming out of him." The gun was suddenly pointed at Bain, and everything was spinning out of control. The room was shifting, weapons were being pointed at everyone, my heart was hammering, and panic was slowly taking me under.

"Stop it!" I shouted, stomping my foot down on the wooden plank beside me. Tiny dust particles flew up, surrounding me in my wake. I glared at Slave with his wicked little smile and asked the simple question that would change everything. "Why was I up for sale? And why did you want me?"

I could never say that no one wanted me again, the only problem was that this was not what I had expected as a young child when all I wanted was to be adopted.

"Because your mother had cheated on Callum." He nodded to Bain's father, the man who still had a gun pointed at his son. "He put you up for sale to get back at her."

Callum stared at Bain as he spoke to me. "I thought it would hurt her more to know you were living a shitty life without her than killing you along with your father. He was nothing but a local restaurant owner." Callum smiled as he revisited the past. "I had him make me a meal before I killed him with the same knife he cut my steak with."

A tremor ran down my spine, shaking me to my core. I mourned the loss of someone I didn't even know.

I shifted my attention back to Slave, not able to look at the fear in Cade's eyes because I knew the fear wasn't because there was a knife to his throat. It was because he could see my decisions before I even saw them myself. "Why did you buy me? What could a man like you want with a baby?"

"Well"—he smiled at me as if he were a kind and decent man—"I was going to sell you on the black market. American girls are a hot commodity."

Bain must have seen the confusion on my face, because he explained it quickly, ignoring the gun pointed in his direction. "Slave owns one of the biggest sex-trafficking rings in the United States. Selling women and children all over the world for sex purposes."

My face fell, and my watery eyes were instantly drawn to Cade. I was deadbolted right there. *What do we do?* It was so much worse than I had expected. This was never something I could have imagined when I was younger, and I had imagined a lot of different reasons as to why I was placed in an orphanage.

"And now?" Cade asked. His voice shook me out of my stupor, and when I regained my ability to focus again, he mouthed, *Breathe, baby.*

My breaths were short puffs, but at least they were viable.

"Up until ten minutes ago, I was still going to sell her and make a nice chunk of change."

"You've made plenty over the years, getting a percentage of the gun sales for my debt with you."

Slave's scowl deepened. "I got a percentage of the sales in exchange for not killing you, remember?" He shifted his attention back to me, and it was a burning cut to my skin. "But he's right. I did make a lot of money on the sales, so I don't think I'm going to sell you anymore. I think I'm going to keep you."

Something sour coated my tongue, but I would rather have taken that knife and opened up the old wounds on my arms before allowing these men to see me scared.

"I'm sorry to say it..." Bain stepped forward, and the room

fell silent as he walked all the way over to his father, an inch away from the barrel of the gun. It was as if everyone else faded away, and Bain and his father were the only ones in the room, a spotlight shining down on a very damaged father-and-son relationship. "But that isn't going to happen."

A gulp was lodged in my throat like I'd swallowed a golf ball, and I shifted past Bain's firm jaw and landed on Cade. His eyes widened, just barely, but enough for me to understand that something was about to happen, and I needed to be ready.

Slave laughed. "Excuse me?"

Bain stared into his father's eyes, ignoring Slave. "I will gut you if you think you're going to sell my fucking sister to him. I don't give a fuck if you hate my mother for fucking someone behind your back. I don't give a fuck if I die trying. I won't let you take her. Mom's last dying wish to protect her only daughter is so much richer than anything you have to offer, *Dad*."

I knew what was going to happen next, so I put my hands over my ears and caused a distraction by yelling, "I'll go with them! Just stop! No one else has to get hurt trying to...to... save me!"

Silence fell upon us, and that was when I flashed a stern look in Cade's direction, and what was once a feud between Bain and Cade turned into something else entirely. The two of them formed an invisible bond, and I knew this was the moment we were all waiting for.

Chaos erupted when I caught a glimpse of bright blood on the tip of Slave's knife, and then I was running straight for Callum's gun that Bain had kicked off to the side.

CHAPTER THIRTY-EIGHT

CADE

THE ONLY WAY TO become the hero was to be selfless, and I didn't mean in the Tommy Walker way. I meant it in the way that I would give up anything for Journey because she deserved it and was worthy of it.

I knew it from the moment I met her; her love was hidden and quiet but also strong. There was a charisma about her, this soft spot inside of her that made me want to crawl underneath it and stay there forever. She'd give up her life for someone else. That was why she was caught here in the middle of a fucking storm that was created for her.

I'll go with them.

Over my dead body—and apparently, Bain's dead body, too.

The back of my head throbbed as I slipped out of Slave's grasp, gaining a knife slice at the bottom of my neck and on my shoulder. It was a plan I'd already come up with, but Journey was the one to set it into motion. The gun in Callum's hand skittered across the dust-covered floor as Bain advanced on him, landing several feet from Journey, who I'd hoped would run the fuck out of here, but again, the girl's love was strong—she wouldn't leave me here even if I begged her.

And I wanted to. I didn't want her in here witnessing what was about to go down, because one of two things were going to happen: Bain and I were going to come out on top, or Slave and Callum were. And if they were the ones to win this, she needed to get as far away from here as possible.

An uppercut to my jaw caused my line of sight to tilt, and I dove underneath the next punch to land on the knife that was stained in red. My back connected with it, and I knew that there was another cut, but I quickly fumbled to my feet when I gripped one end of the blade, cutting me again.

"Stop it!" Journey screamed.

"Journey, fucking run!" Bain shouted as his father pulled another gun out. He drove a fist into Callum's stomach, jutting him quickly, and blood suddenly began staining his shirt. "How's that stab wound feeling? My sister has good aim, yeah?" *He's the one who tried to take her?*

I saw the hunger in Slave's scrutiny, and I knew that he was feeling a little stabby, too. If I'd known that this was how the night was going to end, I would have been double-armed, but bringing a gun near a prison didn't seem like the best idea, so here I was, holding a bloody knife with a man who looked at this fight as a form of child's play.

"Journey," I gritted. "Listen to Bain. Go. Now. We've got this."

Slave and I circled one another as Callum threw his head back and laughed. There was a trickle of blood dribbling from his mouth. "You've got this, do you?" His laugh faded, and the devil took over. *Fucking shit.* I knew what was coming. Callum's hand raised with the barrel of the gun directed at Bain, but he stood his ground. To my benefit, Slave paused, too, to watch the show, but one look of horror on Journey's face had me winging the knife in his direction so I could slam into Bain before Journey had to watch her *only* family die in front of her eyes.

A gunshot reverberated in my eardrums, and it didn't matter how many times I had heard that sound, it was still a shock to the core when it was such a short distance away. It was the chorus of my childhood, drenched in pleas and blood.

Bain and I fell to the floor, and we both scrambled to our feet to see who'd been shot. "Oh my God." The pain in her voice gutted me, and for a moment, I thought I was the one who'd been shot, but when I saw her standing there with a gun in her hand, shaking back and forth as if the metal weighed more than she did, I rushed for her and lowered the black weapon to the floor.

"Drop it, baby. Give it to me." Her bloodshot, stormy gaze flew to mine in shock, and it stole my breath away. A choked sob left her, and my bloody hand wrapped around hers so tightly I felt more blood rush out. "Breathe, Journey. Breathe."

"I... I... I..." she gasped, and I panicked. I wanted to slap my hands onto her hollow, wet cheeks and blow air into her mouth to make her take a breath.

"Journey, it's okay. Breathe."

"I shot him. Did I kill him?" She tried to peel out of my arms to look at Callum, but I quickly pulled her back.

"Cade, get her the fuck out of here."

I looked over at Bain, and he was straddling Slave, who had blood sputtering out of his mouth. The knife that I'd thrown was pulled out of his side and in Bain's hands. *There's too much blood.* Someone was gasping for life. I felt Journey buckle, and I caught her at the last second.

Her lifeless, weak body was scooped up into my arms, and

then I left her half-brother in an abandoned building bathed in blood and got her the fuck out.

———

"B‍REATHE. J‍UST BREATHE." Journey was on my lap, clinging to me for dear life, as Headmaster Ellison paced the small space of his living room over and over again. At one point, I'd looked down at the rug beneath his feet to see if a hole had formed yet. I had a feeling he had done this numerous times over the last month.

"What were you thinking?" Tate stopped pacing and placed his hands on his hips, staring directly at his daughter, Gemma. "You *just* became safe, and now I find out you go with Journey to an abandoned building to find a nun who is missing? Is this a joke? You walked right into a trap!"

"We didn't know it was a trap." Gemma was pacing just like her father, but she was behind the couch Journey and I were sitting on. "And what was I supposed to do? Just let Journey go alone and possibly die?"

Isaiah let out a hefty breath and slammed the back of his head on the couch. "It's done now, Tate. Let it go."

"Let it go?" he shouted, making Journey jump.

"Tate," I gritted, giving him a stern look. His attention flew to Journey, and then he pinched the bridge of his nose.

"Gemma, you're grounded."

Isaiah's laugh filled the room, and although the situation was completely fucked up, and my insides were traumatized and mangled, I had to bury my face in Journey's hair to keep my smile hidden.

"You can't ground her. She's fucking eighteen. And she doesn't even live here."

He threw his hands up. "What the fuck am I doing? I'm the worst father and...the worst headmaster, too. I got the security system to prevent these things from happening, and here we are. One student has multiple wounds. Another is fucking traumatized. Bain is currently MIA, doing God knows what. Most of the authorities are corrupt in this town, and I would die a happy man if the FBI never contacted me again."

Before we knew what was happening, Gemma rounded the side of the couch and threw her small frame around her father's middle, wrapping her arms around him tightly. "I'm sorry." Tate's expression went from angry, to confused, to relieved. Silence filled the room, and eventually, Tate put his arms around his daughter.

"It's okay. I just need you to stop finding yourself in these situations. I just found out about you and Tobias, and I can't take the panic of losing you or someone else taking you. *Again.*" He looked at Journey. "And you, too, Journey."

She peeked up at him, and although her face was clear of tears, I still felt the instant pain and remorse in her heart. I was certain that her mind was going in a million different directions, and the shock of shooting someone was probably replaying over and over again in her head. "I'm so sorry. This is all my fault."

She and Gemma caught gazes, and Gemma was seconds from opening her mouth to say something when Shiner, Brantley, and Bain walked into the living room.

Bain took one look at Journey and said, "It's not your fault. It's mine."

<hr>

CHAPTER THIRTY-NINE

<hr>

JOURNEY

MY EXPRESSION FELL, and I sobered up real quick when Bain walked through the living room of the headmaster's house. I tensed on Cade's lap, and he must have felt it because he wrapped his arms tighter around me. I didn't allow myself to cave into the fear and avoidance that I wanted to escape in, and I knew that being in Cade's arms helped keep me steady in front of my...*half-brother?*

I need answers. A lot of them.

The conversations were replaying in my head, and my hands shook with the feel of the metal still in them. *I shot someone.* Shivers coated me from the top of my head down to my toes, and Cade's hands ran down my arms, warming me up. *And Sister Mary. Where is she?*

"I would love a fucking explanation," the headmaster said, locking his arms over his rising chest, glaring across the room at Bain. The flames of the fireplace behind him roared as he stomped farther away to put distance between them, but Bain didn't seem fazed by the headmaster's anger at all.

"Me, too," Cade said from behind me.

It was Bain on one side of the room; the Rebels, myself, and Gemma on the couch; and then the headmaster a safe distance from us all.

"Was it you that fucking locked me in my room?" Shiner leaned forward, the couch dipping as he placed his elbows on his knees like he was ready to snap Bain's neck in half. I'd always known Shiner as the flirty, amusing one of the Rebels, the one who made everyone laugh when we were supposed to be serious, but right now, he was angry.

"You didn't seem to mind with your face buried in pussy. It was only after that you noticed."

I felt the rise in temperature from Shiner, so I quickly placed a trembling hand on his knee, and he instantly fell back into the couch. There was too much violence tonight. There was too much of everything.

"Was it you?" I asked, sounding more like a mouse than anything else. My blurry vision hit the floor as I continued feasting on all the knowledge I'd learned in the last few hours. My hands were still shaking, and I swore I could still hear the ringing of the bullet flying from the gun inside my ears.

"Was what me?" Bain asked, expression softening as he stared at me from across the room.

I leaned forward, unwrapping myself from Cade so I could shove my sleeves up to my elbows, showing off my long scars. "Did you do this to me?"

His eyes instantly grew dark, and the muscles along his shoulders bundled, looking as if he was wearing armor underneath his t-shirt. "Yes."

I was placed on my feet a heartbeat later, and Cade was suddenly storming over to him before I even realized his reaction. Isaiah and Brantley were beside him as Bain stood there, unmoving and completely unbothered.

"I'm going to snap your fucking hands off and then kill

you afterward." The threat was unrestrained and as clear as if he were speaking over the intercom of St. Mary's.

The headmaster threw his hands up in disbelief, but Bain stared right at Cade and said, "You can snap my hands off, but you won't kill me."

"If you think that, then you don't know me very well."

"I'm her only family. You're not going to fucking kill me, Cade."

Cade's jaw tightened as he looked away. Frustration flew off of him in thunderous waves.

"Cade," I whispered hardly loud enough for anyone to hear. Bain's attention flew to mine as Cade turned around to look at me. "Will you come back over here?" *I need him.* I needed him to get through this.

A piece of light-colored hair had swayed down onto his tight face. His golden-brown eyes looked brighter and full of something wild with the flames behind him. When he walked closer to me, I was able to breathe again.

He sat down and pulled me onto his lap, burying his face in my tangled hair. We inhaled at the same time. "I'm sorry."

Bain cleared his throat before crossing his arms over his chest and kicking a leg behind him to rest against the wall. He met my eye, and I refused to look away.

"Yes, I was the one that cut your wrists."

Panic made me burn. "Why?" I asked in disbelief. My heart climbed higher and higher until he answered. The thumping was deafening, and the room was slowly caving in. *He cut me. He was the one to attack me.*

Bain's dark chuckle flew out into the living room before he said, "Because dead girls never talk, and if you were presumed dead, like when you were an infant, no one would ever find out who you were."

It was a special kind of torture, looking at a person who attacked you, knowing you should've hated them, but instead you found yourself understanding and accepting the pain they'd caused you. *What is wrong with me?* Was it all just too much to handle? Was I just completely numb from what had happened earlier? I said nothing as I sat on Cade's lap, blinking every few seconds.

Isaiah was the one to feed into his confession. "So, you weren't trying to kill her? Instead, you were trying to show someone else that she was dead?"

Bain nodded. "My father was in town that night, doing some business with Richard at the Covens."

Gemma bristled at the sound of Richard's name as Bain continued.

"He knew I was distracted, so he came to the school, and that was when he found me watching her. I was waiting to see if Cade showed up. My father didn't know who she was at the time, and assuming she was my distraction, he was going to hurt her to make a point. Instead, I acted desperate for his approval, and I said I'd kill her so he knew my loyalty was to him and that I wasn't distracted like he thought. I cut her wrists, knowing I missed the radial artery, but he was too hungry to see blood to even realize."

My throat tightened, and my breathing had picked up. I pictured myself getting up and plowing my small fist into Bain's face or, at the very least, shoving him and yelling at him for putting me through such a trauma, but instead, I remained on Cade's lap, feeling confused over the fact that my understanding outweighed my anger.

Cade placed a tiny kiss to the side of my neck before asking, "So you're the one who sent me the threats, yeah?"

"I needed her to be far away from my father, and considering the fact that you all were involved in the illicit gun business, I knew that he'd stumble upon her eventually, and I couldn't risk it."

Bain glanced at me. "You look just like Mom."

I was in a chokehold, hardly able to breathe correctly with everything he was admitting. The more it was explained to me, the more I wished I would have kept my past a secret. I was still an orphan, only now, I knew the story behind it, and it was worse than I ever could have imagined. Sister Mary's face popped into my head, and fear kept my mouth closed. I was too afraid to ask if Bain knew where she was, not sure if my heart could handle anything else.

"So..." Gemma stood up and began pacing back and forth between us and Bain, just like her father was doing moments ago as he fumed over our whereabouts. "Let me get this straight. You and Journey"—she pointed to him and then me—"are half-brother and sister. You guys have the same mom but different dads. According to what Cade had told us a little while ago, your mother cheated on your father, and in his rage, he *sold* Journey as a baby to Slave to get back at her."

Bain nodded. "But my mom had told him Journey died at birth, which obviously wasn't true, but it made my father even more angry." He paused, looking away. "He ended up raping her shortly after Journey was born, because of course, she wanted *nothing* to do with him after everything. That was how she ended up pregnant with me." Bain finally looked at me. "We're only ten months apart. She faked your death and dropped you on Sister Mary's front stoop a day after you were born."

I sat up a little taller, knowing I had to get the worst of this over with. My voice was wobbly, and my stomach hurt. "Is..." I cleared my throat, already knowing the answer to the question. "Is Sister Mary..." *Shit.* I hurriedly rushed the rest of the sentence out. "Is she dead?"

His long pause told me what I needed to know, and my heart slammed to the floor, stealing a gasp from my core. "Yes." Silence filled the room, and it was so loud I wanted to cover my ears. Tears swarmed me, and I was drowning. My lips smashed together, and my chest was tight as I refused the oxygen. "I knew she was dead the moment the police showed up and said they had found blood. That's when I knew my father had learned of you."

I clasped my hands and put them up to my forehead, finally giving in to the screaming in my lungs. *She's dead because of me.*

"No." The stern voice made the hair on my arms stand up. Bain's voice was closer now, but I refused to look at anyone. Cade's arms tightened around me as I began to shake. "Sister Mary knew what she had signed up for. She knew the consequences, Journey."

"It's still my fault!" I yelled, breaking free of Cade's comforting hold. I took Gemma's spot in the middle of the living room and stomped back and forth, feeling my blood heat up with too many emotions piling on top. "She's dead because of me, and although your dad was a fucking psycho, he's dead because of me too! I shot him! And what happened to our mom? Did I somehow kill her, too?!"

My hands covered my eyes, and I gasped, feeling confused and embarrassed all together. I felt Cade before his arms corralled me, and that was when a broken sob tore out of my chest. *Why is this happening?*

"This is not your fault. Stop. Please stop." *It still hurts. Sister Mary is gone. Did she die in pain?*

My sentences came out in rasps. "I want them to take it all back. I don't want to know any more. I don't care. I just..." I inhaled the stiff air in the living room, coughing through a cry. "I just want it to be done. I just want to go to the roof of this school and lie with you under the stars like we did last year before any of this happened."

Cade turned me around and placed his strong hands on the side of my face, furiously wiping my tears. I realized the room was empty now except for me, Cade, and Bain.

"We will lie under the fucking stars every single night, if that's what will make you stop hurting." The agony within Cade's features mirrored mine. The desperation to make me stop feeling this way was palpable, and I nodded desperately before placing my forehead against his lips.

"It's just going to take time," Bain said quietly. "And no, you didn't kill our mom. That fucking psycho you shot killed her. Every single day since the moment he sold you, he slowly killed her. You were just a casualty trapped in between a heartless man and a desperate woman."

I peeked over Cade's shoulders and locked onto my half-brother's saddened eyes. All of a sudden, there was a burning connection with him that I had never felt before. We now shared the same pain, and it coursed around the room like a whip.

"I'm sorry that this is how it played out," he whispered. "You were never supposed to be a part of this world."

Shutting my eyes, I pressed my forehead back onto Cade's lips and submerged myself in the safety I felt with him, knowing that whatever came next, I didn't have to do it alone. Cade pulled back, and I wasn't sure if Bain was still in the room or not, but Cade's soothing voice locked all my emotions into place. "Don't worry, Journ. You have me, okay? You had me even when you didn't know it."

I nodded and clung onto him even harder.

EPILOGUE

JOURNEY

"What do you think he did with the bodies?" I asked, bending down and grabbing a handful of snow.

It had only been a couple of weeks of learning that I *was,* in fact, an orphan and had no living relatives other than my half-brother, who just so happened to be my boyfriend's arch enemy up until recently, but there were still so many questions I wanted answered.

Cade's cool chuckle filtered through the air as he sat back on the lacrosse bench with a black beanie on, making his sharp features stand out even more. "There are clean-up crews out there. My father had them on speed-dial."

I was still packing the snow into a little ball as my lips parted in shock. "It's alarming how nonchalant you are about that. Not only do I have a boyfriend who has lived this lifestyle but also a half-brother who has, too." *Bizarre.*

Cade shrugged. "It's not all that outlandish to me with how I grew up, and the same for Bain. Why do you think my mother skipped town so quickly?"

There was a bump in my chest at the obvious hint of pain. Cade could play off his emotions to anyone else *except* me. The few times he had mentioned his mother with an evident dip in his tone told me that this was something that was affecting him, whether he wanted to admit that or not.

"Cadeeeee."

His warm eyes sized me up and down. "Journeyyyyy."

There was a flip in my belly, but I shut down the instant butterflies from his flirty voice. "Let's call your mom."

His smile fell. "No."

My boots crunched over the snowy field, leaving a trail of footprints behind me. The second I got close to him, his legs spread, and his cold, red hands flitted to my waist. His chin was tipped up, and I peered down into his eyes, suddenly becoming swept up in the overpowering amount of safety and contentment that I felt within them. *I want him to feel that, too.*

"Yes," I said, dropping the snowball I had planned to throw at him before wrapping my hands around his cold cheeks. The rosy color matched his lips, and I found myself staring down at them. "If anything...to just close the gap."

"There is no gap."

My hands grew tense on his cheeks, feeling the subtle scruff on his skin. "There is. You owe it to yourself to tell her what kind of man you are."

"And what kind of man am I, Journey Smith?"

My lips curved, and I pushed in closer to him, letting his arms wrap around my waist even tighter. "You're loyal to those who deserve it, you are selfless beyond belief, you're caring and sweet when you want to be, and you are determined to be righteous even when all you've known is evil."

A cloud of warm breath flew from his mouth before he picked me up by my thighs and sat me down on his lap. I straddled him as my legs hung off the back side of the bench.

His lips graced my neck as he whispered into my ear, "I think you just filled the gap."

"Nice try," I whispered back, bringing our faces closer together. "If I'm going to work on a relationship with my half-brother who cut my wrists to make it look like I was suicidal and kept me locked away in a psych ward so no one would know I was alive, then you can call your mom and start working on things, too." I paused. "Not to mention, aren't you the one who keeps preaching to me that others' actions are not my fault? Like blaming myself for the death of Sister Mary?" The thought of her still hurt, the feeling nestling deep in my belly and coming out at the worst times, like when Cade and I volunteered at the orphanage on the weekends. "You are not your father. His actions should not reflect on you."

He growled as he thrust his hardened middle to meet mine, coaxing a rushed gasp to leave me. "Fine," he bit out, darting his tongue out to lick my bottom lip. "But first..." My back was in the snow as his mouth hovered, putting a pause on everything else. "I'm *starving*."

The End

AFTERWORD

For more of the Rebels (and to find answers for those questions I know you have for others characters), head to Amazon to preorder book four in the St. Mary's Series: **Heartless Boys Never Kiss** (Tobias and Sloane's book). Their book will be coming in the Fall of 2022. What to expect: Grumpy/sunshine, enemies/bully feel, best friend's brother trope!

Haven't read the St. Mary's Duet and want to see how Gemma and Isaiah got their happily ever after? Head to Amazon to purchase book one: **Good Girls Never Rise!**

ALSO BY SJ SYLVIS

English Prep Series

All the Little Lies

All the Little Secrets

All the Little Truths

St. Mary's Series

Good Girls Never Rise

Bad Boys Never Fall

Dead Girls Never Talk

Heartless Boys Never Kiss

Standalones

Three Summers

Yours Truly, Cammie

Chasing Ivy

Falling for Fallon

Truth

You can find all books on Amazon or at sjsylvis.com

S.J. Sylvis is an Amazon Top 50 bestselling romance author who is best known for her angsty new adult romances. She currently resides in Arizona with her husband, two small kiddos, and dog. She is obsessed with coffee, becomes easily attached to fictional characters, and spends most of her evenings buried in a book!

sjsylvis.com

ACKNOWLEDGMENTS

To my sweet, sweet, family—I love you more than words can say and thank you for being my favorite people in the entire world. I love spending my days with you.

My amazing author/reader friends: THANK YOU for your continued support and encouragement. You mean so much to me and I am forever thankful for you! I would be lost without our daily voice messages. Love you lots!!

To my alpha/betas (Lil, Danah, Emma, Megan, Erica, and Meagan): Thank you so incredibly much for your help with plot holes and any inconsistencies in Cade and Journey's story. I will forever be grateful for your advice and sharp eyes. XO.

Ellie—you are an absolute gem of a human and thank you making me put a dedication in my book. It's for you <3

Mary, my PA, where would I be without you? Thank you for keeping my head on straight and reminding me of things that I forget three seconds after we chat about them. I would not be where I am today if it weren't for you and your help!!

To my editor, Jenn, THANK YOU ALWAYS. So grateful our paths have crossed!! Xo

To my Agent— Bethany, thank you for going the extra

mile for my books and getting them into the hands of audio companies and foreign publishers! Thankful for you!

Lastly, thank you to every reader, blogger, tiktoker, bookstagrammer, etc. I appreciate every single share, tag, or review that I get. Truly! It means SO much to me and I am forever grateful for our support and I am SO thankful you enjoy my books.

Xoxo,

SJ

www.ingramcontent.com/pod-product-compliance
Lightning Source LLC
Chambersburg PA
CBHW021438310726
48971CB00005B/1413